AWEN STORM

ALSO BY O. J. BARRÉ:

Awen Rising: Book One of the Awen Trilogy
The Druids of Marduk, Part I: An Awen Prequel
The Druids of Marduk, Part II: UnderEarth

AWEN STORM

O. J. Barré

PeaceMakers Publishing

PEACEMAKERS PUBLISHING, MAY 2020

PeaceMakers Publishing
9169 W State St #3332
Garden City, ID 83714

olivia@ojbarre.com

For information about special discounts and orders by trade bookstores, wholesalers, book clubs; or for film options, translation rights, etc, please contact the publisher.

PeaceMakers Publishing Paperback ISBN: 978-1-7332736-2-6

Cover Design © 2020 by 100Covers

First Printing, 2020
Printed in the United States of America

TO DON & CHERYL (CHERRY) ORDES

My brother-in-law and sister. For five decades, you have never failed to be there for me, and for that, I am eternally grateful.

ACKNOWLEDGMENTS

First of all, I'd like to thank my mama and daddy, Jean and Yank Herrell, for doing the deed that brought me into this world. Daddy, thank you for instilling your love for the earth and its glorious creatures; Mama for passing on your love of the written word, and for always being there when I needed you. To my brothers, Bill and Jon, you have left this planet to join our parents, but you will ever live inside my heart.

To my sister, Cherry (whom everyone calls Cheryl), thank you for being my childhood reading buddy, my lifelong friend and sounding board, and a shining example for us all. Your and Don's undying love and support have kept me going through good times and bad.

Grandmother Willoughby Herrell, you always knew that I was special. Thank you for encouraging my curiosity, answering my endless questions, and for teaching me the names of every plant, flower, and growing thing in your vast yard. But more, thank you for being a veritable force at a time when women weren't allowed.

To my ninth grade English teacher Mrs. Lucy Harris, thank you for recognizing my gift with words. I wish I had understood the import of your revelation, rather than waiting a lifetime to start writing. To the college English Comp teacher whose name I don't remember, thank you. You raised my hackles *and* my awareness, and taught me to write an essay or argument that can stand the test of time. I only hope that holds true for novels.

To Andrew Post, Roland Yeomans, the late Eric Trant, Elliot Grace, and all the other authors and kind souls who read *That Rebel with a Blog*, thank you. Your feedback helped me find my voice, that elusive quality every writer must have. To you, I owe my writing life. Without you, this book might not exist.

Thank you to my writing partner Debra Holm, and to my friend, bodyworker, Janine Willey, for helping shape the final story.

Lastly, thank you to Philip and Stephanie Carr-Gomm for providing the inspiration for the Awen Trilogy's animal characters via your book *The Druid Animal Oracle*.

MAILING LIST/FREE BOOKS

I send newsletters to my fans and readers a few times a year, sharing details about new releases, freebies, special offers, and other stuff. The emails are typically short and related to writing, books, life, and the latest goings-on in the Awen Universe.

If you would like to get these, subscribe to my mailing list via one of the links below. And, bonus—you will also receive a free eBook of the first Awen prequel, *The Druids of Marduk, Part I.*

If you would like to sign up, here's the HTML link and QR Code:

https://www.subscribepage.com/awentrilogy

Welcome to the Awen Universe!

Happy Reading! Olivia/O. J. Barré

TABLE OF CONTENTS

AWEN:

Life Essence, Inspiration,
Divine Creative Energy

"We didn't come here to fight monsters, we're not equipped for it."

~ Creature from the Black Lagoon

NOT BY A LONG SHOT

The air stank of sulfur and noxious fumes spat out by the volcano while civil defense sirens caterwauled, announcing danger to all within a twenty-mile radius of Zoo Atlanta. Emily Hester was one of those in danger. She perched atop a ledge that had sprung up from the earth and now extended far above the Gorilla Compound.

Like Emily, her companions were bloody and disheveled, but miraculously, alive. Cu the Irish wolfhound barked beside her, while Lugh MacBrayer peered over the edge. Brian, his nephew, turned a slow three-sixty, gawking at the devastation.

The typically-inactive Brevard Fault had ripped asunder, creating the lofty peak on which they balanced. Lava still pooled near the Reptile House, and below them, frightened animals reeled from the shock. Some huddled inside manmade structures behind glass or bars, but others weren't so fortunate. A screech ended mid-cry, tearing at Emily's tender heart and punctuating the desolation.

The early-afternoon sun broke through banking cumulus clouds transforming the dust and ashes into an incandescent soup. Peering through it, Emily whispered a druid spell to calm the animals and another to cleanse the air.

A welcome breeze lifted the sweat-dampened curls clinging to her temples. She swiped at her face and realized her jacket was no longer tied around her waist. Her purse must've met a similar fate.

But the spell was dissipating the thick haze, thankfully taking the stench along with it.

Turning her gaze to ground zero, Emily searched for the dragon with flaming wings. It had vanished when her spell quieted the volcano, but when Lugh kissed her afterward, she had caught a glimpse of its crimson eyes. Remembering them now, Emily shuddered. It was apparently gone, but how would they get down from this mountain?

The wind picked up, clearing the remaining haze and revealing the extent of the wreckage. Employees rounded up escaped animals and tended the wounded. Firefighters battled a blaze near the Reptile House, while rescue workers loaded injured people into ambulances. Sirens screamed as they careened from the park.

A roar rose above the din, announcing several National Guard helicopters. They flew in formation toward the melee and hovered above the reptile house, all except the one that banked to approach the promontory.

Excited, Emily squealed, then wobbled precariously near the edge when the downwash of its rotors beat against them. Lugh grabbed her arm and pulled her to safety, and she clung to him as a ladder emerged from the copter's belly. Relieved, she cheered and held on to Lugh.

"YAY!" Brian yelled. "They're rescuing us!"

"Yes!" Lugh shouted.

Cu barked madly, and their heads craned upwards as the ladder descended slowly from the helicopter. A uniformed medic leaned from the craft with a bullhorn.

"Climb up the ladder one at a time. Women and children first. We'll send a sling for the dog."

At that, Cu let go of a series of yaps that carried the shrill edge of hysteria they all felt.

Suddenly, the peak trembled, and an otherworldly wail sprang from the earth. Emily's heart thudded. It was the earth dragon, Draig Talav.

She clenched Lugh's hand and hollered at the ladder inching toward them, "Hurry, dammit! HURRY!"

But Talav's wail grew in intensity, nearly drowning the thunder of the copter, and Emily's anxiety inched toward panic. She let go of Lugh to fight it, flapping her hands at her sides and sucking in deep breaths.

Then, the ledge shuddered and wobbled harder. Emily screamed and grabbed Lugh. Below them, disaster-weary survivors screamed too. Then, Brian yelled something Emily couldn't make out, and Cu's bark deepened.

The ladder dangled above their heads.

Lugh stretched on his tiptoes to catch the lifeline, but a stream of fire shot through the air, and the ladder ignited. The flame ran up it, and the helicopter jerked higher and away.

Above the lava by the Reptile House, the dragon rose, body blazing. The fire had spurted from its massive jaws. Emily screamed and collapsed to the ground. Then it screeched, and she clapped her hands over her ears.

An answering shriek emanated from the bowels of the earth as the whole zoo quivered.

"It's the dragon!" she yelled, pointing a trembling finger, and the peak rocked harder.

Brian fell to his knees beside Emily. His eyes brimmed with fear, a reflection of hers. Cu whimpered and crowded near. Then Lugh's arms surrounded them, holding them together.

They all stared at the dragon for a few harrowing seconds while swaying above the zoo, then the peak groaned and crumbled. Emily slipped from their grasp, grappling to hang on to anything, but there was nothing but air beneath her.

Pain ratcheted through every body part that slammed into the slope as she bounced down it, being further battered by falling rocks and debris. Finally, Emily skidded to a stop, belly down, at the edge of a shelf.

Emily crawled to the brink and nearly passed out. Below her was a yawning abyss. She stared into the rent earth, shuddering, grateful she had stopped when she did. But then something slammed her from behind, shoving her over the rim.

Agony bloomed as she somersaulted into a living nightmare. It was probably moments, but it seemed an eternity before Emily landed in a broken heap at the bottom of the chasm the earthquake had carved into the zoo.

But that wasn't the end. Falling rocks, branches, and concrete pummeled Emily as she chanted the "calming" spell into the dirt. Talav's shriek trumpeted inside the earth. It quieted to a low moan, and the world stilled.

Raising her head, Emily ventured a peek. Lugh scrabbled down the chasm toward her, with Cu close behind. Blood covered the druid priest's face. Alarmed, Emily tried to crawl through the shifting rocks to reach him, but the stones beneath her began vibrating violently.

Her blood chilled. She might not be dead yet, but she was about to be.

Panicked, she flailed in the unstable rubble, struggling to climb out. But her bruised elbows and knees could find no purchase. The stones churned and quickened into a whirling pool of grinding, biting rock. Then, a vortex opened beneath her, and Emily screamed as it sucked her into the bowels of the earth.

☀☀☀

Brian MacBrayer wasn't ready to die. He dangled from the mangled fence, desperate to reach the top. But his hands were sweaty, and he kept sliding to the end of the pole. Spying an exposed tree root, he stretched his arm and almost had it but lost his grip.

Clawing at the empty air, he screamed bloody murder and plunged toward the steep slope. But his skateboarding muscle memory kicked in at the last moment, and he twisted in midair to land hands-first on a chunk of buckled concrete.

When he saw the upside-down bottom rushing toward him, Brian shrieked. Then getting his feet beneath him, he rode the broken concrete section over the cascading rocks.

For a split second, it was almost fun. Then Emily disappeared, and a boulder bounced and struck Cu in the head.

"Noooo! Cuuuuu!" Brian screamed, leaping from the slab to grab hold of his pet. But as his fingers sank into Cu's wiry hair, the ground opened at Brian's feet and sucked him under.

☀☀☀

Lugh watched as his nephew circled the same pit that had claimed Emily, the love of Lugh's life and the head of the Awen Order. Without hesitation or thought for his safety, he dove into the whirlpool, frantic to save Brian and Emily.

He fell a long way, then Lugh landed in the dark, gagging. It smelled like a backed-up sewer down here.

WORST FEARS

Emily blinked. Or thought she did. No glimmer of light penetrated the darkness. Was she dead? The absence of pain said probably so. Still, she would keep her eyes closed, otherwise, her phobias would kick her ass. If alive, she needed her wits.

Getting up on all fours was too easy. If she was other than worm food, wouldn't she be in pain? Or at least feel something? She groped the cramped space, half expecting to find her dead body, broken and battered like in the movies.

Pent-up tears trickled down her cheeks and her wail echoed off the walls of her prison. Just her luck. After twenty-nine years, she had finally found a place where she belonged. A place where she mattered and that mattered to her. A place of acceptance. A place of love.

Were the others dead, too? As a disaster specialist, Emily knew the odds. She sobbed a prayer for them anyway.

Attempting to rise on unsteady limbs, she slipped and took a shard to the knee. Pitching forward, she landed on hands that were already bruised and raw. Physical pain found her then and she collapsed in the rubble.

She wasn't dead after all. Again she had been spared, while those she loved died.

Giving in to the anguish, Emily keened. And in the rubble of yet another catastrophe, she hugged her knees and rocked like a child. Hot tears stung her ravaged face like a swarm of bees.

The earth rumbled menacingly, and the ground vibrated beneath her. Emily's heart raced.

She stopped rocking to listen. If the walls came down, she would be crushed. She had to get out of here. If she didn't, who would lead the druids against the Darkness?

The earth rumbled again, louder this time.

No one was coming. As usual, Emily would have to save herself.

Pushing back at the panic that conjured all sorts of frightful endings, Emily squeezed her eyes tight and sat up to assess her situation. She was underground. In the dark. In a claustrophobic space. And those who knew her whereabouts were likely dead.

All her worst nightmares come true.

Saliva pooled in the back of her throat. She pitched forward and heaved what was left of the hot dog she had eaten for lunch. It hadn't been that great going down. It was worse coming up.

When the nausea finally passed, Emily wiped her mouth with a ripped sleeve and rose on shaky legs to feel her way around the perimeter. Her ankle would barely hold her weight, but at least she could stand without banging her head.

Her skilled hands edged along granite walls that gave way to glassy dampness. Forgetting for a moment, she opened her eyes to inspect the surface. A shiver ripped through her as the nyctophobia struck, knocking the wind from her and dashing the little nerve she had mustered.

Squeezing her eyes shut again, Emily gulped musty air and rested her brow on the cool, notched surface. She called on God and every ounce of training she'd ever had to calm her nerves. She was alive. Someone would find her. They had to.

Soon the panic faded to a dull thud, and the flop-sweat dried.

From far away, Emily could feel more than hear a pulsation, similar to that of the ley lines. Only this was rhythmic. Man-made. Was it an earthmover? Were they digging for her? A ray of hope pierced her despair.

"Maybe the others did make it," she whispered aloud. Her gut knew better, but then she should be history too. If not found soon, she would be. The walls would cave in. Or her oxygen would run out. Her heart raced and pounded hard as the panic threatened again.

She fumbled for a rock and reared back to bang it against the wall, but her ankle gave way on the uneven ground. Mind-numbing pain shot up her leg and she lost her balance.

Crying out for help she knew wouldn't come, Emily fell and struck her head on a rocky outcrop.

NATHAIR

Hijacked by the spirit of a wandering druid, Nathair ascended the tunnel at a pace impossible for most snakes. The ground warmed as the path steepened. He paused as it groaned and shook violently.

Fortune had smiled on Alexis Mayhall. After wandering the Underworld longer than she could remember, a vain earth dragon pressed her into service, promising a reprieve should she complete one task.

Anxious to escape never-ending misery in a realm that allowed no redemption, Alexis had snapped at the chance. Here in the Underworld, nothing was real but pain. And though she had consciously chosen this lot in life, she hoped for salvation. Even if it meant inhabiting a snake.

But Talav, the clumsy earth dragon, had released more than Alexis—molten magma now coursed through the Underworld. With luck, it would remain below her and not travel any higher. She might be dead, but pain was her penance. She'd rather not endure the agony of being burnt to a crisp.

The passageway narrowed, becoming little more than a tiny crevice. As Nathair, Alexis shimmied through it, relishing the sensation of tight skin ripping from her long, lithe form. Leaving it behind, she slithered toward the figure lying in a heap on the rocky ground and stopped short.

It was the child she had failed to protect in life. A child now grown and hovering precariously between worlds. But *she* was not her allotted task.

Reaching into the Otherworld, Alexis called the dragon. Talav would help. Talav could save the girl. Alexis could not.

Weaving in and out of consciousness, Emily flickered between worlds. The line between them was tenuous, both dark and frightening, both full of recrimination. She had saved Atlanta, but couldn't save herself. And what about her friends and her Da? Were they safe? Or were they dead?

Probably the latter. And it was her fault. If she had listened to her father, they would all be alive. Still, she didn't deserve this—a slow, painful death, alone and underground in the dark. Every one of Emily's worst nightmares had come true.

She slipped into a delirious dream as her life-force ebbed.

"Help," she cried.

From the recesses of the cave, a voice whispered back. "Help is here."

Emily's fear subsided. "Here where?"

A soft hiss arose, like pressurized air escaping a tiny hole. A way out?

With great effort, Emily crawled toward the sound until she reached a narrow tunnel. The hiss was barely audible from the other end. Desperate to escape what was likely her tomb, she crept through the ever-narrowing crack. The ground groaned and shook violently.

With her last ounce of strength, Emily squeezed through to the other side. Her skin peeled away like a snake's.

Emily shivered awake. She was cold and lethargic. The damp had seeped into her bones, making her dangerously hypothermic. All she wanted to do was go back to sleep. But the still-reasoning part of her brain knew death would follow.

She groped in her pocket for Awen's ring, then realized it was on her finger. Too weak for anything more than a whisper, she held it to her chest and implored, "Awen, please save us."

The cave filled with a heavenly glow and her ancestor appeared. Dressed in a green gown over a white bodice, Awen knelt to caress Emily's cheek. Her long, luxurious hair cascaded in waves around Emily's face.

"It's about time you called. I thought you never would." Awen settled beside Emily and lifted her head gently onto her lap to stroke her face. "I am always here, within you." She smiled sweetly and touched Emily's heart. "You need only seek me out."

Her nose and eyes crinkled. "Your independence keeps me at bay. But your desire, your acceptance—these allow me *and* my power to manifest through you. But you are afraid of me. You believe I will take over, that you will not be in control. Your fear denies me expression. It keeps me locked away, impotent and unable to help."

Awen's eyes—the eyes Emily saw in the mirror every day—filled with sadness, compassion, and longing. The emotions reverberated within Emily's soul. She nodded to Awen.

From the corner of the vault came a soft hiss.

"There. Nathair calls. Follow him. Your destiny awaits at the other end." Awen bent to kiss Emily's forehead, then disappeared.

Half submerged in the dream, Emily crawled through the dark toward the snake Elder, one agonizing inch at a time.

TRAPPED LIKE A RAT

Tremors rattled the earth. A boulder jarred loose and landed inches from Brian's temple. He clenched his eyes tight and thanked Brigit, the goddess to whom he had prayed since childhood. Somehow he knew Brigit would save him. He was too young to die.

But his legs were pinned under a pile of rocks. He had tried repeatedly to move them, but they wouldn't budge. Now the pain and feeling were draining away. His throat was raw from screaming for help, and all the dirt he had swallowed. The others weren't near, or they would've heard him by now.

Unless they were all dead.

Terror squeezed his insides. He might die too, half-buried beneath a pile of rocks. How long would it take? Would rats eat him alive?

His head swam and he thought he might puke. He held his breath to keep from hyperventilating. Why hadn't he listened to Uncle Lugh and stayed home with Cu? They would both be alive. And watching it on the news.

A sob escaped, followed by another. If he lived to be a hundred, Brian would never forget Cu's scream or the sight of that boulder bashing in his head. He shivered and brought the handful of hair to his nose to breathe in Cu's scent. Then he stuffed it in his pocket and wrapped his arms around himself.

He thought of his mama and hiccupped on a sob. He didn't tell her goodbye. The floodgate opened in earnest, now. Cybele MacBrayer would come unglued. First, his dad had disappeared. Now Brian. He stared up at what he supposed to be the ceiling, though he couldn't see it in the dark. The tears stung his scraped cheeks.

A scrabbling noise made his heart pound. He lifted his aching head and groaned when the room spun round and round.

It was useless anyway. All he could see was black. But what was that noise?

"Probably a rat."

A chill ran through Brian. The voice was familiar. He squirmed to escape and every bone in his body screamed. The rocks held him pinned like a fly in a science exhibit.

"Wh-wh-who's there?"

"It's me. Hamilton. The good news is, there are signs of habitation. We might get out of this sticky wicket alive."

"Where are you? I thought Cu died. That boulder nearly took his head off."

"My friend Cu didn't make it, son. But I did. And I have you to thank. I'm sorry about jumping aboard without asking, but there was no time. I hope you don't mind. You saved my life."

His whole body began to shake. His teeth chattered. "You're inside me?" he squeaked. "You jumped inside *me*? You didn't ask. Is that allowed?" The shudder went all the way to Brian's toes.

"I'm sorry, Brian. It's typically frowned upon. But in emergencies, the lines are blurred. And I should let you know that I can hear your thoughts. And feel your feelings. Right now you're feeling violated, and you're afraid my presence might harm you in some way. I can assure you, it won't. And yes, you're still you."

Ever since his father had taught him how to shape-shift, or inhabit a body other than his own, Brian's worst nightmare was getting stuck. Now someone was stuck in him.

"I promise I'll jump ship at the first opportunity."

Well, that was something.

Brian quivered, taking stock. Other than Hamilton's thoughts in his head, he didn't feel all that different. Maybe it wouldn't be as bad as he'd always imagined. Especially if Hamilton could get them out of here.

"Can you?" he asked.

"Working on it," Hamilton said. "I can at least get these rocks off our legs. I mean, your legs."

"That's okay. You can say 'ours'. Do you feel how much it hurts? Even with the numbness?"

"Oh yeah. I'm trying to ignore it."

Brian's snicker sounded more like a sob. "I know, right?"

The crushing weight was nearly unbearable. Had the rocks broken his legs? Would they work again? Assuming, of course, they got out of this mess.

"I told you we would. A little faith, huh?"

"I guess," Brian mumbled, then something occurred to him. "At least I'm not alone. Well, yeah. I guess I am. But you know what I mean."

"Yes, kid. I do."

"Heeeey."

"What is it?"

"For some reason, you living my worst nightmare makes it better somehow. But it's still creepy. I'm sorry you don't have a body. If it's anything like I imagine, it must be pretty awful."

"Actually, not so much. You get used to it after a while. You're still you, no matter the vessel. And it beats pushing up daisies in a decaying corpse. Well. Maybe not. If you hadn't grabbed hold of Cu, I'd be sipping rare cognac and smoking a doobie with friends on the other side. Instead, I get to stick around and help you and my daughter save the world. Now, let's figure out how to get out of here. Starting with our legs."

ANIMALS AMUCK

Lugh MacBrayer woke bloody and bruised on a pile of gravel and red Georgia clay. Dank and close, it reeked of sulfur and open sewage. Emily and Brian were nowhere about. Nor was Cu.

He had failed them all. Now it appeared he needed saving, too.

Praying they had survived despite the odds, Lugh stood gingerly and brushed dirt from his clothes. Light leaked in from somewhere, allowing him to barely see his surroundings.

He studied the room, if it could be called that. The structure did appear man-made. Dust-covered canned goods and spider webs lined wooden shelves in one corner.

Was it an old root cellar? A fall-out shelter? Whatever it was, it hadn't been used in a long time. He took one step and shuddered when a mouse skittered across the floor in front of him. As a restauranteur, Lugh abhorred mice.

Spying the outline of a door, he tried to pry it open, but it wouldn't budge. Lugh circled the room. In the far corner, he found a roughed-out closet. Light leaked around the edges of a trap door mounted in the ceiling. Cement blocks were conveniently stacked underneath.

Lugh mounted the makeshift step and yelped when pain speared his hip. Taking his weight on the good leg, he shoved and felt the trap door give. Moving it to one side, he peered over the edge and put a finger to his nose to keep from sneezing.

Disturbed dust swirled in the light. Barrels of feed, stacked hay, and alfalfa bales meant the space was likely zoo storage.

Grunting, Lugh used his arms to haul his body through the trap door. He gave silent thanks he was in excellent shape. His druid training made sure of that. Other than a wrenched hip, cuts, scrapes and what felt like a million bruises, he had fared well, considering he'd lived through an earthquake *and* a volcanic eruption. He hoped Emily, Brian, and Cu had survived, too.

Outside the storeroom was a long hallway. Anxious to find the others, Lugh limped as fast as he could, sending dust into the air. He sneezed until his head pounded. Up a long flight of stairs, then another, Lugh climbed, until he was finally outside in the zoo.

A cacophony of sights and sounds assaulted his keen druid senses. Bedlam reigned. A cheetah shrieked and rushed past, chasing an injured orangutan that crashed through the underbrush.

Horrified, Lugh saw it strike. With one powerful leap, the big cat knocked the screaming primate to the ground. With brutal precision, the cheetah ripped out the ape's throat, then dragged it behind a building to feed.

A peacock screeched. Not a proud, preening call, but a dying one. Around the zoo, escaped animals fell to predators set free by the earthquake.

Over his head, helicopters from every news station from Atlanta to Savannah buzzed. Uniformed troops poured from the belly of one on the ground that sported a National Guard insignia. They joined zoo employees, darting frantic animals, bandaging wounds, and giving orders.

Lugh waded through the commotion until he found himself at the far end of the gorilla compound, opposite where they were when the quake struck the zoo. He ran toward the chasm, hip screaming agony with every step. Wiping his face, Lugh ignored the blood that came away on his hand. Whatever was wrong, he would deal with it later. First, he had to find Emily, Brian, and Cu.

On the opposite side of the rift, rescue workers maneuvered a backhoe into place, disturbing the shifting talus. Rocks skittered down the sharp incline and gathered momentum.

He squinted up at the newly-formed peak and recalled the thrill of riding it into the air. Then the terror of falling when the top crumbled. Turning, Lugh peered down into the chasm where the others had disappeared.

At the bottom, he spied what looked like a gorilla partially buried in the ruins. The others huddled in a makeshift enclosure above the fissure.

Hearing a roar from somewhere behind him, he turned to see a lioness and a lynx battling over a dead hyena. Lugh's head swam.

Bending forward, he drew a ragged breath and sought the still place inside of him. Breathing fouled air, he felt the quiet grow. Calm slowed his racing pulse. The ache in his gut lessened, and his hip eased.

From this place of power, Lugh reached out with his senses and searched for Emily's energy signature. It was faint, but steady. Next, he found Brian's trace. His was slightly askew, but pulsing strong. Cu, Lugh couldn't sense at all. Nor his hitchhiker, the former Grand Druid, Hamilton Hester.

For one sorrowful moment, Lugh let himself grieve for the majestic dog and the man who had always treated him as an equal.

A baby emu nipped by, chased by a coyote. Roused from his melancholy, Lugh drew an imaginary circle in the wreckage, took three deep breaths, and spoke a spell to subdue the animals.

Their cries quieted. One-by-one, the frightened beasts returned to their cages. A cry went up from rescue workers as they witnessed what some might call a miracle. Grateful for the small triumph, Lugh hung his head for the ones he couldn't save, including his companions.

A flash glinted off something in the fracture zone, and hopeful adrenaline flooded his limbs. Without care for his safety, he slid down the slope, dislodging rocks and debris. A paramedic waved and yelled something Lugh couldn't hear over the whump of the helicopters and the backhoe's maneuvering.

Slipping and sliding, he picked his way down the tricky talus. By the time he reached the bottom, his head was throbbing and his vision had gone slightly blurry. But he recognized Cu's collar.

Falling to his knees, he frantically dug rocks and dirt from his buried pet. Tears dripped on the backs of his bloody hands, and he couldn't help thinking of the first time he'd seen the dog lounging on an old blanket in front of his fireplace.

He'd been so opposed to keeping him. Now all Lugh could think was how much he would miss the big lug. And that if Cu was gone, Hamilton Hester's spirit was gone too. Which didn't bode well for the Awen Order.

Or the world.

Debris rattled down to land beside Lugh. The paramedic that had yelled at him earlier picked his way gingerly down the hill. Ignoring the stout man, Lugh continued pushing rubble off Cu until he freed the dog's head. He scooted closer and rocked it like a baby.

As the burly paramedic neared, he yelled over the din, "Sir, you're hurt. Let me help you."

"I'm fine. Just help me dig my dog out." Lugh looked up from his dead pet.

The paramedic squinted against the sun and studied Lugh's face. Lugh stared back, wondering what else could be wrong.

"Sir, I need to examine that gash."

Placing a hand on Lugh's shoulder, the paramedic spoke into a wrist unit, urgency punctuating every word. "Bertram, get down here with a Stokes basket. We have a head injury. A bad one, from the looks of it."

Lugh touched his crown. It was a gooey mess. Nausea hit him, and the world went wonky. He slumped to the ground.

The not-so-gentle paramedic shook Lugh's shoulder. "Stay with me, Sir. Keep your eyes open." He tapped Lugh's cheek. "Sir! Look at me!"

But the effort was too great. A gentle fog stole through Lugh's body and he sank into the bliss of unawareness.

DANGER IN AGARTHA

Nergal crept along the alley, intent on reaching the medical clinic. Shibboleth, the warlord from Gamma Reux had claimed command of Nergal's forces, and his goons had beaten Nergal to a bloody pulp. They'd left him for dead in the chutes outside Irkalla. The doctora in charge of the clinic was purported to hold no sympathies for Shibboleth *or* his new regime.

Keeping his stolen hood raised and his head down, Nergal hid in a doorway and peered from behind the hood. Wanted posters bearing his image papered the streets, and though a gaping wound marred his features, he was still recognizable. Still, no one had challenged him.

Hearing the sound of a throng approaching, Nergal limped to the end of the alley and shrank into the shadows. A contingent of Draconian soldiers outfitted in full battle gear appeared on the street.

Faraway, an explosion like the one he'd heard earlier, shook Agartha. Something big was going down. The rumbling intensified and the alley pitched from side to side, slamming Nergal to the ground.

Biting his black tongue against the pain, he molded his tortured body to the base of the jittering building. Mere meters away, the soldiers marched past on drunken feet. They weaved, cursing, but remained upright to surge over the bucking earth.

Straining to hear any news they might reveal, Nergal caught a grunted exchange. Enough to learn that something powerful had created a rift in the earth's mantle, releasing kilotons of magma toward the surface.

But for some reason, the crust had remained intact. The molten slurry was subverting and spreading through the chute system. Nergal thought of the hundreds of chutes that riddled Agartha, and the ones that connected it to all points of UnderEarth.

Were he still in power, he would divert the flow to the nearest volcanic upshaft. Make it the humans' problem. Instead, he was cowering in an alley, on the run in his own empire. A pariah with a price on his head.

The magma was Shibboleth's problem now. Unless Nergal happened to be in its path. Which would be ironic, considering he had just managed to reach Agartha without being captured or killed. Or dying from the wounds inflicted by Shibboleth's goons.

Struggling upright, he embraced the pain that lanced through his back, setting it afire. He would not give in to the pain *or* to Shibboleth. He would regain his strength and take his rightful place as leader of all Earth—after butchering the odious warlord and his henchmen.

But first, Nergal's injuries must be tended.

As if in agreement, the earth quieted. The rumbling shake abated to a quiver.

Hiding his welted face behind the hood, Nergal limped to the deserted street. He stooped to rifle a fallen pack dropped in the troop's haste. His effort secured him a stunner and two concussive devices. Nergal tucked the weapons in the lining of his cloak. Making sure he hadn't been seen, he hobbled to the shadows and continued to the clinic.

Soon, he spied the bold Draconian letters rolling across a flashing neon sign. *Qualified Medic. Always Open. Low Fee. No Questions. No Hassle.*

He slunk to the entrance and peered one last time through the gathering gloom. Few were around. Those that were hastened about their business.

Lifting the latch, Nergal shoved the slab aside and entered the small, well-lit clinic. He ignored the riff-raff crowding the waiting area, and shuffled to the counter where he demanded to see the doctora. The frightened receptionist skittered to the back.

Nergal limped to a nearby bench and accidentally stepped on the tail of a slender Draca, a female even more battered than him. Offering no apology or acknowledgment, he sank to the bench to huddle behind his robe and fight the pain.

"Sir?" the receptionist squeaked. She held the inner door ajar and motioned to him. Nergal rose.

The Draca beside him gasped. "NERGAL?"

Recognizing the voice, he wheeled to confront the wench responsible for his near-murder in Irkalla. But the room tilted on a roaring boom and he crashed into her. Scrambling upright, Nergal disentangled from the wily enchantress, only to be slammed by the heaving earth against the receptionist cage on the opposite wall.

An ominous rumble shook the building. Ceiling tiles rained upon the occupants of the waiting room. They climbed over one another, squealing and grunting, trying to reach the exit. The stench of fear and foul fumes thickened the air.

Springing to action, Nergal hauled the receptionist off the floor and pushed Inanna before them past two slimy arthropods. He thrust them out the door and dove back inside. Without the doctora, he would die of his injuries.

The rumble intensified. A crack ran up the far wall and the ceiling crumbled, giving way in the corner. Nergal limped to the back room. A Draca in medical scrubs worked to free an aging Fomorian from a tube that had been crushed beneath ceiling debris. The room lurched and the tube skittered sideways, sending the doctora face-first to the floor.

Patrika Tolbert tossed and turned in a troubled sleep. She had left Shalane Carpenter's tour in Atlanta, and would rejoin her after her brother's wedding. But in her dream, she was a man. And not just any man—a lizard-man in a dark cloak caught in an underground earthquake.

Patty jolted awake. She peered around the bedroom and laid back, relieved. She was not in a strange city nor an earthquake. She was in her mother and step-father's house in California.

Holding her hands in the air, she inspected them and the French manicure she'd gotten the day before, then jumped up to look in the mirror. Her reflection was human, not lizard. Thank God.

Shuddering, Patty climbed in the tall bed and stared at the ceiling.

Head propped on one hand, Ishkur, Nergal's Vice Major, stared at the Fomorian connected to the target Shalane Carpenter. He'd been in the lab since early that morning, shaken from a drunken stupor by an assistant bearing word that General Nergal was somehow dead.

Now Shibboleth, the warlord from Gamma Reux, was on his way to inspect Xibalba IX. More specifically, the experimental Human Domination program Ishkur had engineered for Nergal.

Reaching for a beaker of strong chicory, Ishkur groaned. His head felt the size of an Octedron's, and just as thick. But Shibboleth was coming. And from what Ishkur had heard of the infamous warlord, drunkenness was grounds for punishment by death.

He chugged the hot liquid and his throat constricted further. What he needed was a good, stiff drink. Turning back to the connector, Iskur moaned and grabbed his head.

The Fomorian's body lurched, then quieted. Ishkur logged the movement. Most likely an involuntary muscle twitch. The connection between the Fomorian and Carpenter was deactivated. At least, for now. But the beast would remain here, kept alive by feeding tube—a prisoner until he died, or his usefulness ceased.

Ishkur ran his tongue over his dry lips and checked the wall chronometer. It would be hours before Shibboleth and his crew arrived. Several hours. Plenty of time. One drink wouldn't hurt.

Reaching into his bottom drawer, Ishkur retrieved the bottle of Furroot he kept for such occasions. Unstoppering it, he tilted the bottle and guzzled the fermented fizz, letting it slide down the back of his craw. Replacing the cork, Ishkur belched and put the bottle in the drawer.

He stared at the Fomorian and wondered what was to become of them now that Nergal was dead

DRAIG TALAV

When Emily came to, it was darker than the darkest night and her head was one big, throbbing ache. She could no longer hear the steady thrumming that had meant someone was trying to rescue her. Had they given up already? How long had she been out?

She tried to stretch her legs and found she couldn't. Fear constricted her throat. Were they paralyzed? The fear intensified.

Putting a cautious hand out, she started when the crystalline surface gave way beneath her palm. That was odd. She feathered her fingers over the faceted stones. Had she landed in a bed of quartzite? The wall heaved abruptly, freeing her legs. Then the quartzite burped.

Jerking her hand away, she stumbled and tried to stand. Instead, she went sprawling face-first into the jagged rock. A sudden brilliance filled the room, blinding Emily. She cringed and clapped her hand over her eyes to squint between her fingers.

And wished she hadn't. What she thought was a bed of quartz was not. She lay atop a dragon, exposed in the glow of its fiery breath.

Scrambling to the ground, Emily flattened her back against the granite wall. Flames sprang to life around the ceiling and the dragon fire ceased. When her eyes adjusted, she looked about frantically for a hiding place. But there was nowhere to run.

Trembling, she faced the enormous creature. The cat Elder Hope had insisted the dragons were on Emily's side. This one twinkled like a Christmas tree and bore little resemblance to a-Ur or the fire dragon from the zoo. It had soulful golden eyes that glistened with interest more than appetite. And without the neck ruff or spikes, it didn't seem as intimidating.

Emily relaxed a little, grateful for the light now that her eyes had adjusted. When it tucked its legs under in a stance reminiscent of her cat's Buddha pose, she noticed it had no wings. Which struck her as funny. Uneasy laughter bubbled over though she pressed a knuckle to her bruised lips.

The dragon peered at her with something akin to wonder. "Awen," it sighed.

The melodious notes landed in the chamber like pearls of hope. This wasn't the first time Emily had been called that.

Uncertain, she responded. "Yes?"

Refracted color danced off the mirrored scales as the dragon dipped forward in a bow. "I am Talav, Queen of the Earth Dragons and Keeper of the Earth. At your service, Awen, as ever."

"You look different from the other dragons," Emily sputtered. "Where are your wings?"

The snake-like head whipped back in a roar, and the dragon reared on powerful hindquarters. "And where are your manners?"

Stones dislodged and skittered down the walls to rest at Emily's feet. She was reminded, a little late, that dragons are vain and easily offended. Or so she had been told.

When Talav quieted, Emily apologized for her breach in manners. The fire faded from the queen's eyes, replaced by a glow so brilliant Emily had to lower her lashes.

"I've been searching for you, my lady."

"I am honored, wise one. Can you get me out of here?"

Talav shifted. Light rainbowed off her jeweled breast. "Of course I can. But here is where you are supposed to be."

"Here? Hardly." Emily wanted nothing more than to get out of here.

"There are things the druids cannot teach. I will help you discover that which you seek."

Emily moved a step closer and collapsed against the wall when pain shot through her ankle and up her leg. "And what is it I seek?" she groaned.

"A way to save the world."

The words floated on a puff of dragon's breath that was warm and surprisingly inoffensive. And very familiar. Which on inspection, seemed absurd.

"I have searched for you for four long years," Talav explained. "You're a hard one to reach." Tendrils of dread shimmied up Emily's spine. "Now, as prophesied, we are here at the end of the world."

Emily's heart pounded and her throat tightened. "You know the prophecy?"

"Aye."

Brushing her bushy hair out of her face, Emily leaned against the wall, careful to keep her weight on her good foot. "So you say. What do you know?"

"I was there when the earth was made. And a thousand years ago, I heard the prophecy uttered."

"You were? You did?"

"I was. And I did."

"Then you must know about my companions. Are they alive? Did they make it out?" Emily pointed to her ankle. "Can you heal my wounds?"

"I can help." The dragon blinked and the worst of Emily's discomfort vanished.

"You know magic!" She rotated her foot and touched her face. The gashes had receded and the pain was gone.

"That's not all I know, deary," the dragon crooned.

Desperation ratcheted Emily's plea. "Then will you tell me about my friends? Can you save them?"

"No deary, only you."

The cold enveloped Emily's heart. She hung her head, wondering what to say that might change the dragon's mind. Grief welled up for her father and friends. What if they were dead? Or dying? She thought of Da's warning, his insistence something was wrong.

Tears trickled down Emily's face. Some savior she'd turned out to be. The zoo had been her idea. Perpetually pigheaded and mired in self, Emily had not listened. She had endangered them all.

Huffing steam on already-glittering jewels, Talav produced a tanned hide from a nearby shelf and rubbed her scales lovingly. Her sad eyes flicked from her precious gems to Emily.

"No, you are no savior. But you will be. Or can be. That is entirely up to you." Like a mother reassuring a child, the dragon's tone was calm and soothing.

But what had Emily been saying? Something about her companions.

"They are no longer your concern, little wren."

The familiar epithet plucked Emily's heartstrings. But she'd not be deterred. "Can you at least tell me if they are safe?"

"Safe is a relative term."

Talav's frustrating vagueness did not surprise Emily. All the animal Elders she had met during her brief, but eventful, druid training, shared the same annoying trait. Interpreting their words meant reading between the lines. And asking a lot of probing questions.

"Are they alive?"

"Alive, too, is relative."

Emily groaned on a yawn and fought to keep her eyelids open.

"The sooner you learn these things," the dragon waved a slightly-feminine forepaw around the cave, "the sooner we can get you out of here."

Fear congealed in Emily's stomach. "So now I'm your prisoner? You said you would help."

"Shhhh," the queen soothed, pressing a shiny claw to leathery lips. She began humming an ancient tune that filled the cave, as surreal as it was haunting.

Emily opened her mouth to speak but forgot what it was she was going to say. All she could think of was a comfortable bed and a warm down comforter. She strained to stay awake, but her body relaxed. Her lids drooped. The tension drained out of her jaw, and her shoulders sagged.

Despite her best efforts, Emily succumbed to sleep and floated on a bubble of bliss, buoyed by the dragon's narcotic song.

CONCUSSION

Through the fog of a raging headache, Lugh zeroed in on the beeping alarm. He reached for the snooze, but his arm wouldn't move. Opening bleary eyes, he realized he was in a hospital bed with his arm strapped down. He strained to gather his thoughts. Why would he be in the hospital?

Mitchell Wainwright appeared in his line of sight. And why would Mitch be here?

"How are you, buddy?" His tone was solicitous, but Lugh's once-friend was angry. At Lugh. Lugh turned his head away and groaned.

"That good, huh?" the attorney growled. "Well, imagine how your Grand Druid must be feeling. Oh, wait. She's probably dead and feeling nothing. Isn't the high priest sworn to protect our leader?"

Eyes clenched tight, Lugh lay there remembering.

Every word Mitch spoke was true. Not only had Lugh lost the woman he loved, but he'd also lost Brian and Cu. *And* the disembodied spirit of Emily's father, Hamilton Hester. The Order's erstwhile leader.

Tears escaped, first one, then another. Lugh let them fall. To hell with Mitch. It was a miracle Lugh hadn't perished, too.

"Don't listen to him, Lughnasadh." The southern-drenched syllables were those of Morgan Foster, the stately, but formidable, head of druid security and Emily's aunt. Lugh turned his head, and the pain was like an exquisitely sharp dagger twisting in his temple.

"We're beside ourselves, Sugar. Including, believe it or not, Mr. Wainwright here. He hopped the first plane from Rome and drove straight to the hospital from the airport. Didn't you, dear?" Morgan shoved Mitch, and the attorney grunted.

Her quick smile didn't reach her eyes. "Finn says you're okay. Or relatively so. You have a mild skull fracture and a moderate-to-severe concussion. You won't be out of the woods for several days. But you will live. Brian and Emily, on the other hand, are missing and presumed dead. Please tell us different, Lughnasadh. What happened out there?"

In as few words as possible, Lugh recounted what he remembered, beginning with the earthquake. When he was done, the two druids remained silent. Morgan was drawn. Mitch seemed surprisingly upbeat, though Lugh had offered no new information. Lugh turned his face to the wall, gasping when the knife-edge seared his temple.

A ghostly hand reached out to stroke his brow—warm, soft, and light as a feather—easing the pain. When Lugh opened his tortured eyes, the others were gone. The angelic face of his dead mother floated above him, singing, "Sleep, my little Lughnasadh, sleep." A narcotic-induced slumber towed him under.

☼☼☼

When Lugh woke again, the room was empty. A glance at the window told him night had fallen. He stirred and tried to sit up straight, but the leads and IV held him in place. He thought of ripping the needles from his arm and bolting from the hospital. But he was in Critical Care with a cracked skull and a severe concussion. Leaving now was a fool's plan. And Lugh MacBrayer was no fool.

Better to lie still. With rest, would come recovery. He stared at the low ceiling and wondered whose voice was in his head. Maybe the doctor or nurse had whispered it to him.

But Brian and Emily were out there somewhere and needed help. His addled brain tried various rescue schemes, but not one of them changed the facts. He was too weak to do anything but lay here and heal.

Lugh drifted for a while, unaware that he slept, and woke alert in the wee hours of morning. The monitors still beeped in the same monotonous tone. He looked around the room, taking in the IV trolley, empty Naugahyde chair, and the portable bedtable with its cup and pitcher just out of reach.

He eyed the cup and tried to lick his thick, dry lips, debating whether to use the call button. But Brian and Emily had no water. Assuming they were alive.

He put a tentative hand to his throbbing forehead and fingered the butterfly dressing. The gash was a good two inches long and cut across the corner of his right brow. His cheekbone felt bruised, puffy, and raw. Someone had said he'd lost a lot of blood.

Lugh thought of their day at Zoo Atlanta and chills ran up and down his spine. The animals had declared fealty to Emily, calling her Queen Awen. Each had been reverent, bowing in its way. Never in Lugh's life had he seen or heard anything like it. Not even in the tomes of druid lore he had devoured over the years.

And to think they'd been celebrating when it happened. Emily's spells had stopped both the earthquake and volcano, fooling them into believing the nightmare was over. Instead, it had sucked them into the earth.

A tall male nurse bustled in. He flipped on the too-bright overhead light, and began checking Lugh's bandages and vitals. "How are you feeling, Mr. MacBrayer?"

"Awful," Lugh croaked. Which was exactly what he deserved. "My head is throbbing and my mouth feels like sandpaper."

The long-limbed man poured water into the cup and held it so Lugh could drink from the straw. Commandeering it, Lugh slurped the entire contents and immediately wished he hadn't. Brain freeze jabbed an ice pick through his already-aching skull.

When it passed, he grinned weakly and held the cup out for more.

With slanted brows, the young man poured, snapped the lid on and handed it back. "Careful, dude," he ribbed good-naturedly. "Don't hurt that pretty little head of yours."

Lugh managed a thin smile, sipped, and handed it back. A breeze stirred and Finn the resident neurosurgeon and Emily's cousin, bustled to Lugh's side.

"Lugh-Mac, you scared the bejesus outta us. Welcome back. You've got one hell of a concussion." He lifted Lugh's hand between both of his and rubbed vigorously, conferring a welcome glow.

"Will I live, doc?" Might as well get to the point.

"I believe so. But we're keeping you here under observation for a day or two." Finn glanced at the antique tank Cartier watch hiding beneath the sleeve of his white coat. "I want you to relax and sleep as much as you can. We're administering medium-chain fatty acids through the IV, and will soon begin the cold laser treatments. By the time you leave, you should be nearly new. A bit shaky until your body recovers from the beating it took, but well enough."

Lugh grabbed the druid doctor's arm and held on tight. "Finn, I have to go after them. It's our Grand Druid. *And* my brother's kid. Mitch is right. This is on me. I'm the one that lost them. Get me out of here so I can find them."

The doctor took Lugh's hand and leaned close. "No Lugh-Mac. Your only job at the moment is to get well. We need you. Let Morgan worry about finding Emily and Brian. Security is all over it."

Lugh's agitation melted under the healer's touch. Letting go of a heavy sigh, he closed his eyes. Morgan and the others would find his charges. Finn would get him out of here as soon as possible, and nearly as good as new. He'd said so.

Cu's regal face flashed in Lugh's mind and a vice-grip wrenched his heart. His eyes flew open. He grabbed the hem of Finn's white coat. "What about Cu? Did someone bring him home?"

The doctor's face sagged a little. "They took Cu to Jocko's and put him in the back of the deep-freezer away from the food. He's wrapped tight, and will stay there until you can give him a proper burial."

Tears sprang to Lugh's eyes, then faded as the meds kicked in. "Night buddy."

The voice came from far away. Lugh drifted in a troubled land where he kept losing Brian and Emily to an avalanche, while Cu ran around him in a circle barking.

CURIOSITY

The tragedy unfolded on satellite television as Shalane Carpenter watched. The human toll was minimal, but Zoo Atlanta was split in two. An unknown number of animals were dead, with others free to roam neighboring communities. Civilian troops in combat gear worked to secure the area and rescue the living.

Among the missing and presumed dead was Emily Bridget Hester, sole heir to the extensive Hester Empire. Shalane stared at the redhead, gut twisting. Why did she know that name? Two shock-eyed girls stuttered on camera through copious tears. They described seeing the heiress and a man fall into the crevasse, along with a boy the girls knew from school.

Another eyewitness, Juan the zookeeper, had been fortunate enough to grab hold of an anchored tree root. He had dangled helplessly above the pit as the victims disappeared. In addition to the boy and Emily Hester, a security guard was missing, though his name was withheld pending family notification.

One man survived—a miracle according to the paramedics. The camera panned to the bottom of the fracture zone, where the medics hoisted a thirty-something man with a bandaged head onto a stretcher. Workers toiled to extricate the bodies of a very large dog and a gorilla.

"Not the dog," Shalane wailed.

A fat tear rolled down her cheek. A gaping hole had opened inside of her. But why? The disaster was a boon. It would fill the seats of the Fox Theater. And that was a good thing. Advance ticket sales had been bleak. Southern Baptists weren't as forgiving of Shalane's lifestyle as the rest of the country.

She stared at the screen and tried to swallow past the constriction in her throat. What was wrong with her? Disasters usually had the opposite effect, but for some reason she felt a deep sense of loss. What was different about this?

Giving in to the impulse she'd had since waking, she threw a jacket over her street clothes and left the charming inn. She had checked into it the day before, needing a break from her crew and a real bed and full-sized shower.

It was twelve-oh-one. Seven hours until curtain call. Plenty of time to get to the zoo, then to the Fox Theater. She had to know why she was feeling this way.

She programmed her destination into the rental car's GPS and searched the radio for the latest news. Halfway to Atlanta, a call from Cecil interrupted. She punched the hands-free.

"Yes?"

"I'm here, where are you?" her husband demanded. "Your room is empty. I only agreed to stay in Villa Rica because you promised to go with me to the gold museum. What happened to our lunch at Chat & Choo? You said you liked that restaurant. And you promised, Shay-Shay."

She had forgotten. Seeing Cecil's number had reminded her. But his tone had her seeing red, and Lord help her, she snapped.

"Dammit Cecil, can't you let me have one stinking minute without you or anyone else climbing up my butt? Just one lousy minute? Is that too much to ask?" She growled and ended the call, then felt guilty for hanging up on the one person who loved and accepted her for the freak that she was.

"DAMMIT!" she shrieked at the top of her lungs, fresh tears streaming down her less-than-cherubic face. She didn't want Cecil. She wanted…what? Something she couldn't have. But what? Neither the screeching nor the temper could fill the mysterious, expanding hole in her heart.

The zoo was closed when Shalane arrived. National guards and civilian troops swarmed the front entrance. She would have to find another way in. She detoured around the Cyclorama and left the grounds to traipse through Grant Park, grateful she'd had the presence of mind to wear comfortable shoes. Other than looky-loo's, helicopters, and blaring sirens, Shalane detected no sign of an earthquake.

She came upon a gap in the fence and looked around. No one was watching, so she slipped inside. Zoo employees scurried along the trail, impervious to her presence. When they passed from sight, Shalane slipped from the bushes and followed the same path.

Soon she came upon a buckled sidewalk. From there, all she had to do was follow the wreckage. Matchstick-size splinters that had once been mature bamboo trees littered the landscape. Employees and troops worked side by side, still rescuing animals whose habitats were destroyed.

A peafowl cried. Another answered from farther away. Shalane rounded a corner and stopped when she spied the broken peak from which Emily Hester and the others had fallen. It looked taller from here than it had on TV.

The fissure below it was easily a hundred yards long, and a quarter as wide. Emergency personnel spilled over the pinnacle. Forming a human chain, they were manually cleared rubble from the site. Which she thought was odd, until she spied a backhoe that had fallen into the crevasse.

The bottom of the pit was deserted. Reinforcing the spell to make her inconspicuous, Shalane circled the ridge. She had to get down there or she would burst from not knowing what was drawing her.

The air reeked of sulfur, destruction, and death. A perfect combination for winning souls. Glee warred with Shalane's horror. The weekend services were sure to sell out. From the opposite side, she picked her way down the unstable slope, trying not to disturb the rocks or call attention to herself.

In no time at all, she was huffing from exertion. And only halfway to the bottom. She rested on a boulder and took a swig of the water she'd brought with her. Despite the slightly overcast day, her cheeks blazed. She peeled off her jacket and tied it around her waist, mopped the sweat from her brow, and took another pull from the water bottle.

From this vantage point, Shalane could see the top of the crater and the line of workers. All else was hidden by the rise. Broken concrete and asphalt, trees, and mangled fences littered the slope. She thanked God there were no dead bodies. Her belly rumbled, reminding her she had skipped breakfast in favor of this odd, unscheduled jaunt.

Picking her way around a tangle of barbed wire, she slid on loose gravel and grabbed the root of an upturned tree. She hung in midair for a long couple of seconds before gaining a foothold. Letting go, she scrabbled the rest of the way to the bottom and looked up. It was a daunting ten stories to the top. Or more.

She pushed away thoughts of scaling it and focused her attention on the fracture zone. As far as she could tell, the cave-in had started somewhere else, then ripped through here and kept going.

According to the news reports, this was where Emily Hester and her friends had disappeared. But there was something else Shalane had not expected. Ancient magic imbued the land. And it was overlain and countermanded by another sort of magic, one she'd never encountered.

She knelt and laid her hand on the loose stones. Ripples of energy wafted over her. Baffled, Shalane changed positions and took another reading. The result was the same. Inconclusive. She sat back on her heels, wiped her brow, and took a sip of water. Never had she encountered either brand of magic.

Conscious she was taking longer than planned, she called on Archangel Michael, then listened with all her senses. But no answers came. Only more questions.

Raising her eyes to the heavens, Shalane sighed and hauled her bulk upright. No wiser than she'd been before, she began the treacherous climb to the top.

OUT OF THE FRYING PAN

To Brian's amazement, the spell worked—the pile of rocks rolled right off his legs. And with Hamilton's healing charm, his legs were as good as new. Maybe this togetherness thing wasn't so bad. He had learned more magic in the last few minutes than in weeks of training. He should talk to someone about adding it to their curriculum.

"I think you just did." Hamilton's voice inside his head reminded Brian he wasn't alone.

His stomach grumbled and he thought about what he'd been trying to forget. "So what's the game plan? I'm hungry," he answered silently.

"Me too."

They both laughed. It was weird having another experience your bodily functions.

"Notice anything different about our surroundings?"

Brian opened his eyes. He'd been keeping them closed, a trick he had learned from the therapist his mother made him see after his dad left. It hadn't gotten rid of his separation anxiety, but it had helped with his fear of the dark.

"It's lighter. But why?"

"Not sure," Ham said aloud. "Is that a knife in your pocket? How'd you get it through zoo security?"

Brian shrugged. "I don't know. I just figured it was too small. Nobody's ever bothered me about it."

"Well good for us. We have a knife, even if it's a little one. Too bad you didn't throw some matches in your pocket. Or a lighter. Those would help."

"Well excuse me for not bringing my Cub Scout survival kit to the zoo," Brian huffed. "Believe me, if I had known, I'd have stuffed a couple of candy bars in my pocket."

"I know, kid. But cheer up. Judging from the light, we must be close to the surface. Which means help is near. Ready to explore?"

Brian peered into the darkness. It might be lighter, but not much. "No. I'm not. But if it's the only way we're getting out of here, let's go."

"Walk slowly and be on the lookout for low ceilings and bottomless pits. And we should probably keep the chatter inside your head."

Shivering, Brian hunched his shoulders and whispered a prayer of protection to Brigit. He put his hand to the wall and reached out with one foot to test the ground before proceeding. When he had trudged downhill for what seemed hours and miles, Hamilton prompted him to stop and listen.

A low-pitched hum whirred up ahead. And farther away, someone was talking. Brian's heart sang. Rushing toward them, his legs locked and he pitched forward.

"Why'd you do that?" he whined, picking himself up. "There are people. We're saved!"

"No, I don't think so. The language sounds alien. It might be a trap."

"Know a lot about aliens?" Brian snickered.

"A little. Enough to know to be careful. Shush!"

That hit home. Brian flattened his back to the tunnel wall. The voices were louder and approached at a fast pace. Panicking, he turned to retreat but Hamilton stopped him again.

"Shhh. Don't move," the druid said inside Brian's head. "Aliens have acute hearing."

Brian froze. The voices were low and gruff, clipped and scary. Hamilton was right. These were no humans. Brian wrapped his arms around his shoulders and realized he was shaking. Ham mumbled something and his trembling quieted. The fear eased, but only a little.

"Those things are headed our way," Ham whispered in his head. "We need a plan. Some aliens are friendly. Others, not so much. These live underground, so they probably belong to the second category. Either way, your youth could be an advantage. Play it up. Cry. Bawl. Tell them about the earthquake and how you got here. Don't be threatening, and maybe, just maybe, they will let us live. Got it, son?"

In the shadows, two tall beings approached carrying on a steady stream of conversation. It sounded like nothing particularly important, like they were passing the time, shooting the breeze. Brian prayed they were friendly. Oh, goddess. What if they wanted to eat him? To boil him alive and fight over his carcass?

"Hold it together," Hamilton warned. "Here they come."

A brilliant beam of light pierced the darkness, joined by another. The exchange ceased as the beams found Brian's face. Screeching in pain, he covered his eyes and doubled over. Then wailing as instructed, he crumpled to his knees and cowered on the floor with his arms over his head.

"Don't hurt me," he sobbed with genuine fear. "I was trapped by the earthquake. I'm lost and need help. Can you help me? I'm just a child. Please don't hurt me." From the corner of one tear-filled eye, Brian watched the creatures. He was glad Hamilton had warned him, else he might've crapped his pants.

More than seven-feet tall, the aliens stood upright and had greenish scales and snake-like faces that reminded him of Lizard from the old Spider Man movie. Or Killer Croc from Suicide Squad. Brian and his friends played those video games a lot.

The aliens looked back and forth at Brian and each other. They wore nothing but wide belts with gadgets hanging from them. Above the belts, the breast and abdominal plates were much larger, and a lighter shade of green. The creatures were thin and muscular, with clawed hands and feet that could easily rip Brian apart with one swipe.

He lifted his head to peer up at them. "Please, can you help me? Can you get me home?"

The leader grunted something. The other responded.

Would they let him live? Neither had drawn a weapon from those belts. Not that they needed one. The biggest guttered something meant for Brian. Not knowing how to respond, he remained silent. It grunted again and motioned for Brian to stand.

When he did, the other twisted Brian's arms behind his back and clamped something on his wrists.

"Good job, Brian," Ham whispered in his thoughts. "They're not going to kill us. At least not yet. Otherwise, no need for restraints."

The brute shoved him and pain shot up his back. He yelped and nearly fell in the dirt. The creature prodded again, this time higher and not as hard. Brian took a tentative step. Were they taking him to their headquarters? Would they make him battle some ferocious monster to the death?

"Doubtful," Hamilton chimed. "But you do have quite an imagination, Brian. Ever think about a writing career?"

"Writing? Are you kidding?" Brian stumbled ahead of the Croc-man. "I'm about to be eaten alive and you're talking to me about books? What is wrong with you? I thought you were supposed to be some big-deal druid master and you're talking to me about what I want to do with my life? Well, listen up, *Sir*. I may not be around much longer, in case you haven't noticed. So unless you have something useful to say, like where they might be taking me, or how I can escape, then maybe you shouldn't talk right now."

The druid had the nerve to chuckle in Brian's head. Either the gravity of their situation wasn't registering with Ham, or all the shifting between bodies had affected his brain. Or maybe, considering he could jump into an alien if need be, Hamilton wasn't all that concerned about Brian.

"What an awful thing to think!" Ham sounded genuinely hurt.

"Alright, I take it back. But promise I won't end up lizard food."

"I have a few tricks up my sleeve. Or rather, your sleeve. Just stick to the plan, keep up the harmless, help-me routine, and with luck, we'll live."

Brian smacked his lips. "I need water," he said over his shoulder to the creatures. "And food. I'm thirsty and starving." His plea fell on deaf ears.

The tunnel opened to another that was wider and brightly-lit from an unseen source. Something about it looked familiar. The floor was as slick and clean as the walls. Brian had heard about underground mazes and knew the druid nation had an extensive network. But this was not the same. These had been carved from bedrock and polished to a high sheen.

The long corridor slanted downward, opening onto many side routes that veered off to who-knew where. The deeper they went, the hotter it grew.

The leader hissed something into a handheld communications device. Brian paused, only to get shoved again. Grunting, he stumbled forward, wishing he could wipe the sweat from his brow. A hundred yards later, they turned left at a bank of elevators.

What the hay? Was this an old bunker, abandoned and forgotten after the World Wars?

The leader's communicator beeped. He answered and growled something to the other brute, who turned and hurried back the way they'd come. One of the elevator doors slid open. Yelling gibberish, the alien shoved Brian so hard he flew across the threshold into a vacuum tube.

Brian had just enough time to wonder why the alien hadn't come with him before the door slammed shut. The car flew, down, down, down, until the heat became unbearable, and the tube bucked and shook. It continued hurtling downward for what seemed an eternity, then stopped abruptly. Brian slammed into the floor of the tight enclosure and something snapped. Had his wrist broken? If so, it didn't hurt.

"Well that wasn't pleasant," Hamilton said over the rumbling of the earth.

"You can say that again."

"Well, that wasn't pleasant."

"What? Are you five?" Brian stood to see what bones were broken and found his hands were free. The snap had been the wrist restraints breaking. He jabbed the air with both fists. Beneath his feet, the rumble intensified, then moved away through deeper chambers. The floor stilled. "Don't you know we're in danger?"

"Of course, but I thought a teenager would appreciate my attempt at humor in what is certainly a dire situation. Lighten up, little raven. At least we're free." Hamilton gave him the internal equivalent of a prod. "I have a feeling this is not where they meant us to end up. We've been waylaid."

"And I smell those rotten eggs again. Is that why it's so freaking hot down here?" Hamilton was silent. Brian mopped his face with his sleeve.

They were not in a dungeon as Brian had feared, but a dirt cave. Or maybe this was what they used for a dungeon. Something about it, too, seemed familiar. He spied a dimly-lit passage and followed it until he reached a place where three tunnels intersected. Two were blocked by crude doors.

"And now I'm getting the feeling we're being herded." Hamilton cleared his throat.

There were no knobs, levers, or finger holds in the doors, nothing carved out to assist in getting to the other side. Brian shoved against them, but neither budged.

"It looks like it's either go back or down that tunnel," he said out loud. Something about it seemed slightly sinister. Even more than where they'd already been.

"I vote tunnel," mumbled the druid master.

"Okay," Brian gulped. "Here goes."

He walked as quietly as possible. It helped that the floor was hard-packed clay, soft and spongy beneath his sneakers. It muffled any sound he might've made. In places, the clay was damp and slippery, making progress slow. He soon figured out that water was seeping around the edges where the floor met the wall on his right. A plink sounded and echoed in the void, like glass or thin metal clinking together.

Straightening slowly, Brian searched the dim tunnel. It all looked the same, but his awareness ratcheted up a notch. On high alert, he put one foot in front of the other until he reached the place he thought the noise had sounded. Inspecting the walls and floor, he found nothing. Just dust on the left side, sticky clay to his right.

In his head, Hamilton said, "I'm with you, partner. That sound wasn't natural. Let's hurry, shall we?"

Brian needed no further motivation. Remaining cautious, he quickened his pace until he spied a brightening at the end of the tunnel.

"The sun!" he cried and hurried toward it, glee building. Until his legs buckled and Brian collapsed in a heap with a grunt. "What'd you do that for?"

"I didn't," his hitchhiker said in his head. "You tripped."

"Did not." Brian stood, dust flying as he patted his pants and wiped his hands on his ripped shirt. "My legs collapsed. There's a distinct difference. But it's probably a good thing. There might be more monsters out there."

He inched to the opening and leaned far enough to peer around the corner. What he saw made Brian jerk back.

They weren't out of danger. Quite the opposite.

THE DOCTORA

With only seconds to spare, Nergal shoved the doctora through the door and barely cleared it himself before the building collapsed with a shockwave that sent them cartwheeling into the street. The ground shuddered. Dust billowed from the flattened structure, clogging the air and blinding Nergal. Rising to all fours, he located the doctora and yanked her from the rubble.

"Can you walk?" he grunted.

Dazed, she teetered in the wreckage and pointed to one ear slit.

Another tremor hit, rocking the buildings that were still standing. Then a thunderous explosion sounded in the direction of the base. Nergal's base. Or it had been.

A Breesnak screeched and charged from a building, flames engulfing its hairy back. Nergal grabbed the horrified doctora's arm and dragged her to the alley, limping as fast as his pain and bowed-posture would allow. She yanked her arm from his grasp and planted her feet. A line of lavender blood trickled down one cheek.

Leaning closer so she could hear him over the din, Nergal bellowed, "Come. My hideout is on higher ground. It should put us above the danger."

Her tortured countenance swiveled from side to side, gawking at the death and destruction. Another explosion sounded louder and closer. A steam vent spewed noxious gas. He had a momentary thought of cold-cocking the Draca, but in his current condition, Nergal wouldn't be able to carry her. And he needed her skills.

He grabbed her arm and dragged her behind him, picking his way over fallen rubble, and fighting past crazed survivors to the end of the alleyway. Drawing his hood tight, Nergal peeked around the corner. The main intersection was a heaving cauldron of reptiles and other beings hurrying to escape the quaking rumble that was growing stronger and louder.

Reeking of fear and antiseptic, the petite doctora nudged Nergal's shoulder and nodded to a nearby drain. The vent spewed, blasting toxic steam in their direction. He cleared a path through the hysterical crowd, bowling them over like pinquots with his good shoulder. The rumble intensified and the doctora urged him to hurry.

The ground undulated in a side-to-side roll that flung them on top of a pile of writhing bodies. She scrambled up first and grabbed Nergal's cape to free him from the grasp of a wailing Jahquad. Slinging the offender into the throng, Nergal trampled another and limped with the doctora away from the melee.

Over their heads, an imperious screech drowned out everything else. Glancing up, Nergal faltered. It was the double-crossing drake. The one who had sealed the volcano shaft near Xibalba IX and ended Nergal's forays into AboveEarth. For a moment, he prepared to do battle. Then reality sank in. He was much too weak to challenge the dragon.

Instead of answering with his own primal roar, Nergal kept his head down and led the doctora through a maze of wrecked buildings, blistering-hot steam vents, and past flowing magma. The dragon's raucous cries shredded Nergal's nerves as it zigzagged above the village, strafing anything left standing by the quake. Fires burned out of control.

Still, they pushed on, winding away from the dragon and town, ever in the direction of the cave. Nergal limped as fast as he could, bolstered by the doctora. She had apparently decided he was safer than the magma, the rabid crowd, and the vengeful dragon. Which was a good thing. He needed her help.

They reached the first steep hummock, and Nergal slumped to the ground. They weren't safe yet, but he had to rest. Behind them, the dragon flew back and forth over the outskirts of Agartha. The villagers scrabbled to escape its fiery attack, hiding in ruins that were already scorched.

The stench of burnt flesh and sulfur fouled air already thick with smoke, making it difficult to breathe. Nergal calculated the distance to the cave. They would have to hide until his strength returned. It had been hard enough coming down. With his energy depleted, he was no match for the grueling climb.

"Come. You can make it." The first words the doctora had spoken were delivered in a rolling accent like none Nergal had heard.

He looked at her closely. Her pupils were violet, a vivid shade that sent a shockwave through him. Nergal glanced back toward the city.

Few of the high-rise buildings were left standing, and the firedrake had passed from sight, though its eerie screech echoed through the valley.

With the doctora's help, Nergal stood on legs that begged to give out. He leaned heavily on the small, but seemingly strong Draca. When the climb proved too difficult, they scrabbled up the rest of the hill lizard-style. They rested briefly at the top, then slid down on their backsides, grinding to a stop by a stand of trees.

It was quieter here and though the ground trembled, the rumble was no longer deafening. The dragon's cry had gone silent. Nergal dragged himself up by an exposed tree root and directed the doctora through the trees to the next set of hillocks.

☼☼☼

Patty thrashed about in her bed, unable to escape the dream. In it, she fell to the ground, exhausted. Pain shivved through her, but the lizard-doctor urged her to rise and climb. At the limits of her endurance, she gritted her pointed teeth and dragged herself up with the doctora's help.

Or as close to upright as she could get. Her back screamed bloody murder and the high-pitched roar of some frightful air-beast nearly buckled her knees again. The doctora clutched at her scaled arm, then crooked it over her shoulders, supporting and half-dragging Patty up the rise.

Only her name was Nergal. And she was badly injured and close to death. The air stank of burning flesh and brimstone. Was it her wounds she smelled? Or something even worse?

She labored up one hill and down another, half-conscious, and half-delirious. The doctora drove her on, coaxing, haranguing, and cheering her efforts. Without her, and possibly even with, Nergal-Patty knew he wasn't long for this world.

But he made it up and over every hill. They eventually found themselves at a nearly-invisible entrance, the approach to the cave he had discovered two days earlier. They navigated the winding entry, and the doctora rolled the boulder into place, sealing the world outside.

Patty woke with a start and shuddered. She was covered in sweat, her sheets drenched. The dream had been real, so real she could smell the sulfur and burning flesh and hear the explosions and dragon-roar. She wrapped her arms around her shoulders and stared at the ceiling. Why did she keep dreaming she was a monster?

DRAGON'S LAIR

Emily stretched and yawned in a luxurious bed so huge it could've been made for a giant. So it hadn't been a dream. She peered about anxiously. The dimmed torches softened the cave so that it appeared almost homey. Almost.

Scooting to the edge, she slung her legs over the side of the bed, and a blast of cold air curled around her. The dragon slid through an opening she hadn't noticed before.

"What time is it?" Emily asked through a yawn.

Talav stared and blinked her leathery eyelids. "There is no time in the Underworld, deary. Not as humans know time."

"The Underworld?" Emily hugged herself, shivering. "That's a real thing?"

"Of course it's real. You're in it now, aren't you?"

Scrubbing her face in her hands, Emily shuddered and wished she could wake up at Wren's Roost in her own bed. But when she opened her eyes, Talav's enormous head hung over her.

Emily dragged the thick comforter around her shoulders and stared back at the dragon. "Or I'm in a cave. As far as I know, the Underworld is a myth found in legends and fairy tales."

"Of course, little wren. Truth too difficult to understand is presented to the uninitiated as myth. But the truth it remains, nonetheless."

This just kept getting better. "Hey, you put me to sleep last night."

"Your point?"

"I was asking about my father and friends. You cold-cocked me with your dragon juju.

"Hmm…"

Emily stuck her fingers in her ears, determined not to be manipulated again. "Don't you dare."

Talav laughed. It was a pretty sound, like a rainbow arcing across a meadow. It bounced around the room, echoing from one rounded wall to another.

Despite her annoyance, Emily chuckled. "Don't handle me."

The dragon reared. "I'm doing nothing of the sort. The giddiness and tricksies are common side effects of interacting with a dragon. They will pass once you have time to adjust. Most never get to even see a dragon. If they do, they don't remember. But you, Awen. You are different."

"How so?"

"Like us, you were here when Earth was divided, when humans were given dominion over the land and the lizard-men that of inner Earth." Emily sucked in a sharp breath. "It was you who insisted the Federation allow the dragons to patrol Earth's borders and keep the reptilians separate and humans safe. You, Awen, have been, and ever will be, the Keeper of the Kingdoms and our Dragon Master."

"The Keeper of Kingdoms?" Emily's head reeled. "Dragon Master?" This was all too surreal to comprehend. She leaned forward and waited for her equilibrium to settle. Talav eyed her with compassion and a touch of sadness.

Emily held her head and pushed through the wooziness. "You would have me believe that there is a race of reptilian beings living inside Earth and that dragons roam freely? Explain yourself. How could humans not know about this?"

"It would be easier to show you." The dragon extended its gemmed forearm to touch Emily's head with the back of a claw. Emily shrank away, not certain she wanted to be coupled in some mind-meld with a tricksy dragon. She thrust out her chin.

"Will it hurt?"

Talav wagged her giant head and guffawed, a ratcheting, yet lilting and ethereal sound that escaped her sharp teeth and lifted the melancholy within the chamber.

"Are you ready?" The dragon asked.

Emily propped against the massive headboard. "What should I do?"

"Just relax and enjoy the ride."

"Ride?" Emily jerked upright. "Where are we going?"

"It's a figure of speech, deary."

She was still reeling from Talav's news and that "Keeper of the Kingdoms" thing. But her tension eased. "How long did you say you've been down here? That's a fairly new phrase."

"Eons. But I've been searching for you for four years. I learned the new idioms. You know," Talav muttered, "I think I'll answer your questions in reverse order. Let me show you what I found, what incited me to shake the earth to reach you."

"What?" Emily gasped. "You caused that earthquake? My father and friends could be dead because of you. And all of Atlanta could have been annihilated."

The dragon hung its head. "You don't know that. *You* lived. I'm sure they did, too."

Emily stomped the bed angrily. "I was lucky, Talav. And you found me, making me doubly lucky. If you killed them, I swear I'll—" She let go an exasperated breath, unable to think of a threat the dragon would heed.

Talav watched, lips pursed.

"So did you?" Emily wailed. "Did you cause the earthquake?"

"Not on purpose, little wren. It was for your own good. And that of the planet."

In her mind's eye, Emily saw the gorilla tumbling into the abyss. She heard the cries of the dying birds and animals. "Of all the self-absorbed, irresponsible things. People were hurt, Talav. Maybe even killed. Plus, all those animals. Dammit, dammit, *dammit!*" Wiping the tears from her eyes, she glowered at the dragon. "I insist you find and rescue my friends. If you don't, I will never speak to you again."

Talav's head snapped up, shame melting into indignation. "You are perfectly capable of finding them yourself, Awen. You don't need me for that. Now, stop wasting the precious time we have left and let me show you what we're up against."

Emily returned the dragon's piercing gaze, anger shimmering hot within her. "No. I do not trust you. I will not let you inside my head. Am I, or am I not, the Dragon Master? I *command* you to rescue my friends."

Talav snorted and slapped her tail against the wall. Pebbles dislodged and rattled to the floor "Good try. But that's not how it works. I answer to the Awen's power. Try again once you've taken up her mantle."

Score one for the dragon. No, make that two. Emily gave Talav a grudging nod. "Then tell me how to do it myself."

Talav eyed Emily sideways. "After my news."

HOME AGAIN

Lugh's clothes were ripped and reeked of catastrophe. Why hadn't he thought to give someone a key so they could fetch him clean ones? Putting them on made his stomach queasy. When the congealed blood smeared on the back of his hand, he gagged and almost threw up. Which sent excruciating pain through his head.

He waited for it to pass, then tucked in his shirt and tossed the shredded jacket aside. He hoped it wasn't too cold out there. In his pants pocket, he found his keys and wallet. He'd ask Mitch to run him by the zoo for his SUV. Assuming the attorney ever got done talking to Finn.

But Mitch immediately nixed his idea, arguing that Lugh was in no shape to drive. Doctor's orders. On the short ride home, Lugh stewed in silence, pondering his next move. His mother's face popped in his head and he decided he would ask his parents' ghosts.

He sagged against the leather seat and hummed a few bars of the rock song playing on the high-end stereo. Mitch reached over and turned up the volume. Rolling his eyes, Lugh sang the words, wishing for one vulnerable moment they could be friends again.

When Mitch's slightly off-key alto joined in, Lugh grinned. For the first time since high school, they shared a companionable moment. But soon they were in Lugh's driveway and Mitch was helping him climb the front steps.

It seemed an eternity since Lugh had left, angry at his nephew and dog for ruining his first date with Emily Hester. He limped through the too-quiet house, thinking about Cu. He'd been a pain in Lugh's butt and pocketbook, but the wolfhound was part of the family. When Hamilton was dying, Cu had offered his body as a vehicle for Ham's spirit. They had coexisted inside Cu until the earthquake. The wolfhound deserved a proper druid burial.

Lugh sank to the bed. Had he locked the front door? Surely he must have. And he was so thirsty. Was it the medicine?

Groaning, he held his head between his hands and with a gargantuan effort, stood to shuffle to the hall. Then changed his mind. Kicking off his tennis shoes, Lugh climbed into bed, nasty clothes and all, beyond caring about anything as mundane as dirty sheets.

His heart pounded in both ears, especially the left. Which, oddly enough, was the side opposite the injury. Worming his way beneath the covers, he listened to his heartbeat settle into a strong, reassuring, steady rhythm.

Lugh fell into a restless sleep in which he wandered Zoo Atlanta searching for his companions and trying to explain to Jake and Cybele that their only son, the nephew they'd entrusted to Lugh's care, was likely dead.

A NEW OBSESSION

Shalane detoured from her route to the Fox Theater and followed the rental car's GPS to the last location she'd entered the day before. She wound through busy streets and turned into an older, upper-class neighborhood. It all looked familiar, but she had no recollection of having driven this way.

She turned down a street called Wren's Way, but there was no house where the GPS indicated. Making a U-turn, she traversed the lane again, with no better luck. Still, the forest seemed vaguely familiar. She followed it for a while, then turned right, pulling over to let an impatient driver pass. A park appeared ahead. Deepdene Park, according to a directional sign.

Now *that* she remembered. She idled along beside it, ignoring the line of cars honking behind her. Pulling into the steep driveway where she'd found her car yesterday, she made sure to engage the emergency brake.

Climbing out, she crossed to the park and followed the trail to the woods. Nodding to a line of joggers, Shalane walked a short way to the clearing. Near a granite boulder, she found the bench.

Sitting, she stretched her arms along the back. It was peaceful here. Even the noise from the street seemed faint and far away, and she could hear the tinkle of a nearby stream. Shalane closed her eyes and took three long, deep breaths. She let her mind empty, then sat quietly, waiting for the memory to unfold.

The woman with shocking-red hair had been here, and they had argued. An exquisite pain squeezed Shalane's heart. Tears poured from her closed eyes, but she fought to stay with the meditation. The fog cleared and she could see a face. Ebby Panera, though her hair was different. And she knew magic.

Shalane's eyes flew open. She remembered Ebby, or at least her face. But something important loomed close, receded, then was gone. The woman did mean something to Shalane. Only what? And why the hell couldn't she remember?

She hadn't been drinking, so it wasn't a blackout. And her memory of Ebby went back to California. Only the particulars weren't there.

Frustrated, she walked back to the car. What could Ebby Panera have meant to her? From the ache in her heart, it must've been big.

☼☼☼

A mob milled in front of the Fox Theater.

"Is that for me?" Shalane wondered aloud. Her crew had arrived early and was inside getting ready for her opening performance.

Settling her soda in the cup holder, she belched and rolled down the window to peer anxiously at the gathering crowd. They held signs and jostled one another, vying for space on the densely-packed sidewalk. How was her audience supposed to get in for the show? Anger licked at Shalane's gut.

"They can shove those signs up their tight asses."

She sent a quick text to Cecil demanding that he have the cops remove the offenders, and contemplated pulling to the curb to give the milling hicks a piece of her mind. A mental picture of being swarmed and kicked to death made her dismiss the idea.

A tall, thin man carrying an electronic board threaded between her car and the crowd. Shalane stared at the sign. It depicted her face on the body of a snake-like devil with a forked, hissing tongue. The protester forced his way through an opening and disappeared, but his sign bobbled and jigged above the crowd, moving ever inward through the long foyer until it was out of sight.

The light must've changed because the line of cars inched forward. At least the mob seemed amicable enough. Traffic stopped again when the news van in front of Shalane pulled to the curb. A reporter leapt out, followed by a camerawoman. Horns blared in protest.

"Morons," she mumbled, eyeing her rearview mirror.

There was a commotion on the sidewalk as the reporter and camerawoman claimed space amidst the throng. Shalane thrummed her fingers on the dash and read the closest signs.

"FORNICATOR GO HOME!" "SHALANE CARPENTER IS A WITCH & A WHORE!" "DEVIL INCARNATE!" "GO HOME GOD HATER!" "WE DON'T NEED NO SHE-DEVIL!"

Her favorite was a picture of her sitting on her throne chair. But instead of straight blond hair, golden snakes emanated from Shalane's head, and she had a flat nose, enormous red eyes, and a scaly snake face. Chuckling and shaking her head, Shalane moved with traffic as the van pulled away.

She turned right onto North Avenue and caught a glimpse of a directional sign for The Varsity, the fast-food restaurant Cecil had raved about yesterday. The throng extended around to this side, too. Some of the protestors had gathered across the street in a parking lot belonging to Emory's Midtown Hospital.

Blowing her horn, Shalane waved and leered, then gunned it when a big brute of a man charged her car, followed by other angry protestors. She lost sight of her would-be attackers in traffic and circled to the back entrance, where she showed her credentials to the parking attendant and pulled in next to her tour bus. Gathering her travel case and purse, she called Cecil and waited for him to come out to get her.

Once inside, Shalane began clearing negative energy in the auditorium, while Cecil went out front to have the entrance cleared. When her cell phone vibrated, she was in the loge praying, asking God to fill the hall with joy and redemption. Expecting it to be a crew member asking a stupid last-minute question, she yanked it from her pocket and grunted, "What?"

"Reverend Carpenter?" The male voice was strong and pleasant. And vaguely familiar. A restless flutter stirred inside her. She softened her tone.

"Yes?"

"This is Attorney Mitchell Albom Wainwright the Third." She knew that name from somewhere. "We agreed to touch base once you made it to town. This is me reaching out to touch you."

Loaded with sexual innuendo, the man's words triggered Shalane's wet response. Her hand went to her crotch. The following silence was fraught with carnal tension. Her nipples tingled as she touched her vibrating clit through her pants. Another word from that sexy voice and she'd come spontaneously.

"Hello?"

Shalane shivered from head to toe and fell into a seat to hook a finger into her honey hole. A circular motion had her vibrating like a jackhammer. With a silent moan, she clutched the phone to her ear.

"Yes, I'm here. What can I do for you, sir?" The last word shuddered out as she convulsed on her wayward finger.

"Looks like Emily Hester may be gone for good."

Now that was a buzzkill. Pulling her hand out of her pants, Shalane wiped her cum on the cloth seat and sat up, all business.

"The woman who was killed in the earthquake? I don't know who you are, or why you think I care, but let's discuss this in person. I have a show this evening at the Fox Theater. I will leave you a ticket at Will Call with a backstage pass. Come to my dressing room after the show."

"You want me to come…there?" The voice sounded slightly breathless. "Can't you tell me on the phone? I'm a busy man, Miz Carpenter."

The hitch was almost imperceptible, but Shalane recognized it, having just had one of her own. The attorney was jerking off! She drew out her response, teasing now that she knew what he was doing.

"No, Mr. Wainwright. Come tonight. We'll talk after the show. I'm looking forward to it." Peering up at the lifelike stars sparkling on the ceiling, Shalane ended the call and came again.

☼☼☼

Mitchell hung up the phone and caught a glimpse of his reflection in the glass of the computer screen. The leer was classic Mitch Wainwright, post-coitus. He rearranged his package and zipped his pants. Throwing the catch towel in the trash, he leaned toward the screen to type in Shalane Carpenter's name. He'd checked her out one other time but didn't remember much of what he'd read.

There were ninety million references. That was mind-blowing in itself. Mitch clicked on the first, then paged through the list, skimming. Depending on the site, Shalane was a sorceress, a

53

budding evangelist, a murdering witch, a Hollywood love-child, and his favorite—an omnisexual nymphomaniac.

There was a whole website dedicated to Shalane's effect on men, with instructions on how to avoid falling under her spell. According to it, just being in the witch's presence was enough to make men do crazy things. And not some men. All of them. And women too, if what he read was true.

A vague unease stirred in Mitch's gut. Hadn't he just experienced that very thing? Merely hearing her voice across the phone had turned him into a pervert. He burst out laughing. As if he wasn't one already. He read a few more anecdotes, then clicked on the link about how to block her mojo, snorting when it asked him to enter contact information.

"Hardly," he mumbled, clicking back out. He'd read everything about Shalane he needed to know. Knowledge was power and Mitch had stalled the advances of many a determined woman over the years. He was sure he could handle the evangelist-witch.

But his disquiet continued into the afternoon as Mitch tried to go about his law firm business. When the office began closing in around him, he gave up the hope of being productive. Bidding his secretary adieu, Mitch drove to the courthouse to file a motion. But his eyes wandered to the Beemer's digital clock and he calculated the time until Shalane's curtain call.

He shoved the thought aside. He was not going to that witch's performance. Not tonight or any other night. Having had money and privilege his entire life, Mitch refused to be led around by his dick. Ramming the shifter into third, he squealed the high-performance tires.

Thirty minutes later he was at Phipps Plaza in the Men's Shop, trying on suits. Though he told himself he needed a new one, the niggling agitation said otherwise. He pushed thoughts of the provocative minx away and shimmied into a pair of black peg-leg trousers that, buttoned and zipped, proved to be exactly right.

The clerk handed him a pale pink shirt. Mitch held it to his chest. Liking the effect, he put it on with the pants. He donned the matching, severely-cut jacket with thin lapels and the outfit was complete. He turned from side to side, then moved to the larger mirror, craning his neck to see his ass.

"Well, look at that." He broke into a grin and squared back to face the mirror. "Not bad, if I say so myself."

But it needed something. A tie perhaps? Or maybe he'd leave the top two buttons open and show a little chest. Mitch was no bodybuilder, but he did stay fit at the gym.

The clerk appeared with several neckties. He tried each but decided he liked it better without. He was dressed, without being over-the-top. Or looking like an attorney on the prowl. Not that he was going to Shalane's performance. But he had new duds just in case.

MAGDALENA

Using the flint and gauze from a tuft she kept in her pack, Magdalena lit the dry twigs she'd gathered outside. The flames caught and grew brighter. Smoke tendrils reached for the flue-like opening tucked in the corner of the forward chamber. She had yet to explore the dark nether regions of the cave, preferring to stay close to the entrance for now.

The fire grew stronger and Magdalena added deadfall from the willow-grove outside the cave. When it was hot enough, she added denser branches until the fire blazed. Pouring water from the nearby spring into a collapsible metal cup, she placed it on the coals and glanced over at Nergal the Destroyer. He rested on the bed of newly-greened boughs she'd laid for him.

Magdalena had recognized the general the moment he'd charged into her office. He was the last being she would have chosen to be her rescuer, but she was grateful nonetheless. The fearsome Draco had collapsed as soon as Magdalena laid the branches, falling into a fitful sleep.

By the light of the fire and the opening in the ceiling, she inspected the livid gashes across Nergal's face and chest. They oozed blood and pus, having opened during their flight from Agartha. She must clean and treat them. With luck, the infection had yet to go internal. If it did, the general would most assuredly die.

Bubbles appeared on the surface of the water and Magdalena removed the cup with a tong from her bag. Adding a pinch of powdered elderberries, she stirred the brew gently with a twig of yew and set it to steep with the twig. After a short while, she removed a shallow dish and poured a measure of the decoction. She lay two wads of gauze in the dish and replaced the cup over the coals to keep it hot.

Returning to Nergal, Magda dribbled the cooling brew into the face wound. The general stirred, then quieted again as she delicately spread the gauze over the laceration. When she placed the second swatch over his chest and pressed, Nergal lashed out, knocking her backward onto her hindquarters. She returned to Nergal's side and placed the back of her claw on his forehead. The Draco's fever raged.

Guarding against another attack, Magdalena prodded Nergal awake and bade him drink the rest of the healing draught. With more patience than she felt, she sat with him, coaxing down one sip at a time until he'd consumed the lot. By the time he finished, his forehead felt clammy, and the great lizard shivered violently.

It took all her might, but Magdalena slid him and the bed closer to the fire and laid down beside him, conforming her body to his. To warm him faster, she told herself, though the proximity to the macho Draco aroused something in Magda she hadn't known was there. When his shivers abated, she rose on all fours and studied Nergal's bandaged face. Revulsion warred with the newfound feelings.

She leapt up and hurried through the convoluted entrance to the grove of willows. The stench of sulfur and burning flesh still clogged the air, triggering her gag reflex. She climbed the first hill, the tallest between the cave and Agartha. From its crest, she peered beyond the other peaks to the city. Fires raged, and the cries of the dying, though muted and faraway, tugged at Magdalena's heart.

She was not like Nergal or the other Dracos. Magdalena had a soul, inherited from her half-human father. Or so her mother had said. Magdalena never met him. And never would. He had died long ago, his life ended by a Draco intolerant of his half-blood status. One of General Nergal's soldiers, according to her mother.

Magdalena had harbored a deep distrust for Nergal and his kind ever since. She'd kept her heritage to herself for fear of persecution and had even paid to have her official records altered to protect her secret.

On reaching majority, Magda had abandoned the requisite
warrior training to be a healer. That earned her a shunning by her
mother and littermates. Unable to bear the emotional and physical
exile, Magda left the rich northern regions. She wandered long and
settled in Araf for a short while before taking up residence in
Agartha.

A local doctor took her on in both places. Eventually, the one
in Agartha died and left his practice to Magdalena. She worked
hard to turn it into a safe place for the less fortunate. And had
rejected few throughout the years, working day and night, if the
need presented.

Which had left little time for romance, other than the
occasional fling. She found most males too callous, or too
enamored of themselves. So Magdalena had spent her life helping
others. All in all, it had been a good, if lonely, existence. And it
had kept her off the Dracos' radar.

Above the city, smoke billowed into a mushroom shape and
spread out along the plain. Tears formed and slipped down
Magda's cheeks. What would she do now? Dejected, she turned
and picked her way through the pines to the bottom of the slope,
recalling her old mantra. One day at a time.

For the moment, her lot was tied to Nergal's. Assuming he
lived. He needed powerful medicine, more than she could provide
from her emergency stores. If only she had access to her office,
assuming it still stood.

One day at a time. One moment at a time.

Meanwhile, she would scour the countryside for healing herbs
and barks. Without them, the Draco would die.

☼☼☼

A thousand spears stabbed at Patty, some razor-sharp, others
dull and wretched. She was in Nergal's body. His face throbbed
and she tried to sit up, but his chest screamed bloody agony and
his back refused to obey. She laid there instead, a mighty Draco,
helpless and unable to move.

But Nergal must. Or he would die.

Using his arms as levers, Nergal shrieked and collapsed. Every
muscle in his back clenched to the point of anguish. Trying again,
he managed to make it to a seated position and looked around
panting. He was in the antechamber of the cave. But how had he

gotten here? The last he remembered was leaving the city with the doctora.

The doctora.

Patty-as-Nergal peered through the twilight. A fire crackled nearby, but the smoke had not filled the cave. How had the doctora managed that? His gaze followed wispy coils to the top of the chamber where the smoke exited the low ceiling. There was more to the doctora than met the eye.

His pain spiked when he pushed the thin metallic sheet she had stretched over him to one side. He slowly scooted crab-style to the nearest wall, then waited for the agony to subside. When it eased a little, he braced against the pain and dragged himself, grunting and groaning, claw over claw, up the rough wall.

But his legs wouldn't hold. He bellowed in agony and crumpled to the floor, almost losing consciousness. Involuntary tears coursed down the scales of Patty's flat cheeks. She gritted razor-sharp teeth and pulled herself up the wall again, centimeter by centimeter.

Intense pain shot down her legs. Nergal-Patty fell to the ground, where he wallowed in the dirt like the maggot he'd become. Where was the damn doctora? Had she sentenced him to death? With the last of his strength, Nergal rolled to his back and consciousness fled.

Patty shuddered awake in her own bed and hugged her shoulders. If the Nergal dreams didn't stop soon, she just might go mad.

MAGICAL MIND

Emily propped against the headboard, mind spinning. Not only had Talav caused the hum, but there were evil alien lizard-men living inside the earth. She knew intuitively they were the danger about which the druid Elders had warned.

"Can you tell me more about them?" she asked. "I believe I saw one in another's mind the other day."

"You read minds!" Talav gurgled. "I knew you couldn't be totally powerless."

Emily nearly choked on her own saliva. "Gee, thanks. No, I do not read minds. I merely checked a witch's pulse and had a vision of the lizard-man."

Talav stopped her awkward shuffle-stepped dance. "That's reading minds, Awen. Even if you didn't try."

Emily rolled her eyes. "Whatever. Tell me about the lizard-men."

"They are known by many names, but call themselves Reptilians, Draconians, or Dracos for short. You humans simply call them aliens. They live within Earth's mantle, in what they call UnderEarth." Talav's lips wrinkled in a dragon pout.

"*That* is what I remember. I know there's more, but the rest is a total blank. Like someone or something wiped my memory clean. I get occasional flashes, but they come to naught. It is disturbing to be so afflicted. Dragons are normally immune to such conditions. Only powerful magic could've done this. Which is even more disturbing."

"I'm still wrapping my brain around the presence of dragons and aliens on Earth. Now you tell me someone magicked away your memories? Who could do such a thing? The aliens?"

"Maybe." Talav hesitated, then shook her head. "But not likely. They cannot see us dragons. Or more accurately, can't remember seeing us. To the Dracos I do not exist. Same as to humans."

"I see you."

The dragon queen batted lashes Emily hadn't noticed before. "Yes, but you are an exception, Awen. To answer your question, I detected no magic while in the reptiles' midst. I believe it had to be someone else. Someone powerful enough to wipe a dragon's memory."

"Who is that powerful?"

"Only the Awen." Talav wagged a baffled snout. "But what do I know? My memory has been ransacked."

Goosebumps raced up and down Emily's body. She was sure these lizard-men were the threat the druids faced. The dragon queen gave an approving nod.

"Are you listening to my thoughts?" Emily rose to her knees and thrust her chin at the dragon, who batted leathery eyelids and feigned innocence. "How rude! I did not give you permission."

"And you wouldn't, would you? Dragons have no shame when it comes to listening. It's a veritable compunction. And one of the perils of hanging out with us." Talav shook her jewel-encrusted head and colored lights danced from floor to ceiling and back again. "We can't help it."

"And that makes it okay?" Emily sank back on her heels, hugged her knees, and glared.

"Of course it does. If it is one's nature to do a certain thing, it shows a lack of integrity to do otherwise. Isn't it worse to deny one's propensity? To neglect to embrace that with which one is gifted?"

Unable to argue with the dragon's logic, Emily expelled a loud breath of displeasure.

"While I searched for you, I kept an eye on the Dracos. They like to fight, even with each other. Nasty creatures the whole lot."

"And creepy looking." Emily shuddered, imagining what it would be like if the earth was overrun by the warring creatures.

"Like a lizard or snake mated with a human. As you saw, most are around seven feet tall, though a few are much taller. There are shorter ones, too, with larger heads. They are all scaled, mostly in varying shades of green. The leaders are ashier. Albino maybe. And they have bony prominences that run from flattened brows at a forty-five-degree angle to the back of conical heads. And red eyes. Except the short ones have black eyes that flash red."

Emily shuddered again. She had to get out of here and sound the alarm. It was scary seeing the lizard-men through Talav's mind-meld. She certainly didn't want to meet one in person.

"But you will," Talav insisted. "It is your calling. Only you can stop them should they escape UnderEarth. Which is why it was imperative that I find you, Awen. Why did you keep ignoring my call?"

"Your call?" Emily's thoughts went her last jog on the beach in California. "Was that you in Venice Beach? By the pier?"

Talav's expression went blank, then her eyes widened hopefully. "That must've been Draig Ooschu. The Water Keeper."

"The water keeper."

"Aye. I did call you a few weeks ago. Then again yesterday, before I shook the earth.

Emily scooted across the bed and slid off. "You mean that day at the mall? The Hum? That was you?"

Talav picked at a gem on her chest. "The hum?"

"The screechy-humming noise that comes from the earth on occasion. Ohhh," Emily gasped. "So *that's* what I heard. And why it kept happening in my presence. It was you!" She pondered the enormity and wondered what she would have done had she known the Hum was a dragon. Run, most likely. Like she had done every time.

Distaste pooched the dragon's lips. "My voice sounds screechy?"

"Ear-splitting screechy. Like a pair of rusty shears cutting through rustier metal."

"No wonder you ran." Talav stretched and plodded to the entrance. Each step vibrated the walls. She stopped and turned her head to face Emily. "Awen, you are partially to blame for that earthquake. Had you not been so obtuse, we would have met years ago."

"Me? How was I to know?" Emily growled, offended. "My mother never told me the truth. I didn't know about my heritage or being a druid, much less about you. I did feel a tug. Your call resonated and created a strong urge inside me to do something. But I never knew what. So I ran away. Like everyone else."

Sadness permeated the cave. The dragon hung her head. "Such is my lot."

"Talav, I am sorry. I will answer from now on, I promise."

"If you don't forget again?"

"Forget? Did I know you before?"

"Of course, silly girl. I told you. You were with us from the beginning. Have you fallen victim to the memory veil, too?" Talav stared off into space. "That would explain so much."

"Can you tell me more about the curse?"

Talav looked out the opening, then back at Emily. "The forgetfulness curse and memory veil are two separate things. I believe you are asking about the veil. When most species, including humans, are born, your memories are wiped and only return when you are ready. Most never are. But your time has come, and not a moment too soon. We have much to do to prepare you, little wren."

"Why do you call me 'little wren'? My Da and the animal Elders call me that."

"Because the form you most take as Awen is that of the humble wren," the dragon explained. "Wrens build upon the successes of others and achieve heights to which few can attain."

"I read that story. The 'king of birds' title was to be given to the one that flew the highest. The wren won by hiding beneath the eagle's feathers. When the eagle reached the pinnacle of flight and proclaimed itself king, the wren popped out and flew a few inches higher, thereby gaining the honor."

"Aye. That is right. But did you know that the wren is the most sacred of all birds to the druids? Its proper name is Drui-en, the Druid Bird. That's you. Little wren."

The moniker sat well with Emily. As much as she would like to be an eagle, she wasn't that bold when it came to most things. She *was* good at figuring things out and taking it to the next level. Like the wren.

Her stomach growled and she remembered she hadn't eaten since the zoo—a long time ago. Why wasn't she hungry?

"Would you like something to eat?"

"Stop reading my mind! What I want is to get out of here. I have more training to do. And you promised to rescue my father and friends. You have shared your news. Now, help me find them."

"First, I promised nothing. Second, there is something else you must know."

"You said you would save them. Pay up."

"No. I did not. I said you could do it yourself. Come." Talav lumbered to the back of the cave. A gilt mirror materialized from thin air, as big as the wall.

"How'd you do that?"

"Dragon magic. Come stand beside me."

Emily did. The dragon's reflection sparkled in the mirror. But there was nothing where Emily stood. Fear bloomed raw inside her gut.

"I don't understand." Was she dead after all? She turned to confront the dragon. "Is this a trick? A magic mirror?"

Talav stared at her silently. A tear dripped from one ochre eye.

"So, I am dead." Emily's legs nearly buckled. Talav steadied her with her tail.

"No. Not dead. But you walk the Otherworld, a place outside of life and death. A place that exists yet does not exist."

"And that's better than being dead? You made me believe I'm alive. Oh, why did I listen to a dragon?" Emily scrubbed her face in her hands and looked in the mirror again. She still wasn't there.

"Because humans believe what they want to believe, even when it bears little resemblance to the truth. You, my dear, are not dead. Not in the traditional sense of the word."

Misery sucked at Emily's core. What good did it do to have the acquaintance of a dragon if she was dead? Or drifting in some world outside of life and death? Was there any way back to the real world?

Talav left Emily to her tears and morbid thoughts, though her eyes were full of compassion. The more Emily sniffed, the more Talav ignored her, resuming the cleaning of her sparkling jewels. Presently, a melodic hum filled the air. It was the song Talav had sung the night before.

A lightness crept into Emily's being. Curious, she studied the new sensation and found it quite pleasant. What if she dwelt here, rather than in misery? If she was supposed to be the master of her emotions alive, then why not dead? Or almost dead?

"Exactly!" Talav interjected, paying closer attention than it had appeared. "Now we're getting somewhere!" She stopped polishing her accoutrement.

"So taking responsibility for my feelings is all I need to do to get out of here?"

"Well. Not all." The dragon shifted, claws clicking against the mirror. Her eyes glittered as bright as her jewels. "You must take charge of your thoughts, deary. Change your beliefs. Belief is what holds you in one world or the other—what keeps you alive or kills you. Or rather, allows you to die."

"Oh. Is that all?" Emily climbed onto the high bed. It was the only seat in the house.

"Changing your thoughts and beliefs is not a small thing, little wren," the dragon cautioned.

"I was being facetious." Emily fluffed her hair and found it matted with sticks and pea gravel.

"You humans are hard to read sometimes."

"Us? We are hard to read? How about you? You've given me nothing but lies, half-truths, and innuendo. How would I know if you're telling the truth?"

"Harrumph," the dragon snorted. "Stop hearing what you want to hear and listen to what is said. Or not said. Drop your filters. Stop coloring everything with your preconceived notions. Learn to be objective. Only then will you know."

"So you haven't lied. It's me, twisting your words. Typical."

The dragon roared. "Mother of all that is holy, woman. Why are you so thick-headed? You're wasting our precious time." She swept through the door, leaving a wisp of irony in the air.

Climbing down, Emily ran after Talav. She was her only hope of escaping, her only chance of finding the others. But outside the door was inky darkness. Paralyzed, Emily shivered in the corridor, unable to take another step. Then Talav's counsel came back to her.

"This is just an illusion," Emily said as matter-of-factly as she could. "It is only dark because I believe it's dark. If what Talav said is true, I am creating the whole thing. And danger is only dangerous if I believe it to be true. Or something to that effect." But still, she couldn't move.

Closing her eyes, she imagined a brightly-lit hallway and running through it perfectly safe. Emily opened her eyes and gasped. The tunnel before her was lit from the other end. Was it the sun? Elated, she ran toward the light.

But the passageway was longer than it appeared. Each time Emily neared the end, there would be another twist or turn, and the light appeared further down the corridor. When her faith faltered, the light grew dim. Each time, Emily stopped to close her eyes and tell herself the dark was an illusion powered by her thoughts. Then the darkness would recede, allowing her to continue.

When the light faded for the fourth time, Emily imagined the tunnel ending just ahead and the dragon waiting at the exit. The vision grew stronger in her mind. She opened her eyes to dancing, disco-ball, colored reflections along the length of the corridor. Determined the dragon would be at the end, Emily trotted forward.

Sure enough, where the twinkles originated stood Draig Talav decked out in all her queenly glory, dripping with jewels and a sardonic grin.

"What took you so long?" Talav drawled.

INTO THE FIRE

What was going on down here? Brian gawked, careful to stay concealed behind the tunnel opening. Several lizard-men stood at attention in a polished chamber, claws clasped behind scaled backs. They faced the leader of the duo that had apprehended Brian earlier.

The beings were tall and lean, with muscles that rippled under dark green scales. Their chests and abs were like plates of armor, and slightly lighter in color. But it was their heads that creeped him out the most—like snakeheads with two rows of horn-like knobs that curved to the back and huge eyes with glowing red pupils, and slits for nose and ears.

On the far wall, an image appeared. Brian recoiled. This lizard-man was even bigger and meaner-looking than the others. It towered over the room and was obviously in charge. When it snarled something in reptile-speak, the creatures stiffened and smacked their chests in what appeared to be a salute.

At that moment, something heavy landed on Brian's shoulder and scurried down his back. He yelped and danced a drunken jig to dislodge what felt to be an enormous rat. It leapt to the ground and stared up at him for a millisecond before disappearing through a crack. Brian shuddered and wrapped his arms around his shoulders. Then remembered the aliens.

He flattened against the wall, but it was too late. The razor-clawed lizards charged the tunnel. Brian sprinted in the opposite direction, weaving and zig-zagging to avoid their claws. The plinking noise sounded and a partition appeared, cutting off his escape. Brian turned toward his pursuers and raised his arms in surrender.

The creatures halted a few feet away. One barked something in lizard-speak and Brian fell to his knees, hands in the air. The brute yanked him to his feet, and dragged him to the gleaming, whirring gallery of fear, and shoved him to the floor. Spread-eagled on the cold surface, Brian waited for the worst.

The screen-image growled. Two of the monsters hauled Brian up and shoved him forward. Trembling, he kept his eyes averted and studied the twisted face. Its scales were cream-colored, its snout longer and tapered at the end. And it had white eyes that flashed red. Waving muscled arms, it let loose a series of grunts and howls. Brian was glad it wasn't there in person. He'd probably pass out. Or crap his pants.

Hamilton whispered in his head, "Buck up, Bri. You're on."

In his most forlorn voice, Brian whimpered, "Hello, I'm Brian. Can you help me? I was lost in the earthquake and need to get back home."

The avatar roared. It sounded like strangled laughter, only more obscene. It must not have liked Brian's suggestion.

He tried another. "Could I have some food? And water?" He pointed to his mouth and rubbed his belly in a circular motion, then put his hand to the matted knot on his head. "And maybe a doctor?" Brian didn't have to fake sincerity.

"Good move," Hamilton whispered. "The guy on the screen is the leader. Don't piss him off."

"Way ahead of you, dude."

The image barked a command. The lizard that had captured Brian made him spin in place, then paraded him back and forth like he was on a runway in one of his mom's modeling shows. His chin lifted in defiance and he stared the screen-monster in the eyes. It roared and Brian looked down, preferring life over the satisfaction of spitting in its face.

An exchange between the screen-leader and the one in the room ensued, then ended abruptly. The avatar spoke directly to Brian, only this time in guttural English.

"Why have you come to Agartha? To spy on us?"

"Make it good, kid," Hamilton mumbled.

"Shhh," Brian warned. Out loud, he said, "My name is Brian and I live in Atlanta, just above here." He pointed to the lofty ceiling. "I lost my uncle and dog in the earthquake. I think they were killed. Your soldiers saved me. I am in your debt." He bowed and straightened. "Thank you for saving my life."

The monster roared again. Was it laughing or angry? They sounded the same to Brian's untrained ear.

"You are related to this woman?" The image changed and Brian stared at a photograph of Emily Hester.

Hamilton hissed, "Don't react. He's fishing."

Brian kept his face impassive as he whispered to Ham, "But he knows about Emily? What should I say?"

"Tell the truth. You know her. But not well. She's your uncle's friend and they were both lost in the earthquake. Do not mention druids, magic, or anything else. Keep it simple and basic. Now go." Brian did.

After interrogating him for an eternity, the beast ordered his henchmen to throw Brian in a cell. Which would have been scary, but after the lizard-men, he was actually relieved. Still, it was dark and dank and about as pleasant as the hole the chute had dumped them in earlier. One of the creatures tossed in a flash-like container before slamming the door.

Pleased to find it held water, Brian guzzled most of the contents, then studied the cell. The head honcho was sending someone to fetch him. Or torture him. Brian wasn't sure which. But, oh goodie, wouldn't that be lovely.

"We can't wait," Hamilton said. "They'll extract every ounce of information from you, and then some."

Suddenly, Brian didn't feel so good. He doubled over retching and stumbled to the wall to puke. Nothing came out but digested hot dog and chips. Which made him gag and retch again. Tears sprang to his eyes and Brian sagged to the floor.

He hadn't asked for this. He should be at Uncle Lugh's eating pizza and playing D & D Online with his friends.

He sat up in his snivel, adrenaline shooting through his veins.

That was it. Dungeons and Dragons 2040. That's where Brian had seen that tunnel. And the three-way intersection. There were even chutes that shuttled the avatars and demons from place to place and a grand hall similar to the one they'd had him in, complete with overhead display.

"Good job, son," the druid crowed. "What else do you remember?"

"All of it." Brian grinned. "I remember all of it." He stood to look for an exit point. "Every. Last. Level."

SHIBBOLETH'S COMMAND

"**A**ttention all personnel. Report to the main hall immediately. Commander Shibboleth will address troops and support staff in ten minutes. Attention. All personnel. Report to the main hall immediately." The terse voice boomed through the loudspeaker.

Ishkur woke with a start, slumped across his console. Lamia would be fuming. He'd never made it home from his gambling spree. Rising from the bench, Ishkur cradled his head and groaned. This might be the mother of all hangovers. Ignoring the consequences, he reached in his drawer and grabbed the bottle of Furroot.

Damn. It was empty. No wonder he'd passed out. And no telling how much he'd had during the game. Staggering to the door, head down, Ishkur hightailed it to his bunk and cracked the label on a new bottle. He took a healthy swig and detoured to the loo.

He let go of his bladder in the open trench and cast his eye over the other occupants. Two Cymbidians carried on a conversation in a language Ishkur barely understood. He did manage to make out a few words: Shibboleth. Cleansing. Death.

Not liking the conversation, he exited the loo and joined a stream of others. The great hall was crammed to overflowing. Ishkur shoved his way through the throng and took his place in the front of the room directly behind General Nergal's second-in-command.

A nasty-looking Draco with an evil aura stepped to the microphone. The oversized warrior's attire consisted of a half-helmet and wristlets of leather, along with a vest fashioned from an arthropod's shell. His claws were painted blood-red, a practice

Nergal had prohibited in Xibalba IX. Ishkur disliked the arrogant Draco immediately.

A cringe-producing screech was followed by amplified thwacks on the microphone, then a loud, "AHEM."

Ishkur clasped his muscled arms behind his back in a show of respect. He stood shoulder to shoulder with his fellow warriors behind the major who had assumed the role of acting Base Commander upon news of Nergal's demise. The remaining support staff of various species had arranged themselves in order of importance behind the Dracos.

Ishkur stood statue-still, awaiting the announcement. The back of his neck tingled, and his gut burned. He wished he'd eaten. No telling how long the assembly might last, or when he would get an opportunity to fill his belly.

The red-nailed Draco leaned forward and pressed thin lips to the microphone. "Attention Dracos and support staff. Nergal, your commander, is dead."

A murmur went through the hall. Some were getting the news for the first time.

"SILENCE, measly worms!"

An uneasy quiet settled upon the room. Ishkur shifted his weight. His left haunch ached, having been injured a few days earlier when a clever Ecthelion got the jump on him. The hung-over Ishkur had overpowered the fierce creature, making a meal of its innards and brains. His stomach growled, reminding him of the carcass still hanging in his berth.

"I am Maw, right hand to Commander Shibboleth. He is here from World Headquarters in Irkalla, and will address Xibalba IX."

The applause was sketchy.

The malevolent Draco scowled and arched his back. "I repeat, Commander Shibboleth will now address Xibalba IX."

This time, an explosion of applause greeted his words. Even Ishkur clapped and stomped his feet. He didn't want to lose his position, or his life. He had heard that Shibboleth was more ruthless than Nergal. Which was hard to imagine.

"Silence!"

The room quieted as the sinister Draco ceded the microphone to Commander Shibboleth. Although shorter and narrower of form than his spokesman, Shibboleth was an impressive specimen. Rumor had it, the commander was over ten thousand years old. He had aged well, looking no more than a few thousand.

But if the truth be told, the commander wasn't all that terrifying. Until he opened his mouth, revealing a full complement of the sharpest teeth Ishkur had ever seen.

"Major, step forward," Shibboleth barked.

Ishkur imagined the major's turmoil as he stepped toward Shibboleth, exposing Ishkur. The warlord held out a claw as if to clasp the major's. Instead, he yanked him forward and ripped his throat from earhole to earhole. The room exploded in an uproar as Shibboleth raised his bloody hand in victory.

Shocked, Ishkur suppressed the urge to attack. Dread curdled his gut. He was next in line.

Sure enough, Shibboleth called on Ishkur. "Vice Major, report."

Knees shaking uncharacteristically, Ishkur stepped forward. Shoulders square, he stood before Shibboleth, eyes downcast. It wouldn't do to let him see his fear.

When Shibboleth reached out a great, clawed hand, Ishkur hesitated. Then releasing a pent-up breath, he looked into the warlord's eyes and held out his claw. If it was his time to die, then so be it. Shibboleth grasped Ishkur's hand and pulled him to the microphone beside him.

"Ishkur, am I to understand that you are the overseer for the Human Domination project?"

Not knowing what was happening, Ishkur responded, "Yessir."

"Am I also to understand that the idea to link with influential humans was your idea?"

Ishkur gulped. He was about to die. "No sir, it was General Nergal's. He tasked me with engineering the program."

Shibboleth turned to address the hall. "Let's give this Draco a hand. Well done, Vice Major Ishkur." There was a pattering of applause. Shibboleth muttered to Ishkur, "Fall back in formation."

Alarmed, but relieved, Ishkur moved back in line.

Shibboleth continued. "Fellow Draconians, support staff. It is reported that Nergal was mounting an insurgency to overtake my command." A hubbub ensued. Shibboleth glared at the offenders until they quieted.

"An order for his arrest had been issued and a reward offered for his return to Irkalla. Yesterday, we got word that the general is dead. An investigation is underway and you can rest assured those responsible for General Nergal's death will be dealt with swiftly and without mercy."

The applause was thunderous. Ishkur refrained and stood tall, clawed hands behind his back. Good thing, too. All around him, those clapping crumpled to the ground. The thuds of falling bodies filled the room.

What was this madness?

Shaking in earnest, Ishkur kept his eyes on the Commander. Shibboleth towered above the room, a sneer twisting his stern countenance. Behind him stood Maw and another, equally-offensive Draco. Shibboleth's Death Bringers. The rest of Shibboleth's soldiers fanned out behind them.

Ishkur knew, without twisting his head to look, that he was one of but a few left standing.

Shibboleth ordered one of his soldiers to the front. His head was larger and his height nearly half that of most Dracos. Well-developed muscles rippled beneath his scarred vest, and the belt slung low across powerful hips.

"I present Major Azi," Shibboleth boomed. "He will take over Vice Major Ishkur's duties here in Xibalba IX."

Stifling a gasp, Ishkur kept his knees locked and his backbone straight.

"It will be Azi's responsibility to ensure the project is operational within one AboveEarth week."

Ishkur's scales prickled and his claws trembled. He clasped them tighter. If Azi was assuming Ishkur's duty, then what about Ishkur? He needed a drink.

"Ishkur's presence is required in Agartha," the warlord went on. Ishkur's stomach lurched. "He will lead the investigation into Nergal's death, supervise the rebuilding of the Agarthan base, and oversee the rescue of any survivors."

Ishkur swallowed hard. The warlord might be sparing Ishkur's life, but he was sentencing him to a sure death in Agartha. Magma still flowed freely through the chute system beneath and around the Agarthan base. Containment had been minimal.

"Vice Major," Shibboleth commanded, "You will take your Dracos and leave today. My onsite contingent will brief you upon arrival. I expect a full report this evening and regular communications thereafter. Dismissed."

Ishkur saluted and pivoted to leave. To his dismay, only three other Dracos remained standing. The rest were Fomori, Jahkquadi, and Pindejah.

Ishkur clicked his heels together, struck his chest in salute, and stepped over the fallen on his way to the door. The other Xibalba IX Dracos followed suit.

THE PACKAGE

The sun was low and after a long day, there was still no sign of the package. Khenko was in Corr's body staring at the blue hole when a pair of ochre eyes rose from the water. Startled, he leapt into the air and took flight with a sweep of the crane's thirty-inch wings.

Circling at a safe distance, he trumpeted loudly when the creature rose from the azure liquid and lumbered to the bank dripping water. Birds and howler monkeys protested noisily and abandoned nearby perches to flee into the jungle. Squawking, he circled once more and settled on the bank.

The creature ignored him and arranged its bulk in the sand near the jeep. Its neck ended in a tapered head, somewhat like that of a brontosaurus. Only it was brilliantly hued in every color of the rainbow, from its rounded snout to the tip of its powerful-looking tail.

"Where is the package?" Corr asked without ceremony.

The dragon blinked its enormous eyes and stared at something behind Corr. He swiveled his long neck. There was nothing there but rocks and jungle. The path leading to the gravel lane was empty as well. Corr turned to the dragon, who polished its jeweled hide and ignored Corr.

He must have offended it. He'd forgotten how vain dragons were purported to be.

Bowing low to the ground, he eyed the creature. "Hail mighty one. My name is Corr and I bow to your magnificence." When the dragon continued ignoring him, Corr added, "I am here to receive a package, a woman possibly wounded and in need of medical attention. I was told she would be here at the Atlantean blue hole. Are you in possession of this package?"

"Aye," the dragon rumbled, not bothering to look up.

Khenko's annoyance crept into Corr's raucous cry, "So where is she, then? I've been waiting all day." If the woman wasn't coming, he would like to go home. He was ready for dinner. And a cocktail. Plus, he needed to answer the email he'd gotten from a group inquiring about a trip to the vortex.

The dragon rose to its full, impressive height, eyes fixed on Corr. "The druid is in the caves of the blue hole. She roams the Otherworld teetering between life and death and needs medical attention. I have mended her worst injuries, but have not been able to revive her, Crane."

"Can you bring her to me?"

The dragon shook its head, raining saltwater on Corr and the beach. "I need your help to move her."

Corr gazed across the water. So much for Khenko's evening plans. He morphed into human form and returned to the jeep, where he shimmied into the neoprene one-piece. Strapping the first-aid kit around his waist, he slid a skinning knife in one thigh holster and a water-proof revolver in the other. The stun-gun fit into his pocket beside his ever-present Swiss blade.

He checked the air gauges before hefting the full tank onto his back and snapped his mask in place. Hoping he had everything, Khenko stepped into his flippers and frog-walked to the dragon, then waited with forced patience until it deigned to look up.

"Ready?" the dragon asked.

"Ready," Khenko replied.

When the dragon stayed put, Khenko lifted the mask. "Something wrong?"

The dragon's head swayed, looking at Khenko from different angles. "Do I know you?"

Khenko shook his head. "Nope. The last recorded dragon sighting was centuries ago. I'm sure I would remember meeting one." A sensation ran through him, like molten lava was being poured through a hole in the top of Khenko's head. It trickled down until his entire body burned like fire. He fought the urge to rip the wetsuit off and looked askance at the dragon. Was this his doing?

"Hers," the dragon crooned, startling Khenko. The damn thing could read his thoughts.

"I have decided. We *have* met before. But since you don't remember, I will introduce myself." The dragon bowed. "I am Talav, Queen of the Earth Dragons."

Khenko couldn't help being impressed. He bowed low. "Khenko Blitherstone, cultural anthropologist and Iroquois medicine man. I am pleased to make your acquaintance, Queen Talav. You are the most amazing creature I have ever met. I could never forget you."

"My dear," the dragoness crooned, batting impossibly long lashes. "Keep that up and I'll make sure you don't."

Khenko grinned and felt his ears grow hot. He seated the mask over his eyes to hide his discomfort. The dragon's leer told him she hadn't missed a thing.

"Ready?"

Khenko nodded.

Talav swayed on the edge as if loathe to enter, then plunged head-first into the blue, blue water.

MOTHER

Mitchell backed out of the alley and gunned the motor of the G-Series. Which wasn't saying much. The energy-saving coupe, unlike Mitch, was built for economy. Which made running through the gears unsatisfactory. But he was headed to his mother's and it would tickle her pink.

Rona Wainwright was a staunch proponent of environmental preservation, much to her conservative husband's chagrin. While he supported most of her causes, this one he opposed. Such was life with Mitch's father. Mitchell Wainwright Jr. never let anyone forget he was an important man. Not only as a world-class surgeon and Chief of Trauma at Emory University Hospital but also in the community. And worse, in his own mind. The man was a raving narcissist.

Pulling into Canongate, his parent's estate, Mitch parked the tin-can car and hurried up the flagstone walkway to the massive front door. Stilton, the butler his father stole from a neighbor soon after Mitch was born, answered the door and greeted Mitch with fond enthusiasm.

He left his overcoat with Stilton and found his mother in the kitchen, where a symphony of smells greeted Mitch. Despite an entire kitchen staff, she commandeered it often. Mitch admired that in his mother—her complete refusal to conform to societal mores.

He spied Rona in front of the double ovens, a combustible package with coifed blond hair, startling blue eyes, and a smile that could melt a zombie's heart. She fixed it on him, beaming past crinkled red cheeks. Her dimples went deeper than he remembered. When had she started looking older?

"Ma." He enveloped her in a gentle bear hug, careful not to squeeze too hard. He didn't want to rouse the air of sadness that had been her companion of late.

"Mitch," she sighed, returning the embrace. She held him at arm's length and studied his face. "My son, how are you?"

"I'm okay, Ma," Mitch lied, careful to keep his emotions hidden. She knew him too well—the only woman who ever had. Of course, she was the only one he'd ever let in.

She shoveled ingredients into a blender and turned it on, eyeing him over the commotion. When she flicked it off and dumped the soup in a bowl, Mitch swallowed hard and attempted a smile.

"I took Lugh MacBrayer home from the hospital," he began, but seeing the stricken look that flickered in her eyes, he paused. "Are you okay?"

"Of course." She wiped her hands on her apron and turned to the sink. With her back to him, she asked in a low voice, "How is he, hun?"

Mitch rounded the chopping-block and put his arms around her and rested his chin on her shoulder. "Lugh's fine. He always is. A little bruised and shaken up, but past the worst and well enough to be released from the hospital. Finn says he'll be okay."

Rona ducked under Mitch's arm and returned to her preparations. Her relief was evident. "That's good news." She had always liked Lugh and had encouraged their friendship. She'd grown up and gone to school with Lugh's mom and dad. "And the others? Lugh's nephew and the Hester girl? I've had the news on, but you know how they are. Half is pure conjecture, the other half lies."

Mitch chuckled. His mother was right, as she was about most things. "No, Mom. No news. But Lugh saw them go down."

Rona winced and hung her head. "And Jake? Are you still looking for him? He should be told about his son." Jake MacBrayer had been missing for two years. When the federal investigation ended, Mitch began searching. Unofficially, of course. Jake was a friend. And Mitch could never resist a good puzzle. But none of his feelers had panned out.

"Yes, nothing so far. It doesn't look good for Jake's son or the Hester woman, though. The authorities are still combing the wreckage. But the site is unstable. They're having to shore it up as they go and it's taking a lot of time."

Her face drew into a sad knot as Rona finished Mitch's unspoken thought. "And time is something those kids don't have."

"Exactly," Mitch sniffed.

FRIEND OR FOE?

Rumbles echoed through the caverns beneath the dungeon. Brian was wondering if they were aftershocks when the door clicked. The aroma of food had him salivating and rising to attention. When a young woman bustled into the cell pushing a cart, he gaped in wonder. Hallelujah. He wasn't the only human down here. But why would she work for the lizard-men?

Her face bore a welcoming smile, to which Brian responded with a quick grimace. Was he hallucinating? No mortal could be that gorgeous. Thick, brown hair flowed to just above her shoulders and framed a triangular face that was impish, yet haunted. A cap sat atop her head at an angle. It matched her blue jumpsuit and the biggest eyes Brian had ever seen.

He tried to read the gold insignia stitched on her uniform and cap, but the letters were unfamiliar.

"I have food. And medical care." Her voice was melodic. And she spoke English. Brian breathed a sigh of relief. He eyed the tray of what he hoped was people-food and a pitcher of water.

"For me?"

She nodded and pushed the cart to a bench cut into the wall. Brian trailed in the wake of something that smelled wonderfully like chicken. He hadn't eaten in at least a day. No wonder his legs felt rubbery.

At the girl's urging, Brian slid behind the cart onto the bench. When she removed the cover, he almost croaked. Eyeballs stared up at him from the plate.

"What is it?" he gagged.

"It's better than it looks, I promise." He eyed it with doubt and she prodded his arm. "Go ahead. Take a bite." He stared at the dish, nose wrinkled in disdain. She lifted the fork and handed it to him. "Go ahead. You need your strength."

In his head, the druid whispered, "She's right, kid. Better eat. If and when we get out of here, who knows when we'll get another meal."

Brian hesitated. He loved food, but eating new things was not his bag. Especially gross-looking things.

"Is dying of hunger? Eat. I'm hungry."

Ham had a point. With trepidation, Brian held his hand over the eyeballs so he couldn't see them, scooped a tiny amount, and put it to his lips. The flavor wasn't bad and his hunger kicked into overdrive. He took a larger bite, then another and another.

Finally remembering his manners, he glanced up and caught the girl watching him with fascination. She looked away and a pretty shade of pink crept into her delicate features.

"Thank you," he said, and stuffed another forkful in his mouth, mindful of not eating like a barbarian.

"It's okay. I know you're hungry. You probably haven't eaten in a while. I—" She glanced at a camera he hadn't noticed.

He ate another bite and tried to ignore the eyes. Finally, he couldn't stand it anymore. Taking a swig of the water, he burped and grabbed his mouth in dismay. Belching was not the way to impress a girl. And he wouldn't mind impressing this one. Her stifled giggle warmed his heart.

"I need to check you for injuries." All serious again, she put her hand to the wall and a keypad appeared. She tapped a button and a ledge bearing a thin mattress shot from the sheer rock face. She motioned Brian to lie down.

He eyed the bed, then the girl. Her blue eyes reassured. She took a medical bag from a shelf beneath her cart and opened it.

"Are you human," he blurted, unable to contain his curiosity any longer. She shook her head vigorously.

Disappointed, he reluctantly lowered his frame to the lumpy mattress. The girl leaned down to tape a device to the underside of his wrist. It beeped ever so often and zapped him with tiny electrical shocks that made Brian's teeth vibrate. He was about to complain when she ripped it off.

"Good job, son," the druid said in his head.

"Go away," Brian warned. "I can't talk to you both at the same time. She'll think I'm crazy." It occurred to him then he didn't know the girl's name. "I'm Brian. Who are you?"

"I am known here as Number Three." When his eyebrows went up, she hurried to add, "Because I am the third member of my family to be—" She glanced at the camera. "Conscripted." She stumbled over the last word and her expression hardened. Enunciating clearly, she repeated, "My name is Number Three."

Brian held out his hand. She ignored it and spoke into a handheld device.

"Human subject has abrasions and contusions, mostly minor, with one large knot on the crown of his head where the blood has coagulated. There is the likelihood of a mild-to-moderate concussion. His faculties appear intact, vital signs normal for a human male of—" She looked at Brian. "How old are you?"

"Just turned fourteen," he muttered. "How old are you?" Number Three ignored his question.

"Vitals normal for a human male of fourteen years." Brian smiled like a dope. "Subject should be kept under observation for at least twenty-four hours to assess signs of disintegration. Further recommendations will be made at that time."

A tone sounded overhead and Number Three's handheld device vibrated. The guttural voice of a lizard-man growled, "Vice Major Ishkur will be here in seventeen hours. Make sure the boy's cured before his arrival. That's an order, Fomorian."

"Yessir," Number Three chirped and motioned Brian to stand.

He scrambled from the bed and awaited instruction. "What's a Fomorian?"

She ignored his question and methodically stowed the plate, the pitcher, and the medical bag into the cart. Then straightening from a crouch, she glided to the camera and opened a keypad beneath it to type in a series of codes.

Moments later the voice exploded through both speakers. Number Three punched a key on her device and it quieted. The other continued crackling. "Slave, report in immediately. The camera has gone dark. What's going on down there?"

"I don't know, sir. I'm taking the final readings now. Maybe the magma is causing a disturbance in the feed? Number Three Out." As soon as the last words were spoken, she hauled a weapon from beneath the cart and gestured toward the far end of the cell.

Startled, Brian leapt away from her with his hands up.

"This is not for you." She slipped past him to disappear into the shadows. Brian stood motionless, hands still in the air.

"Are you coming, human? Or does the prospect of being eaten by a Draco appeal to you?"

Brian shuddered at the thought. "You're rescuing me?"

The big eyes blinked from the shadows. "You'd better move your feet, or we'll both need rescuing."

He hurried to her and water sloshed beneath one foot. As his eyes adjusted, he could make out a rivulet that ran along the base of the wall for a few feet, then vanished underground.

Number Three activated another keypad. A narrow passageway opened before them, so low they had to duck to slip through. The door plinked closed behind them. Low lights revealed a dimly-lit tunnel much smaller than the ones he'd been in earlier.

"Where are you taking me?" Brian whispered.

"Away from these monsters." Her hoarse answer brightened his mood. "Now remain quiet until we are out of here."

He followed Number Three through a series of tunnels that switched back on one another until Brian had no idea if they were coming or going. Occasionally he caught a whiff of her scent, which conjured his favorite meadow atop the Wasatch Mountains near his home in Utah.

Soon they reached a staircase. Or rather, notches carved into a sheer wall. Brian stopped to catch his breath and craned his neck. Surely they weren't going that way. But the Fomorian pointed up with her weapon, then holstered it on her back.

"You want me to go up there?" The whine escaped before Brian could stop it. He wasn't big on high places. Or falling from them.

"Yes. You first. I'll be behind you in case the Dracos are following. If my computer virus worked, they shouldn't be able to track us. But that's a big IF."

Brian hesitated, weighing the risk of falling from the steep wall against that of being eaten by a lizard-man. But it was a no-brainer. Mumbling a prayer to Brigit, he put his hand in one slot and his foot in another, and slowly scaled the wall. When they finally reached the next level, he climbed onto the ledge. Here another corridor opened.

"So far, so good," Number Three whispered. "I'll have you out soon. Wait here. I'll be back."

He wanted to protest, wanted to rush after Number Three, rather than stay in the dark by himself. Then Hamilton whispered to remind Brian he wasn't alone.

Presently, she returned and shoved something wooden in Brian's hand. He thought it was a club until she produced a flame and it blazed to life. He was holding a torch, the kind you only see in old movies. Number Three took it and led him through more tunnels and up more stairs, until it seemed they'd been at it forever. Finally, they reached a wall with a narrow crack through which light shone.

"Ready?" She held her weapon in her leading hand and the torch in the other.

Gulping, Brian nodded and mimicked her sideways stance, then shimmied one crab step at a time behind Number Three. It was a good thing they were both skinny. He winced as the unforgiving walls grated the skin from his nose and knuckles, and even his knees through his jeans.

The air thickened, making it hard to breathe. "Can we rest?" he gasped.

"No, keep going," Number Three commanded sharply. "We'll pass out from the fumes."

That was motivation enough. Brian quickened his pace, pushing Number Three until they popped out on the other end. The air was even worse here, stinking of putrefying eggs, and the ground was so hot he gagged and hopped from one foot to the other.

There was a loud whoosh near his elbow. Brian jerked away and stumbled into Number Three, shoving her into a nosedive. He grabbed the back of her jumpsuit just in time and yanked her onto the trail.

Good thing, too. The steaming tar burst into flames, ignited by the torch she'd dropped. Startled, they giggled hysterically in each other's arms. Number Three sobered first. She took Brian's hand and pulled him away from the tar pit.

After that, he stuck even closer to her. He smelled, rather than saw, each nasty quagmire in the dim light. Soon, the marsh gave way to solid ground, and the acrid smell diminished. Either that or Brian had gotten used to the stink.

The reddish light grew brighter and he could just make out a forest up ahead, with a rocky field in between. His heart beat faster. "Yippee, we made it!"

"Shhhh," Number Three hissed.

Something big gave a deep snort and pounded the ground behind them.

"RUN!" she yelled and tore out for the trees.

Brian sped over the rocky terrain, but the creature's breath ruffled his hair. He screeched and zipped past Number Three, who had stopped some yards ahead to level her weapon at the beast.

Brian hesitated and turned. The animal resembled an angry rhinoceros, only much larger. It had stopped and crouched, snorting and kicking up clods of dirt and rocks. Then it bellowed and charged.

Number Three's weapon pinged. A thud meant it found its mark. The beast toppled over, legs twitching. He was grateful not to be rhino-meat, but Brian couldn't help thinking of the Black Rhino in Zoo Atlanta. The last of its kind. Now this one was dead.

Overhead a bird cawed and circled, quickly joined by more of its kind. Vultures? Down here? Or had they made it to AboveEarth? His heart thrilled at the prospect.

Without acknowledging the kill, Number Three resumed the lead, scurrying over rocks and boulders at a break-neck speed. Razor-sharp weeds and briars tore at Brian's pant legs and scratched his arms through his shirt. A bird sang a lilting aria as it skimmed overhead. Another from the forest answered.

When they finally reached the edge of the dark wood, Brian was huffing and his side ached. With a searching stare toward the brightening red horizon, his rescuer slipped into the thick trees and pulled Brian in with her.

THE HEALING BEGINS

"Nergal, wake up."

The Draco squinted at the doctora through a waking haze. He made an effort to sit up, but his body shrieked bloody agony. A pleasant aroma wafted to him. Something light and airy. The doctora's scent. Nergal squinted up at the wide, violet eyes.

"Can you sit?" She leaned over him with a cup in one hand and a determined expression tightening her face.

Nergal blinked until his vision cleared. He reached for the cup, but the effort was too great. He could barely raise his arm. The doctora sank to the ground beside him and lifted his head onto her lap. The slight movement sent pain shivving down his back. But her presence was comforting. At least he wouldn't die alone.

The thought shocked Nergal. He'd never needed anyone. Angry and ashamed, he tried to turn his head away, but conceded once again to the pain.

"This will dull the discomfort. Can you drink?" Her tone soothed, and her eyes glittered like compassionate pools.

When something in him responded to her gentle manner, he hated himself. But he nodded once.

The doctora held the cup to Nergal's lips and tilted the warm, vile liquid down his gullet. He swallowed, keeping his eyes on hers. She tilted the cup again, and he gulped the rest. Anything to ease this wretched pain.

The petite Draca set the cup aside. "Sleep now. Soon you'll feel better."

✵✵✵

When Nergal woke again, there was no sign of the doctora. The fire blazed, sending fingers of light dancing on the walls. Nergal's bladder felt it might burst. He thought of letting it go but decided he'd rather not lay in his waste.

He rolled to one side, surprised when the pain didn't take his breath. Managing to get his claws under him, then his knees, Nergal pushed himself upright using the wall. He staggered and almost fell, but slumped against the wall to search for a stick to use as support.

Seeing nothing, he took a tentative step toward the cave entrance. His legs held. Nergal let go of the wall and took another halting step. Then another, and another, until he reached the mouth.

Slowly navigating the circuitous entrance, Nergal made his way to the willow grove. With a last, gargantuan effort, he hobbled a few more meters and let go his bladder into the bushes. Feeling pain before relief, Nergal groaned, then sighed. The nasty draught had done its deed. His pain was a shade of its former intensity.

But where was the doctora? His stomach growled.

The day had begun, though the pall of smoke concealed the sun. The air, while thick, was breathable. Nergal limped to the spring and slowly kneeled to drink. He skimmed ashes from the surface and drank his fill of the clear water, then lowered his aching body to the dense grass. He rolled to his back and stared up through the weeping boughs to the gray canopy.

His lids grew heavy and Nergal succumbed to sleep. In his dreams, he pursued an evil Draco, one with a vicious left hook and painted-red claws. Overhead, a dragon spewed fire on both.

☼☼☼

The doctora stood over Nergal, ogling him with a calculating eye. He sat up so abruptly, his head swam. She knelt to support him until the spinning stopped, then helped him to his feet.

"Feeling better." It was a statement, more than a question.

Nergal's nod made him woozy. He gripped the doctora's arm.

"We're having roasted Furbian for lunch. Are you hungry? I'm a decent cook."

At the mention of food, Nergal's stomach growled. He had never eaten cooked meat, but at this point, anything would suffice.

With the doctora's support, the walk to the cave was faster than coming out.

He accepted the thin plate on which she had piled cooked meat and root vegetables. Nergal took a tentative bite, surprised at the flavor. He took another, then shoved food into his mouth with both hands. Finished, he belched and drank the doctora's draught, then gazed into the fire with his back to the wall.

She cleared away the meal and swept the floor with the old willow branches and left the cave, returning with fresh boughs which she spread on the ground before Nergal.

"Lay down, General. You are far from well. Your wounds are deep and infected. With rest, they should heal and your strength return."

The news was most welcome. His eyelids and body had grown heavy again. Hating his weakness, he stretched out on the fresh bed.

"I plan to explore the hinter regions of this cave."

Nergal struggled to rise. He had wanted to investigate but had lacked the strength. He despised himself for that, too.

"Not you," the doctora ordered. "Your body is too weak. Stay here. Heal."

Nergal grunted and slumped to the bed of spring leaves, and though he willed his eyes to stay open, they closed.

"If you wake before I return, drink the rest of this brew." His eye slits opened enough to see that she pointed to the cup by the fire. "It's a decoction of the myrrh I found growing near the spring. It will ease your pain and help you heal faster. Now, sleep." Nergal did.

TIME TO ACT

Catching a glimpse of Talav's rapidly-receding tail, Khenko entered the blue hole flippers first. About forty feet down, the blue gave way to an eerie red as Khenko entered the toxic haze of hydrogen sulfide that guarded the deeper reaches. A wave of nausea hit him, and he quickened his pace through the silvery net of noxious cobwebs.

Breaking through into black water, Khenko paddled back and forth in a throng of air bubbles searching for Talav. Her head popped out of the curtain of calcite obscuring the entrance. Beckoning, Talav turned and vanished again. Careful not to disturb the delicate beauty of the calcite straws, Khenko glided through the opening.

A triangular vaulted ceiling soared above the dark floor of the underwater cave. He anchored a guidewire for the return trip, then followed the dragon through the lightless corridor. A profound calm descended upon him as they wove through a surreal maze of stalagmites and stalactites. Tiny fish and frilly shrimp darted through the beam of his headlamp. The floor rose gradually until he was in shallow water.

Khenko used his hands to walk along the sandy bottom. When his head broke the waterline, he searched the inky darkness for Talav. His light found her amid a rainbow of sparkles.

A stream of flame shot from her mouth and Khenko leapt backward into the water. Torches flared to life around the cave and he felt a tad silly. Stepping onto the bank, he unbuckled his belt, dropping the extra mask and equipment to the floor, then removed his gear. The dragon waited while he slid his feet from his flippers and donned his water shoes.

"How much further?" he asked.

"Not far." Talav turned and shuffled down a narrow passageway.

They traversed one tunnel after another until Khenko wondered what the dragon considered far. According to his watch, they'd been meandering in the corridors carved into the bedrock for fifteen minutes. The only light was from Khenko's headlamp, and they were deep in the bowels of the earth. His heart pounded at the thought, so he focused on the dragon's tail. She disappeared, and Khenko hurried to catch up.

Finally, the hallway opened to a large chamber lit by a circle of lanterns. In the middle of the room stood a massive, four-poster bed occupied by a slip of a woman. Scarlet-gold hair framed a tranquil face that was marred by scabs and yellowing contusions. Her chest rose and fell in a slow, steady rhythm.

Talav's gems flashed colored streamers of light as she moved to the bed. "Your assessment, Healer?"

Khenko joined her and shook his head. "It's hard to say. She looks pretty banged up." He took a closer gander. "Has she displayed symptoms of a head wound?"

"Other than the bloody knot and being out cold?" the dragon retorted. "None that I could find."

"I thought you said she was annoyingly vocal?"

"I did. She is. But in the Otherworld." The dragon's eyes went vague as she touched the woman with a clawed forepaw and Khenko with the other. The woman sprang to life before his eyes, though the body remained unmoving in the bed. Khenko jerked away and the animated version disappeared.

"What the—?" he gasped.

"You just got a glimpse into the Otherworld, which is populated by the dead, the near-dead, and the unfortunates wandering and lost in life. It is tricky to negotiate, even for dragons, though we are creatures of all worlds. Even for us, getting distracted in there could mean years of wandering in the mist. Or lifetimes."

Pity stirred Khenko to action. He opened his doctor's bag and began a thorough examination. Lifting the woman's head elicited a small cry, then a loud sigh. He found a lump above the right temple and probed gently. The wound had healed over, leaving dried blood and a small swelling. Khenko lifted her eyelids and his breath caught. Her eyes were as green as the sacred Heart of Atlantis.

A gurgling startled him and he looked up. The dragon held a bowl beneath a rivulet in the far corner. Turning back to his patient, Khenko lowered the comforter and lifted her shirt to press the flattened tips of both hands into her abdomen. When she didn't react, he put his stethoscope to her chest and listened to her heart and lungs, then pressed it against her belly. All the sounds were within acceptable parameters.

When he was done, he straightened to address Talav. "Like you, I find nothing overt. But since she's in a coma, I recommend we get her to the hospital." The little medical facility in Zephyr Cay could hardly be called that, but it was the best they could do at the moment.

The dragon reared and wagged her head. "No hospitals. Only you."

"But she—"

"No hospitals."

"But her life may depend upon it," Khenko implored.

"Her life also depends on her remaining hidden. I will concede only if it becomes necessary. And if an alias is used to protect her identity."

"Which is?"

"In this lifetime, her name is Emily, Emily Bridget Hester. To the world, she is Awen. THE Awen."

A shiver passed over Khenko. What had his totem gotten him into? He leaned closer. "Hello, Awen. I'm Khenko. How 'bout we get you back to the center?"

Talav had a quick conversation with the invisible spirit, then used magic to lift her into the air. Khenko followed the dragon and floating body through one tunnel after another, until they were back at the entrance to the blue hole.

Khenko outfitted Awen in the extra mask and tank. When he was sure she was breathing without distress, he donned his own and signaled Talav. She hesitated and Khenko could swear she was gathering courage. Which made him wonder if there were things even a dragon feared.

Talav arched her long neck and glared. "I fear nothing, healer. But I am an earth dragon, not a water dragon."

Khenko shuddered. The dragon could read his mind. He turned to attach the tow rope to the woman. Talav wagged her head and motioned him toward the blue liquid.

"You go first. I will follow with the Awen."

"Are you sure? I can tow her."

"Aye, healer. I am sure."

He entered the water and followed the nylon cord through liquid-black corridors. Periodically he looked back to make sure Talav followed with Awen. Soon they reached the delicate, calcite curtain disguising the entrance. Clipping the guide reel to his belt, he pointed up, and Talav nodded readiness. Khenko ascended slowly, passing through the murk, then the red hydrogen-sulfide haze.

When he finally hauled himself out of the water, night had fallen. By the scant light of the sickle moon, he changed into street clothes and threw an old blanket across the back seat of the jeep. He made a pillow from a towel and returned to the blue hole as the dragon climbed out.

Khenko removed the woman's gear, and Talav levitated her into the back of the jeep. A groan escaped the Awen's lips as she sagged into the battered seat. Her wet hair and torn clothes clung to her petite form. He positioned her head on the towel and tucked another around her dripping body. The air would be chilling in the open jeep, though it was a humid seventy-something degrees Fahrenheit.

"Contact me when she wakes." Talav rumbled.

"How do I do that?"

"Call my name and I'll appear." The ochre eyes went somber. "But understand, this is no mere woman. The Awen is Earth's only hope in the days to come. Her life, and that of every being on the planet, is in your hands, Healer. Do you understand?"

Daunted by the enormity of Talav's pronouncement, Khenko wavered. "Not really. Are you serious?"

"Dead serious." Talav shook her bejeweled head, raining water everywhere. "You, Khenko, blessed of Corr, have been called to service. It is your duty as a peacemaker and medicine man to heal this woman and ensure she makes it to her next destination. There is little time, and I have matters to attend. Do you understand?"

Icy fear traced the curve of Khenko's spine. He nodded slowly. "That, I understand."

"It is my job to help Awen achieve her appointed task. As soon as she is strong enough, you will return her to my care. Keep me informed. Keep her identity secret. And allow no calls or hospitals. It is important the world thinks her dead."

Sadness filled the dragon's eyes. She lowered her snout into the jeep and gently nudged the girl. "Fare thee well, sweet Awen. Call me if you need me. I will answer."

Talav turned to Khenko. "Khenko of Corr, to you I say it is time to cease your wanderings. Time to fulfill the destiny to which you were born."

The dragon's words touched something deep within Khenko, opening a well he had been afraid to tap. Long had he led a vagabond's life; long had he denied his calling. But in his bones Khenko Rainman Blitherstone knew—and had since the stork appeared in his dreams—his wanderings had indeed come to an end. It was time to return to the Iroquois.

Then the most incredible creature Khenko had ever seen strolled to the edge of the blue hole and slipped into the water with a loud splash.

Feeling the weight of the whole world descend upon his shoulders, Khenko climbed behind the steering wheel. He drove along the gravel road at a low speed so as not to disturb his passenger. He could no longer think of her as a package.

Cocking the rearview mirror, a thrill ran through him. The Awen's face glowed in the wan moonlight.

THE ATLANTEAN CENTER

Emily found herself in a small room. Was she still in the Otherworld? Or was she dreaming? The room spun around when she tried to sit. She laid back carefully and studied her surroundings.

A steady sluicing outside the open window sounded like surf. At least she was no longer in a cave. Unless this was an illusion created by her mind. Or the tricksy dragon. Had she dreamed the whole thing?

Emily got out of bed slowly and deliberately, keeping a steadying hand on the mattress. When the spinning stopped, she moved to the window and peered through the screen. Moonlit breakers rolled ashore to pound the sand. Her heart soared. She *was* at the beach. But how did she get here?

Shivering, she searched for her shoes to no avail. Lifting the thin blanket from the double bed, she wrapped it around her shoulders and tiptoed to the door to slip into a long hallway. She tiptoed down the hall, glancing in the open doors that lined each side. Every room was empty and identical to the one she'd left.

What was this place? And how had she gotten here?

The hall opened to a large foyer. A cane fan whirred lazily overhead, stirring the tangy air. Community flip-flops of various sizes were arranged neatly by the front door. Emily found a pair that fit her size sevens and slipped them on.

Releasing the deadbolt, she flapped onto the dark porch and down to the yard where a gravel driveway bisected thick jungle. The building appeared to be situated on a promontory overlooking the ocean. The night lent a surreal quality to the surging and receding waves.

Though largely obscured by a palm thicket, lights twinkled from next door. If she squinted, Emily could almost make out the house. She turned back to the building she had exited and spotted a sign by the front door. The Atlantean Center.

Was she in Florida? The Bahamas? Most of those islands had succumbed to the rising seas.

Several structures surrounded the main building, including a garage and some sort of utility building. A wooden cabana opened onto the beach, with chairs and umbrellas stacked in one corner. A light wind fluttered the palm-leaf awning and carried the scent of salt and sea creatures. Her ocean-deprived senses soaked in everything.

Breaking waves churned in the light of a sickle moon, and slapped against the shore before washing out to sea. Her eyes devoured the scene, mesmerized. The spray caressed her cheeks.

Spying a lone director's chair beneath a date palm, Emily dragged it several yards from the waterline and sank into the salt-encrusted canvas. She sat for a spell without moving or thinking, letting the ocean's essence wash over and through her battered self.

In a hypnotic state, she leaned back and looked up at the star-filled sky. Based on the placement of the constellations, she couldn't be far from Atlanta. How long had she been gone? Days? A week? More?

The sting of her losses had miraculously lessened. Somehow she knew the others were okay. All was as it should be. For the moment, anyway.

Emily closed her eyes and let the pounding of the surf scour her senses. She fell asleep, head cocked to one side. Her soft snores blended with the ocean sounds. Slowly, one by one, the creatures of the deep left their hiding places and gathered nearby.

☼☼☼

Talav eyed the sleeping Awen. Getting her out of the caverns had been exactly what she needed. She still walked the Otherworld, but she was growing stronger. Strong enough that the sea creatures were drawn to her presence—a good sign. Talav lingered until the sun approached the horizon and night gave way to dawn.

With a satisfied sigh, she eased into the ocean and struck out for the blue hole, leaving a trace of earth magic on the waves.

DEATH SENTENCE

Ishkur hefted his pack and donned his fiercest headgear. Fashioned from a hawk he had defeated in battle, Ishkur wore it with pride. The raptor had terrorized a rural community outside Xibalba before Ishkur caught wind of it in a poker game. He'd lost a week's pay taking time for the hunt, but had gained his most prized possession. Thus attired, he set out to meet the others in the central square.

The three Dracos, Kaijin, Mokele-Mbembe, and Nahuelito, were waiting for Ishkur on the platform. They stood at attention and saluted—a quick, closed-fist smack to the chest. Ishkur returned the gesture and shouldered past them, intent on catching the next car out before Shibboleth changed his mind. The further he could get from the warlord, the better Ishkur would feel.

Chute cars whizzed by, going east and west. The north-south lines were at the far end. Giving no thought to the Dracos trailing behind him, Ishkur made a beeline for the station pub. Tossing credits on the bar, he requested a froksch and downed it in one swallow, then slammed the empty stein on the counter and nodded for the barkeep to draw another. Leaning on the tap, the Pharechi filled his mug, then hurried to the other end of the bar.

All around him, patrons whispered, likely about Shibboleth. Or Nergal's death. Two things Ishkur had no control over. Shame deepened his pale-olive scales to turtle green. He gulped the chilled ale, pivoted, and strode out of the bar.

The others waited outside.

"What the hell?" Mbembe muttered. "Couldn't you wait until we got on the chute? How 'bout staying sober for once? Our lives might depend on it."

"Yeah," Nahuelito growled. "Put a cork in it. At least 'til we get outta Xibalba. That warlord means business."

It took all Ishkur's restraint not to strike them down on the spot. But they had a point. He resolved to hold it together, at least until they arrived at Agartha and he'd had time to assess the situation.

He thought of Lamia, his familiar, and their two little ones. Would he ever see them again? After news of Nergal's death, Ishkur had sent them to the country in case things got ugly.

"Attention," the intercom blared. "The Agarthan Express is approaching the station. Please stand back. It will debark at Gate Nine, and depart in fifteen minutes."

Snatching his pack from the platform, Ishkur slung it over one shoulder and settled his hat more securely on his head. The chute chugged past, a deluxe sleeper. Which meant a bar and a casino. Just the distraction Ishkur needed to quiet his anxious gut.

Because Shibboleth had spared him for one reason—he didn't want to risk the safety of his own Dracos. Agartha and its spreading magma was a death sentence.

☼☼☼

Azi entered the dark lab, the center of Nergal's Human Domination project. A thrill of excitement raced through him. Supine on an onyx bench in the corner was the first successful intermediary, a lowly Fomorian. A lab tech occupied an adjacent terminal.

Acknowledging her, Azi moved to the glass enclosure. The Fomorian's chest barely moved. Azi considered activating its paused connection with Shalane Carpenter to study how it worked. All the others were modeled on this one, and Shibboleth's orders to Azi were to implement Nergal's program worldwide.

But it was not yet past the experimental phase, and he had given Azi only one week.

Azi's claws clattered over the main console's keyboard. The technology and methods used to identify and tag the targets, as well as connect and download their information to the main brain, was nothing short of genius. Azi memorized the project specs and all its particulars, itching to try the system. But that would have to wait until tomorrow.

He accessed the extensive target list and included it in a communique to the corresponding coordinators around UnderEarth. In it, he outlined Shibboleth's orders and scheduled a virtual meeting with them for the next morning.

When he was satisfied with the evening's work, Azi bid his tech good morrow and went in search of his quarters. He would be living in Xibalba IX for the foreseeable future. At least until they perfected the domination technique and breached AboveEarth, a daunting task for most. But for Azi, it was a challenge worthy of his superior intellect.

CYBELE

The sight of Jocko's Pizza was a balm for Lugh's spirit. Before going in, he admired the upgrades they had made last month after tornadoes demolished the front wall. The new brick was stronger and safer, and still boasted a generous array of windows. They had also rearranged the dining room, picking up enough space to add an extra booth and table.

Unlocking the front door, Lugh left the "Closed" sign hanging. The restaurant wouldn't open for several hours, and he planned to be quick, just long enough to check on Cu and hopefully talk to his parents.

He circled the restaurant and ran loving fingers over the shellacked countertop. He found and traced the initials he and his brother Jake had carved with a pocketknife. Pinky, the bartender, had caught them in the act and dragged them to the kitchen, where Mama lectured them on the bad manners of destroying property. Papa's punishment was a leather belt.

How Lugh had hated those whippings, more sensitive to the sting of shame than that of the strap. Jake was older and blamed everything on him, a habit that backfired as much as not. Then one day Jake left and didn't come back.

Lugh's heart ached as he stopped beside the table Emily had occupied when Mitch brought her to Jocko's. The first time Lugh saw her he'd known he would marry her. Now, like Jake, she was gone.

He looked around the dining room, and a surge of gratitude brought tears to his eyes. So many memories had been made here over the years. Despite all that had happened, Jocko's had survived. As had Lugh.

But not his nephew. Or Emily. Or her father. Like Cu, they were probably dead.

The thought bent Lugh double, a punch to the gut. He crumpled to his knees and put his forehead in the wooden chair. And there, in the middle of his family's restaurant, Lugh howled like a wounded animal. What was the goddess thinking?

Anger flooded in, scuttling the despair. He dashed away tears. Cybele had entrusted Brian to Lugh's care, and it had been two days since the earthquake. He had to call her. What if she had seen the news? No. She would've called. But how could Cybele forgive him? How would he ever forgive himself?

"Oh Goddess, give me words," he begged, tapping Cybele's photograph on his phone.

As always, her voice mail answered right away. Never once, in all the years Lugh had known Cybele MacBrayer had she answered a phone. Leaving an urgent message, Lugh hung up and swallowed. It was time to talk to his parents and see Cu.

He shoved through the swinging doors, but the kitchen was empty. Disappointment tugged at his heavy heart. He'd hoped to see Ma and Pa's spirits bustling about, waiting for Lugh to open the place.

He glanced at the mementos on the walls—a Hamsa from Rabbi Soflinski, who had eaten at Jocko's every Thursday until he died, the ceramic triskele they'd brought back from Europe the year Lugh turned twelve, and the bronze bust of St Brigit purchased in Ireland on the same trip.

Lugh fingered the frilly apron still hanging where his mother had placed it the day they turned the restaurant over to him. They had planned to travel, had even purchased a motor home. But they died that March in a traffic collision, making the transition bittersweet.

Burying his face in the apron, Lugh groaned, "Ma, I don't know what to do. You told me to help Emily, but I couldn't. Now she's gone. Brian, too, and they both might be dead. I left a message for Cybele. But how do I tell Jake, if he's even alive? Ma, what should I do?"

"Nothing, my son," his mom whispered behind him. "You wait. And do nothing,"

Lugh swung to face her, arms open for one of her famous hugs. Catching nothing but air, he teetered on tiptoes.

"Nothing?" That was the last thing he wanted to hear. "I can't do nothing, Ma. I lost Brian. *And* our Grand Druid."

"No, dear. You did not. You did everything in your power to save your nephew. And your girl. Let them go, Lugh. They're in the gods' hands. Even I cannot see them." She reached a distraught arm toward him.

He turned his back, miserable as only the damned can be. Hot anger churned inside his gut. So they *were* dead. And according to his mother, there was nothing Lugh could do.

"Mi Amor," she crooned, "do not despair. Just because I can't see them doesn't mean they are dead. There are places even I cannot see." Lugh winced and she rushed to add, "Not all of them are bad, my sweet, sensitive boy."

His Pa's stern voice boomed across the room. "Lughnasadh Bran MacBrayer, are those tears I see?" His father was a man's man. Not one to coddle or condone waterworks.

Lugh blinked back the tears as the rotund man joined his mother by Lugh's side. Since their last meeting, he had donned a clean apron, but the ever-present dusting of flour rode high on one cheek.

Unashamed, Lugh admitted, "Yes Papa, I am crying. I lost Brian and Emily. And you may have noticed that Cu is dead in the deep freeze. Maybe Hamilton Hester, too." His Pa's thick eyebrows arched, and his mother gasped.

"No," Lugh sighed. "Mr. Hester is not in our deep freeze. He transferred to Cu's body a few weeks ago when his own gave out. But now Cu is dead and in the freezer."

The two knitted foreheads smoothed, but only a little. They sighed in unison, as linked in death as they were in life.

Lugh's phone vibrated and he jumped several inches. Recovering, he retrieved it from his jeans pocket. "Lugh MacBrayer."

"Lugh, this is Cybele. What in the world? Are you crazy leaving a message like that? Brian is missing? For the love of all that is sacred and holy, tell me my son is okay!" Her voice was shrill and near hysteria.

The truth caught in Lugh's throat. On the other end, Cybele sobbed. He listened, feeling helpless. Soon came the bleat of her blowing nose. Hopefully, she had passed the hard part. That's why he'd left the news in his earlier message.

But Lugh hadn't. He worked his frozen jaws, but couldn't say the words. All he managed was a guilt-ridden, "Cybele—" followed by snuffles of his own.

"Lugh, get it together. Or, I'm really going to lose it," Cybele choked out. The woman had never taken bunk from anyone. She was a good mom. And Jake had loved her like crazy.

Lugh closed his eyes to gather his composure, then said in one long breath, "Cybele, I was there. I couldn't save them." The recurring dream he'd had as a child came to mind. The circumstances changed each time, but the result was always the same—Lugh helpless, unable to do anything but watch horrified as something awful happened. Only this time, it was real. There was no waking.

"Cybele?" he whispered. "Are you there?"

Her strangled response sounded tortured. "Yes."

"Say something. Anything."

When she remained silent save the muffled sobs, Lugh begged, "Please, Cybele. Say something. Say I'm awful. Say anything. But dammit, say something." Lugh slammed his fist into the cellar door, then cradled his bruised knuckles.

"Let me call you back." The line went dead, and Lugh sank to the floor. He stayed there staring off at nothing until his phone rang a few minutes later.

"Cybele?" He answered on the first tone.

"Lugh MacBrayer, my son is not dead," she spit into the phone. "I may not be a practicing druid any more, but dammit, get yer head outta yer ass and feel for yourself. Brian is not dead. I can feel my boy. He's out there somewhere. You go get him, Lughnasadh. I believe in you. Find our boy."

For the first time since the earthquake, Lugh wept for real, wept for the missing, for the broken and the dead. And he wept for the one thing that could never be broken—hope. An image of the tabby appeared in his mind's eye.

"That's it! Cybele, you are brilliant!"

She laugh and cried. "What? What did I say?"

"You reminded me of Hope, the druid Elder. Hope will know what to do."

Cybele laughed for real this time. There was the slightest disdain at his mention of Hope, but her laughter eased his tension.

"Should I come to Atlanta? We're in the middle of production and I need to see this through. But if you need me, I'll be there straight away."

Lugh hesitated. "No. Just pray. And if he contacts you, call me."

"I will, Lugh. Jake always said you could be trusted for anything. I believed in Jake, and I believe in you. Now, go find our boy."

Lugh's sense of relief was immense. He hadn't realized he'd been holding it together for Cybele. And strength was something he was short on at the moment.

"Whatever you think. And Cybele?"

"Yes?" she sounded far away.

"Thank you for not hating me—" Lugh's voice caught.

After a short silence, Cybele spoke slowly, enunciating every word. "Lugh, there are many emotions I am feeling right now. But anger at you is not one of them. At God, yes. I won't deny that. But not at you. Brian thinks the world of you. I know he whines and complains, but my son is happier with you than he has been in years. And that means the world to me."

Lugh smiled. He was well aware of the belly-aching to which Cybele referred. "Well, I'd be lying if I didn't say the feeling is mutual," Lugh admitted. "But don't tell Brian." He winced and could've kicked himself. "Never mind. Do. Tell Brian just that. Or hell, I will. Cybele, thank you. I will keep you posted."

"I know you will. And, Lugh?"

"Yes?"

"Remember that year we went to Zoo Atlanta with your Ma and Pa? When Brian was four?"

"Uh-huh." Not long after that, Cybele had taken Brian and moved to Utah, leaving Jake and the rest of the family behind.

"Something happened that day, or more to the truth, Jake told me something. I need to share it with you, but not on the phone. Next time we're together." Alarms clanged in the recesses of Lugh's brain. "In the meantime, keep me posted about Brian, and give him a huge hug from his mama when you find him."

"Done, Cybele. Thank you."

Lugh ended the call and stared at his mother's apron still clutched in his hand. Shaking it out, he hung it beside his dad's and walked to the deep freeze. Dread curled in the pit of his stomach.

Taking a deep breath, Lugh pulled the handle and peeked into the walk-in freezer. He spied a large package in the back corner, propped against a rack that held frozen desserts.

He wanted to look, had intended to look. Instead, he wavered in the doorway, icy tendrils sneaking around him to escape into the warm kitchen. Perplexed at his reluctance, Lugh backed out of the freezer and slammed it shut.

He must talk to Hope.

☼☼☼

Cybele slumped in the chair and stared into a future too cloudy to see. After a time, she rose to brew a pot of coffee. It was going to be a long night. Now, not only was her ex-husband missing but their son too. She fingered the swatch of cotton she had saved when his baby blanket bit the dust. Brian had clung to it long past the usual time. Cybele hadn't been able to let go, either. Not entirely.

Folding the ragged cloth into the box of keepsakes, Cybele wiped away the tears before they could trickle down her cheek. Brian wasn't dead. She would know. A mother would know. Especially one as intuitive as Cybele Cray MacBrayer.

She removed the scrying ball from her suitcase and cleaned it carefully with the chamois cloth. She placed it gently in its cradle and carried it to the tiny table. Settling in front of the crystal ball, Cybele lit the candle stub and a half-burned chunk of dhoop to purify the air. Calling on the Celtic goddess Brigit to reveal her son Brian, Cybele waited, breathing the sweet, spicy scent of sandalwood and frankincense.

Presently, a vision appeared—a tall, pale woman, young in years and gentle of heart. Her slender ears pointed upward, and her wide lips moved in hushed tones speaking to someone outside the field of vision.

Cybele's mother-heart thrilled. She knew it was Brian. And had no doubt.

She watched until the image faded and passed her hand over the ball in a cleansing motion. With loving care, she polished the crystal again before replacing it in its cradle. This time she asked to be shown Jake, her ex-husband, and the love of Cybele's life.

Crimson flames appeared inside the orb.

For a long time, Cybele sat in contemplation. The flames appeared every time she had tried to scry Jake's whereabouts. If she believed in a biblical hell, she might think he had died and ended up there.

"But if that were the case," she reasoned, for the thousandth time, "I wouldn't feel this strong pull. Jake MacBrayer, I know you are out there. Where are you, my love?"

Returning the orb to its velvet bag, Cybele gathered the paraphernalia and stowed it in its diminutive trunk. Spinning the dials to change the combination, she returned the trunk to its hiding place inside her Pullman.

Holstering her sidearm, Cybele donned a raincoat and pulled the hood forward to hide her face. Making sure no one was about, she slipped out the door of the cheap inn. It was time to rendezvous with the handsome arms dealer. The one who claimed to have information about Jake.

BEST LAID PLANS

Despite his intentions to the contrary, Mitch called a limousine. If he drove, he couldn't drink, and he planned on getting sloshed. Plus, he wouldn't have to find a parking place or worry about a roving gang snatching his Beemer.

A text heralded the limo's arrival and Mitch changed his mind again. He had no desire to spend time listening to a born-again evangelist, even a sexy female one. But when the sleek car pulled up at his door, Mitch got in.

"Fox Theater, sir?" The driver eyed him in the rearview mirror. Still torn, Mitch grunted an affirmation.

As it turned out, Shalane Carpenter was a gifted speaker. Her orchestra was first-class and her singing voice, divine. By the time it was all over, Mitch was ready to give his soul to God.

"Oh wait," he mumbled. "It's already His." He chuckled to allay his unease. There was nothing wrong with kindling a God-fire in people. It felt good to have a connection.

Mitch wiped his sweaty palms on a handkerchief and waded upstream through the throng of patrons leaving the theater. He'd been backstage at the Fox before, but never had Mitch been this nervous. Even as a kid. He presented his pass to a burly guard and wound his way behind the stage.

Shalane's dressing room was easy to find. Her name was emblazoned in scarlet sequined letters across the door. Mitch's knock came off sounding like a timid schoolboy, so he tried again, this time a man on a mission.

The door opened and a wave of perfume washed over him, sultry and sweet and seductive. A hand snaked out and caught hold of his wrist, pulling him in. Shalane didn't let go until he was inside, where she raked him up and down with her eyes.

"Let me get a look at you." Her voice was low and husky. And devoid of accent, other than sex. She had kicked off her shoes and was dressed in the diaphanous purple getup she'd worn on stage. Her thin blond hair was damp from exertion. Her eyes were a bit glassy, and the room smelled of hashish or some really good herb. A thread of smoke rose from the pipe she held out to him.

"Care for a hit?"

He hesitated. It'd been a long time. But when in Rome. "Sure, why not?"

Putting the stem to his lips, Mitch took a long pull and barely managed to hold it in his lungs. His eyes bugged out, but he held on, then exhaled a thick cloud of smoke.

"I'm Mitch Wainwright. Pleased to meet you." He handed the pipe back.

"And you as well." Shalane nodded distractedly. "Care for a drink? I have beer and brandy, anything else we'll have to order out."

"They do that here?"

"For me?" she chuckled. "Hell yeah, handsome. Name your poison."

Mitch needed to keep his wits about him. He had no intention of becoming Shalane's pawn. Or play toy. Or any of the things he'd read about. "What kind of beer?"

"The cold kind." She fished a tall bottle from a compact refrigerator and handed it to him, taking one for herself.

He twisted the top and took a swig of the bitter brew, then stifled a belch. Catching Shalane's eye, Mitch returned her grin. But to himself, he recited Georgia Law Code to counteract what was happening in his pants.

"So, Reverend Carpenter. What do you know about Emily Hester's disappearance?"

The evangelist batted heavily-mascaraed eyelids. "You mean the woman that died in the earthquake this morning? I don't believe I know her, but her name and face seem vaguely familiar. Who is she?" She fixed Mitch with a measuring stare.

Mitch stared back. What was she playing at? He rubbed his face in both hands, then tried again. "You said you knew her as Ebby Panera." There was a flicker in the blue eyes.

"Nope. No bells. But since you're here, and I'm here…" Her voice trailed off, laden with seduction.

He eyed her speculatively. "No doll. Seems you've gotten me here under false pretenses. I don't play games."

Shalane ran a finger lightly down his sleeve and a trail of electricity followed, making his cock twitch. He yanked his arm away and turned toward the door.

"Look, I don't know this person you're talking about. But I believe you when you say I should." She sounded earnest. "Since I saw the news this morning, it's been nagging at me. I even visited the quake site. And I'm wondering if someone messed with my memory."

That got Mitch's attention. He *had* given Shalane the Wren's Roost address. But he doubted Emily Hester's skills were advanced enough to wipe anyone's memory.

Shalane clutched at his sleeve. "Will you help me remember?"

He studied the witch-turned-evangelist. Without the airs, she was just another needy woman, something Mitch could never stomach. "Yeah, no. I don't think so."

She drew to full height, which couldn't be more than five foot two, but the room shrank around her. "Then why are you here?" The blue eyes flashed, and she twisted her hands. As her agitation multiplied, Mitch's misgivings quieted.

"I am Mitchell Albom Wainwright the Third," he stated calmly. "But you already know that. You also know that I'm here about Emily Hester. More than a month ago, you called my office looking for her and we've talked several times since then. Hell, I even gave you her address the other day."

Shalane blanched and moved to repack the pipe. Mitch had learned from his father not to reveal intimate details to adversaries, strangers, and new friends. It was unclear which category Shalane fell in. But at least her deadly sex-beam was no longer pointed at him.

Was she telling the truth? From earlier indications, she'd been obsessed with Emily. Now she denied even knowing her. Still, Shalane could be of some use. Other than for sex. The thought brought a grim smile to his lips. He was not going there.

"You do have beautiful blue eyes, you know." Shalane batted her lashes and tittered. Mitch wasn't sure what a titter was supposed to sound like, but coming from Shalane, it was exquisite.

Astonished, he paused to replay his last thought. Titter? Exquisite sound? What the hell? He searched his memory for an obscure law code and came up with one about cousins marrying.

But the vixen turned the pipe around, stuck the bowl in her mouth, and blew a trail of smoke, expecting him to inhale. Mitch hadn't partaken of pot in years, much less shotgun-style. Against his own volition, he leaned in and sucked the smoke deep into his lungs. Reaching maximum excursion, he backed away.

Which would've been fine, only the pot was potent, or possibly laced with hashish. It expanded in his lungs and exploded out of him in a violent coughing fit. Blinded by tears, he coughed and struggled to get a breath.

"Can't hold it, don't toke it," the woman cackled, obviously enjoying Mitch's discomfort.

"You *cough cough* did *cough* that *cough cough cough* on purpose." He spit saliva on the last syllable, then collapsed on the sofa in another round of hacking.

"Water," he choked. She handed him his beer. Mitch took a tiny sip, and when it calmed the hacking for a few seconds, took another. The third he spit out coughing, but by the fourth, Mitch had regained tentative lung control.

"Bitch," he swore when she tried to hand him the pipe again, "keep that shit away from me. Can't you see I'm dying here?" Another spate of coughing seized him. He glared at Shalane when she laughingly took a hit and blew it in his face.

"Are you always this *cough* insufferable?"

"Pretty much." She puffed and exhaled in Mitch's face.

He stood abruptly, anger rising. "Look, you said you had information about Emily Hester. Do you, or do you not, have said information? If so, get to it. If not, I'm leaving." He spun on one shiny-loafered sole and crossed to the door in two strides.

"Don't go," Shalane pled, blocking his path. Her big blue eyes welled up with tears, and she looked genuinely stricken.

Moved despite his resolve to the contrary, Mitch hesitated, hand on the doorknob.

"I need company. Hang out with me this evening?" Her lashes batted seductively, and she rolled her shoulder so that the strap of her gown slid down to reveal the curve of one buxom breast.

Mitchell's cock perked up. "Tell me about Emily Hester and I might consider staying."

The plump face reddened and Shalane snapped, "Who the hell *is* this Emily Hester? And why do you think I know her?"

"Because you phoned me about her more than a month ago," he snapped back, then blew out a long, exasperated breath. "You bribed me, Shalane. Got me to do your dirty work. Then you ordered me to appear here, like a peon summoned to court. All under the guise of having information about Emily and her whereabouts. So what's your angle? Who is Emily to you? Come to con her out of her newly-inherited fortune?"

The woman went white. "Get out of here!" she screeched and shoved him toward the door.

"Gladly," Mitch snarled. He slipped through the opening and slammed it hard.

Hurrying down the corridor, he glanced over his shoulder. The hall was empty. The witch hadn't followed. He slowed to a saunter and exited a side door.

Outside on North Avenue, rock music poured from a nearby tavern. He thought about texting his driver to go home. But he was too riled to even think about sleep. Mitch nipped into the bar instead.

THE FOMORI

The trees in the dense forest were gnarled and ancient. Grateful to be away from the lizard-men, Brian followed Number Three along a barely perceptible trail. His rescuer's limbs were long and lean, her movements effortless and never tiring. She crossed the distance with noiseless strides.

Brian trotted to keep up, at times breaking into a run. But he was exhausted. And sleepy. And desperately needed rest. The food he had gobbled had long since cleared his grumbling stomach. Fixed on his misery, Brian tripped on a root and stumbled into Number Three.

Not missing a beat, she continued the flight into the heart of the woods. The hooded cape she had produced along the trail hid her flowing brown hair and turned her silhouette into a ghostly vision in the filtered morning light.

Who was this lovely creature, and why was she helping him?

A variety of birds called to one another, and one of the largest squirrels Brian had ever seen scampered across the trail and up a tall, spindly tree.

The foreboding forest gave way to a stand of evergreens. Here the path was padded with needle-fall. Every step sent the spicy scent of pine wafting into the air, along with the musty mold of decay. Brian breathed it all in, grateful to be out from under the earth and back into the light of day, even if it was dimmer than he remembered.

He thought of the time his father had visited him in Utah and taken him caving. They had explored several caverns searching for buried treasure, or so Brian had pretended. His dad had drawn pictures and scribbled notes on a hand-sketched map. When his mother found out, she went ballistic, forbidding his dad from seeing him again.

Brian shivered. He had forgotten that part.

Number Three turned and gave him a quick smile—her first. He grinned and walked taller, sneakered feet barely touching the ground. Until he realized he was smirking, and missed a step. Had he gone gaga over an alien girl?

"Snap out of it," he mumbled to himself. It wouldn't do to let Number Three know he was interested.

"Oh, I don't know."

Hearing Hamilton's voice in his head made him stumble again, only this time Brian caught himself. Number Three flashed another quick smile over her shoulder.

"We're almost there. Another ten minutes, barring complications."

"Complications?" he gulped, then wished he hadn't sounded like a frightened kid.

"The Reptilians normally steer clear of these woods, but they've become bolder during daylight hours. They sometimes lie in wait, capturing Fomore and other races to make us their slaves."

The sense of relief the woods had given Brian fled. He looked around, wary now. "Aliens live above the earth, too?"

"Aliens?" Her head whipped toward him, and she stopped and stared. "I am no more an alien than you, Brian MacBrayer. Nor are my people. We are originally from Ireland. Have you not heard of the Fomore? My ancestors migrated here long ago. Unfortunately, the lizard-men, as you call them, got here first. They are enemies to all us gentle-folk."

"UnderEarth? What is that?" Brian was worried he might know the answer.

There was a loud cracking noise up in the trees. They crouched and Number Three grabbed her weapon. A thick tree branch slipped through the canopy and crashed to the ground. Rising, she holstered it, wide eyes reflecting the dappled light.

"Just a broken branch. Let's hurry. I'll explain when we get inside."

Within minutes, the evergreens thinned to a large pasture. A sheep baaed and cows mooed. Number Three halted. A large red-tailed hawk swooped low to snatch a rodent from the field, then flew off with it dangling from its claws.

They had to be back up top. There wouldn't be sunlight inside the earth. Nor hawks and crows and cows and sheep.

His rescuer searched the woods, then approached a boulder. She tapped it three times with a booted toe, and spoke words Brian didn't understand. The stone rolled back to reveal a hole in the ground. The wide eyes gazed at him intently.

"You first."

Brian peered into the dark hole. "Do we have to? We just got out."

She nodded, and Brian gulped.

Gathering his nerve, he sat and dangled his legs into the hole. He was preparing to jump when she touched his shoulder.

"It'll be easier if you turn around." At his quizzical look, Number Three explained, "There's a ladder in there."

"Ahh." Feeling stupid, Brian felt for the ladder with his foot, then turned to face it. One thin rung at a time, he descended into darkness. The pretty Fomorian followed.

A small circular room waited at the bottom. Number Three punched a series of codes into her handheld device. There was a snick, and a door opened out of the bedrock. Inside that was a grand entrance.

Brian gawked at the magnificent chamber. "Where are we?"

"A Fomorian stronghold. One of the few remaining in this part of UnderEarth."

"What is UnderEarth? You keep mentioning it."

Number Three said flatly, "We are *in* UnderEarth. My home. The realm within earth's mantle."

Brian felt the blood drain from his face. "So we really are inside the earth? Not on top where I live?" Tears gathered behind his eyes and clogged his throat.

"I'm sorry." Ethnui touched his shoulder.

"But there are trees. And birds and animals. And a sun. If we are inside the earth, where does the light come from?" Would he never escape this nightmare? He smushed his face with his hands, making his eyes and mouth pop out like a fish. Number Three's laugh lifted his spirits. He chuckled, too.

"My little human." The Fomorian smiled apologetically. "I know how you must feel."

"How could you?" He swallowed hard to push the lump back down. "This is your home."

She settled on one end of a cushioned bench. Tired to the bone, Brian sank beside her and wrapped his arms around his chest. He focused on the rough-hewn stone floor that for some reason, was incredibly warm. Perspiration beaded on his upper lip. He wiped it away and tugged off his jacket. The rips and bloodstains reminded him of Uncle Lugh, and Emily, and Cu.

And Hamilton Hester.

"Sir, where are you?" he whispered in his mind. "Have you abandoned me?"

"I'm here. Pay attention. She's about to tell you what we need to know. Get a grip, son."

"Get a grip? You've got to be kidding me."

The woman watched Brian with interest. When she had his attention, she leaned closer. "Like you, I once lived in AboveEarth. I grew up on an island off the coast of Ireland." Shyness crept into her lyrical voice. "After they brought me here, I had the same problem as you. Where did the light come from? Why were there birds? And how could there be a sky beneath the ground?"

"Exactly."

"The answer is simple. Life up there originated down here."

Brian almost choked. "Huh?"

"UnderEarth has been inhabited for time untold. When the outer conditions improved to livable, species began migrating to the surface. The earth you see is a reflection of that which is down here."

"And the sun?"

"Is not a sun, but radiation from the earth's core. It cycles, so we have day and night. The air above us is what we call 'sky'. And it rains, too. We have wind, and even electrical storms, though not that often. I've heard there are oceans, but I've never seen one. And a few enormous rivers, and lakes galore. Oh, and fish! Most of the animals are much bigger than up top. I know you're going to ask why, but I don't know."

Brian stared, not sure whether to believe Ethnui or not. But why would she lie? "So you're okay with never going back to Ireland?"

Ethnui shrugged. "I was young when we left, and don't remember much—mostly that I was different from everyone else, including my family. It was the reason we were on the island in the first place. Me and my mother."

She reached for her cap. It still perched at a jaunty angle, undisturbed by their travails or the hood that now rested against her back. Removing the clips, Number Three took it off and lowered her head.

Brian gasped. "You have horns!"

Fascinated, he studied her more closely. The eyes he'd thought blue, now reflected brown hues from the robe and wall. Fear and self-loathing, two emotions Brian knew well, pooled within their depths.

"But they're tiny. Nubs really," he rushed to reassure. "Can I touch them?"

Number Three lowered her head. He ran his fingers lightly over the tips peeking through her thick brown hair.

"Don't they have names? These stubby little horns?"

She recoiled, face blazing. Had he offended her?

"Only if you name them," she sniffed. "Otherwise, they're just horns."

Brian's face grew hot. Then his mythology lessons kicked in.

"Ooo, ooo I know." He leapt from the bench. "You're a satyr! A demi-god!"

His rescuer stared at him, horrified. "Heavens no." She spit the words out like they tasted bad, and shook her head vehemently. "At least not the satyr part."

"But you are a demi-god?"

"If you insist on calling it that." Her tone went cold and in the blink of an eye, Number Three disappeared. She simply folded and closed in upon herself like a roly-poly bug. All that was left was a round ball with a shell.

"How'd you do that?" He tapped the shiny, buff-colored casing, and laid an open palm on the warm surface. When she unfurled like a flower bud, he leapt backward. "Whoa. That's a pretty amazing trick, Number Three. But that can't be your real name."

"No, you're right. I am Ethnui."

"That's a pretty unusual skill, Ethnui. Should I bow to your awesome goddess-ness?"

She burst out laughing and bent double, one hand on her chest. "Of course not! It is I who should bow to you."

"Because?"

"Because of you, we have finally cloaked the Dracos' security system. The DNA of a human was the only strand missing from the program."

Brian shot off the bench and backed away. So she'd wanted him for his DNA. What else might they need?

"Is that why you rescued me? Why you brought me here?"

Ethnui's eyes narrowed. "You are perceptive for a human. I promise we mean you no harm. I only needed your DNA to complete the program. Since I wrote it, I was chosen to upload it to their mainframe. Plus, I had the uniform." She pointed at her outfit. "When I was enslaved by the Reptilians, I acquired experience as a medic. This is what I had on when I escaped. It helped me pass through their security undetected."

"So you're a computer geek?"

Ethnui's cheeks blazed. "Is that a bad thing?" She was cute when flustered, though he wasn't sure about that roly-poly thing.

"Goddess, no. It's an awesome thing. Tell me more about this program. What does it do, exactly?"

The Fomorian looked pleased. "It blinds their cameras and blanks out surveillance tapes and recordings. It can also remove all traces of one's presence in UnderEarth."

"That's brilliant," Brian crowed. "Does that mean any footage they had of me is now erased?"

"That's the idea. Of course, I never had a chance to test it on their system. So I don't know for sure." She looked at him shyly. "Do you really think I would have left you in that dungeon? Or that I mean you harm?" Her shoulders drooped, and he suddenly realized her ears were pointed.

She noticed him looking and quickly covered them with her long, slender fingers and stared at the floor. Brian pulled her hands away.

"Don't. They're yours. And I think they're cool. Don't be ashamed."

The big eyes swam, but Ethnui smiled.

"Where is everyone?" They'd encountered no one since leaving the dungeon. "Is it time to eat? I'm starving."

"Most remain conscripted. Only those who have escaped the Dracos' dungeons live here. Our numbers are small." She led him to another hallway, where a chandelier blazed overhead. Number Three stopped.

"This is as far as you can go without permission from my superiors." She motioned Brian to a bench. "This shouldn't take long. You are expected."

"I am expected? What does *that* mean?" Adrenaline surged through him. He went up on his tiptoes, poised to flee.

The Fomorian's crystalline laugh echoed through the chamber. "They sent me, silly."

Goosebumps crept up Brian's back. "But why? Why would they risk you to rescue me? Why not save your people instead?"

He backed toward the doorway, once more unsure of his welfare. But where would he go? Running wasn't much of an option. He was in a strange land with strange inhabitants and wild creatures that would eat him for breakfast. Not to mention Godzilla's evil relatives.

Ethnui gazed at Brian with a mixture of pity and annoyance. "Look, you're safe here. No one is going to hurt you. I'll be right back." And with that, she slipped through the door and was gone.

"Hamilton?" he whispered. "Where are you?" He was greeted by silence.

The door opened. Ethnui was back already. The look on her face chilled Brian to the bone.

"What is it?"

"They're gone. All of them."

THE ALMOST DEAD

The raucous cries of hungry gulls jarred Emily awake. She opened her eyes to the glorious sight of the ocean gently lapping the shore. The tide had gone out and tiny Sanderlings played tag with the waves. A thin layer of clouds hugged the horizon in a brightening sky still painted with swaths of pinks and purples.

Emily stretched in the creaky canvas chair and sand crabs scuttled away from her feet. The day was already warm. How long had she slept? She looked around and yawned. Had the dragon magicked her to this glorious place?

Last she remembered, she was chasing Talav through an endless maze of tunnels. She stood and turned a circle, inspecting her surroundings, then slowly ambled to the building relishing the feel of the sand on her bare feet. The sign on the door said Atlantean Center. Whatever that was.

Emily took the steps two at a time and kicked the flip flops into the corner by the door. She eyed the long hall with the numbered doors. Ceiling fans turned lazily overhead, the only things stirring. Where was everyone? She tiptoed to her room. Was this a hospital? A hostel?

Neither seemed likely. It was too nice to be the second and didn't smell like the first. Besides, wouldn't there be people working? She slipped into her room and stopped short, hand on the knob.

Someone was asleep in Emily's bed. Gasping, she hurried out and huddled in the hall trembling. Then reason returned. She checked the next room thinking she'd forgotten which was hers. But behind every door was an empty bed. Baffled, Emily returned to the occupied room and eased the door open. She approached the bed silently and barely suppressed her surprised squeal. The battered face was her own.

With trepidation, Emily lifted the covers. The woman wore the same outfit as she, only it was soiled and ripped, and her face and arms sported nasty bruises.

What in holy hell? She stood transfixed, staring at the apparition, unable to move or look away. The "Emily" in the bed lay very still. Her chest rose and fell, and her cheeks, though drawn and scabbed, were a pale pink.

The doorknob rattled and Emily barely had time to slip behind the curtains before it creaked open. A strawberry-blond man dressed in cut-off Levi's and a faded tee ducked through the doorway. He crossed to the bed and took the other Emily's pulse. Done, he laid the back of his hand on her forehead. A good six-foot-six in bare feet, the man's informal dress nixed hospital. He was shaggy and unkempt, but not bad looking.

Clearing her throat, Emily croaked, "Pardon me. Are you in charge?"

The lanky man jerked as if he'd been struck. "Who's there?" Could he not see her?

"Emily Hester. Who are you?"

"Emily? Did you say Emily? Where are you?" The man moved around the room, checking the closet and beneath the bed. He even looked past her out the window. Why was he acting like she wasn't there? She watched him search feverishly.

The "her" in the bed moaned. It was barely discernible, but the tall man hurried to her side. He lifted a hand and held it between his.

"Emily? Are you trying to reach me?"

Something fluttered inside her. She waved her arms. "I'm here! By the window!"

He scanned the room, shook his head and said, "There's no one by the window."

"I don't understand."

"Nor do I." He looked up at her with solemn eyes.

"You see me!" she crowed. His wagging head said no. "Oh. You hear me."

The man nodded and wrapped a blood pressure cuff around the arm he held. He pumped it full of air and placed the bell of a stethoscope in the crook of the elbow.

Emily moved closer. She touched the other face with her fingertips, a light caress on the cheek. There was a stirring on her own and she jerked her hand away. The pressure on her cheek disappeared. Chills ran up her spine.

"What did you do?" Excitement sharpened the man's tone.

"Nothing."

"No. Something happened. You responded. Your cheek flinched. Do it again."

Surprised, Emily stroked the face and once again felt the pressure on her own. Flabbergasted, she stared at the body in the bed.

"Do something else."

She closed her eyes and ran a gentle hand over the matted curls, amazed to feel the sensation of being petted.

"You're waking! Keep going!"

His excitement fired hers and when the image of her Bebe giving her the druid kiss popped in Emily's mind, she leaned forward and took her face in her hands. With the utmost care, she kissed the familiar forehead, nose, chin, eyes, and cheeks—and felt both the giving and receiving ends. With her last caress to the lips, the eyelids fluttered.

The tall medic whooped. "YES! Come on, Emily! You can do it! Wake up!"

The sun shone brightly on the coral shells littering the thin bedspread. Emily's heart thudded. Then suddenly, she was lying beneath the covers, blinking her eyes against the blinding light.

☼☼☼

Few could see into the Otherworld according to the dragon, yet Khenko had heard the woman speak—before she woke from the coma. Now she stared at him from the bed in the Jade Room with the prettiest green eyes he had ever seen. When a quick smile lit her bruised face, Khenko's breath caught. Then she was a confused woman again, fighting her way back from near-death.

"Water," she mouthed.

He hurried to the pitcher he'd filled the night before and poured her a glass. Her arm fell limp to the bed, so he squatted beside her and held the glass to her lips. The glittering eyes peered into his when he elevated her head.

She sipped and nodded "done".

Gently, Khenko laid her head on the pillow and watched her expressive face.

"Where am I?" she croaked. "Who are you?"

The knot inside Khenko's chest relaxed. The woman was coherent. Now to see if she had her faculties and memory. A dragon could remove both.

"My name is Khenko Blitherstone. No really," he added when her brows arched. "I get that a lot. I thought about changing it, but my dad freaked out. So, I'm stuck with Blitherstone. What's your name?"

The brows shot higher, and her thin lips twisted into a tiny smile. "And your first name? Surely he didn't name you after an office supply store?"

That smile flashed again and Khenko's heart skipped a beat. He didn't even mind that she'd opened with his least favorite slur.

"I'm named after my totem. You call him Corr the Crane, but his Iroquois name is Khenko. Spelled with a capital kay-aitch-ee. Not kay-aye, like the office store."

"Ahh," she breathed. "My given name is Emily. Emily Hester. Or so I've recently learned."

"Well," Khenko chuckled. "Nice to meet you, Emily Hester." His gaze traveled to the hand he knew was ringless. "Are you married?" The corners of her eyes crinkled. "No?" He smiled uneasily. He was experiencing an odd attraction to the redhead. "Dating?"

Emily recoiled, if only slightly.

"Okay, okay," Khenko chuckled. "Sorry, I got carried away."

"Could you tell me where I am?" She looked past him toward the window. "I was in a cave. And there was a…" Her brows knit, then her cute, uptilted nose scrunched.

"What? There was a what?" Did she remember the dragon?

But his patient changed the subject. "Why were you asking me all those things?"

He decided to let it go for the moment. "I'm sorry. I'm not usually into women. I need a cup of coffee. Let's start again. You've been in a coma. How do you feel, Emily Hester?"

She stretched beneath the covers, groaning in stretch-ese. Slowly, she moved her hips and shoulders and neck as if trying them out for the first time. "I'm stiff. Sore. A bit lightheaded. And my bladder is about to explode. Is there a bathroom?"

"Of course. I'll help you."

Khenko lifted Emily out of bed and steadied her. She took a halting step, leaning heavily on him. After a couple more, he wrapped her arm around his waist and half-carried her to the bathroom.

Soon, the toilet flushed and water ran in the sink. The door opened. Emily stood, holding onto the doorknob. Her quick smile flashed and his heart went kaboom.

"Hungry?" He held his hand out to her.

"Famished." She let him help her to the kitchen where the smell of fresh-brewed coffee greeted them. He steadied her while she lowered to a chair, then pushed it to the table.

"I'm afraid there's not much. I missed market-day waiting for you at the blue hole." The auburn eyebrows raised, but he didn't bother explaining. "I have oranges, pineapple, apples." He gathered the ingredients. "How about a smoothie? It's nutritious and easy to digest. Especially after not eating for a couple of days."

"Mmm." Her eyes brightened. "Do you have coconut?"

Khenko grabbed a fresh carton of coconut milk and the jar of coconut butter. Ladling each ingredient into the blender, he added spinach and several tablespoons of hemp seeds. Blending it to liquid, he handed Emily the tumbler, wondering how much she remembered.

AGARTHA

Upon arrival in Agartha, Ishkur's contingent was delayed. Ishkur was whisked to the base expecting to be presented with the human Shibboleth had questioned the night before. He clicked down a polished corridor, flanked by the warlord's troops.

Unbeknownst to him, a decree had been issued the day before. Officials previously under Nergal's command must be accompanied by Shibboleth's guard. Ishkur's blood boiled at this latest travesty. He turned a sharp corner, and one of them clipped him from behind.

Striking instinctively, Ishkur slashed the idiot's chest. Not deep enough to be deadly, but severe enough to put him out of commission for a few days, and to teach them all a lesson.

Feeling better having exerted his power, Ishkur signaled the guards to tend to the Draco. Which left fewer tagging along behind Ishkur. He stood tall as he swept into the Agarthan command center, identical to the one in Xibalba IX. The major who'd been responsible for capturing the young male saluted Ishkur, as did the others in the room.

Hungover and fifty thousand credits poorer after a night in the game car, Ishkur was not in the mood for pleasantries. "Bring the prisoner to me."

The major nodded to his vice major. The smaller Draco saluted and left the room. The remaining guards continued to stand at attention, staring straight ahead. Ishkur signaled them to stand down. The guards remained at attention.

Not bothering to hide his displeasure, Ishkur turned his back to access his handheld. He skimmed through the meager information on the prisoner. The boy's father was listed as a missing person, the mother as a journalist somewhere in Europe. The boy currently resided with an uncle who had been injured in the earthquake. Ishkur studied the photographs, noting the familial resemblance.

A buzzer sounded and he looked up from his handheld. The major roared and bolted from the command center. Ishkur followed. He would not be duped, nor allow Shibboleth's goons to hide whatever mess they made. He would see for himself.

The guards streamed behind Ishkur as he followed the Agarthan major down one corridor and then another. When the major hopped a chute, Ishkur entered too, and they whisked to a dark, dank part of the compound—the place reserved for prisoners and slaves.

Without waiting for his entourage, Ishkur followed the major through the torturous turns until they stepped into an open area where pandemonium reigned.

"What's going on?" Ishkur roared. The Dracos ran about like disturbed ants. "Silence!" he bellowed. That got their attention.

They lined up in formation behind their major. Fear and consternation oozed from the lot. From the looks on their faces, Ishkur could tell they had lost the boy. They remained silent, save for the shuffling of feet.

"Explain!" he commanded.

His escort arrived and piled into the quad behind Ishkur, fanning out in pecking order. The least of the Dracos were closest to him. He *had* gotten their attention. When the commotion died down, Shibboleth's vice major stepped forward.

"The prisoner was held in this cell." He gestured to a small opening. "But when I came to collect him, he was gone."

Ishkur roared. "Of all the incompetent, idiotic things you could say to me, 'he's gone' is not the one I would hear. How, in the name of Enki, is that possible? This place is supposed to be an impenetrable fortress. Is it not?"

The Dracos' heads hung low.

"Sir, if I may," the major began and waited for permission to speak. Ishkur nodded.

"This has never happened before. I have dispatched my troops to search high and low. There is no other opening in the cell, except the one through which the water flows. At only a few centimeters, unless the human can change into a mouse, there could be no escape."

Ishkur sneered. It was ludicrous to think a human could shapeshift, though there were accounts in their history texts. For a child to be accomplished at such a feat was farfetched.

"Are you certain he is not hiding?" Ishkur stepped inside the cell. The contingent crowded behind him, trying to fit through the door all at once.

"Stand back!" he barked, shoving the closest guards.

They left the cell, and Ishkur and the major searched for crevices, footprints, and holes, anything that might give a clue as to the boy's whereabouts. With one clawed foot, Ishkur felt along the floor line where the water rushed but found no outlet.

Knowing he would be blamed for losing the prisoner, Ishkur turned on one heel and stomped from the cell. Shibboleth's arrogant guards lounged in the outer area, poking fun at Nergal's lax security. Livid, Ishkur tore into the chamber.

Using claws, teeth, and tail, Ishkur ripped open bellies, throats, and faces, until all that was left in the quad besides Ishkur, were entrails and bloody remains. Satisfied for the first time since Shibboleth's arrival in Xibalba IX, Ishkur licked his antagonists' gore from his claws and exited the dungeons.

He hopped the chute back to the command center and strode to the console. Calling up the schematics for the dungeon and compounds, he combed through them searching for a weakness or escape point.

"Impenetrable, my ass," Ishkur muttered. "This is not good. If Agartha is vulnerable, then the other strongholds of UnderEarth are, too. If a human child can find its way out, then others can get in."

And that was much worse than losing a human, one that would probably die of starvation, or burn alive in the magma coursing unchecked through the maze of tunnels surrounding the base.

Alone in the command center, Ishkur unclipped his hip flask and took a generous swig, glad to be shed of Shibboleth's imbeciles. Their disrespect was infuriating. He settled in front of the console and relayed a message to the warlord about the prisoner's escape, demanding Shibboleth's guards be held accountable.

He eyed the computer curiously. The sophisticated system should have flagged any suspicious activity. He entered a command to begin a new search of the entire Agarthan stronghold. The program began running, and he paced the hall, mind racing.

If the computer yielded no information about the prisoner's whereabouts, Ishkur would send his own Dracos to search the compound. Assuming they ever arrived.

AZI'S SECRET

zi hung his vest and belt on a hook in his assigned quarters. The suite was large enough to accommodate a family, though Azi had no partner or offspring. He'd been intent on science and electronics, not consorting with females or engaging in the endless drills of brute strength the other Dracos enjoyed.

They had picked on Azi mercilessly. His brain and head were larger than most Dracos. That and his diminutive stature made Azi a target. His intellect and don't-give-a-damn attitude infuriated them further.

A natural scientist, Azi was happiest exploring and pushing the boundaries of the already-vast Reptilian knowledge base. In electronics, he had recently pioneered a self-actualized chute system, the technology of which was being applied to other areas with great success.

Ideas like that just came to Azi. Usually when he was able to daydream, or as he liked to call it, lollygag. As a result, the credits had accumulated so quickly he had ceased peeking at his rising balance. He was a simple Draco, with simple tastes. All that capital in his account made him nervous.

He devoured a meal of leftover Ecthelion stored in the cooler, then slipped outside to explore the nearby forest.

The compound was deserted. Most of Nergal's personnel had been slain by Shibboleth. Wasteful, considering the Dracos' ranks were severely depleted. They'd never rebounded from the proton wave directed at them by the Procyon System last century. But Shibboleth had no heart. No mercy. No soul matrix.

Unfortunately, Azi did. Souls were even more abominable to Dracos than small stature. Should Shibboleth or his minions discover his secret, Azi would likely be executed. Reptilians with souls didn't live long in UnderEarth. The no-souls found them too human-like to stomach. So, Azi concealed his inner softness.

A Fomorian scuttled by, head down. Azi thought of its kin, lying supine on the onyx bench plugged into a human host. His heart panged. Did the creature have a family? Did it feel pain? He was pretty sure it did.

He followed the narrow footpath in the failing light and soon arrived at the watering hole he had seen on the map. The only occupant was an aging Draco from Nergal's command, a survivor of Shibboleth's wrath. The old-timer exited the hole quickly for one so ancient. He struck his chest in a sign of respect, then hobbled toward the base.

Azi slid into the pool feet-first. He submerged his body and swished water in his mouth and through his teeth. Surfacing, he spat it in an arcing stream and rolled to his back. He floated on the surface and stared at the outline of dark clouds unfurling against the inky sky.

Surely there was a better way to breach the worlds. For thousands of years, the Reptilians and other aliens had been relegated to UnderEarth. For those without developed brains, and some with, that was enough. UnderEarth was beautiful in its own right.

But there were no real stars in the night sky. Only pretend ones. And endless darkness. Expelling the air from his lungs, Azi sank beneath the water, eyes open. Sparkles of lamplight glittered on the surface—like twinkling stars.

The memory of celestial lights plagued Azi. His soul yearned to see them again. He wanted, needed, craved, more. Hence the inner void from which the new inventions and discoveries poured.

Surfacing, Azi hefted his form onto the edge and sat with his legs dangling in the pond. He stayed that way a long time, watching the diamond-stars dance upon the ripples created by his paddling feet.

SCRATCHING AN ITCH

Shalane dug in the drawer for the pain meds. She hadn't needed them in quite a while, but after the odd visit from Mitch Wainwright, her eye socket raged. Tossing two of the pills on the back of her throat, she swallowed them with her last sip of beer and lobbed the empty bottle at the trash.

She missed by a good foot. Shalane ignored it and fished another from the fridge, guzzled half, and belched loudly.

What had possessed her? Why had she invited the attorney here?

His sexy voice. That was why. Just hearing it on the phone made her orgasm. That's why she'd invited him. But she was also curious about Emily Hester, aka Ebby Panera.

Shalane settled on the loveseat, sipping beer and letting her mind wander. It didn't go far. The headache made sure of that. She wished she hadn't canceled her appointment at Emory. But she'd had cat scans, pet scans, MRIs, and other tests with elaborate names. All showed her brain was fine.

When the headache lessened to a dull ache, Shalane's restlessness returned. She had given her assistant the night off, and Cecil and the crew knew she'd be indisposed. She had not expected the attorney to go cold. She would have to find another way to take the edge off. Someone else to scratch her itch. But first things first.

Opening her tablet, Shalane scanned backward through her calendar, searching for references to Emily Hester or Ebby Panera. There was nothing for the last year, but when she accessed the calendar for 2040, there it was—Ebby Panera. The woman had taken a meditation class and then several private lessons.

She searched the web for Ebby Panera and waded through several pages of sites claiming to provide the dirty on individuals. For a price, of course. Shalane combed through them for valid links. On page seven, she found a reference to one Ebby Panera employed by the U. S. Disaster Recovery Agency out of Los Angeles, California.

Adding that information to her keyword search, Shalane found a newspaper article about a cyclone in Malaysia that had killed a man named Trey Serra. Ebby Panera's fiancé. In the photograph, Ebby was wrapped in a silver emergency blanket and huddled in the middle of several people.

The woman was attractive and Shalane's junior by a good ten years. She had straight, blond hair that clung to her face. A face Shalane remembered. If only she could bring back the rest.

She accessed the picture of Emily Hester. The face was the same, thinner maybe. But the hair was different, curly and a shocking shade of red. Shalane would remember that hair, wouldn't she? Refilling the pipe, she took a hit hoping it would fill the hole in her gut.

But nothing was helping. Not tonight. She retrieved her phone and called Patty. It went straight to voice mail; Patty's brother's wedding was today. Her call to Cecil went to voice mail, too. Shalane hung up without leaving a message.

Sad, lonely, and deeply dejected, Shalane changed into street clothes, gathered her things and called a security guard to escort her to the tour bus. She removed leftover curry from the refrigerator, popped it in the microwave, and took the meal to her room.

Thirty minutes later, she was out the door—restless, irritable, and discontent—and seeking a cure. For her, that meant loud music, strong liquor, and wild, wanton sex. She strolled the sidewalk, oblivious to the cars.

It was after eleven, and Atlanta's nightlife was going strong. Shalane passed in front of the Fox Theater, surprised to see people still leaving the show. They threaded through a rope line, behind which police held the protesters. She was in full disguise and kept her eyes trained on the sidewalk. It was part of the game. And she wasn't in the mood for a confrontation.

Past the theater, she spied a late-night coffee shop. Next to that, a Vietnamese restaurant. Both were full, and neither offered what she needed tonight. At the corner, she surveyed her options. On one side the Georgian Hotel advertised two separate bars. Catty-corner to that was the Emory-affiliated hospital.

No. And, *hell* no.

She turned right and gazed up at the Fox Theater's soaring parapets. Built more than a hundred years ago in 1929, its Arabic architecture and Yaarab influence were legendary. Shalane had been excited about bringing her tour here, despite the protesters.

Further down, a blues band played, drawing Shalane's attention. Patrons spilled onto the sidewalk from an old-fashioned honky-tonk directly below the theater. Jostling her way through the crowd, she batted her eyes and rubbed her boobs on men and women, ignoring the glares from their partners.

Shalane eyed the couples gyrating on the dance floor, and sidled up to the bar.

"What ya drinking?" the red-faced bartender growled.

"Johnny Walker Black. Neat," she said, then wondered why. She abhorred straight bourbon. He poured and set the drink in front of her, along with the check. A masculine hand reached in and snatched the glass.

Shalane rounded on the asshole and found herself staring into the steel blue eyes of Mitchell Wainwright.

"Hi, doll. You look different. Thanks for the drink." He lifted it in salute.

She raked him with a withering glare and signaled to the barkeep. This time she ordered her usual scotch. Mitch grinned from the barstool and guzzled her bourbon.

The bartender returned and Wainwright placed the empty glass and a fifty-dollar bill beside the scotch. In spite of her annoyance, Shalane found the brazen attorney refreshing. Most men, not counting Cecil and her manager, kowtowed to Shalane's every whim. She loved to be pampered, but sometimes it was nice to be a normal person.

She nodded a reluctant thanks and turned to watch the band. The guitarist humped his Stratocaster in a rousing rendition of "Superstitious". Dancers ground against one another in a time-honored ritual.

Compared to Mitchell, she found the other men lacking. She wasn't all that impressed by the women either. Shalane downed her drink and signaled the bartender. Mitch slid off the stool.

"Have a seat," he murmured, leaning too close.

Neck tingling, Shalane hesitated, then took his chair. She'd rather not stand. Especially after a hard day's work. She eyed the man. He had deep blue eyes a woman could swim in, and a physique that screamed good stock and regular workouts at the gym. She leaned toward him.

"Thank you. I wouldn't have pegged you for a gentleman."

The eyes searched Shalane's face and dropped to her chest. "And you would have been correct. Want to get out of here?" The attorney touched her thigh, igniting a fire.

Her heart thudded. That was Shalane's line. Slowly, he inched his hand toward her groin. She swayed on the barstool for one exquisite moment feeling the warmth suffuse her panty-less crotch, then shuddered when he removed his hand.

She straightened and gathered her composure as the band started another song. The dance floor emptied and filled again. Shalane slid off the stool and crooked a finger. The attorney followed.

Outside, a gust of cold wind slammed against them. Mitch turned his collar up and flashed Shalane that sardonic grin. Something deep inside her melted. Something that seemed to have been waiting for the right moment. And maybe the right man.

As if in a dream, Shalane let him guide her up a wide staircase that looked like something out of *Gone with the Wind*. In the cubby at the top, Mitch shoved her against the side door of the Fox Theater and ravaged her lips in a deep, lingering kiss.

When he stuck his tongue down the back of her throat and ground his knee against her twat, Shalane groaned and collapsed against him, grinding and moaning as her hair-trigger clitoris orgasmed again and again.

Near swooning, she dragged her mouth away and shoved him from her, retreating down the steps to catch her breath. The attorney was having an odd effect on her, one she hadn't experienced in a long time. But, vulnerability and lack of control were two things Shalane could scant afford.

Mitch Wainwright stood at the top of the sweeping staircase, hips thrust out and waiting. His eyes held a dangerous glint. Was it welcome or warning?

A DIRTY SECRET

Mitch rolled out from under Shalane. She burrowed deeper under the covers. The bitch had fallen asleep in the middle of riding him like a Preakness jockey. He studied her in the lamplight, and something sinister curled in his belly.

Dressing in a hurry, he slung his jacket over one shoulder and tiptoed from the room he'd rented despite being determined not to get mixed up with Shalane. Once again, his cock had overridden his reason.

He texted his driver and received a prompt reply: "Be there in five."

Exiting through a side door of the Hotel Georgian, Mitch shrugged his jacket on and shivered in the damp wind. His smartwatch said it was 3:37 am. Traffic had petered off, though the after-hour clubs would be in full swing. He studied his reflection in the mirrored hotel and slicked down his hair, then huddled inside his thin suit jacket. Moments later, the sleek limo pulled to the curb.

Too wired to sleep, Mitch had the driver swing by Manual's Tavern. It was closed, so he settled for the bar next door. He ducked into the dive and chose an empty seat at the crowded bar. Despite the late hour, the place was packed with businessmen and ladies of the night.

Ordering a Johnny Walker Black, Mitch tossed it back and ordered another. He couldn't shake the feeling that something bad was going to happen. Considering his inability to resist Shalane, maybe it already had.

He drank the second shot and ordered another, then wobbled to a table in the far back corner where it stank of beer and spoiled whiskey. His stomach roiled. He hadn't eaten since lunch yesterday.

Peering at the menu, Mitch flagged a scantily-clad, and possibly-underage, waitress. Surprisingly, his cock remained limp in his britches. The witch had drained all the desire from him. For the moment, anyway.

When the girl brought his burger and a cold Budweiser, he paid and tipped her generously. Then Mitch tucked into the less-than-appealing fare, ravenous now that it was in front of him. At the next table, three older men swapped stories of bygone days. When Hamilton Hester's name came up, Mitch stopped chewing to listen.

"Can I get you anything else?" The waitress startled him. He waved her away, and leaned toward the adjoining table, chasing down his mouthful of burger with beer.

"—Yeah, I had a chance to be rich. Ham Hester approached me about screwing my wife, too. But unlike you, I turned him down…"

Mitch's ears pricked up. What the hell?

"Did your wife conceive?" the man asked.

"Nah," his friend shook his grizzled head. "Well, yeah. But she had a boy. Hester insisted it had to be a girl, so he only paid us ten grand, rather than the whole shebang. Chadd here struck it rich." He playfully backhanded the fellow next to him who chugalugged a beer and thumped it on the table.

"Yeah, but our daughter wasn't good enough. Just as well. Hester woulda taken her and raised her as his own. I don't know what I'd a done without our Aaliyah. She may not carry my genes, but she's my daughter through and through."

"Does she know?" The first man's beady eyes bored into his friend.

"Hell naw!" Chadd slapped the table with both hands. Which startled Mitch, who choked on a mouthful of Budweiser.

"Y'all better not tell anyone either. Not EVER. That's a secret me'n my wife planned to take to the grave. If she knew I told you-uns, she'd skin me alive." He glanced over at Mitch who was hacking up his guts. "Y'okay over there?"

Mitch nodded and took an unimpeded breath, then dropped his eyes to the now-cold burger. Downing the beer, he shoved away from the table.

HELP FROM HOME

Khenko had debated all morning whether to call his parents. He needed advice, and the best way to get it was to talk to them. But it went against his nature *and* his wishes. Caving in, he sucked in a deep breath and placed the call.

It rang once before Val Blitherstone appeared on the other end, dark hair swept back in a ponytail. He must've caught her fresh from the tennis court.

"Khenko!" she beamed, slightly off-center on the screen. "What a pleasant surprise. Yvette and I were just talking about you." His mother's best friend stuck her face in front of the camera and broke into a smile.

"Mon cheri," she crooned, "it is good to see your handsome face. And my, so brown. That Bahamian sun loves you, cher." There was a good-natured shoving match, then Yvette ceded ground. His mother appeared onscreen again.

Warm, fuzzy love tightened Khenko's voice to a near-whisper. "Hi, mom. I've missed you."

"I've miss you too, son. Are you in trouble? You look worried. Can I fly to Zephyr Cay and bring you home?"

Khenko chuckled and shook his head.

"Then what is so important as to make you break your own 'No Talk' rule?"

"I do have a little situation," he admitted. "But go visit with 'Vette and call me later."

"It's okay, Bird. I'm heading out," Yvette called. "No, don't get up, Val. I'll lock the door behind me." Her face appeared on the screen beside his mother's. "Bye, Big Bird." She lowered her voice to a conspiratorial tone. "Please come home. Your mother won't admit it, but she needs you desperately."

Val bumped her friend away. In the background, Yvette hollered, "Bye, Big Bird. I love you."

"Bye 'Vette. I love you too."

His mother leaned so close all he could see was her dark eyes. "Now. You have my undivided attention." Fear tightened the lines of her smooth, olive complexion. "Are you okay, sweetie?"

"Yes. At least I think so." It hadn't occurred to Khenko until that moment that he might not be. "Do you know something I don't?"

She leaned back and her full face appeared. Her lips loosened in the faintest of smiles.

"Of course I do, son. But that's beside the point. You never call and said you wouldn't. Now you *have* called, and say you need to talk. A mother worries. Even yours."

Khenko winced. The remark struck home. His absence had been hard on his mother and sister. He hung his head. "I know, Ma. I'm sorry. I do miss seeing the two of you."

"And your father? He worries too, you know." It was half accusation, half attempt to console. But that ship had sailed many years ago.

A door opened and shut down the hall. Emily was up; he'd have to be quick.

"As you know, I don't practice the Iroquois ways. But a few nights ago, I was visited by the crane." Khenko paused for her reaction but Val remained silent, her face impassive. "Corr appeared to me in a dream. He told me to go to the blue hole to receive a package. So I did."

The blank expression shifted. A light emerged in his mother's eyes.

Needing to finish before Emily interrupted or wandered away, he poured the rest out, omitting nothing but the dragon and its instructions. That part he'd documented on his laptop, in a private file for Khenko's eyes only, in case Talav changed her mind and imposed the memory spell.

Val touched the camera as if it were his face. "My son, what an auspicious gift. It is the greatest of honors to be called upon by one's totem. Not many are. And few have the courage or strength to answer. I am proud of you, Khenko. But for something this significant, I must confer with your father."

His displeasure must have shown because she hurried to finish. "You did right to call, son. Let us help." He still wasn't sure that's what he wanted, especially from his father. But he didn't know where else to turn.

"I will speak to him tonight."

Khenko huffed, disappointed. He had hoped to get an answer right away.

"He's at Princeton teaching and has a meeting after that. I promise I'll speak to him as soon as he gets home, and call you right after. Will that work?"

A low knock sounded on Khenko's door—three taps, a pause, and three more.

"Just a minute," he called, then mumbled to his mother, "Guess it'll have to. Gotta go, mom. Call me soon?"

"I promise, Bird. I love you. Be safe and take care of yourself and your patient."

☼☼☼

Khenko closed his laptop. "Come on in."

A shy smile lit his charge's otherwise glum face as she opened the door.

"What's up, princess? Have a seat."

She slid into a chair opposite the desk and leaned toward him. "I need to contact my family. Let them know I'm alive and where I am."

Khenko tapped his fingers on the desk, wondering how to tell her she couldn't. Quick and to-the-point would probably be best. But first, he needed to know what she knew.

"Emily, do you remember what happened before you woke at the center?" He reached for her restless hands and sandwiched them between his.

"In a nutshell?"

Khenko nodded.

As if reading something from a signboard, Emily spoke mechanically. "I was at the zoo in Atlanta with my friends. There was an earthquake—" she faltered and chewed her lip. "I got sucked into the ground." She stopped again and stared off at

140

something far away. Khenko massaged the backs of her hands with his thumbs.

Emily's gaze drifted back to lock with his and her eyes were terrified. "I woke alone. In the pitch dark." Khenko tightened his grip. "My worst nightmare come true." Her cold hands trembled in his. "I was alone in the dark, surrounded by fallen boulders. It should have killed me." Her voice hitched. "I thought it had."

"Hush yo' mouth, honey child," he chided in a silly voice. It had the desired effect. Emily giggled.

"Then I tripped over a dragon," she added. Khenko relaxed. She remembered Talav.

"You're not surprised? You believe I saw a dragon?"

He chuckled, remembering his reaction upon seeing Talav. "Two days ago, I would have said no. But today, yes. I believe you, Emily." The stunned-look lingered on the battered face. "Do you remember anything else?" Color rushed to her cheeks.

"I remember it all. The dragon saved me, Khenko. She caused the quake, then she saved me. "

He sat up straight.

"Oh, God," she wailed, rubbing her face in her hands. "The dark was awful, even worse than the quake. That happened so fast I had no time to think, and shock held the pain at bay. But that dark cave, omigod. I thought I was dead."

"What do you mean, the dragon caused the quake?"

Emily stared at him, wild-eyed. "She caused the quake. She even admitted it. She shook the very foundations of the zoo until the earth crumbled and split apart. Then I fell in. I still don't know what happened to my boyfriend. Or his nephew and dog and my father."

She had a boyfriend. The air left Khenko in a rush. His homosexuality would remain intact. "I'm sorry," was all he could think to say. "Did Talav mention how close to death you were?"

"No. Was I?" Her somber eyes stared.

"Yes. Talav used her powers to heal what she could. But you remained in a coma. She called it lingering in the Otherworld."

Understanding flared in the green eyes. "Yes, she did tell me I was in the Otherworld. But she also said I was in the Underworld. Wherever I was, it seemed oddly like this world." She squinted as if comparing. "There really wasn't any difference at all. Except my reflection didn't show up in Talav's mirror." Her brows shot

skyward and she sat up straight. "You! You were there." She leapt
from the chair and backed away. "You're in cahoots with the
dragon!"

Khenko busted out laughing. "In cahoots?" he snorted. "Who
says 'in cahoots'?" He guffawed until tears dampened his eyes.
When Emily stamped her feet, he slapped his sides in another
round of gaiety. By the time he gained a degree of sobriety, she
was hopping mad and stared down at him, hands on hips, green
daggers for eyes.

"I-I'm sorry," he managed to get out without laughing. "I did
come to the cave, but to rescue you. To bring you back here.
Surely you didn't want to stay with the dragon?"

The red drained from Emily's face. "No, I did not."

"Well then, there you go." He was offended she would think
he meant her harm. He'd never hurt a soul, not on purpose.
"Thanks to me and that dragon, you are back in the real world. In
the land of the living."

Emily sighed loudly. "And few make it back." This time,
gratitude swam in her liquid eyes. "Thank you, Khenko. You did
save me, didn't you?"

He couldn't help squirming. It had been an assignment. One
Khenko had tried his damnedest to ignore.

"You did," she concluded. "Thank you."

"You're welcome. But I have to tell you something, and you're
not going to like it. Steel yourself."

"Steel myself? That's a good one," she grinned. "Almost as
good as 'in cahoots'. What is it?"

"You cannot contact anyone. By order of the dragon."

"But—"

Khenko held up an index finger. "Wait. Let me finish."

Emily scrubbed her face in her hands and looked up
impatiently, bottom lip caught between her teeth.

"Talav insisted. She said your family and the world must
continue to believe you dead. Or at least, missing." Emily frowned
and her nose wrinkled. "I *can* tell you that the MacBrayer man
made it out alive. The boy is missing. But the only mention the
news made of your father is that his death preceded the
earthquake by several weeks."

"And Cu?" she squeaked. "The wolfhound?"

"The dog did not survive. His body was recovered." Emily crumpled into tears and Khenko hated himself. "I can also tell you that Talav revealed the identity of your family. You come from a long line of powerful druids. And the world's existence depends on you."

She lurched like a gazelle poised to run.

"It's okay," Khenko assured her. "I am here to help. I am not druid-born, but I hail from another long line of peacemakers. The Iroquois Nation. We answer to the same ancestors, though we call them by different names."

Emily relaxed a little, though her inquisitive look remained.

"I was trained as an Iroquois medicine man. Two days ago, Corr the Crane appeared in my dreams. He told me to go to the blue hole and wait for a package, so I did. When Talav finally appeared, she led me to you. The rest, you know."

"But why can't I call home?" Emily groaned. "At least let me call Lugh. He's the priest of my Order and would keep our secret."

Khenko shook his head. "According to Talav, it has something to do with the end of the world."

Emily blanched, then reddened. "Oh. That."

"Yeah. That."

"I'm freaking tired of being threatened with Armageddon." She flounced into the chair. "If I can't let my family know I'm alive, then what, pray tell, is the plan?"

INANNA

The compulsion to get out of the compound became too much for Ishkur to bear. Once Shibboleth heard about the decimation of his guards, the warlord's retaliation would be swift and merciless. Ishkur would rather not be there when that happened.

His three Dracos from Xibalba IX were still missing. Ishkur had dispatched an attaché to discover their whereabouts but had received no word. He eyed the interactive map of the city, searching for a pub not gutted by the creeping magma. Noting a cantina on the south side of town, Ishkur scribbled the coordinates on a slip of paper and exited his berth.

The lights were dim in the empty hallway. He strode to the chute system and ignored the occupants that skittered to avoid him. At the far end of the station, he accessed the keypad. Minutes later, a southbound transpo zipped into the station and stopped. The auto-door slid open. No one exited.

Ishkur stepped into the car with a couple of Fomorians and a Breesnak. He stood, rather than sit with the lesser species, and gripped the hand strap as the chute sped through the compound. They emerged to the sight of the setting sun. The sky was awash. Purples, reds, and blues glowed through the ashen haze.

It reminded him of his familiar Lamia and their female-issue, Lamalita. They loved nature and had taught Ishkur to appreciate its beauty. Snapping a picture with his handheld, he sent it to Lamia with a promise to make contact that evening. But first Ishkur would have a well-deserved drink.

He left the chute and gagged. The stench of burnt flesh and rotting corpses was formidable, the devastation mind-boggling.

Ishkur strode down the ravaged street, gaping at the eerie scene. The computer images had been nothing compared to the actuality. Charred skeletons were all that remained of the once-thriving city, save a few scorched buildings amid the smoldering ruins.

Few living beings were about. Those that were, hurried along. An itch began at the base of Ishkur's spine and crept slowly up his back. Spinning, he scanned the burnt-out doorways for signs of danger or pursuit. Encountering nothing but shadow and stink, Ishkur picked his way through the rubble with caution.

Rounding a corner, he stopped short. In the middle of the street, a Draco feasted on the bowels of a charred Ecthelion. Disgusted, Ishkur drew his leather cloak close and hurried past, gut queasy.

A flash of neon lifted his spirits. His insides eased. An ugly Draco-mutant leaned against the open pub door, cigar hanging from its cracked lips.

"Two credits," the bouncer muttered.

Ishkur hesitated, unused to paying to enter a drinking establishment. He'd be shelling out plenty enough inside. Grumbling, he reached in his belt for coins. With credits, the computer would track his drinking and whereabouts. And Shibboleth was sure to be on his trail.

Bellying to the bar, Ishkur ordered a Furroot. He chugged it and slammed the stein on the counter to signal for another. This, he carried to a dark corner. He claimed a stool at a high-top table and kept his head down, nursing his drink. He stared at the creatures occupying the bar. Only a handful were Draconian, the rest a hodgepodge of species.

Ishkur sipped the Furroot and consulted his handheld. The attaché had located his companions. They had apparently debarked early to deal with a troublesome issue in the countryside. He grimaced, remembering the unscheduled stop. He'd been in the middle of an especially-spectacular winning streak. Patting the winnings in his belt, Ishkur tipped his mug and downed the potent brew.

The itchy sensation crawled up his spine. Ishkur glanced around the room. His back was to the corner, but he still felt exposed. Knowing Shibboleth would be looking for him made Ishkur even more jumpy than usual. A shadow darkened the entrance and the tingling intensified.

A tall Draca ducked through the door and hesitated to glance discreetly around the smoke-filled room. A cloak concealed her features, and it appeared she was alone. She stepped inside, made another sweep of the room, then disappeared behind the curve of the bar.

A server moved through the crowd. Ishkur raised his glass for a refill. Moments later, the Draca reappeared. She muscled through the crowd and claimed a small table not far from Ishkur. With a quick scan of the room, she settled on the stool. The waiter brought Ishkur's Furroot and bustled to the newcomer as she dropped her hood.

Ishkur gasped. He knew that face. Her image had appeared in the base alerts, wanted for questioning in Nergal's death. As his body had yet to be recovered, no warrant had been issued for her arrest. She glanced Ishkur's way, and the itch grew stronger.

A shrill voice pierced the hubbub from a gaming table in the back of the tavern. A weasel-like creature rose to challenge its opponent and the two tore at each other's throats. One fell to the ground with a thunk, then the game continued. The din resumed.

Ishkur stared into his bubbly brown Furroot. Should he confront the Draca? He guzzled the fiery liquid and decided against it. He had already signed his death warrant. Why bother doing a job he likely no longer held?

At a commotion by the door, he looked up to see a Cerulean dressed in enforcement garb surveying the crowd. The merc spotted the Draca, and Ishkur coughed loudly. Her head snapped up. The Cerulean charged. Eyes wide, she reached behind her for a scythe-like weapon. Ishkur slid from his perch and rushed her table. Planting his bulk between it and the Cerulean, he raised his fists. The Furroot had kicked in, and he was spoiling for a fight.

"This Draca's mine!" he roared.

The Cerulean hesitated, then retreated to the bar to eye Ishkur with malice born of greed.

The Draca hissed in Ishkur's ear, "I don't need your help. I take care of myself."

Ishkur wheeled, spine tingling. Her voice, like her face, was familiar. "I am not helping. I'm taking you in."

The Draca extended her fist in greeting. "I'm Inanna. Have we met?"

Ishkur returned the gesture, surprised when the Draca's claw engulfed his.

"I recognize you from the alerts. You're Shibboleth's female-spawn. You're wanted for questioning in General Nergal's death."

The Draca shrank away. "You shouldn't believe all you hear. Who are you?"

Ishkur drew to full height. "Vice Major Ishkur of Xibalba IX. On assignment to Agartha. I am here to investigate General Nergal's death. What have you to say for yourself?"

The Draca blinked and stared past him at the door as if she would bolt. She was attractive, even with her recent injuries. It would be a shame to mar her features further.

With a heavy sigh, she capitulated. "I am innocent of those charges. If you promise not to arrest me, I will explain my part. I am as much a victim as General Nergal. Who, by the way, is not dead."

That got Ishkur's attention. "You know this how?"

The Draca drained her glass and set it on the table. "Buy me a drink."

Signaling the server, Ishkur slid into a chair at her table and ordered two Furroots. They sat in silence until the Zynog set the drinks on the table. Half emptying his, Ishkur belched. Inanna sipped. After a long minute, she set her mug on the table and eyed Ishkur.

"The Agarthan populace has no love for my sire. Should he try to impose his will, they will rebel. For that reason alone, I dare show my face. But how do I know you won't turn me over to Shibboleth? Or kill me yourself? If you, Vice Major Ishkur, cannot promise me safety, I must take my leave."

Ishkur rose and laid a fist over his heart. "In this matter, my loyalties are with General Nergal, not Shibboleth, though I am here at his command. My interest is in finding the truth. As long as you assist, I will not harm you. Nor will I turn you over to the warlord."

The Draca's taut posture relaxed. She cradled the Furroot and took another sip, then looked up at Ishkur and smiled.

His heart melted. He thought briefly of Lamia, then dismissed her from his mind. She would be bedding another if Ishkur lingered in Agartha long. He had no illusions about that. Inanna placed her hand on Ishkur's knee. His groin tightened. He hadn't bedded anyone but Lamia in a long while.

He tried to listen to the Draca relate what had happened to Nergal the night he disappeared. But the tightness in Ishkur's loin increased until his man part twitched. Licking lips that had gone dry, he reached for the Furroot and drained his mug, nearly choking when Inanna trailed her hand higher.

A fire ignited in Ishkur's groin. His member grew harder beneath its flap until his entire being ached. When Inanna's clawed fingers untucked his cock, Ishkur's breath caught. He gasped and leaned closer. Sensation washed over him, and the orgasm exploded. With a sigh, Ishkur slumped in his stool, loin tingling.

A smirk played on Inanna's lips. She licked her claws, one by one, then reached beneath the table. The Draca convulsed and her eyes rolled back. She squeaked a little, then slumped against the wall.

Sitting up straight, she laid a wet claw over Ishkur's. "Thanks. I needed that. Now, what were we saying?"

With a supreme effort, Ishkur tore his attention from her lips and rearranged his man part. What had she been saying? Nergal was alive? Ishkur's erection softened and retreated into its flap.

"How do you know Nergal is alive? And why I should believe you?"

The Draca scoffed and took a large swallow of Furroot, eyeing him over the top of her mug. "I saw Nergal."

"When?"

"The day of the earthquake. The day Shibboleth's army marched through Agartha." Inanna hesitated, eyes vague in remembrance. "I was in a doctora's office waiting to be treated when Nergal appeared. It shocked me to no end because Shibboleth's goons had bragged about killing him before they gave me these." Her honey-gold complexion deepened, and she pointed to her wounds.

"Then the quake struck. Nergal shoved me through the front door and ran back for the doctora. They barely made it out before the building collapsed. He took off in one direction, dragging her. I ran in the other. Everyone was seeking shelter from the quake."

"So, two days ago?"

Inanna nodded.

Ishkur pondered the implications. This could change everything. With Nergal alive, they could reassemble what was left of his army and challenge Shibboleth.

Inanna twisted her hands together. "Nergal looked awful. If his internal injuries were as grave as his visible ones, he may not survive for much longer."

"Nergal *is* a survivor. That Draco has endured things over the years that would kill a lesser Draco."

Unshed tears gleamed in Inanna's eyes.

A chill ran up Ishkur's arms. Did this lovely creature have a connection with the general? In spite of Lamia, Ishkur found himself hoping not. Then the kernel of an idea formed.

"Can you take me to the doctora's office where you saw Nergal?"

An odd look passed over Inanna's marred face. "I can, but it will be to no avail. That sector was demolished. What the quake didn't destroy, the magma has burned."

Resolve congealed in Ishkur's chest. Half his mission in Agartha was to find Nergal. So, find him, he would.

HOPE

Wren's Roost was an imposing, two-story Tudor Revival mansion built in the early 1900's. Lugh parked his SUV in the circular drive and started up the brick staircase to find Hope, the druid animal Elder.

As luck would have it, the Scottish Wildcat lazed in the sun on the top landing. One might easily mistake Hope for an oversized tabby. Only the animal Elder talked, and had been in and out-of-body for at least as far back as the original Awen.

The cat stretched and blinked chartreuse eyes holding unspoken truths. The hole in Lugh's insides shrank just a little.

"Hope," he said simply, a multitude of emotions riding on the one word.

"You are troubled, Lughnasadh. Come. Speak." Hope swiped at a shoulder with her scratchy pink tongue, and he settled on the steps beside her.

"Cu is gone. He died in the quake. It—" his voice broke when sorrow flickered in the cat's eyes. The wolfhound had been her faithful companion for a millennium. But Hope said nothing. Lugh swallowed hard and tried again.

"Emily and Brian are missing. And I fear Hamilton's spirit passed with Cu."

The cat stared off into the distance. "Emily is alive. If not, I'd be as gone as Cu. Or as gone as Cu appears to be. There are rumblings in the Otherworld about the Awen, and about the boy. They are both alive."

A fraction of the weight was lifted from Lugh. It was weird to hear Emily called by that name. Yet she was descended from, and a dead ringer for, the original Awen. He leapt from his perch, ready to search Hades or the moon if it meant bringing Emily and Brian home.

"Any idea how to find them?"

The cat wagged her head. "More than this, I do not know. Except that Hamilton's spirit wanders yet. He came to me in the dark of night after the earthquake."

The hole in Lugh's gut closed a little more.

"Hamilton sensed something bad would happen. He warned me, Hope. I felt nothing myself, so I refused to listen." He shoved his bangs out of his eyes. "I was caught up in Emily and my own selfish interests. I should have listened. I know better."

Lugh hung his head and the hair flopped into his eyes again. "I should abdicate the priesthood. I am unworthy of my station."

Hope scoffed. "Lugh, you did nothing wrong. As your Elder, I command you to cease worrying about Emily and your nephew. They will both be fine without you."

But he wasn't convinced.

The cat stood and stretched. "We have much to do to get ready for the invasion. Oh yes," she said at Lugh's sharp intake of breath. "The time grows short. The Elders whisper of a race of beings banished and forgotten long ago—monsters living inside the planet. They would destroy all human life and take Earth for themselves."

"But that's where Emily and Brian are." A two-by-four couldn't have hit Lugh harder. He sank to the step from which he'd risen and cradled his head, wishing the pain would go away. His heart raced thinking of Emily and Brian at the mercy of monsters. "Hope, we have to get them out."

"There are more than monsters down there, Lugh." Her fat tail twitched, stirring the thick Georgia air. "Remember the Tuatha Dé Danaan?"

Lugh nodded. Hope peered at him until understanding dawned. "You mean the Great Ones? Is that who you think is under Earth with Brian and Emily?"

"And Hamilton," the cat nodded. "Lughnasadh, you must listen closely. Your path lies not below the earth. You must go with me to Beli to seek out the crone and the dragons."

Lugh recoiled. Dread curdled his stomach. "Not on your life. Beli is a myth, not a real place. I am not going on a dragon quest. Not now, not ever. No way."

Hope's stare remained fixed.

"No. Uh-uh." Lugh shook his head vehemently.

The tabby laughed, a thick, throaty sound that filled the space between them, and tickled the corners of Lugh's lips. Soon he was smiling, then chuckling at Hope's infectious gurgle.

Something brushed against the cobwebs of his mind. His brother Jake had always believed in the existence of dragons. When Jake disappeared, Lugh had had a hunch that he'd gone searching for the mythical creatures.

"Seriously, Hope? I can't go traipsing around the world, searching for mythical beasts. I have a missing nephew. And Order rituals to perform. Beltane will be here soon. And even if we found Beli, assuming it exists, and the dragons, assuming they exist, it still won't help us find Emily. Or help her command the dragons. There's a forgetfulness curse. Remember?"

"Yes," Hope conceded. "I'm working on that. But I must go to Beli, nevertheless, and I can't go alone. I require a human companion. And that must be you."

Lugh groaned and shoved his bangs out of his face. "I am not going anywhere. Not until we've found Brian and I've buried Cu. Plus, I have to make arrangements for Jocko's. At least give me that."

"Get your affairs in order. We have a trip to plan."

NO RESPITE

Brian and Ethnui's search for the missing Fomore yielded no clues. Days had passed since Brian last slept, and the exhaustion was getting the better of him. He could sleep on sharp stones at this point, but Ethnui showed him to a small bedroom.

He plopped down to remove his sneakers and found it quite cushy. Crawling under the soft covers, he pulled them to his chin and sighed, grateful to finally stretch out flat. But he was too keyed-up for sleep.

He eyed the dark ceiling, thinking of all that had happened since the earthquake and wondered if Lugh and Emily had made it out alive. Cu hadn't. A tear trickled down Brian's cheek to the thin pillow. He sent a feeler to Hamilton, who didn't answer. Had the druid tired of him and jumped into Ethnui?

Alarmed, he whispered aloud, "Hamilton? Are you there?"

"I'm here." The voice sounded far away. "Sleep, little raven. You've earned it."

Assured he wasn't alone, Brian drifted off to a peaceful sleep in which mermaids romped in a deep blue sea, and a dragon swam lazily through their midst.

☼☼☼

For the past two days, Hamilton had been intent on keeping alive Brian. Now the lad was asleep, and they were relatively safe. Ham was free to roam. He was certain Lugh had escaped the quake. But Emily was down here somewhere. He just had to find her.

He entered the perilous Otherworld and combed through the zoo wreckage before diving beneath the surface. Skimming the

153

rip-rap and large boulders, he reached the bottom of a dark cave and spied something. Hurrying to the spot, he found a scrap of material from Emily's blouse. Encouraged, he circled the chamber. She was not here.

Hamilton spotted a crack, and threaded through it to reach a corridor large enough for a person to walk. Presently it met with another passageway lit by smoldering torches. Thinking he'd found one of the Draconian tunnels, Ham sped along it, hoping against hope that he would find Emily alive. Better to be in the lizard's clutches than crushed under tons of displaced rock.

Eventually, Ham ended up in a large cave. Emily was not here, but her energy signature remained. He circled the room, and his spirit soared. This was no Draconian stronghold. No danger lurked in its rock walls. He was in a dragon's lair.

A dragon had found Emily. Which should mean his daughter was safe. Only where had the dragon taken her?

☼☼☼

Emily rolled to her back in the small bed. She grounded for meditation and focused on reaching out to her father. Talav had said she could contact her family. It was time to try.

Ignoring all else, she quieted her mind and thought of her Da presenting Aóme to her while conferring the title of Grand Druid, and him declaring his eternal love. She thought of the day he had transferred from his dying body to that of the wolfhound Cu. His first druid lesson was that same afternoon. He'd taught her and Brian to sing Amergin's song, the one about Taliesin.

Something inside Emily loosened, then her Da appeared. Only he looked like Brian.

"Da!" she cooed. "It's Emily Bridget. Are you okay? Where is Cu?"

"Yes, I'm okay, but Cu is gone. I'm with Brian. Where are you?"

"In the Bahamas on an island called Zephyr Cay. Talav, the earth dragon found me and brought me here, to a healer named Khenko Blitherstone. I'm glad you're with Brian. I've been worried about you two. Where are you, Da?"

He rolled Brian's dark eyes, and it was Brian who answered. "We're in a place called UnderEarth. There's a whole, amazing world down here, Emily. And all sorts of creatures. We were

154

captured by lizard-men, then we got lucky. A nice Fomorian lady rescued us."

Emily's Da cut in. "We're out of danger for the moment, but we're stuck here until we can find a way back to the surface. Assuming the Dracos don't find us first. Can you get word to the Order? They need to prepare for what's going on down here."

There was a loud knock, and Emily came to in the bedroom in the Atlantean Center. With a sigh that was both annoyed and triumphant, she called out for Khenko to enter.

☼☼☼

For a year, Ethnui had worked on the computer virus and had been eager to upload it to the Dracos' server. It was designed to blind the reptiles to the comings and goings of any but themselves. But the invisible program would also open a subroutine.

She tapped a few keys and the Reptilians' data streamed to her mainframe. She checked her handheld and found it there, too. And all without detection or trace. Ethnui allowed herself a momentary smile at her utter brilliance. Her program was working.

Not only had she and the human left the compound unseen, she now had access to the Dracos' data. Without her virus, she would likely have been captured, and would now be rotting in that cell beside Brian. Or they'd both be dead.

Her neck prickled. Brian was not like the boys Ethnui knew. An intelligence smoldered behind the obsidian-colored eyes, and she kept wanting to touch his thick hair. Being near him stirred feelings she hadn't experienced before. A sparkle. A tingle. A flutter of the heart.

Her fingers flew over the keys, pulling up feeds for the compound. The command center was empty. Zooming in on the computer console, she studied the layout and configuration. Ethnui would need to get into its guts to know for sure, but the Reptilian technology appeared similar to that used by the Fomore.

Accessing their database, she searched for information on the human. The data was sketchy. She clicked out of his file and perused the compound feeds. They rotated through several vantage points, including the cells in the dungeon where Brian had been held.

155

In the foyer outside his cell, two lizard-men cleared away piles of remains. Blood and guts were everywhere. Ethnui gagged and switched to another chamber. A Draco slept on the side bench, snoring and out cold. Ethnui clicked through the other feeds, finding no sign of her missing colleagues. Were they in the outer prisons?

She went back to the feed of the command center, where guards now gathered around a holographic image of a nasty-looking Draco. He was decked out in full battle gear, wearing a half-helmet and wristlets of leather, along with a thick, shell vest. His claws were painted blood-red.

Ethnui shivered and activated translate mode. The lizard barked commands and insults, threatening to do worse if they failed as miserably as the guards who had died the day before.

So that's what the lizards had been cleaning up. Ethnui retched and hung her head over the side of the chair. She practiced a Fomorian calming technique, breathing deeply. On the monitor, Dracos poured into the command center. Their ranks swelled as they jostled one another to cram into the hall.

They didn't know how the human could have escaped and had written him off as unimportant. Instead, they were focusing on finding two of their own—a Draco named Ishkur, and another named Nergal.

Ethnui sat up straight. Nergal was the monster that had imprisoned her father and then Ethnui. But what were they saying? Magma released by the earthquake had pierced the chute system and was spreading rapidly through the base and the town. Served them right.

But what she heard next was more chilling. Dracos had been dispatched to search the city and all the known Fomorian hideouts. Ethnui's heart skipped a beat.

They must leave. And now. If it wasn't already too late.

Thinking longingly of sleep, she hurried to Brian's chamber and knocked lightly, in spite of the urgency. When he didn't answer, she opened the door a crack.

"Brian?" A light snore answered. She entered to prod the boy's shoulder. "Wake up. We must go."

The long lashes flew open, and a hand snaked out to grab Ethnui's wrist, holding her in place. Then the eyes came to life, and Brian let go.

"Hullo." His voice was low and sleep-drenched.

Detailing their predicament, Ethnui blushed when he leapt out of bed wearing nothing but briefs. She turned her back and finished her explanation while he dressed, then led him to the kitchen. Grabbing the two packs filled with foodstuffs and water, and disinfectant tablets in case the water ran out, she retrieved her handheld and its dock from the processor, then signaled Brian to follow.

"Where are we going?" He took one of the packs and slung it over his shoulder.

"There's a spring at the edge of Fomori territory with a dry cave. We can hide there."

Brian shouldered one of the packs. "How far is it from their base?"

"Hopefully far enough. About a hundred kilometers."

They exited what had been Ethnui's home for the last eighteen months, and a shiver passed through her. She wasn't sure if it was fear or excitement.

"Stay close," she warned. "This journey is treacherous, even without the Dracos on high-alert. The computer virus should continue to hide us from their security network. But as I told you before, they can see and smell us in person."

She didn't tell him what they might find beyond the border. Based on the stories Ethnui had heard, it was a dangerous realm from which none had returned.

☼☼☼

Azi perused the seventeen-page report assembled by his team. It listed possible access points between Under and AboveEarth. With all the possibilities, the Dracos should be able to breach the barrier. They just had to find the right ones. He scanned the summary eagerly.

According to the report, the primary entrances were at the North and South Poles. The openings were so large they could be seen from outer space—2100 and 1500-kilometers respectively. To keep them secret, the humans had allowed no commercial fly-overs since early in their 20th century.

There were also cave entrances in the Sierra and the Rocky Mountains of the western United States, and in the Appalachian and Ozark Mountains in the east. Other access points peppered the Alps, Himalayas, Andes, and Caribbean Isles.

There were even portals beneath the ocean. These could be found in the deep trenches of the Pacific Ocean and the Caribbean Sea, and the submarine ranges of the Atlantic Ocean, especially around the Azores, Canary Islands, and Falklands.

There were also created entrances beneath the Denver airport in the western United States, the Giza Plateau in Egypt, US Air Force worldwide complexes, and in sacred temples in India and China. All the known AboveEarth openings were guarded by the humans' governments and military forces.

At Azi's direction, the team had referenced each AboveEarth point to the corresponding UnderEarth coordinate. He flipped through the report to the map section and spread it on the marble counter. Locating Xibalba IX, his current location, Azi noted the nearest openings. The closest was beneath the Sierra Mountains. And only a few kilometers from the base.

Azi leapt from his chair and sprinted through the compound. He would take his trusted assistant and investigate.

DISAPPEARING CORPSE

Lugh sat up in bed to answer his cell. His head chef never called, especially at this hour.

"Lugh, this is Spence. Did you come by and get the dog?"

"Huh?"

"Your dog. He's not in the deep freeze. Did you pick him up today?"

Lugh scrambled from the bed, yanking on his jeans with one hand and juggling his cell with the other. "No, Spence. I wouldn't do that without letting you know." He switched his phone to speaker-mode and laced his sneakers, pausing when a thought occurred to him. "Wait! Are you getting me back for putting Cu in there without telling you? If so, you woke me from a dead sleep, and frankly Spence, this isn't funny."

His head chef groaned. "I'm serious, Lugh. Cu's gone."

"Did you search the freezer? Maybe someone moved him."

"If they did, they left the blanket and bag. They're piled in the corner where Cu was propped. Where else could he be?"

"Not a clue. But I'll be there in ten."

Lugh ran a brush through his unruly hair and threw a jacket over his clothes. He left through the front door without looking at the living room as he passed through. It was too empty without Brian and Cu.

In less than ten minutes, he pulled into Jocko's parking lot. Two minutes later, he stared into an empty freezer. Not empty-empty, it was filled with meat and frozen goods. But the wolfhound was gone. In the corner where Cu had been awaiting burial, lay the blanket and vinyl body-bag.

Lugh gaped at Spence, then back at the vacant corner. Who would've moved his dog? And to where?

"I looked everywhere," Spence said apologetically, "including the supply closet and the cellar. I can't imagine who would have the cojones to take him. Or how they would've gotten him out of here without me knowing."

The thought of Mitch Wainwright creeping into Jocko's ran through Lugh's mind, but he dismissed it as ridiculous. Blaming his old nemesis for something he would have no reason to do was grasping at straws.

"Was he here when you got to work?"

"Yessir. And he was here this afternoon when I ducked in the freezer to cool off. That woulda been around four or five. I didn't notice he was gone until closing."

As Spence spoke, Lugh remembered Hope's words. The lives of both animals were tied to the Awen. And since Hope was alive, Emily was too. Maybe Cu had come back from the dead? But if so, where was he? Under the earth with Emily and Brian?

Lugh hoped so. Maybe Cu could help them escape.

"Pack 'er up, Spence, it's late. We'll unravel this mystery tomorrow. In the meantime, go home and get some sleep. Cu's dead, so no harm, no foul. Right?"

Spence cocked one brow. "Guess not, boss. I'm sorry I woke you up. Sleep in tomorrow, okay?"

Lugh slapped his back. "I have never slept late a day in my life, but the meds make me drowsy, so who knows. Maybe I will. Want me to stay and lock up?"

"Nope, I've got it. You go on home. I'll grab my stuff and be right behind you."

On the drive home, Lugh pondered his theory. As crazy as it sounded, it made the most sense. They had witnessed the cat and dog's initial appearances—seemingly out of nowhere. With luck, the hound had returned and would rescue Emily and Brian.

At home, Lugh shucked his overcoat and walked through the house, looking for Cu and Brian out of habit. Feeling blue and a bit creeped out, he kicked off his shoes and climbed in bed. He thought about taking a pain pill, but rolled over and plumped his pillow instead.

Only sleep wouldn't come. Lugh lay in bed, reliving the horror of the earthquake and volcano. He was grateful Emily's magic had saved him and the entire Atlanta area, but dammit all to hell, why couldn't *he* have saved *her*? Or Brian? Or Cu and Hamilton?

Lugh was almost asleep when he heard a noise. The tree service had trimmed the black walnut, so it wasn't that. He rolled over and was drifting off when he heard it again. Only this time it came from the dining room.

Groaning, Lugh dragged himself out of bed and padded down the hall in the dark, nearly jumping out of his skin when a crash sounded on the patio. Heart pounding, he grabbed his baseball bat and tiptoed to the slider. Sucking in a breath, he flicked on the light and peeked through the blinds.

There, alive and in glorious color, was Cu the Irish wolfhound, who exploded into loud, frantic barking and reared to put his paws on the door. In seconds, Lugh had removed the two-by-four and opened the slider.

"Cu!" he gurgled, happier than he'd been since the earthquake.

One hundred and forty pounds of dog bounded in, knocking him to the floor. Laughing, Lugh tried to wiggle away, but the dog slathered him everywhere with his long tongue. Clutching Cu in a bear hug, Lugh rolled on the floor with the gangly wolfhound.

Cu yelped with joy, then squirmed free to skitter back-and-forth between the kitchen and living room barking.

"How'd you get here, dude? You were dead!"

Cu shoved his empty bowl across the floor and barked.

Laughing, Lugh snagged it and filled it with kibble. Cu's bark grew shriller. Lugh set the bowl in its usual spot and the barking was replaced by the frantic crunch of kibble.

"Death and reincarnation made you hungry, huh boy?" Lugh stared in wonder. Cu was alive. Really and truly alive.

Filling the other bowl with filtered water, Lugh chuckled when Cu lapped it noisily. He bent to hug the dog close and ran his hands over his curls. Cu whined and went back to eating.

"So how *did* you do it?" Lugh asked, though he knew the lives of the animal Elders were tied to the Awen. Hope was alive, and now Cu was alive. By extension, that meant Emily was too. Grabbing his cell from its dock on the counter, Lugh sent a text to Morgan and Arthur, despite the late hour.

WATER DRAGON

Emily gazed out the window at the waves crashing against the shore. She ached to curl in a ball in the morning sun and sleep for a hundred, no, a thousand years. But even a short nap would be nice. She eyed the lanky American Indian.

Khenko had told her he was a shaman of the first degree, trained as an Iroquois medicine man to minister to his people. But he had abandoned that calling after some terrible experience he refused to share. He'd run from the responsibilities thrust upon him, leaving the tribe and his family back in Princeton, New Jersey. Emily could relate.

How many times in her almost thirty years had she done the same? And how often had she wanted to leave since learning of her world-saving burden? So many, she couldn't begin to count. She had no right to judge this man for doing the same.

But, Khenko Blitherstone was avoiding her question. When his expression remained blank, she prodded. "There is no plan, is there?"

His answer was flat and emotionless. "Not really, no."

"There's something important you're not telling me. Spill, Khenko."

Evading her gaze, he cleared the remains of breakfast from the kitchen.

"Would you at least tell me how I'm supposed to get back to Atlanta? You say that you know who I am, but do you also know that the druids are depending on me? That I have to finish my training so I can help avert some world-ending disaster?"

The medicine man looked down at feet the size of diving flippers. A shock of strawberry hair slid across his face. "According to Draig Talav, you are to remain with me until you regain your strength. She says the dragons will teach you what the druids cannot. Past this, I've not been told. Past this, I cannot see."

"Dragons?" Emily squeaked. "Where are the others?"

"Beats me," Khenko said, wiping the table. "I have only met Talav. But she said dragons, plural. She called them Keepers. Does that mean anything to you?"

Emily nodded, remembering what Hope had told them that night in the Wren's Roost library. "The Keepers keep watch over Earth and her inhabitants. They save us from ourselves and one another." Then she thought of Talav's explanation. "Oh wait. Talav said the Keepers keep us humans safe from reptilian aliens that live inside Earth. And there's something called a forgetfulness curse. The Keepers are responsible for that too. Or so I think."

"Aliens live inside the earth?" Khenko pulled at his long chin. "Talav didn't mention anything like that. She did tell me about the forgetfulness curse. She threatened me with it and made a big deal of letting me keep my memory. If she hadn't needed my help to save you, I doubt I would remember a thing. She let you remember, too," he added. "You must be special."

"Not so much," Emily mumbled. "According to her, I am one of a few who are immune to the dragons' forgetfulness curse." She yawned, not bothering to cover her mouth. Her eyelids felt heavy, and her head heavier as it sank toward her chest.

Khenko rounded the table to put an arm around her waist. "Let's get you back in bed, princess."

"No, no," she protested and pointed to the sea churning outside the window. "Can I go out to the beach? I'd love to curl up on the sand, assuming that's okay with you and the dragons."

Her sarcasm landed. Khenko blushed, though the change in color was difficult to discern on his permanently-tanned face.

"Of course, madam." He swept into a bow. "Your wish is my command."

"In that case, take me home. Or let me use your cell phone."

The medicine man snorted. "You know I can't. But I *can* take you out to the cabana. Then I want to hear about those aliens when you wake up."

Exiting the vortex, Draig Ooschu, the water dragon, paddled toward the isle of Zephyr Cay. Her bumbling sister had managed to corral the Awen, though Ooschu had failed. That burned within her like Tienu's fire. But the Awen was injured, and another human was now involved in what should be a clandestine operation.

Slicing through some of the clearest water in the world, Ooschu spotted a large squid, her favorite delicacy. The translucent creature scooted along the ocean floor, barely discernable against the creamy-white layer of crushed seashells. Unable to resist, she dove for the snack before continuing her journey.

The closer she got to her destination, the stronger she could feel the Awen's pull. Slowing to a halt, Ooschu trod water to survey the land. The lee side was covered in dense vegetation, mostly mangroves and scrub palms so thick that even the diminutive key deer would have trouble picking through them. Sea turtles sunned on a fallen palm trunk, and colorful parrots chattered in the trees. But the structures Talav had mentioned were nowhere to be seen.

Ooschu circled the promontory until she spied another outcrop. Wooden structures with thatched roofs rose from the jungle, facing east and south. She sank into the warm, shallow water and resisted the urge to pursue a colony of squid that darted away.

Along with the presence of the Awen, Ooschu sensed dragon magic as she closed the distance. Rising above the surface, she scanned the island, then submerged to swim the last hundred meters to the mangrove-dense shore. This time her eyes were rewarded.

The Awen languished on a blanket spread across the fine, white sand, snoring loud enough to wake the gods. Ooschu stared. This was the Awen she had tracked back and forth across Earth's globe?

Despair raked at Draig Ooschu. She sank beneath the waves, momentarily daunted. How were they supposed to save the world with a puny, untrained Awen? They had almost failed a thousand years ago when she was seasoned and in command of her powers. Something bumped hard into Ooschu's shoulder.

She swung around, sensing more than seeing the large creature before it disappeared. Then it rammed her hard from behind. Ooschu struck out defensively with her tail and razor-clawed feet, but caught nothing but water. She turned a tight circle and spied the threat. It swam toward her, moving fast.

Ooschu stared, not believing what she was seeing. Earth dragons didn't swim. Yet here was Talav, underwater, leering at her. In the dragons' long history on Gaia, Ooschu had never known Talav to tolerate the water. Similarly, Ooschu couldn't stand being on land.

Ooschu surfaced with a gasp to gulp air. Talav came up beside her.

"Talav, you're swimming!" The earth dragon swam in a circle around Ooschu, slicing through the water like a pro. "You old she-devil. Where did you learn to swim like that?"

Talav laughed and splashed water in Ooschu's face. "It's amazing what happens when necessity presents." Talav swam to shore and trudged onto the beach to settle beside the Awen. Taunting Ooschu, she challenged, "Your turn, sister."

SOCIAL CLIMBER

"You seem different," Patty whined. "Did something happen while I was in L.A.?"

Shalane frowned. "A lot happened. But what do you mean? Different how?"

"Oh, I don't know. You're stand-offish, less attentive. You don't laugh at my jokes or my funny faces. And when I try to initiate sex, you push me away. You've never done that."

Shalane stared up at a picture on the wall. Something *was* wrong with her. For the first time in her adult life, she didn't want sex from anyone. And she had no idea why. "I'm tired, is all. This headache takes a lot out of me."

"But you had the headache before. And you wanted me all the time. Do you not like me anymore?" Patty's lips twisted in a jealous sneer. "Or is it that Ebby Panera? Did you hook up with her while I was gone?"

That got Shalane's attention. "What do you know about Ebby Panera?"

"N-nothing. Only that you get all googly-eyed when you talk about her."

Then why couldn't Shalane remember the woman?

She looked Patty up and down, barely recognizing the Marilyn-wannabe she'd rescued from a bar in California. Her sexuality still oozed, but there was a new, sharp edge of sophistication. Her breasts were larger, for one thing. Shalane had paid for the augmentation in Las Vegas after Patty threw a hissy fit. Personally, Shalane liked them better before.

But that wasn't the problem. Shalane felt nothing for the girl. And she hadn't since Patty had come back from California. Her eye twitched, and a pain shot through it like a bolt of lightning. Shalane grabbed her head and rocked, riding it out.

"Are you okay?" Patty asked, suddenly attentive.

When it eased a little, Shalane slumped in her chair. "Do I *look* okay?"

"Well, you don't have to be shitty." Tiny lines crinkled across the girl's forehead and between her brows. "I'm worried about you. It's not like you to turn down sex."

So they were back to that. "Look, Patrika. I feel like crap. Stop making this about you." But Cecil had said the same thing.

"Nothing is about me where you are concerned." Face flaming, the girl flounced from the room fluffing the new hairdo Shalane had paid for and wagging her ass in the expensive jeans Shalane bought. Patty had turned into a greedy monster. She ought to send her back home for good.

Shalane checked her cell phone. In the last few minutes since she'd looked at it before, the attorney had neither called or texted. But heat gathered in her loins. She sighed, relieved. At least she wasn't dead down there. She had begun to wonder.

Only she hadn't heard from Mitch since that night in Atlanta. He'd been gone when she woke the next morning and hadn't contacted her since. She thought about calling or texting him again, then decided against it. People chased Shalane, not the other way around.

☼☼☼

Patty crammed her clothes into the new suitcase. She had agreed to come on the road with Shalane to escape the shithole she'd lived in after leaving her mother and stepfather's house. But if she wanted to be treated like a piece of trash, she could've stayed home. There, she was invisible. Unless her stepfather was drunk.

At least he hadn't come to her room while she was there for the wedding. She'd been terrified he would. He was probably afraid she would draw a butcher knife on him again. The last time he raped her, she'd told her mother and threatened to go to the police. She shuddered, remembering.

Her mother had turned on Patty. She insisted she'd manufactured an elaborate lie to get attention, and had even threatened to throw her out. At fifteen, Patty had nowhere to go.

167

So she recanted and kept the knife beneath her mattress, and slept with her door locked.

Good thing, too. He'd come to her room one more time, shit-faced drunk. She'd been asleep. He'd ripped her panties off before Patty could get her hand on the knife. Luckily, she didn't have to use it. He fell over his own feet, hit his head, and blacked out. Patty fled to a friend's house and never went back.

But she was used to pretty things. She'd gotten her hands on a fake driver's license, and took a job as a waitress. The tips were good, but not enough to support Patty in the way she was accustomed. Determined to be the pampered princess she was meant to be, she earned extra money sleeping with wealthy customers.

Which was why she had gone with Shalane in the first place. Patty had never been with a woman, but Shalane was supposed to be her ticket out. In the beginning, she'd made Patty feel special. Then she expected her to perform on demand, just like her stepfather. But ignoring Patty was even worse.

Well, screw that. She had made it on her own once she could do it again. If Shalane didn't start treating her better, Patty would leave. But not without Shalane's money.

MEDICAL SUPPLIES

Three long nights and days had passed since the earthquake. While Nergal slept, the doctora spent most of her time foraging the hills for herbs to make poultices and teas. They were rank-smelling and tasted of rotted piss, but her decoctions had tonified Nergal's blood and lifted his spirits. Each day his wounds healed a little more.

On the evening of the third day, the doctora declared Nergal strong enough to tackle the journey, and the two set out for Agartha. If her office still stood, they would scavenge anything that could aid in Nergal's healing. The first hill wasn't too difficult. Nor the second, or even the third. But each one after that became more laborious. They had to stop often for him to rest, but Nergal made it to the city on his own.

Inside the scorched gate, the stench of death and sulfur rendered the air untenable. The once-imposing city had been annihilated; the charred metro area half-razed, with vents spewing steam here and there. The air and ground was blistering hot.

Nergal gritted his teeth against the pain and repositioned the empty pack. He let Magdalena lead as they picked their way through the stinking, steaming ruins. But reaching her office took longer than expected. Each time they found a path through the wreckage, another peril blocked their progress.

About halfway in, a band of thugs appeared from a dark alley and surrounded them. Nergal threw back his hood, probably a bad idea considering he was a wanted Draco, but the brutes melted into the shadows and gave them a wide berth.

Soon, they came to the doctora's street. Nergal cheered silently, then cursed himself, despising the weakling he had become. They approached what was once her office. The doctora cried out in dismay and rushed into its shell.

The stench of rotting flesh assaulted them. The waiting area was unrecognizable beneath the rubble, but at least the magma had not encroached here. Holding one hand against her nose, the doctora yanked an intact cabinet open, and came up with lightsticks and an emergency kit. Nergal placed the kit in the empty pack. The lights they used to pick their way to the back.

Here the walls and roof had only partially buckled, but the Fomorian rotted in the crushed tube, and it stank unbearably. Nergal gagged and followed the doctora to the hindmost office where one partially-smashed cabinet yielded instruments, braces, ointments, and unguents.

When she found her safe unharmed, the doctora cheered. It held the main object of their trip—narcotics and powerful anti-inflammatories. In the dim glow of a lightstick, Magdalena searched the rest of the office while Nergal stuffed her finds in the packs. They scavenged everything possible, then waded through the rubble-filled waiting room.

Extinguishing the lightstick, Nergal made sure the way was clear. As they exited quietly to the dark street, a spotlight clicked on, pointed straight at them.

DEMIGODS

The arduous flight north took all of one day and the following night. Running on next to no sleep, Ethnui and Brian neared the edge of the Fomore's known territory. When the sun broke the horizon on UnderEarth, they stopped for a brief rest. Brian fell asleep immediately.

Ethnui drank water and studied him in the dim light. They had made good time. The human was in excellent shape and had only complained once or twice. After a while, she stood and slung her pack over her shoulder, then jostled him awake.

Brian protested but rose and scrubbed his face in his hands. "We're nearly there, right? I can't go much farther without a good night's sleep."

"Cheer up, human." She checked her handheld, though she already knew the answer. "Only a few more clicks."

Shouldering his pack, Brian gave her a grim nod and fell in line behind Ethnui.

The trail had climbed steadily for the last part of the journey. Now it rose at an even steeper angle. Picking her way through limestone karst littered with potholes and towering monoliths, Ethnui's heartbeat quickened. The steady susurration they'd been hearing deepened, and there was a new, rhythmic, crashing whoosh.

They neared the summit. Ethnui slid her weapon from her belt and motioned Brian to do the same. For the last few meters, they walked side-by-side on the narrow trail. At the top, they stopped and looked at one another, then mounted the summit.

Brian gasped and Ethnui stared. Before them spread an enormous body of water, larger than any Ethnui had seen.

"It's the ocean!" Brian crowed and threw a companionable arm over her shoulders. "I've only seen the Pacific in Oregon, but that's what this is. I'll bet anything."

Ethnui stared in wonder and trepidation. She'd known that her birthplace in Ireland was surrounded by ocean. But she hadn't been prepared for the profound sight. Awe, immense and sharp, overpowered her. Tears sprang to her eyes and Ethnui fell to her knees in the prickly sand.

☼☼☼

They pitched camp in a cave by the ocean. Brian set up the lighting and portable heater and hurried from the cave.

"Be careful out there," Ethnui called behind him.

She unfurled the thin, eiderdown sleeping bags and spread them on either side of the heater. Then she moved to the cave entrance to keep an eye on Brian. In case of trouble, she told herself.

Her stomach flip-flopped when the human squatted beside the perilous sea. He scooped water to wash his face and hands, then wet his unruly hair, slicking it back behind his ears. When he proceeded to have a conversation with himself, Ethnui strained to hear. But she couldn't distinguish his words over the surf.

Sitting with her back to the cave entrance, Ethnui dug her handheld from her pants pocket and plugged it into the kinetic charger. She accessed the interactive map she had engineered for the Fomorians and checked their bearings.

They were at the edge of known territory, far from Agartha. Other than local fauna, the only sentient lifeforms in a fifty-kilometer radius were Ethnui and Brian. She glanced up. Brian had settled on the sand. Sitting cross-legged, he threw stones into the water, lips still moving, speaking to himself.

Ethnui checked in with her headquarters, but none of her comrades had made it back, increasing her worry exponentially. When Brian returned to the cave, she'd laid food on a thin, metallic sheet. The fare was simple but filling. The boy chewed contemplatively as they ate in silence. Finally, he looked up.

"The longer I'm down here in what you call UnderEarth, the more it seems I'm back home. You even have a sun, though it's a reddish color and not nearly as bright as ours. And there are animals and birds, and even an ocean. How can that be?"

172

Ethnui pondered a moment, unsure of the answer. "Wouldn't each be a mirror-image of the other? That would make the most sense to me."

Brian stared at something on the wall behind her. "Yeah, probably. But from what I learned in Biology classes, species evolve to reflect their environment."

"Is the environment here all that different from up there?"

"When I was underground I thought so. But once I saw daylight, I thought I was back home until you told me I wasn't. So, no. It's not that different at all."

Tears sprang to Ethnui's eyes. "I wish I could see your world. UnderEarth is all I've ever known. Or, all I can remember. I wonder if I still have kin in Ireland."

"Can you tell me more about your people?" Brian flopped onto his stomach facing her.

She had wondered if he was as curious about her as she about him. "The Fomori?"

He nodded. "Until now, I'd never heard of your people. Are you—" he gulped.

Ethnui held her breath, waiting for the label she feared was coming.

"Human?" He said it in a near whisper, eyes soft and searching. No judgment lurked in their dark shadows.

"Yes," she sighed, "and no."

At his intake of breath, Ethnui smiled. Patience was not one of Brian's virtues. "According to legend, the Fomori are a semi-divine race that inhabited Ireland in ancient times. Like the Greek Titans, it was believed the Fomori preceded the Dagda and the other Celtic gods."

Brian's eyes danced. "So you *admit* you're a demigod!"

Ethnui squirmed. "No more than you. The original Fomori were gods of storms and rough weather. Some of us still wield that power." He looked thoughtful, and she hurried to add, "No, not me. Nor anyone I know. Though my mother could summon storms and calm them." Sadness squeezed her heart. "My parents were captured before me. I still don't know their whereabouts—or if they are alive."

"I'm sorry, Ethnui." His gentle tone soothed some of her sadness.

"Have you heard of the Tuatha De' Danaan?"

"Yes!" Brian sat up. "My family and I are descended from the Tuatha. What about them?"

"Though the Tuatha are more well-known as the gods of civilization, we Fomorians predate them. The original Fomori had the body of a human with the head of a goat. That's why I have horns. I can also fold myself into a ball that has outer armor. My mother couldn't do that."

Brian's eyes grew wide, but he didn't comment.

"There are accounts of Fomori with one eye, one arm, and one leg. But others were very beautiful. Like Bres and his father, Prince Elatha. Fortunately, I descend from that line, a fact for which am eternally grateful."

"Why?"

"Because the others are hideous, with pointy teeth and ears." Brian eyed hers and Ethnui shook her head. "No, much pointier. Like elves."

"You have elves down here?"

She threw back her head and laughed. "Not that I know of. But the tales are still whispered. Does it bother you that I'm descended from goat-people?"

Brian hesitated, then shook his head. "Not really. I mean, you have built-in armor. How cool is that?"

"Very cool. But I didn't always think so. Imagine growing up looking different than everyone else. I hated my differences. Every one of them. Of three sisters and one brother, I was the only one who took after Mother." As she said it out loud, Ethnui realized the fact no longer stung.

"Over the centuries and millennia, the Fomori and Tuatha interbred. Now, thousands of years later, we are of one blood. Some look Fomori, others Tuatha. Thankfully, I am a strong blend of the latter."

"So we're related?" The words rolled slowly from Brian's tongue.

Of all she had revealed, that was what he grasped?

"No, not really. And yes. We are related in the way all humans are."

"Ahh." He sounded relieved.

Ethnui winced. It was clear Brian didn't want to be related to her. He thought her defective. Or worse, a monster. She fought the reflex to close in on herself.

"I didn't know any of this until I was captured by the Dracos. They threw me in a dungeon complex similar to yours, only it was filled with Fomori. Mostly from the other side of the family tree. They despised me and would have killed me."

She swallowed hard, shoving back the memory. She had hated them with a passion. Until Progen changed their minds. And helped her to understand, if not to forgive, how her kin had treated her.

"How awful," Brian growled. "I'm glad you escaped. How did you get out?" His anger dulled her hurt.

"Progen saved me. Because he is different like me, he convinced the others that we share a common ancestry and history. Then one day, he told me of the grand hall abandoned and forgotten by the other races. He got us out, and we fled to the compound."

There was a commotion outside the cave. They scrambled to attention. Finger to her lips, Ethnui drew her weapon and crept closer to the opening.

"What's out there?" Brian whispered, making her jump.

She hadn't realized he'd moved with her. His graze heightened Ethnui's senses. She peered out carefully to search for the source of the disturbance.

"Stay here." She stepped from the cave, weapon drawn. A pair of cygnets bathed in the surf, wings flapping. Seeing nothing else, she rejoined Brian at the hidden entrance.

"Just a pair of swans. But we must remain watchful for the Dracos and stay ahead of the scum."

The human's eyes widened. "That's your plan? Stay ahead of those beasts? After what they've done to you and your people? We've got to do more than that, Ethnui. We have to stop them. If we can get back to my world, we can warn the druids. Let them know what's going on." Brian pointed toward skyward. "But to do that, we have to get up there."

Chills ran down Ethnui's spine. Escaping UnderEarth scared the daylights out of her. Not that life down here had been so great. But, she wasn't sure she wanted to help Brian leave. Or how to go about it, even if she did.

A GATHERING OF DRUIDS

April had set upon Atlanta with a vengeance. Sheets of rain pounded the tin roof at Wren's Roost, where seventy-plus druids crowded the great room and spilled over into the dining room and hall. Lugh MacBrayer stood in front of the grand fireplace looking out at the druids. He knew each by name, most since childhood.

The time for silence was over. Hope and Cu stood beside Lugh, pressed against his legs. Many had commented about Cu's incredible return. It was time to share what that meant.

Lugh cleared his throat and announced, "You all know that Cu was killed in the earthquake that took our Grand Druid and my nephew. Yet, he stands beside me, as does Hope." A murmur passed through the room.

"We know only a fraction of what the druids knew in the days of the Tuatha and Fomore peoples. And even less of what the Ancient Ones knew. We do know they gave us the druid way of life and seeded other peacekeeping tribes around the world. As young druids, we studied these sister-cultures."

Heads nodded around the packed room.

"Most of these cultures share commonalities, including ancestors who could shift into animal form, and animal Elders with magical powers. We of the Awen Order were taught that Cu and Hope," he pointed to each, "completed the original Awen's training, and reincarnate with her when the world's existence is threatened."

"That's true?" Francine Walters shouted from the back, ever a skeptic.

"Yes," Lugh assured. Her expression remained doubtful. Beside him, Hope twisted to lick her already-pristine coat. "I, too, believed this to be a myth. But Hope and Cu have been around a thousand years, maybe more."

A collective groan went up from the room.

"I know, I know," Lugh hurried to say. "I had trouble with this, too. But regardless of what we all believe, these two," Lugh glanced at each of the Elders, "reincarnate with every new Awen. When Emily came home to Wren's Roost, they reappeared."

The cat meowed and Cu yipped. Lugh stood back to let them speak.

"'ello, my fine friends." Hope's French accent was heavier than usual. "What your priest says is true. A couple of months ago, after being gone for decades, I found myself at Wren's Roost. I was called 'ere by zee Awen's presence. Since zen, I have supervised Emily's training. Some of you already knew zis." Druid heads nodded.

"I am still 'ere and have not, what you call, expired. Because of zis, I know Emily Bridget to be alive, as well." Cu barked, and Hope continued. "Zee day of zee earthquake, Cu was struck in zee 'ead and died. But 'e returned last night to Lughnasadh's home, where 'e 'ad been living before zee quake."

Bedlam ensued. Lugh's raised hand had little effect. "That's impossible," someone yelled over the din. "No, it's not," another answered, and the decibel level rose. "Reincarnation is real, and magic makes all things possible," someone else hollered.

The acting Grand Druid, Arthur Creeley, stood to bring them back to order. When the room quieted, he said, "Please continue, Hope. You have the floor."

"Yes, yes," Hope hissed. "Be not so quick to doubt, dear ones. As one of you said, with magic and belief, anything is possible. And since I am alive, and Cu 'as returned, we know Emily Bridget also lives." The ticking of the grandmother clock filled the room.

"Are you saying that Emily Bridget is alive?" Sheba Black, whose family was originally from Johannesburg, stood. "If she survived the quake, where is she?"

"Yes, where is she?" the druids yelled.

Arthur drew to full height. "That we do not know."

"Then how do we know she's not dead?" The question came from Milo Stroud, an Aussie from Queensland, in Atlanta on a temporary assignment.

"That's what we've been trying to tell you," Arthur groaned. "The animals' lives are bound to that of the Awen. We know Emily is alive because Hope and Cu are both alive. When the Awen incarnates, so do they. When the Awen dies, they die; only to return when the Awen returns."

Sean Hester shouldered through the crowd and stopped in front of Arthur. "So it's not a myth."

"No, Sean. It's true."

A loud whoop went up from the druids and a brief, but vocal, celebration ensued. When the room quieted again, the acting Grand Druid cleared his throat.

"Now that you all understand, it is imperative we find Emily and Brian. Who here is willing to help Morgan's crew?"

After more discussion and explanation, Arthur divided the druids into groups according to individual strengths. Tasks were assigned, ranging from electronic surveillance to combing through the wreckage. Those prolific in location charms and telepathy were also put to work.

When the meeting adjourned, the head of security, Morgan Foster, requested to speak with Lugh in private. They climbed the stairs to the library. He settled on the sofa; she sank into an upholstered chair.

Lugh leaned toward her. "You have news about Ham's murder?"

"I have news, yes. But no evidence of a homicide. The hospital found no trace of poison, and the medical examiner's autopsy revealed nothing suspicious." The patrician eyebrows arched. "Tell me again why you think Mitchell Wainwright killed my brother."

Lugh hesitated. He had promised not to tell anyone Ham was alive. Or his spirit, anyway. "Ham mentioned it before he passed."

"My brother was in a coma, Lugh."

"Yes. He was. But he communicated with me, nonetheless. He told Emily the same thing. And he was adamant."

"Did he say he had proof?"

Lugh wagged his head. "No. Just that he knew it somehow."

"Well, that's not enough. We can't charge the man on suspicion, Lugh, much less get a conviction. I'm closing the investigation. Bring me proof, and I will reopen the case."

Lugh exhaled, relieved. As annoying as Mitch was, he hadn't wanted to believe that his once-friend could've killed the head of their Order. "What about Awen's gems? Any clues yet to their whereabouts?"

"No. We're working down the list Emily provided of Alexis's addresses, but we're not even sure it was she who stole them. I have two of my best agents searching for clues. If anything pops, I will let you know." Morgan rose from the chair and stared up at the portrait of Awen and the Elders.

Lugh cradled his head in his hands, and a whimper escaped. Morgan wheeled toward him.

"You okay, Lugh?"

"Not really. My head is killing me." He struggled to stand and sank back down.

"You don't look so good. Why don't you lay on the couch and rest? I'll send Mary up on my way out."

"I think I just might," he groaned.

"Can I get you anything?"

"Not unless you can conjure a glass of water."

He dumped two of the pain pills in his palm while Morgan glided to a compact refrigerator hiding in one corner. She brought him a bottle, cracked the top, and handed it to him.

He nodded thanks, popped the pills in his mouth, and chased them down.

Extracting a throw blanket from a closet, Morgan brought it to him. "Here. This will keep you comfy. Can I get you anything else?"

"A new head?" He held his up with his hands.

Morgan feathered her hand lightly through his hair. "Oh, but this one is so handsome." She grinned, then a faraway look darkened her features.

"Morgan?"

She blinked and her focus returned. "Shall I turn the lights off?"

"That'd be awesome." Lugh closed his eyes and heard her move to the door. "Bye, Morgan. And thanks."

He shucked off his shoes and stretched out on the sofa as Cu bounded into the library. He licked Lugh's hand and flopped to the rug. Hope joined them and curled at Lugh's feet.

Feeling weary deep down to his bones, Lugh gazed up at the portrait of Awen and the Elders. The play of light upon the priestess's face made him feel a bit better. Or maybe the pain pills had started to work.

SURPRISE ENCOUNTER

Blinded by the spotlight, Nergal shoved Magdalena behind him. He dropped the pack and whipped his weapon from his cloak as two hooded forms emerged from a burned-out building. The bark of a familiar voice stayed his claw on the trigger.

"Nergal, it is I, Ishkur. We are here to help."

The smaller Draconian stepped forward and struck her chest in salute. Nergal recoiled when he recognized the familiar features marred by poorly-healing cuts.

"Draca, you have caused me enough grief. Be gone with you," he spat.

The black silhouettes hovered motionless against a blacker night. The male lowered his hood. "General Nergal, it is I. Vice Major Ishkur."

Nergal stiffened and pointed his weapon. Ishkur was likely here to arrest Nergal. But the genius behind Nergal's Human Domination project struck his chest in salute.

Nergal relaxed, but only a little. "Why are you not in Xibalba IX? Who is supervising our project? And what are you doing with this deceiver?"

"There is a pub nearby. Let's get off the street and I will explain all." Ishkur peered to his right and left before twisting to check the dark street behind him. "Come," he barked.

Nergal's mouth watered. He could use a drink. And bar food. The animals Magdalena trapped left much to be desired. But he was a wanted Draco. "I dare not. There is a bounty on my head."

Ishkur's bobbed. "Yes, but despite reports to the contrary, Shibboleth believes you dead. He sent me to Agartha to investigate the rumors. And to find you, should they happen to be true—"

Inanna interrupted, "I, too, am on the run from Shibboleth."

Nergal lunged, but the doctora grabbed him from behind. "Wait, Nergal. Hear her out."

Inanna nodded gratefully. "The residents of Agartha despise Shibboleth and remain sympathetic to you, Nergal, as do I. His minions forced me to set you up, then left me for dead." Inanna struck her chest with a closed fist. "I made a vow to bring vengeance upon our attackers. Should you choose to grant me pardon, I shall declare my allegiance to you as my commanding general."

"I, for one, would be glad for your assistance." The doctora moved forward to stand abreast of Nergal. "We found a few medical supplies, though my office was destroyed in the quake." She reached up to lift Inanna's hood. "Your wounds need tending."

Turning to Nergal, she continued. "I could use a good, stiff drink. I vote we go to the pub. You can leave your hood up. If you feel we are in danger of being discovered, we will all leave."

Too tired to argue, Nergal shifted the uncomfortably-heavy pack. Waving them on, he followed Ishkur, Inanna, and the petite doctora with the violet eyes as they waded through the wreckage, skirting charred remains of buildings and smoldering fetid carcasses. A merciful wind rose, blowing the worst of the stench the opposite way.

Nergal's back throbbed, and the gash on his face burned. But worse was his sense of impending doom. They approached the pub, and he changed his mind. He would not go in. The others prodded and cajoled, then agreed it was for the best. Nergal's presence could bring death to them all.

They filed into the pub, and he squatted in the shadows, pressing his aching back against the sturdy wall. From this vantage point, Nergal could see the alley in both directions, plus keep an eye on the open doorway.

The encounter with Ishkur might prove fortuitous. When he wasn't gambling or drunk, the Draco was a genius. He had designed the Human Domination project based on Nergal's idea and earned a promotion to Vice Major, even though Ishkur was a half-breed.

The wind whistled through the alleyway. Nergal shifted positions and drew the hood tight around his face. A minute or two later, several beings poured out of the pub. They wobbled down the alley, arm in arm. But it was the rich aroma of meat cooking that got Nergal's attention. The doctora had introduced him to the pleasure of roasted-versus-raw, and Nergal was hungry.

The longer he squatted, the more agonizing it became. Fatigue set in and threatened to take over; a side-effect he hoped would be short-lived. The doctora had been noncommittal on the subject.

A stocky Cerulean appeared in the doorway and exited the pub. Nergal shrank into his cloak and lowered his eyelids so no reflection of light would give him away. The Ceruleans were paid brutes, likely for Shibboleth. Striding a short way in the opposite direction, the mercenary leaned against the wall to relieve his bladder.

Nergal suspected the ones from the dive in Irkalla had delivered his near-fatal beating. Inanna had just said as much. Not about the Ceruleans, but the set-up. Despite her part, Nergal found his animosity toward the Draca dwindling. But her litter-father Shibboleth made his blood boil.

A curt, guttural voice shredded the silence. Nergal jerked to attention. The Cerulean was speaking into his handheld. Nergal heard enough to discern the mercenary's intention. He was there to capture Inanna for the bounty.

Not on Nergal's watch.

Hate for the warlord burned in his chest. Until Shibboleth had come out of retirement, making proclamations and commandeering his army, Nergal had been in charge. Now Nergal skulked in a burnt-out city that he used to command, cowering in the shadows. He straightened with supreme effort and bit his lip to keep from moaning.

The Cerulean strode back to the pub. When he hesitated in the doorway, Nergal leapt from his hiding place and slashed the blue giant's midsection with a scavenged dagger. Blood spurted. The Cerulean roared and fought back. Nergal feinted retreat, then drove the blade deep into the blue chest and twisted hard. The merc gasped and coughed blood, eyes widening when he recognized Nergal. Then his life-force ebbed and the eyes went dark.

Ignoring the pain ravaging his own body, Nergal dragged him to the shadows. He quickly removed holster and weapons, fastened them around his waist, and covered the body with charred planks. He thought of chowing down on an arm. But Ceruleans tended to run in pairs. His partner was likely inside the pub. Which meant they were all in danger—including the doctora.

Holding his hood close, Nergal peered inside. A dense smoke haze shrouded beings of every species, but nowhere did he see Magdalena or the other Cerulean. Nergal entered and shouldered his way through the crowd.

In the back corner, Nergal spied the doctora. She was conversing with a Pharechi in firefighter's garb and appeared to be tipsy. Inanna and Ishkur occupied an adjacent bench, engaged in a round of heavy petting. The nerve of them partying while he cowered outside.

Nergal stormed the table and barely resisted flipping it over. Instead, he lifted one mug after the other, chugging the contents. They all eyed him with consternation. Even Magdalena. He clutched at his hood and slammed the last cup on the table.

"Party's over. Time to go." He kept his growl low.

Stuffing the remains of an Ecthelion burger in his mouth, he herded his accomplices to the door. Just outside, the second Cerulean materialized from the shadows, automatic weapon leveled on them.

"Halt!" the merc barked. "Hands where I can see them."

Eight reluctant arms lifted into the air.

"Vice Major Ishkur, you are under arrest by order of Lord Shibboleth for the unprovoked slaying of twelve of his soldiers. Inanna, you are wanted for questioning in General Nergal's disappearance. Surrender your weapons and come with me."

Nergal coiled to retaliate, but Inanna and Ishkur reacted first, making short order of the merc. Congratulating one other, they debated whether to drag his carcass back to the cave for food, then decided the burden would slow them down. They swiped his weapons, and tossed the dead Cerulean under the planks beside his partner, then high-tailed it for the safety of the caves.

☼☼☼

The renegades reached the city gates without further incident and picked their way through the outskirts of Agartha. Inanna and

184

the doctora took the lead. Ishkur followed, supporting Nergal and seething with recrimination. If he had minded his temper and not slaughtered Shibboleth's guards, his life would likely be quite different.

He *had* found Nergal. And Inanna was a rare delight. But Ishkur was now a wanted criminal. Any further actions would be outside the law. If they lived that long. They came to a short hill and he stopped to switch Nergal's weight to his other shoulder.

On the downhill side, Ishkur breathed a sigh of relief. The air here was sweeter, the night alive with cricket song and frog's croak. A light rain began to fall.

Inanna fell back to walk silently beside him, then moved to his other side. She dragged the general's muscled arm along the top of her shoulders and hefted some of his considerable weight.

Together they climbed the next hill. Ishkur nodded thanks and caught a glimpse of Nergal's twisted countenance. His agony was evident in the thin dawn light, leaving little evidence of the leader's former glory. But for better or worse, Ishkur had joined the defeated general. He only hoped their ending would be better than their present.

DOCUMENTATION

It took most of the morning for Khenko to compose the journal entry. Reading through it, he made a few minor changes in wording and grammar. Spellcheck did the rest. Since Emily's arrival, he had been documenting the happenings in detail on the chance something happened to him or his memory.

On this island, one never knew. Since bouncing back from Hurricane Dorian in 2019, weird things had been known to happen. Closing his laptop, Khenko slid his feet into his favorite leather thongs and went to check on his ward. He'd kept an eye on her through the window while he worked. She was healing, but had a long way to go.

Minutes earlier, Talav had emerged from the blue-green soup and now lazed on the beach beside the sleeping woman. Khenko exited the back door and stopped in his tracks. Another dragon rolled in the surf. It spied Khenko, and sank beneath the surface, disappearing with barely a ripple.

Khenko hurried to the beach.

"Hello, young crane." The earth dragon didn't bother to rise. "I see you've managed to revive our girl. She's sleeping like a hibernating bear."

"Welcome, Talav," Khenko rejoined. "I see you've brought a friend."

The sun broke through a cloud, and flashes of color shot from Talav's scales. Khenko tipped his ball-cap to shield his eyes and dragged a weathered chair from the pile in the cabana. He placed it beside Emily, who was stretched out on the sand, face cushioned by an oversized beach towel. A touch of pink had returned to her cheeks.

Khenko adjusted the umbrella that flapped in the ocean breeze, moving it to shade the druid princess. At a soft kerplunk, he glanced up. An enormous dragon rose from the sea and wavered in place. Saucer-sized eyes blinked at Khenko.

"Speak, human," the dragon commanded in a fearsome voice. "What say you?"

Khenko's heart leapt to his throat. Swallowing, he managed, "Hail dragon, guardian of the deep. Welcome to the Atlantean Center, my refuge and home. My name is Khenko Blitherstone and I am honored to make your acquaintance."

Talav roared in mirth, obviously enjoying Khenko's discomfiture. The dragon stood in the shallows as if undecided whether to stay or go. Talav's laughter took on a more mocking tone. Looking uneasy, it lumbered closer and crouched at the edge of the sluicing sea. Water rushed from its blue-green scales and willowy spikes.

"Healer," Talav rumbled, "meet my sister and Water Keeper, Draig Ooschu. Ooschu, meet Khenko Blitherstone, the medicine man who revived Awen."

Ooschu nodded her head and showered Khenko with salty water that fogged his sunglasses. Running a hand through his hair, he realized it hadn't seen a brush in a while. Not that a dragon would care about that. He slipped off his thongs and buried his feet in the damp sand. The Bahamian day was hot as usual, and the sand felt cool on his toes.

"So now what?" he asked.

Talav snorted. "Now we wait. And let her sleep."

They waited in silence for the better part of an hour. Or so it seemed. No self-respecting islander would wear a watch. While they waited, Emily snored, gulls screeched, and the sun tipped past its zenith.

When Emily finally stirred, the tide had turned back toward the sea. She moaned and stretched, then rolled toward Khenko and opened one eye. Seeing him there, she sat up quickly and grabbed her head moaning. "Water."

He leaned close to retrieve the insulated tumbler he'd planted in the sand for her earlier. The ice had mostly melted, leaving cold, filtered water. He handed it to Emily. She gulped until water dribbled down her chin, then handed it back, before screeching and grabbing her head. Her thumbs pressed into her eye sockets.

"Brain freeze?" he asked, hoping it wasn't more.

The green eyes rolled and Emily nodded, still holding her head and moaning.

"Gods help us all," Ooschu's deep voice boomed. "This is the Awen?" She rose on her haunches. "This is the warrior who would save our world? Are you sure, Talav? She looks like the Awen, but is she? This girl is green. In no way is she suited to fight the coming Darkness."

Talav roared, and Khenko nearly jumped out of his skin. It was a deep, angry rumble that resounded in his chest. "Manners, Ooschu," the earth dragon growled. "She's frightened enough."

Emily sat up straight. "Who is this?"

Ooschu wailed. "Who am I?" She rounded on Talav. "This woman doesn't even know who I am. She can't possibly be the Awen."

"Hush," Talav warned. "The veil is still upon her. You know this. She needs training, which is why we're here. Once she is ready, we will take her to Beli."

Ooschu's mighty tail slapped the water, sending spray showering upon the occupants of the beach. A bluish-white crane flapped overhead and settled on the sand between the dragons and Emily. It was the crane from Khenko's dream.

"Mind your manners, water drake," the majestic bird screeched. "And bow to your Awen. It is your duty to stand by her. She is younger, yes. And has been deprived of her destiny. But she is the Awen, nonetheless. Who are you to question your duty? Have you no heart? No eyes? Can you not see this woman has suffered and needs time to heal, to ripen, to come into her own? As always, you let your self-centered emotions rule your words."

The water dragon wilted and hung her head. Great tears leaked from the aqua eyes to roll down her horns into the sea. Bending one knee, she knelt before Emily crying great racking sobs that echoed through the palm trees and bounced across the water.

Emily's face reflected a shock that echoed Khenko's. She transferred her weight to kneel in the sand. Stretching a hand toward the remorseful dragon, she brushed the bowed snout with the tips of her fingers.

"It's okay, Ooschu. I understand your reluctance. I feel the same about my lack of experience. But I can assure you that I have learned much in a short time and remain teachable if you and Talav would do me the honor."

Turning to the crane standing on one leg, Emily bowed. "Greetings Corr, thank you for recruiting Khenko to help save me. I am ever in your debt, as well as Talav's and Khenko's." She looked at each of them as she said their names.

Corr flapped his wings. "My job, druid queen, is to ferry souls between worlds—usually in the other direction. But it is not your time. There is much you have yet to do in this life. I will assist you in any way I can; just call my name and I will appear. Now, these two have a schedule to keep. I'll be going."

Turning to the dragons, Corr uttered something in a language Khenko did not understand, then flapped ten-foot wings and flew out to sea.

Ooschu harrumphed and slapped her tail again, but her anger had dissipated. Facing Emily, she settled into sphinx position, forelegs out in front, back legs in a crouch.

"My apologies, Awen. For years, I tracked you all over the globe, becoming increasingly frustrated when you ignored my calls. I am known for emotional outbursts and I lost my temper. For that, I am sorry. I meant no disrespect."

"Ha!" Talav snorted. "I, too, have tracked the Awen for four years. But if you knew what this poor girl has been through, Ooschu, you would be doubly-sorry."

Making a decision he hoped he wouldn't later regret, Khenko rose from his chair and kneeled beside Emily to lay a hand on her shoulder. He glared at the two dragons, determined to have his say without interruption. When neither spoke, Khenko turned his attention to Emily.

"I don't know about these two, but I am with you, Emily. Or Awen. Whatever your name. It has been foretold in the lore of my people that this time would come, and we would be judged, not on our creed or color, our past words or deeds, but on what resides in our hearts.

"In my thirty-five years, I have met many who proclaim to be leaders and giants among men. But none have had half the sinew you possess, nor a fraction of the heart that beats in your chest. Awen, Queen of the Druids, I bow to you and your greatness." Khenko bowed low on one knee.

"I offer my loyalty and all of my faculties, including a strong back and mind and my abilities as a medicine man. I declare allegiance to you, Awen, and promise to follow you, to defend you, to die for you. I willingly make this oath on my behalf, but also on the behalf of my people, the Iroquois nation." Khenko let his arms fall by his sides. He looked into eyes of splintered jade where tears pooled but held.

Before Emily could utter what was on her lips, the dragons joined in. "Awen, to you, we owe the debt of our lives—past, present, and future. We declare fealty and vow never to forsake you. May you live long, prospering the Earth."

Eyes misty, Emily added her declaration. "On behalf of my ancestor, Awen, she who haunts my existence, I say thank you. To each of you. In exchange for your loyalty, I promise to defend you and Earth to the best of my ability." Rising from the sand, she bowed deeply and rose with a sheepish smile. "Only I have no clue how to do any of that."

ABANDONED SHAFT

Azi and his assistant exited the chute. Consulting the map he had copied to his handheld, Azi made for the northern tunnel. His assistant followed, packing their gear.

They had been walking for some time when a fork appeared that was not on the chart. Azi consulted his compass. The readings fluctuated wildly. Puzzled, he switched back to map mode. The course to the left seemed to head in the right direction, so they followed that.

A quarter kilometer later, a cave-in stalled their progress. Shaking their heads, the two scientists retraced their steps and took the second passage. This, too, lead to a dead-end. The entrance they sought was no longer accessible. Not by this route.

They returned to the chute, where Azi consulted the map. He had hoped to avoid the more treacherous course that wound through Chupacabra territory, but it was their only other option. The Chupacabras were vicious, bloodsucking canids that would stop at nothing to interfere with Draco business. And, while Azi and his assistant were trained for combat, they were more suited to cerebral tasks.

Fearing Shibboleth more than the Chupacabras, he programmed the route on the chute's keypad, and they boarded the car. Soon, they transferred to a second chute and ended up in a narrow and obviously-unused tunnel. With every footfall, dust rose to fill the stale air. Azi sneezed, a loud sharp resounding bark, then sneezed again.

"Shhh!" his assistant hissed.

Azi heard it too. A skittering, scratching noise. They stood silent for half a minute.

Hearing no other sounds, the two continued with greater stealth. The fine silt filled the air, irritating Azi's sensitive nasal passages. He tried breathing through his mouth, hoping not to sneeze again, but the dust collected in his throat as they wound upward along the rock-strewn path. He hacked and swallowed, then hacked again.

The tunnel narrowed further, and Azi's shoulder grazed the wall. Something needle-sharp pierced his scales, sending pain shooting down his arm. He stopped to retrieve a light from the pack his assistant carried.

Beneath the focused beam, the wall sprang to life. Thousands, maybe millions, of tiny quartz creatures crawled over one another to escape the light. Azi grasped one between his claws, intending to inspect it. But when it pierced his scales, he slung it against the wall.

The tunnel exploded with the creatures taking flight. The passage filled with their tiny crystalline bodies, each a stinging needle with a bad attitude. Azi slapped at them and hurried along, hunched over to avoid disturbing the walls.

But the loathsome pests followed, burrowing beneath their scales until a burning sensation filled Azi's senses. Near madness, he pushed on, heartened when light appeared ahead and the creatures retreated. The tunnel gave way to a well-lit chamber and Azi cheered.

His assistant ran past him. Uttering profanities, he threw down the pack and plucked the accursed insects from his hide. Fighting the urge to do the same, Azi consulted the compass and the map. The entrance should be just ahead.

☼☼☼

The fire dragon awakened with a roar, senses on high alert. The lizards approached one of the openings to AboveEarth, across the country from his current position. Whirling the tip of his spiny tail, Tienu created a small whirlwind and blew a fiery breath upon his creation. Glowing orange, the vortex grew larger.

When it filled the chamber beneath the hillock where Tienu had spent the night, he focused his attention on the threatened opening and stepped into the vortex. With a whoosh, the Fire Keeper was whisked into a wormhole, and within minutes, arrived at the abandoned chimney of the long-dormant volcano.

192

Seeing no immediate threat, Tienu lumbered along the tunnels surrounding the vent and reinforced the spell he had woven long ago. His forehead spines tingled. The lizard-men approached.

Taking up a position before the chimney, he faced the direction from whence the interlopers traveled, and planted his powerful haunches and thick forelegs. Tienu wrapped his tail around his bulk, creating an impenetrable fortress.

☼☼☼

After the needle-pest incident, Azi decided it was best not to use the light. Luckily, they'd encountered no Chupacabra. He drank from the container and handed it to his assistant. According to the map and his positioning device, they were nearing the abandoned shaft.

He peered ahead into the dark passageway, dread congealing in his chest. It was a good thing he'd brought his assistant. Otherwise, Azi would turn back now. He was a scientist, not a warrior. Next time, he would stay on the base and send them. He swallowed hard around the lump in his craw and forged onward.

Soon the air changed. It was thinner. And smoky. Like scorched metal. Azi licked his scaled lips and puckered at the metallic feel against his teeth. His assistant crowded close and commented on the change. Azi nodded and kept going, despite the unfamiliar terror that wreaked havoc with his gut.

The closer they got, the more difficult it became to walk—like they were moving against a gravity well of some sort. Soon, they could proceed no further. Perplexed, Azi consulted his GPS. The readings were going wonky again.

He took the light-stick his assistant proffered and turned a tight arc, searching for the entrance. He spied it in a distant corner.

His assistant cheered. "There it is, Azi! We've found it!"

Azi breathed a sigh of relief. They had indeed.

With a monumental effort, he took a small step toward the blocked shaft and bumped into something he couldn't see; something big and prickly and stinking of ore-smelt. Something that roared so loud, and emitted a flame so blistering, Azi passed out on the spot.

THE LAST STRAW

Settling in for meditation, Patty followed Shalane's instructions. She didn't hate it quite as much anymore, but she still didn't get why it was necessary. As instructed, she slid down her energetic roots and connected to the earth. But as she turned to go back up, she found herself in the lizard-man's body again.

This time, there were others like him. They were hurrying to escape Shibboleth, a warlord of great power and cruelty who was plotting to kill the humans and take over Earth. They ran through a burning city with its nauseating odor and foul alien beings. Struggling to wake up, Patty came to with a start.

Shalane's eyes were closed; the backs of her hands rested on her knees. Patty hugged herself and shuddered. Why was she seeing things? The visions were real, as real as Shalane. But why did they keep changing, progressing? Was the earth really in danger? Should she tell Shalane?

As if hearing Patty's thoughts, Shalane opened one eye. "You're staring, Patrika. Why aren't you meditating?"

"Because I saw something. Or rather, *was* something. A lizard-man." Shalane's eyes narrowed and her lips thinned. Patty could feel the disapproval pouring from her. "Remember, Shalane? I told you about it. I keep dreaming about him. Or, about *being* him. I think the lizard-creatures are plotting to overtake Earth."

Shalane eyed her coolly, one eyebrow cocked. "Whatever you say, dear."

Anger shot through Patty. She was sick and tired of being dismissed.

"NO!" she screeched. "This is real, Shalane. It has to be. It is not just a dream. I keep being in his head and body. And it changes every time. Like I'm living his life. Only this time—"

"Shut up," Shalane growled. "I won't listen to this. You're just trying to get a rise out of me. I'm not biting, Patty. If you're done with meditation, please leave so that I can continue in peace."

Patty gaped at her and leapt from the uncomfortable chair. "You know, Shalane? Screw you. You're just as bad as my mom and stepdad. I don't need this shit. First chance I get, I'm outta here."

Shalane's face turned a brilliant shade of scarlet. "Well, Miss Bitch, don't let the door hit you in the ass. Go pack your things. I'm putting you on the next flight to L.A.."

Patty slammed the door behind her and resisted the urge to skip. That had been a lot easier than she thought it would be. She hurried to her bedroom and threw all the clothes and pretty things Shalane had bought her into the expensive suitcase. She rescued childhood pictures from the dresser and her bedraggled bunny from the unmade bed and stuffed them in the suitcase, then wheeled it to the front of the bus.

In the kitchen, Patty quietly opened the freezer door and extracted the fat wad of cash from the fake strawberry bag. She slid it inside her pants pocket, and jump sky-high when her phone dinged.

It was a text from Shalane. *"I'm sorry, Patrika. Please forgive me. I want you to stay."*

HA! Fat chance. Patty pecked out *"HELL NO!"* with an angry-face emoticon and heard something slam against the wall of Shalane's bedroom.

With a satisfied chuckle, Patty ducked out the door and hightailed it for the bus stop she'd scoped out the day before. She was itching to count the wad of money, but she dare not do it until she was safely away.

☼☼☼

Shalane paced her room, furious at Patty, but even more so at herself. What had seemed a good idea at the time—bringing the girl along with her on tour—had proved to be a disastrous mistake. Cecil despised her, creating immense tension, and the girl always wanted something. Shalane had spent thousands of dollars on clothes and accessories, teeth whitening, a boob job, a high-end laptop, an iBlast, and a one-carat tennis bracelet. She'd finally put her foot down when Patty demanded a nose job.

No longer was the girl the sexy, Marilyn Monroe-wannabe Shalane had been attracted to in that bar in California. Patty had acquired a patina, a polish that only money can provide. But her heart had hardened, too. In the beginning, she'd been grateful. And generous with her budding sexuality.

But all that had gone by the wayside. By the second or third week, Patty had turned into a whiny, demanding sycophant. No wonder Shalane was turned off. But despite that, the girl was little more than a child. In a strange city. Disgusted that she cared, Shalane threw on a jacket and went after her.

ON FIRE

Maw strode down the corridor of the Agarthan stronghold, bound for Nergal's old office. He and several others had been dispatched by Shibboleth to arrest Ishkur. The contingent scurried out of his way. He was Shibboleth's right-hand warrior and a particularly nasty Draco in his own right.

While here, they would shore up the compound and investigate the rumors about Nergal. Maw knew there was nothing to substantiate the reports. He and his twin, Mot, had beaten the worm to a bloody pulp. No way had Nergal survived that.

Vice Major Ishkur was another story. Shibboleth had spared him in Xibalba IX and now wanted Ishkur captured alive. But, Maw had other plans for the traitor. A thrill ran through him. He would rip the bastard from navel to nose.

The Agarthan base was a losing proposition. The earthquake had dealt it a devastating blow. The magma no longer poured into the structure, but the Dracos had been unsuccessful in stopping its creep. The dungeons and lower levels were fiery pits, and it was only a matter of time before the upper levels conflagrated.

Maw had directed relief efforts toward shoring up the chute system and defending it from further magma encroachment. The last thing he wanted was to get stuck in this hellhole. They had to keep the magma from crippling the worldwide chute system.

He paced the Agarthan office, pondering his next move. Nergal's minions had already searched the catacombs for survivors. A few had been rescued, the rest had either escaped into the city or been burnt alive. Or so they assumed.

The human male child was no longer a priority, which was too bad. Maw's mouth watered. He had a particular liking for human meat. The younger, and more fear-laced, the better.

He called up the schematics for the base. A ping from his wrist unit signaled an incoming communication from the crew he'd sent into the city to apprehend Ishkur.

"What is it?" he growled.

"A Cerulean mercenary spotted Vice Major Ishkur in a bar in Agartha. He was accompanied by the one called Inanna, and a petite Draca identified as a doctora from the city."

"Capture them and bring them to me," Maw grunted

"But sir," the Draco barked before Maw could end the call. "The targets have escaped and the mercs are dead."

Maw roared. "That is not acceptable. Find them or you will be executed in their place." He cut the communication, seeing red.

His frustration mounted as he fiddled with the keyboard on the general's console. The heat had affected the main computer brain, and the electronics were all going haywire. He resorted to contacting Shibboleth via handheld.

Unable to get a connection there either, Maw dispatched a messenger to Irkalla and assigned a crew to repair and reroute the affected cables and circuits, and to replace those too damaged to reuse. He called up the security monitors and found they too were down.

Maw slammed his fist into the Draco-proof monitor's wavy lines. He was tired of doing nothing. But he was flying blind. Not only could he not see what was happening within the compound, but the chute station and the city were also dark.

Reinforcing his arsenal from Nergal's collection, Maw strode to the chutes. The platform occupants melted into the cracks and crannies, hiding from Maw's fearsome rage.

ELDER BLESSINGS

Long had it been since Losgann had lain eyes on the Awen. Centuries, maybe. Or more. They had been locked in a life-or-death battle with a rogue agent of evil. Had the Awen, aided by the Elders and Dragons, not intervened, the entire populace would likely have been wiped out. This time their foe was less ethereal.

Not all of the Reptilians were prone to violence, but most were blood-thirsty, ruthless, killing machines. This time there would be fighting. Not Losgann's favorite pastime. But fight, they would. It was their collective duty. And destiny.

He shifted positions, careful not to draw the attention of the dragons. Not that they would harm the frog Elder, or bother with him. But he remained at the edge of the jungle, rather than interrupting the Awen's lesson.

Losgann had been chosen by the Elders to confer the blessing of healing upon the Awen. And from the looks of her, she needed healing. The gashes on her face had closed nicely, but her spirit remained deeply wounded. On top of that, she was young and without experience in fighting evil. To this, Losgann would attend.

As the day heated, the frog Elder napped, until he was jarred awake by the Awen's querulous voice. "And exactly how is it we are supposed to get there?"

"The way dragons always travel long-distance. By wormhole," Draig Talav answered.

Losgann was aware of these wormholes but had never traveled through one himself. It was said that to do so, one had to enter the wormhole through an earthly vortex. Such things were not of Losgann's ken. But he listened with interest. One never knew when one might need to hitch a ride. Especially one as small as Losgann.

Presently, Draigs Ooschu and Talav waded into the ocean and disappeared. The Awen stayed behind in a chair, chatting with the human Losgann assumed was the medicine man. He waited a while longer, but when the man showed no signs of leaving, Losgann decided it was time to approach.

The old frog was bigger than most of his kind and covered the distance quickly. But Losgann didn't care for sand, and it made crossing the beach a chore. When he reached the Awen, he croaked loudly—three short croaks, a pause, and three more.

The Awen's gaze locked with his. He could tell she didn't recognize him, though her face lit up in greeting.

He croaked again—three short, a pause, and three more.

"Are you Losgann?" the Awen asked.

This pleased Losgann immensely, though he knew she wasn't sure. "Yes, my lady, I am." He bowed and straightened. "It is good to see you again."

The brows arched and he hurried to add, "I can tell you don't remember me. But I have come to convey a blessing upon you from the Elders and Goddess Brigit. May I approach?"

The man cleared his throat and leaned forward in his chair. "Hello, Losgann. I am Khenko, pleased to meet you."

"Aye," Losgann responded. "The great crane, Corr, told me you helped heal the Awen. We are ever grateful. But there are some wounds only the Goddess can heal. I have come for this purpose."

The Awen and Khenko exchanged glances, then gave Losgann their attention.

"I am honored," the Awen said. "How would you have me receive this blessing?"

"Head bowed, m' lady. Eyes closed." When she did as he'd said, Losgann hopped closer to sit on the top of her foot. The Awen barely moved at the added pressure. He was pleased with her restraint.

Invoking the Goddess, Losgann sang his blessing, conferring hope and healing upon the Awen. When he was finished, he bade her look at him. The crystalline eyes glowed, all the thanks Losgann needed. With a wide smile, he coughed up the blessing stone. Gray, hard, and ridged, it was imbued with his wisdom and his magical powers, along with that of Losgann's kind.

"M' lady, this blessing stone is for you. I have carried it for age upon age, awaiting your time of need. Though not much to look at, the stone holds powerful magic. It will provide added protection when you are in danger. And you can use it to call me and my kin in times of need."

The Awen's eyes shone with tears. One fell on Losgann. Then another. They soaked into his sensitive skin, her return blessing. Losgann's mission was complete. The Awen cradled his stone reverently in one hand and stroked it with the other.

"Thank you, Losgann. I can feel the power pulsing within its depths. I shall cherish your sacred stone and keep it safe with the otter stone and Aóme. And should I be in need, I will use it to call upon you and your kin."

"You do me proud, m' lady. I look forward to the day we fight together, side-by-side, as in days gone by. Until then, I bid you adieu. And you as well, Khenko Corr's-Friend."

"Wait!" the Awen cried. "Can you help my friend, Brian? He is wandering the land beneath the earth, and the dragons refuse to help. Will you find him and help him get home?"

Losgann croaked three times and turned in a circle. "It is done, Awen. I shall find your friend Brian and help him get home."

☼☼☼

Emily showered off the salt and sand and inspected her thin face in the steamy mirror. How much weight had she lost? She'd eaten little solid food since the earthquake and still didn't have much of an appetite. Thank God for Khenko's fruit and smoothies.

She dressed in a borrowed tee-shirt and shorts and retired to her little bedroom. Closing the blinds, she drew the curtains against the sun and climbed in bed to pull the covers over her head. After her lessons with the dragons and meeting Losgann, her energy was spent.

Emily rolled to one side, then flopped to the other. Though she was bone-tired, sleep wouldn't come. She turned onto her back and stuffed a pillow beneath her knees, wishing she could see her chiropractor. Every joint in her body ached.

201

Taking a deep breath, she let it out and sucked in another. She recited the Lord's Prayer, then the Our Father, then focused again on her breathing. Nothing relaxed her keyed-up brain. She thought of Lugh MacBrayer and wished she could talk to him, then remembered Talav's words in the cave. She had contacted her father. Why not Lugh?

Sitting up, Emily leaned her back against the wall and breathed in deeply. She let it go and sent energetic roots to anchor in the earth and a cord up to the heavens. Grounded, she let her mind turn to Lugh, to the first time she had met him. Mitchell Wainwright had taken her to eat at Lugh's restaurant, Jocko's Pizza.

The next time was at the carriage house when the druid leaders came to Wren's Roost for Emily's initiation. Then on the day the tornadoes ripped the roof off Jocko's, Emily had fallen in love with the druid priest while weathering the storm in Jocko's cellar with him and fifty other customers.

A sofa appeared in her mind's eye, the one in the upstairs library of Wren's Roost. A fire blazed in the warm space, and a pair of candelabras lit the portrait of Awen. Emily studied the painting, seeing something she hadn't noticed before. The second stone on Awen's wand was blood-red. She shook her head and the vision disappeared. But she knew it was a sign of some sort.

Starting, she realized Lugh was there. He was vague and far away, but he was there.

"Lugh!" she called, moving closer. But there was someone leaning over him. Someone tall and imposing—Morgan Foster—Emily's aunt and head of security for the Awen Order.

"Aunt Morgan!" she yelled as loud as she could.

Her aunt stiffened and seemed to look inward. Emily lifted her hand to wave, but something dark and dangerous separated from Morgan and moved menacingly toward Emily. Recoiling, she retreated and came out of meditation.

Shuddering, Emily huddled under the thin bedspread covered in seashells. Something evil had a hold on Morgan. Did Morgan know? A coldness crept through Emily. What if Morgan was conspiring with the enemy? She had to find a way to tell Lugh.

ACCESS POINTS

Ethnui shook the boy from sleep and passed him her handheld. Pointing to the file she had uncovered in the Draconian mainframe, Ethnui sat on the mat and peered over his shoulder to read with him.

In India, there is still a strong belief in the reality of Nagas - a subterranean race of serpent people, or lizard men. Described as an advanced species with highly-developed technology, the Nagas harbor a disdain for human beings, whom they are said to abduct, torture, interbreed with, and even to eat. It is said that the Nagas wage war on humans from the subsurface kingdoms of Agartha and Shamballa.

Brian glanced up at Ethnui. "This is talking about the Dracos, isn't it?" His voice trembled, but not with excitement.

"It has to be. The base where they kept you is called Agartha. So is the surrounding city."

"Whoa." Brian's eyes widened. "This looks like it was written in my world. But it has to be about the Reptilians. Does it say anything about how to travel between the worlds?"

They kept reading.

The Nagas reside in underground cities — the two major ones being Bhogavati and Patala. Patala is said to have an entrance below the Well of Sheshna in Benares, India. It has forty steps which descend into a circular depression and then terminate at a closed stone door covered in bas-relief cobras.

There is another major mystical shrine in Tibet. It is said to sit atop an ancient cavern and tunnel system which reaches throughout the Asian continent and possibly beyond. This could be Bhogavati, in the Tibetan Himalayas.

Brian groaned. "These places are on the other side of the world. How in Brigit's name would we get there?"

Ethnui hung her head. How indeed?

"Anything else of use in this database?" He punched keys and clicked a link.

"Like what?" Ethnui tugged the pad away. She didn't like others to use her equipment.

"Like anything about me? Or my family?"

"Not much. Just that you are from the state of Utah, and your mom is in Bali, and your dad is missing…" Her voice trailed off when Brian's face sagged. He looked hurt. "I'm sorry," she offered, then went on quickly, "there's also information about an evangelist named Shalane Carpenter. Ring any bells?"

Brian nodded, dark brows knit.

"And a little about an Emily Mayhall. Or was her name Ebby? I'd have to go back and look. It did say she is dating your uncle, though." Ethnui paused again when Brian wiped his eyes. "I'm sorry. Is this upsetting you?"

Brian sniffed. "I was with Emily and my uncle when the quake happened. But keep going. What else is in there?"

"That's about it. I'll see if I can find more information on the Nagas. Or Agartha." Her fingers flew over the keyboard. "Here's something," she tilted the screen so they both could read.

Agartha is a legendary city said to reside in the Earth's core. The mythical paradise of Shamballa is known by many different names by the Hindus, Chinese, Russians, and some Christian sects. Throughout Asia it is best known by its Sanskrit name, Shambhala, meaning 'the place of peace, of tranquility'.

Brian snorted. "Well, that's clear as mud. Is Agartha the home of evil lizard monsters, or the land of saints? If I wasn't here in the thick of things, I wouldn't believe a word. Where I come from, they would call this hooey, malarkey, and horseshit!"

"Yeah," Ethnui agreed. "To people in AboveEarth, a land down here is nothing more than fiction. Which makes it impossible for us to escape. But we will," she added, determined more than ever to help Brian get home.

"Is there more?"

Ethnui swiped the screen. "Yes! Here it talks about the entrances." She read aloud, hope growing.

"There are allegedly several entrances to the Kingdom of Agartha throughout the world. Some are at planetary grid points—in-wells and out-wells of energy. As the Nagas have an affinity with water, the entrances to their underground palaces are often hidden at the bottom of wells, deep lakes, and rivers."

"Wow," they said at the same time.

"I feel like we're in a Jules Verne novel." Brian stretched and his shadow grew larger on the cave wall.

"I know what you mean. But that's a good thing, right? Jules Verne would write us out of here."

"Good point." Brian jumped up and danced in a little circle. "So, Mr. Verne, how would you get us out of here?"

☼☼☼

The light was growing. Nathair snaked through the coarse grass at the edge of the sand, intent on finding Losgann. A familiar voice wafted to his druid hitchhiker and she whipped his head up.

Was that Hamilton? Hamilton Hester? A rush of nostalgia overtook Alexis. Hamilton remained the love of her life, though he had slept with an untold number of women throughout their marriage. That she'd stolen the girl-heir he'd spent his adult years creating was only one of Alexis Mayhall's sins. But it was by far the one that tortured her the most in life *and* death.

Swinging her head to locate her ex-husband, she spied a dark-haired boy. Alexis moved closer to get a look at his face and jerked away in surprise. The boy was the spitting image of one of Hamilton's many children. Shock reverberated through the snake's body, and Alexis/Nathair regurgitated the field mouse she had devoured earlier.

This didn't make sense. That child would be an adult, older than Emily. Was this Ham's grandson?

"What do you think?" the boy was saying to his invisible companion. "Any idea how to get us home?" His expression changed and Hamilton Hester's voice answered.

"I've been pondering that. If the dragons are helping Emily, maybe they could help us, too."

"Dragons?" The expression changed back to that of the boy. "And how do you suppose we go about finding one of those?" The boy reared back and slung a stone into the surf.

"I told you," Hamilton said. "They're with Emily. I tried to reach her again, but can't get through. There is a veil I cannot see beyond. Nor can I connect with the dragons. I think we should try to find one of those entrances. We could be close to one now."

Alexis/Nathair's tongue flicked the air. Curious. It appeared Ham's spirit was inside the boy. Had his body died? An immense sadness permeated the snake.

"I could take another gander in the Otherworld. Ask around. See what I can find." It was Hamilton's voice again.

The boy scooped up a stone and hurled it into the surf. A large fish broke the surface and made a loud splat when it landed on its side.

"Too bad fish don't talk," the boy said, so low Alexis had to strain to hear.

"Maybe they can," Ham mused.

The boy snorted. "Oh great. Now you speak fish?"

Hamilton laughed, that rich, throaty melody that made Alexis's heart melt. "Something like that. Shall I try?"

The boy laughed. "Why the heck not? I have no better idea." Rising to his knees, he leaned on his hands and peered into the water. "Now what?"

"Now you're just being silly. Sit down and we'll try the Otherworld. If that doesn't work, we can ask the fish."

"Ribbit, ribbit," Losgann the frog croaked, hopping up to Nathair. "What is it you wish from me, Madame Druid?"

☼☼☼

Brian sat cross-legged on the damp sand. The UnderEarth sun morphed from red to a creamy-white as it rose higher and knocked the chill from the air. Until recently, Brian had thought the Otherworld was a myth. Now, Hamilton was going to take him there.

"Ready?" Ham asked.

"Ready." Brian closed his eyes.

"Ribbit."

Exasperated, Brian opened them again. For an important man, Hamilton could be a goofball. But a large frog sat before him, larger than any Brian had ever seen.

"Ribbit." It blinked its bulging eyes.

Brian snickered. "Well, ribbit to you, too."

The frog hopped closer, and Brian resisted the urge to reach out and touch it.

"Losgann, is that you?" Hamilton cried. "You are a most welcome sight."

Brian stared at the frog. He had met a talking dog, cat, zoo animals, and now this frog. His friends in Utah would call him crazy. They wouldn't believe his fantastical experiences in Atlanta, much less the ones he was having beneath the earth.

"It is I, Master Druid," the frog croaked. "I understand you require assistance."

"That we do. We were separated from my daughter, the Awen, and ended up here in UnderEarth. I know that she is with the dragons. But can you help me and my companions find a portal back to AboveEarth?"

"The Awen is with the Dragon Keepers, yes," the frog croaked. "They mean to take her to Beli to restore the dragon-keep."

A stark and utter terror seized Brian. His knees trembled for Emily.

"So things are in motion as they should be," Hamilton commented. "And Emily is safe, which is my primary concern. But we need to get back to AboveEarth without alerting the Reptiles."

"With that, I can help. Ribbit. Not far from here lies a cave system. Its entrance is hidden behind a stand of young yew and willows. Enter the cave and stay to the right. That will lead to a rivulet. Follow that until you reach the sinkhole, and be careful not to fall in.

"Beyond the sinkhole, you will find a crude door. Beyond that, will be a forest leading to an abandoned chute. The reptiles have let it fall into disrepair, so you should be relatively safe. But take caution. Travel only during the day, when the reptiles are more likely to sleep."

"Uh-uh. No way," Brian groaned. "I am not going anywhere near those monsters again."

"Courage, young raven," the frog croaked. "And welcome to the fight. You are in the company of a master druid and will be well-protected. Just keep your eyes open, travel during the daytime, and find a robe or some other disguise."

"So the portal is inside the chute?" Hamilton asked.

The yellow eyes blinked. "Oh no, ribbit. It is miles from there. The closest portal is in the mountains where the smoke rises. You will take the chute headed north and make for a formation known as Blowing Rock. The portal opens beneath the leaping platform. Good luck, Master Druid."

"Could you come with us? Show us the way?" Brian asked in a trembly voice. "I would be happy to carry you."

"No, young raven. I'm afraid not. My path lies in another direction. But I will see you again at your journey's end." The frog turned to leave.

"Wait!" Hamilton cried. "I sense another presence. Can you tell me the whereabouts of the disembodied druid?"

The frog wavered, eyes flicking away, and back again. Away and back. Away and back. Then with a nod toward a nearby boulder and a quick bow, Losgann hopped to the grass and disappeared.

"Welp," Brian said. "I'll go tell Ethnui."

"Wait. Not yet," Hamilton whispered in his head.

At his inner prompting, Brian stood and circled the boulder, unsure of what he was looking for.

"Alexis Mayhall, show yourself," Ham shouted, startling Brian.

The wind hissed and ruffled Brian's hair. An eerie feeling passed through him. Alexis Mayhall was Emily's dead mother. Why did Ham think she'd be here?

BUS STATION

The taxi driver drove Shalane slowly up and down the streets near the Ryman Auditorium. Patty was nowhere to be seen. When Shalane's call went straight to voicemail for the umpteenth time, she remembered the tracking app on her phone. Accessing it, she was surprised to see Cecil holed up in a nearby bar. Patty was in motion, moving slowly toward the bus station. She instructed the driver to take her there.

"Yes, ma'am." He looked at Shalane in the rearview mirror. "Be glad to."

He eased into the next lane and threaded the taxi through the late-morning traffic. A few blocks later, they pulled in front of the depot. Several buses were parked at the curb and one was leaving the station.

"Can you wait for me here?" Shalane climbed out.

"Yes'm," the driver nodded, but she was already shoving the glass door open, searching for Patrika Tolbert and praying she hadn't been on the bus that just left.

"She couldn't be," she told herself. "She was walking a few minutes ago. She's barely had time to buy a ticket, much less leave." She glanced at the app and confirmed that Patty was still in the vicinity.

The terminal was packed. Shalane juked to miss a man who stopped to answer his cell phone and bounced off another who wandered into her path. She'd had no idea this many people rode buses.

Making her way to the ticket counter, she searched the faces. None were Patty's. Damn, damn, DAMN. Her heart pounded, and her ears rang. Shalane scanned the crowd for the petite blond. Where was she, dammit?

The toilet, maybe? She located the directional sign and headed that way. But Patty wasn't there, either. Was there another one? She stopped and asked an attendant, who shook her head and pointed toward the bathroom Shalane had just left.

Frantic now, Shalane stood in the middle of the bus terminal and turned a slow three-sixty. She slid her phone from her pocket and checked the app. Patty was here. But where?

Shalane roamed the gates looking for the red top Patty was wearing. In a corner of the station, she spied big letters announcing "RESTAURANT". Shalane hurried toward it, heart in her throat.

There, at a table in the middle of the room, Patty sat eating a hamburger. Relief flooded Shalane, then the anger returned. The ungrateful bitch could've at least let her know she was okay. She strode to the table and stood over Patty with her hands on her hips.

The girl kept eating. When she look did up, pure fright darkened her eyes. It was quickly replaced by the new, cool, calm Patty. Having found her, Shalane wanted to slap the smug from her face. She reeled in her anger, and slid into the opposite seat.

"Hello, Patty. Going somewhere?"

The girl's eyes widened, and her nostrils flared. "Why? Did you come here to stop me? I'm going home, Shalane. I'm tired of you treating me like shit."

"You belligerent twit. This is the thanks I get for all I've done for you?"

Patty's face reddened. She started to say something, then bit her lip. "I'm sorry Shalane. I should've said thank you before I left. Thank you. But you treat me like I'm your play-toy. You don't mind spending money on me, but how about showing me some respect? Or kindness? Would that kill you?" A tear rolled down Patty's cheek and landed on her new décolletage.

Shalane was unmoved. She had seen the crocodile tears before. Patty used them freely to get her way.

"So that's what you want? Respect? Kindness? I tell you what. You give me back that iBlast and those boobs, and I'll give you all the kindness and respect you can handle. Deal?"

Patty snorted and swiped at the tears. "Screw you, Shalane."

"Now THAT'S a proposition I can get behind."

The girl lashed out, and Shalane grabbed her arm. "Truce?" she said, and let go.

Patty rubbed her wrist and looked away.

"What time's your bus to L.A.?"

"None of your business."

Shalane leaned back in the cheap resin chair. "Well if you'll deign to make it my business, I might be able to help you get there faster."

A light sprang on in the gray eyes. "You would do that for me?"

"I would do it for me." At Patty's quizzical look, Shalane added, "So I don't have to worry. I'm not the monster you seem to think I am." The pretty face pinked. "How much did you pay for your bus ticket?"

"A hundred and ninety-five dollars."

"When does it leave?"

"Not for a couple of hours."

"Then go on up and get a refund. I'll take you to the airport and put you on a flight to L.A.. After that, you're on your own."

Eyes shining, Patty hurried to the ticket counter.

☼☼☼

The chute lurched, waking Azi with a start.

On the floor beside him, his assistant groaned. "What the Hades?"

"What the Hades is right," Azi sputtered and dragged himself up onto the bench. "How'd we get back to the chute?" The rocking of the car made his skull throb.

The light flickered on, sending an ice pick through his temple. Azi squeezed his eyes shut and ran his tongue over his lips. They felt blistered and tasted of metal, reminding Azi of the abandoned entrance.

He straightened gingerly and looked around, blinking. The car vibrated as it gathered speed. According to the chute's overhead display, they were en route to Xibalba IX. Every part of Azi's body ached, and his face felt raw.

"How *did* we get back to the chute?" he wondered aloud.

His assistant wagged his head back and forth. The scales of his face were melted and charred, his eyes vague and short of focus.

What was this madness?

211

THE MIND VEIL

❝Where are the other Keepers?" Emily asked, no longer able to contain her curiosity. "Aren't there four?"

"Four?" An air of vagueness settled on Draig Talav. "There are four, yes."

"So, where are the others? I met Draig a-Ur in Atlanta. Well, I didn't *meet* her. She appeared out of nowhere in the middle of Oakland Cemetery and scared the bejesus out of me. I later found out she is one of the Dragon Keepers."

The dragons blinked and eyed one another. Draig Ooschu spoke.

"a-Ur is an Air Keeper, yes. But she is a he. Who told you he is a Keeper?" Suspicion sharpened Ooschu's tone.

"The Druid Elder, Hope." The dragons stared blankly. "Hope the Scottish Wildcat? She is one of my teachers. But I saw Draig Tienu, too."

Ooschu made a choking noise. "You what? When?"

"A few days ago. The day of the earthquake. I'm pretty sure he had something to do with it."

Talav hung her head and stared at the gems on her chest. Her voice was a low, embarrassed rumble. "Tienu is the other Keeper. And you're right. It is because of his instructions that I disrupted the pocket of magma."

"I knew it," Emily said, spiking the air. But she felt no satisfaction in being right. "Where are they? Will I get to meet them?"

The two dragons blinked in unison, stared at Emily, blinked at one another, then back at Emily. Together they chorused, "We don't know."

That surprised Emily. "I thought dragons knew everything."

Repeating their earlier behavior, the dragons stared, blinked, stared at one another and Emily, then burst into laughter.

"Bwahahahaha. Hohohoho, heeheehee hahaha…" The laughter reverberated through the clearing—great, thunderous mirth—so long and so loud that Khenko ran out the back door to see what was happening. From Big Ben honks to the tinkling of bells, the dragon's merriment ricocheted around them.

Ooschu rolled in the sand; Talav in the shallow waves. On and on, the hilarity continued until Emily could no longer contain her annoyance at being the butt of some joke.

Springing to her feet, she stomped the sand. "Stop laughing! You stop right now!"

Talav hiccupped and sat up in the surf, ochre eyes wide and blinking.

Ooschu slithered to an upright stance, her lovely green scales and face-horns caked in white sand. She did stop laughing, but a lurid grin remained plastered to her snout, revealing long, sharp fangs and rubbery lips covered in gritty sand.

"Are you laughing at me?" Emily demanded.

Attrition turned Ooschu's fins gray, and tears pooled in her liquid eyes. Talav left the surf to collapse in a heap on the beach, still trying to contain her mirth. Khenko Blitherstone watched in amazement.

"Are you?" Emily pressed, seeing red. "Are you laughing at me?"

"No honey," Ooschu sighed. "We are laughing at us."

"Which is ridiculous," Talav moaned, sides still heaving. "Because it's not funny at all."

Emily's anger drained away. "What's not funny? I don't get the joke."

"There is no joke, child." A mournful pall settled on Ooschu. "And it is no laughing matter." She sat on her haunches, hilarity gone. "It's a common misconception that dragons know everything. We do not. But we used to know a lot more." The water dragon paused to glance at Talav who was busy drying and shining her gemmed scales.

"So what happened?" Khenko asked, dropping to the sand.

"Marduk exploded."

"Huh?" Emily stared at the water dragon, not comprehending.

"You know, the planet Marduk? It exploded. That's when the druids and Marduk's other species came to Earth, along with the reptilians. Until then, Gaia was a peaceful planet inhabited by the Ancient Ones and us dragons. Only, we lived inside the earth, not on top of it."

Stunned, Emily gaped at Ooschu, then at Khenko, who dug his toes in the sand to lean closer.

"What are you saying?" The healer's voice trembled with excitement. "There *was* a Marduk? And it really did blow up? I've read that explosion is what altered Earth's trajectory. And made her atmosphere more hospitable to life. Are you saying all those conspiracy theories are true?"

The dragons nodded in unison. Water beaded off Talav's snout, and sand flew from Ooschu.

"Yes!" Talav crowed, obviously impressed with Khenko's knowledge. "When Marduk shattered all those thousands of years ago, the Galactic Federation separated Earth's outer frontier from her inner territories—"

"The Galactic Federation?" Emily sputtered. "You lost me again. Isn't that something out of a Star Trek movie?"

The dragon shushed her. "Let me finish."

Emily squashed the urge to stick out her tongue. Instead, she mimed zipping her lips.

"After a century of trying to live together within Earth, the Human-refugees were awarded Gaia's face because it closely resembled Marduk's atmosphere. The Reptiles were granted access to the inner regions, which had long been home to the Master Race. The Federation believed the Ancient Ones would keep an eye on the Reptiles and prevent them from fouling Gaia and harming the Humans."

"The Ancient Ones?" Khenko interrupted. "Now that's heavy. Are Jehovah and his angels down there? I read that book *The Smoky God* and have wondered ever since."

Ooschu wagged her head, and sand went flying. "Yes, but that's a whole 'nuther story, young stork."

Emily spit the sand from her lips. "If this is all true, why haven't I heard about it?"

"Because you're mainstream," Khenko said. He stood abruptly and dusted the sand from his shorts and legs, then plopped in the other director's chair.

Emily gave him a withering glare.

"Don't look at me like I'm crazy, Emmy. Spend any time on the internet researching Earth's forgotten history, and you'll come across all kinds of so-called conspiracy theories."

At her continued stare, Khenko snorted. "Hells bells, woman. What's not to understand? Marduk was the planet in our solar system originally inhabited by humans. According to Talav, the interior of Earth was populated by the Master Race. The exterior, where we live now, was a barren wasteland. When Marduk exploded, the resultant force caused Earth to tilt on its axis just enough to create the perfect conditions for life.

"At the same time, the spaceship-planet of an intergalactic species of reptiles was migrating to Earth. It was irreparably damaged in Marduk's blast. The survivors from both Marduk and the planetoid were left homeless. With that many dispossessed, the Federation had no choice but to act." With a self-satisfied smirk, Khenko leaned back in his chair and looked up at the sky.

"Well done, medicine man," Ooschu said. "The one thing you left out is that dragons inhabited Earth alongside the Master Race. They recruited us to keep the new immigrants apart, and in exchange, promised we would be left alone by both. The veil was created, or so we thought, to facilitate the separation. And it has mostly worked."

"Yeah. Except for the Yeti sightings. And Big Foot. And Godzilla," Khenko said. Then his eyebrows arched. "Ahhh, so *that's* where Hollywood gets their alien concepts."

Talav cut in. "Remember what I told you the other day, Emily? What I encountered in UnderEarth?"

"The lizard-men?" Emily's throat clogged. She tilted the insulated tumbler to slurp water.

Khenko chuckled. "They can't be much worse than the war-mongering goons we have up here."

Emily snorted, spewing water from her nose. Sputtering, she anchored the tumbler in the sand, and mopped her face. "True dat."

Khenko wiped water from her chin. "Hubba hubba."

"Huh?" She blinked at the medicine man. "What did you say?"

"That they can't be much worse than the war-mongering goons we have up here?"

"No, after that."

Khenko's face reddened. "I didn't say anything after that."

"Not hubba hubba?"

He looked at her oddly.

Ooschu growled. "Can we get back to the veil?"

"Yes, please," Khenko said.

Emily eyed the medicine man. Was she hearing things?

"The Ancient Ones placed a forgetfulness curse on the dragon race. It was designed to do two things. Make the races forget about one another, *and* about us dragons. This made the job of keeping you apart easier. But unbeknownst to us Keepers, our minds and memories were being affected, too. Which was *not* part of our agreement." Ooschu paused for effect.

"With each passing decade, century, and millennia, more and more of our ancient knowledge slips away; first from our thoughts, then our memories, then our minds altogether. This is happening to us individually, and as a race."

Emily and Khenko glanced at one another.

"And the same is happening to humans, too."

This Emily believed. People kept getting dumber and dumber, or so it seemed. The fringe blamed it on fluoridated water and vaccinations, along with chemtrail poisoning, and sensationalized news media, among other things. After studying the evidence, Emily had tended to agree. But was this the real reason?

While Ooschu talked, Draig Talav preened, as obsessive about her jewels as Ralph and Hope about their fur. Sudden grief tore at Emily's heart. She missed her cat Ralph something fierce, and was grateful that Mary and Simon, Wren's Roost's caretakers, would be feeding and keeping an eye on him and Hope.

Blinking back the tears, she asked again, "But what about Tienu? And Draig a-Ur?"

Ooschu snapped her head around to glare at Emily, though the caked-on sand dampened the effect. "You have no patience, do you, deary? Our brother, Tienu, was the official Fire Keeper. Until an awful thing happened." Emily perked up.

"He became bitter and even stooped to colluding with the wicked Reptiles. This, and his precious fire, overwhelmed his senses and consumed his every waking thought. The Awen found out and reduced Tienu to a harmless, mortal version of himself. As penance, she relegated him to a place where she could keep an eye on him until his powers were needed once again."

Talav swished her newly-cleaned tail. Emily noticed budding fins that hadn't been there a few days ago. Like Ooschu's longer, scarier claws.

"And then there is the airy-fairy a-Ur," Talav said. "He developed an attention deficit disorder and was constantly drawn to the currents upon which he rode. He, too, forgot our duty to Earth's races."

"From what we have pieced together," Ooschu interjected, "the Awen set a-Ur in stone to keep him flightless. By the way, there is a powerful secret hidden in that cemetery where you found him, little wren. Not even the Keepers know this secret. Well, a-Ur might. But we don't." The two dragons exchanged a furtive glance.

"So where are a-Ur and Tienu now?" Khenko asked.

The dragons eyed one another.

"We do not know." Talav's sour expression softened. "But the good news is: every Keeper and dragon is programmed to return to the Awen when she calls. As soon as Emily is ready, we will take her to the gathering place in Beli and call a dragon-meet. There we expect she will regain Awen's original powers and memories. Then she can restore ours as well."

"Why don't the animal Elders know about this?" Emily wondered.

"Because they, too, are blinded by the veil. But the Awen has the power to see between the worlds, and even beyond them. We are trying to help you remember this skill. Soon we will enter the Otherworld. There you can look for a-Ur and Tienu, and maybe contact the companions about whom you worry."

Emily levered herself out of the director's chair.

"I'm ready," she declared. "Let's do this thing."

CONNECTING WORLDS

Lugh stretched on the sofa in the Wren's Roost library and rolled to one side. Hope meowed at his feet, eyes flashing yellow in the afternoon light that slanted through the tall, leaded windows. He petted Cu, beside him on the floor, then pulled the handmade throw over his shoulder and secured it with a tuck.

Soon, he fell into a lucid dream. He and Emily Hester were on their first date navigating a bamboo-lined path at Zoo Atlanta. They weren't walking, but floating above the ground, like his parents' ghosts. Only it didn't seem odd. Or strange. Or unnatural.

One by one, the zoo population—birds, animals, and reptiles alike—declared fealty to Emily as Awen, Queen of the Druids. Then the earth heaved and cracked open at their feet. Lava spewed and they clung to one another as the ground shot into the air, propelling them high above the zoo.

Next thing he knew, Lugh was stumbling through a hole. He fell a long way, for a long time until he was in a cave of some sort. And there was Emily! He reached for her, but she slipped through a corner of the rocky vault. His stomach lurched. Once again, his love was gone. In the absolute darkness, he crawled toward the corner, recoiling when he encountered the clammy scales of what had to be a snake.

Now, Lugh MacBrayer was not afraid of snakes. But he didn't love them either. Shuddering, he squeezed through the passage Emily had taken and found himself in another chamber. Her energy filled the room. Unlit lanterns ringed the ceiling. A large four-poster bed towered against the far wall, bedding piled in the center, pillows fluffed against a vast headboard.

And there was something else. Something disturbing. He was in a dragon's lair.

Lugh wasn't sure how he knew, but the dragon had held Emily here. He sat back on his heels. If so, where were they now?

Perplexed, Lugh followed Emily's energy through a labyrinth of tunnels, barely able to see the path. But that no longer mattered. He was one with the dark.

Soon he came to a wall that shimmered like blue liquid. Water, maybe? But what magic kept it from flooding the tunnel? He eased through the osmotic barrier, finding the water warm and wonderful against his skin.

He rose to the surface, where he floated on his back and squinted at sunrays peeking through a cloudy firmament. In one of the beams, Emily danced. Her thick, curly hair formed a red halo around a face that glowed with the light of a thousand hearts.

Then the clouds let go, and crystal rain fell. At first, it was a few droplets, then sheets and torrents pounded Lugh's essence into tiny shards. In joyful abandon, he rode the turbulence until an enormous crane plunged from the sky. With one mighty gulp, it scooped Lugh into its delicate beak and dumped him, unceremoniously, on a beach in front of a rambling structure.

He opened his eyes to see Emily kneeling beside him. She cradled Lugh's face with loving care, then kissed his forehead, nose, chin, eyelids, and cheeks, before lingering on his mouth. Drowning in Emily's sweetness, Lugh floated beyond time and space.

☼☼☼

"Wake up, Lugh." Emily shook the druid priest's shoulder, happy to have found him on her first venture into the Otherworld with the dragons. His black eyes opened, dreamy and vague.

"Can you hear me?" The sleepy eyes fixed on Emily's face, and Lugh nodded. That would do for now.

"This is not a dream. Well, yeah, it is. But you, me," she pointed to the druid priest and then to herself, "we are in the Otherworld. I called, and you came. You found me, Lugh." Stray curls clung to Emily's face. Even here in the Otherworld, the heat was oppressive. She peeled them off.

"Are you alive?" she asked. "Did you survive the quake?"

Lugh nodded and reached both arms toward Emily.

Relieved, she crowed, "Me too!"

A wraith curled around her leg. Heart pounding, she remembered the dragons' instructions and resisted the urge to panic or knock it away. The snake wasn't real. Unless she gave it her attention.

"Focus, Awen, focus." It was Talav's voice in her head.

Ignoring the phantom snake that had slithered hip-high, Emily blurted, "I am in the Bahamas on an island near Nassau. I'm with Talav and Ooschu, two of the Dragon Keepers." The snake wavered, tongue flickering in front of Emily's face. She looked past the apparition, and it disappeared with a poof.

"You're in the Bahamas with the dragons?" Lugh's voice sounded garbled.

Emily strained to remember what they had told her to say. But the Otherworld was tricky. Hard to master. Focusing was difficult. Too many eerie things vied for her attention, each begging Emily to follow. But the dragons had been adamant. She must ignore all but her mission. Or else.

"I'm with the dragons. Draig Ooschu and Talav. The Keepers, remember?"

Understanding flickered in the priest's eyes. He sat up. "Em, I've been so worried. Is this real? Are you truly okay?"

Joy coursed through her. "I am now, but I almost died. Talav caused the earthquake *and* the volcano, though she swears it wasn't on purpose. She rescued me and brought me to the Bahamas to an Iroquois medicine man named Khenko Blitherstone. But what about the others? Have they made it home yet? Are they okay?"

Lugh hung his head. "Cu died." Grief tore at Emily's heart, and she almost missed his next words. "But he came back to life, Em. Just like the legend says. Which made us believe that you are alive. You are, aren't you? This is real?"

She laughed, relieved. "Well, duh. Here I am."

"I'm not dreaming?"

"Nope. Well, yes. But in the Otherworld. I'll explain that when I see you again." Emily swallowed hard. "I'm glad Cu is okay. I talked to Da the other day. He's with Brian, Lugh."

"I wondered." Relief gladdened the druid priest's words. "Brian's mother said he was alive, and Hope insisted they were both okay. But I feared the worst. Do you know where they are?"

Emily shook her head. "If they haven't come home, they're probably somewhere inside the earth."

Lugh brows drew together. "Still trapped?"

She shook her head. "Remember me telling you about 'seeing' a lizard-man when I checked Shalane's pulse at the park that day?"

Lugh nodded.

"The lizard-men are the Darkness, Lugh. They are what the Elders warned us about. There's a whole race of them living beneath the earth. And they're trying to get out. They plan to kill us humans and take over our world."

Lugh's brows arched. "And you know this how?"

"Talav told me. The Keepers are supposed to keep them contained. But the dragons are all missing. And they're being hampered by a memory veil of some sort."

Lugh's eyes turned vague, like he was thinking or something.

She pulled her hair back from her face. "Da told me that he and Brian were captured by those monsters." She shuddered and wrapped her arms around her shoulders. "But they were rescued by some other breed of alien, a Fomorian I think. They're looking for a way to get back home. That's all I know. Would you tell Hope and Cu? And the Order? But don't tell them I'm alive. The dragons will be moving me to Beli soon."

"And when will that be?"

Emily wagged her head. "I don't know. They say there are things only they can teach me—like communicating in the Otherworld. And they won't let me use the phone or email. They want the world to believe me dead."

"Ahh." Guilt and self-loathing colored the priest's single syllable.

"This is not your fault, Lugh. If anything, it's mine. I know you want to come after me, but wait until I get to Beli. And please don't tell anyone but the Elders we've spoken. Okay?"

"We haven't," he said solemnly. "I'm dreaming. Right?"

"Right," Emily chuckled. She yearned to wrap her arms around him and hold on tight. But she was losing her tenuous grasp on the Otherworld. She didn't want either of them to get stuck inside.

"Something's wrong with Morgan, Lugh. Something dark and evil. She was with you earlier when I tried to reach you."

"Emily, get out of there," Ooschu roared inside her head. She caressed Lugh's face.

"The dragons are calling. I have to go. Don't look for me in Zephyr Cay. Meet me in Beli. And don't tell anyone but the Elders that you know I'm alive."

Lugh faded from the beach, and Emily was staring into Ooschu's silver orbs.

NARROW ESCAPE

Dawn came late to the grove by the cave. The wind had changed, and the stench of burnt flesh and electrical components thickened the air. Ishkur relieved his bladder and slurped water from the spring, before climbing the hills to spell Inanna.

A thick cloud covered the valley. Ishkur's keen eyes could detect little else. He wondered about the fire squad. He had seen nothing of them since arriving in Agartha. They should be battling the blazes, knocking them down to save what was left of the charred city. Maybe they'd given up and aimed their efforts toward containing the creeping magma.

Greeting Inanna, Ishkur traded places and settled on the hilltop beneath the towering trees. The frilly leaves were newly green, a welcome contrast to his bleak view. Unclipping the flask from his hip belt, he tilted it up and let the alcohol course through him. His hands ceased shaking. He took another slug and clipped the flask to his belt.

Sighing, Ishkur retrieved his dead handheld from its pocket in his pack. He should have charged it before leaving the compound. But he'd been bent on getting out of there to find a drink. Which was probably a good thing.

Shibboleth's goons would be tracking Ishkur. He thought of the two Ceruleans and the way Inanna had come to his defense. A warm feeling settled upon him. Her loyalty almost made his wanted-status worthwhile.

At least Nergal had chosen an excellent hideout. Looking back toward the cave, Ishkur could see no hint of the willow grove or the cave entrance. After his shift, he would investigate the cave's depths.

The doctora had traversed parts of it searching for outlets before they arrived. She'd found a section of abandoned chutes that she thought might be serviceable. Should they need to make a run for it, the chutes would come in handy.

Besides, they couldn't stay here forever. There was a ready source of water and supplies the doctora had previously scavenged, but they had no other provisions. And finding enough to feed four grown Dracos without drawing attention would be nigh to impossible.

A movement in the city caught Ishkur's attention. He stared at the spot from whence it came. The smoke roiled, thick and dark. Is that what he had seen? He watched a while longer, then slowly rose and slipped behind a tree.

Through the smoke haze, he could barely make out a thin line of Dracos in full battle gear marching toward the city gates. Ishkur counted eleven guards. Leading the procession, strode the Draco that Ishkur had seen in Xibalba IX. Shibboleth's henchman. Not the intellectual one, but the one with the red claws. The one called Maw. The Punisher. Ishkur's stomach lurched.

He watched until they halted outside the city gates. The evil Draco Maw consulted his handheld, then peered up toward the mountains straight at Ishkur, who tucked in tight behind the tree.

When he ventured another peek, they were moving again. The warriors trailed behind Maw, heading straight toward Ishkur and the line of hills protecting the cave.

Of all the rotten luck. Trembling more than he would care to admit, even to himself, Ishkur left his post and scurried down the hill to the willows. Time to make use of those abandoned chutes.

Ishkur shook Nergal awake in the dark cave, and together they roused Inanna and the doctora.

"We've been compromised," Ishkur barked. "Which of you used your handheld?"

The doctora and Nergal shrugged. A sheepish Inanna held hers in the air.

"Get rid of that," he snapped. "Smash it or douse it in water. But disable the damn thing. Maw, Shibboleth's henchman, is headed this way with ten Dracos in full battle gear. We must hurry. They will be here soon."

Inanna scuttled the fire and rushed from the cave. The doctora and Nergal collected the provisions and medicines, while Ishkur

erased evidence of their presence. When Inanna returned, the
exiles shouldered their packs and weapons and retreated into the
depths of the cave system.

HEIR UNAPPARENT

Lugh woke on the sofa in Wren's Roost library. The fire blazed. Someone, probably Mary or Simon, had added wood while he slept. Maybe that's what had jarred him awake. Cu lay spread-eagled on the rug, eyes fixed on Lugh.

"Hey, boy." Reaching over to ruffle the wiry head, Lugh sat up and disturbed the cat at his feet. Hope stretched and leapt to the floor, meowing.

"Well. Did you see her?"

Lugh blinked. "See who?"

The cat laughed, that deep, throaty rumble Lugh would never get used to hearing from a cat. But Hope was no ordinary cat. She blinked solemn eyes.

"Emily. Did you see her?"

His heart lurched. "Emily's here? At Wren's Roost?" Fully awake now, Lugh stared at the cat. Cu barked noisily and pranced in a circle around Hope.

Her throaty laugh bubbled out again. "No, Emily's not here, Lugh. Of course, she's not. She spoke to you. In the Otherworld. Don't you remember?"

He lowered his aching head to his hands. The vivid dream came rushing back. The events at the zoo, falling into the cave, waking with Emily's hands on his face in a druid kiss. Emily alive in the Bahamas on an island called Zephyr Cay. He sprang from the sofa and danced the wolfhound around the room.

Emily was alive. In the Bahamas. With the dragons.

Dragons.

Horrified, he let go of Cu's paws and rounded on Hope. "She said the dragons caused the earthquake, then magicked her to the Bahamas. Should we be worried?"

"Possibly," Hope yawned. "But I think it is a good thing. We know she's alive and we know her whereabouts. We also know the dragons won't hurt her. They are bound to the Awen, as are the rest of the Elders. They must protect and serve."

"She did say the dragons are completing her training," Lugh remembered. "That's how she knew to find me in the Otherworld. Mom and dad visit me on occasion from there, but they're both dead. I didn't realize it was an actual place, or that the living could enter and leave."

The cat growled ominously. "It is not as simple as that, young priest. The Otherworld is a dangerous realm. Most of its inhabitants are not there by choice, and some never escape, much less rest in peace. It is a land of limbo—an in-between land— neither here, nor there. Do not try venturing in by yourself. Not even I enter often, nor linger when I do. What else did she say?"

"That she talked to Hamilton. When Cu got hit by that boulder, Ham shifted to Brian's body." Cu whined and yipped. "I know, boy." Lugh ruffled his head. "I didn't like that either. Emily said Brian was captured by reptilian aliens, then rescued by a female Fomorian. Does that mean anything to you?"

Hope yowled. "This is good news, Lugh. The gods are looking out for Brian and Hamilton. Long ago, the Fomore were defeated by the Tuatha Dé Danaan and driven underground. That was well before Awen's tryst with William the Conqueror. Did she say anything else?"

"Just that Brian and Ham are searching for a way out, and that I shouldn't tell anyone but you and Cu that Emily is alive and we talked. Oh, and the dragons are taking her to Beli to call the dragon-meet." Something inside Lugh unfurled. For the first time since Emily and Brian had disappeared, hope sprang alive in his heart.

"Good, this is good." Hope stretched in front of the crackling fire. "We don't have to find the dragons. The dragons have found our girl. Yes, yes, this is good. Now all that's left is to find Awen's jewels, and get to Beli. Wait!" the cat yowled. "Did you say Emily is in the Bahamas? What are the dragons doing there?"

Lugh searched his memory. "Emily was injured, so they carried her to some shaman. But they are taking her to Beli. Hope, we've got to get there first!" He leapt from the sofa. Fear of the dragons was suddenly replaced by anticipation. He would see Emily again.

And maybe Jake, who'd called him from Wales the night before he disappeared.

"You love her, don't you, Lughnasadh?" Hope purred. He hesitated, and she meowed long and low. "Dear priest, you are meant to be with her. Never has the Awen faced evil alone. Always her William was by her side. Now, it is up to you to fulfill his role."

"What?" Lugh gasped, startled by Hope's revelation. But deep in his bones, he knew it to be true.

"When Awen faces Earth-threatening situations, William also incarnates. He must come through you. You must allow this."

The acrid taste of aluminum filled Lugh's mouth. The vision he'd had after the blizzard when he and Emily were on the sofa in the carriage house came to mind. "William the Conqueror? Wants to come through me?"

"Yes, William's blood runs strong in your family. And now, you must allow him to incarnate through you."

Lugh paced the library, brain ajumble. He stopped to stare at the painting above the fireplace. Awen's fiery hair blew about her in a brisk wind; her cheeks rosy, her lips parted and full. Her eyes sparkled, twin jade stones in a sea of alabaster. At her side were Cu and Hope, as regal and wild as she. Awen's right hand rested on a wand adorned with the emerald that had been set in the ring Aóme, and three other stones the druids had yet to retrieve. Her left hand was lifted to the heavens, palm skyward.

Turning to the cat, Lugh probed, "Are you sure? William is not in this picture. Or in any of our druid literature. Why would you say such a thing?"

Contorting to scratch her shoulder with a hind leg, Hope growled. "Because you are ready. Search your heart, Lughnasadh. All your life you have sought to deny your greatness. But like it or not, you are a descendent of William the Redeemer, the man who helped Awen divert disaster, and went on to unite Europe. I, along with the other Elders, believe you to be William's chosen heir." The cat dipped her head to lick her chest, silent again.

Cu laid his chin on Lugh's shoulder. Jaw slack, Lugh scratched the wolfhound's wiry hair and stared at the cat. He had grown fond of Hope over the past months and had no reason to doubt her. His family had migrated to the new world from Italy. But long before that, they had originated in Normandy. Despite this,

Lugh had not known of his link to William. It filled him with
pride and something else—glee, gratitude, excitement even.

Then his heart sank. "Emily is also descended from William.
That makes us kin."

Hope's throaty chuckle filled the library. "In the way that all
humans are kin, yes. But the bloodlines are so diluted any relation
is negligible. No, Lugh, a liaison between you and Emily would
not be considered incest."

He kneeled and threw his arms around the Scottish Wildcat.
"Thank you, Hope. For everything. But mostly, for believing in
me and Emily. We owe you big."

THE WAY

It took some explaining, including fessing up about his druid history and his hitchhiker, but Brian finally convinced Ethnui *and* himself to return to Reptilian territory. Losgann the Frog Elder had insisted it was the fastest and most direct route out of UnderEarth.

They left the ocean and made their way to the caverns. After a long day's walk, they finally neared the outpost Losgann had foretold. It was indeed in the middle of nowhere and stank of sulfur and old death. Brian gagged and covered his mouth, wishing he had a handkerchief to tie around his head. Or one of his mother's sweet-scented essential oils to rub under his nose.

Ethnui pushed past a pile of skeletons and wailed softly. "These are mostly Fomorian," she choked out. "No wonder we couldn't find my kin. They've been massacred by Draco scum."

While Ethnui blessed the fallen, Brian bowed his head respectfully and tried to ignore the dried blood and guts covering the trail beneath his feet. When she was done, they skirted the pile, picking their way over scattered bones and desiccated remains. He disturbed a particularly gruesome carcass and spewed his breakfast all over the hem of Ethnui's robe.

"Dude!" she squealed. "Seriously? Turn the other way."

Brian leered and wiped his mouth with his sleeve. "You look pretty green yourself, Ethnui. Get us out of here."

She grimaced and resumed the journey, long legs eating up the distance. A fine mist settled upon them, dampening his jacket and shrouding them in an eerie softness. His lashes were wet when Brian spied the structure. He wiped them dry and hurried to join Ethnui.

"It's the terminal," she crowed. "It has to be!"

But the inside was as disgusting as the outpost. Dried blood and guts covered everything, this time mostly Draconian.

"What do you think happened here?"

"Who knows," Ethnui snorted. "The Dracos live to kill. They fight constantly, and not just other species. They are a particularly warlike and arrogant race that thrives on conflict and prides itself in feeling no compassion or other good emotion. They hate any race with a soul. They believe us weak. And thus, inferior."

Brian shuddered. "You mean they don't..." He lowered his voice to a whisper and glanced around. "They don't have souls?"

Her eyes were pools of anguished hate. "Do you really think someone or something with a soul would do this? Or that?" She pointed back toward the remains of her kin.

Dumbfounded, Brian stared. "Are you serious? It happens all the time up there." He pointed toward the sky. "Whole civilizations, millions and billions and gazillions of people, have been wiped out by humans who supposedly have souls."

"Not very good ones," she scoffed. "We were subject to one of those cleanses. That's why the original Fomore migrated down here. But they didn't expect to find an even worse species." Bitterness twisted her fine features.

She turned toward the station. As Losgann had predicted, it appeared to be abandoned. Several cars loomed rusty and empty, lined up one after the other. They approached cautiously, peering through the dirty windows of each. They reached the one in front, and the door slid open with a sucking noise.

The unexpected motion had them leaping into each other's arms. Heat shot through Brian. He released the Fomorian a little too vehemently, propelling her across the threshold. The automatic door slid shut, and he squeezed through, finding himself nose to nose with Ethnui again.

This time, it was she who recoiled. Wishing he hadn't shoved her before, Brian joined her at the map in the front of the car. She pointed to the station farthest north of their position.

"According to your frog, we should take the chute to this station."

"That should work," Hamilton Hester said.

"Who's there?" she squeaked, drawing her weapon.

Brian grinned. "My hitchhiker. The master druid."

"That's true?" Ethnui eyed him up and down.

Brian collapsed on one of the metal benches, rubbing his face with both hands. "Seriously? You think I'd be crazy enough to lie about that?"

The pretty Fomorian had the grace to blush. "You must admit it sounds farfetched."

"Doo doo, doo doo," Brian intoned, pointing his finger at his temple and twirling. "Everything we have encountered on this journey has been Jules Verne bizarro. You said so yourself."

"Point taken." She holstered the weapon and held out her hand. "Nice to meet you, Mr. Hitchhiker. My name is Ethnui."

Ham swept Brian forward in a bow. "My name is Hamilton. Hamilton Hester. The pleasure is all mine."

"Now that you've officially met," Brian groaned, "can we get the heck out of here? This place gives me the creeps." He stood to circle the abandoned car. It was dirty and rusty, but at least the dried gore was limited to spattered and smeared blood.

Suddenly there was a guttural bark. They crouched low and extinguished their lights.

"What was that?" Brian hissed.

"A Draco." Ethnui's fingers flew over the keypad of her handheld, and she gasped. "They're in another part of the caves, but too close for comfort. Let's get out of here."

Choosing a button on the panel, Ethnui pressed. There was a whooshing noise, then a slurping one. The overhead lights blinked on and an electronic voice guttered something in reptile-speak. The car vibrated but remained in place.

They eyed one another.

"Try again," Hamilton said with urgency.

This time there was a whirring and a loud clanking as the gears engaged. The car lurched once, then shuddered mightily. Lurching again, it jerked forward and slowly picked up speed, rusty wheels squealing on grime-covered rails.

Eerie shapes loomed in the murky darkness outside the windows, then disappeared. Ethnui settled on the uncomfortable bench beside Brian and pulled her cap down over her eyes. He glanced sideways and realized she had already fallen asleep.

The interior of the car was remarkably similar to that of human trains. Rows of seats faced forward, interspersed with long-ways benches on the sides. The walls were chrome or some similar material; the floor, a porous substance that had a bit of a spring.

How many reptilians had ridden in the car before it'd been abandoned? Countless, Brian figured.

They picked up speed and the rusty squeal quieted to a whine. The only other sounds were a whirring hum and the occasional clanking thud as they crossed intersecting rails. Soon, the monotony lulled Brian to sleep. In his dreams, he was in AboveEarth watching soul-less men and women rip each other to shreds.

GOOD RIDDANCE

The rain started in earnest, pummeling the windshield of the cab.

"Hold up for a minute," Shalane instructed the driver. The wipers beat furiously as she watched Patty enter the airport. Part of her was sad to see the girl go. But the relief was stronger.

As it turned out, Patrika Tolbert was an energy-sucking vampire, both needy and standoffish at the same time. She'd been an expensive hobby, twenty grand for the boob job, and an untold amount for her hair, face, and wardrobe. But there had been moments of tenderness, moments when the artifice fell away, and Patty was the girl to whom Shalane had been attracted.

"Airport Security is waving me off, ma'am. We gotta go. Where to?"

Jolted from her reverie, Shalane replied, "To the park by Ryman Auditorium. Where you picked me up."

The rain stopped again, and the sun beat down. Shalane donned her sunglasses and turned the vent toward her face. Though it was only April, a merciless heatwave had settled on Nashville and all of the South. She was grateful, not for the first time, for air conditioning.

Pain shot through her eye socket. Shalane moaned and pressed it with her thumb.

"You okay, ma'am?" the aging driver asked, gawking at her in the rearview mirror. Shalane nodded. "You look familiar. Are you famous?"

Her head shot up. He was the first person in the south to ask that question. "A bit, I suppose. I'm Reverend Shalane Carpenter."

Shock and awe stretched the lined features. "I knew it!" he crowed. "Could I get your autograph?"

Groaning inwardly, Shalane smiled sweetly. "Sure. What would you like me to sign?"

Gnarled fingers passed a small, wire-bound notebook over the top of the seat. She removed the pen clipped to the cover. "Do you want it personalized? Or just my signature?"

He pointed to the nav screen where his name was displayed. "Could you write 'To Saloman, the best cab driver in the world'?"

Shalane chuckled and scribbled, "To Saloman, the best cab driver in the world. Best wishes, Reverend Shalane Carpenter" and handed the book back over the top of the seat.

"Thank 'e, ma'am. Here's your stop."

Adding a substantial tip, Shalane paid him and exited the cab.

☼☼☼

With her first-class ticket, Patty breezed through the security line at Nashville International Airport. She gathered her carry-on and purse from the bins and made a beeline to the bathroom to freshen her makeup. With plenty of time before her flight, she hoped to see a famous musician or movie star. Nashville was known to be swarming with them, but up until now, she hadn't met one.

She showed her ticket to the Sky Club attendant, who waved her in. The room was smaller than Patty had expected, and though it was clean and nicely appointed in beiges and salmons and grays, she doubted any celebrities were hanging out here. Many of the single seats were occupied, as were the small tables. Most of the travelers had their noses glued to a book, laptop, or smartphone.

In the far corner, a ravishing woman who appeared vaguely familiar spoke quietly into a Bluetooth device. Patty rolled her carry-on to the seat opposite the woman and settled in. Extracting her cell phone, she posed for a couple of selfies and posted the best to her social media accounts, hashtag "#freeatlast".

She messaged a couple of friends in California to let them know she was heading home, then sent her mother a quick email. She had no intention of going back to La Quinta and planned to stay in L.A. with her old roommate until she found something better.

At a sharp intake of breath, Patty glanced up to find the woman staring. At her.

Patty tried to say hello, but it came out somewhere between a grunt and a burp. Mortified, she covered her mouth and jerked up straight, face blazing.

The woman's eyes crinkled as she suppressed a laugh. "Do I know you?"

Patty looked around to make sure she wasn't talking to someone else.

"No, I don't think so. I'm Patrika Tolbert."

"Hi, Patrika. I'm Latoya Cloud."

The woman's sultry voice was like spun honey. Nervous, Patty fiddled with her hair. She knew that name from somewhere.

"Are you famous?" she asked, embarrassed when her voice cracked again, making her sound like a country hick. In spite of that, the woman seemed genuinely interested.

"I've done a few movies. But I wouldn't say I'm famous."

So she was in the movies. She didn't appear to be starving, either. Which meant she was at least modestly successful. And had money, from the looks of her designer luggage, purse, and shoes. But did Latoya like women?

Patty glanced around the room. A couple of nosy travelers looked away quickly like they'd been listening to their exchange.

She leaned closer and lowered her voice. "Would I have seen any of them?"

Latoya's laugh bubbled up like water from a fountain, and Patty's insides went gooey. She fumbled in her purse and pulled a Kleenex from the package Shalane made her keep and dabbed at her nose. The darn thing had been dripping since arriving in the South.

"Maybe. They're mostly R-rated, so maybe not. How old are you?" There was a glint in Latoya's eye that hadn't been there before.

"Eighteen. But I'm old for my age. Or so Shalane said."

"Shalane?" The narrow eyebrows launched toward the ceiling. "Shalane Carpenter? The witch turned evangelist?"

Patty nodded, wary at the mention of Shalane being a witch. "Do you know her?" She held her breath, waiting for the answer.

"No. But that's why you look familiar. I just saw your picture in the L.A. Times." Latoya reached into her bag and drew out her phone. She opened it and swiped the screen a few times, then turned it around and handed it to Patty.

The title read: *IS AMERICA READY FOR A CHILD-MOLESTING EVANGELIST?*

"Huh," she said flatly. "I had not seen this." In the accompanying picture, Shalane's arm was draped over Patty's shoulder with her hand cupping Patty's boob. "Oh, great," she moaned. They were both high as kites, and you could tell.

Making a mental note of the reporter's name, she glanced at Latoya over the screen, then handed the phone back. Patty didn't need to read the article. She knew all about Shalane *and* her vices. Which were more numerous than a reporter could know.

But she planned to contact a reporter about Nergal once she got back to L.A. It might as well be this one.

Latoya's expression was sad and concerned. She tapped the phone with a silver manicured nail. "I felt bad for you when I saw this. Are you okay?"

Patty gulped and realized her own hands were clenched tight. She relaxed them and gave Latoya the most pitiful look she could muster.

"Yes, mostly. Shalane was nice at first. Lately, not so much. I decided to leave her this morning and made it as far as the bus stop. She found me and dumped me here at the airport with a ticket back to L.A. Once I get there, who knows?" She shrugged and let the corners of her mouth sag.

The actress laid a hand on Patty's wrist. "You poor girl."

Patty rolled her hand over and entwined her fingers with Latoya's long, warm ones. "It's sweet of you to care. Thank you, Ms. Cloud."

Latoya rubbed Patty's hand briskly between hers before letting go. "Call me Latoya. Do you have a ride home from the airport?"

Patty wagged her head and looked down at her own stylish shoes, courtesy of Shalane. With a soft knuckle, Latoya lifted Patty's chin. Their eyes met, and Patty knew she was in.

"You do now. My limo driver will drop you wherever you'd like."

A welcome warmth filled Patty. That had been easy. Almost too easy. "Are you sure? I don't want to be a bother."

"Nonsense." The actress tossed her long brown hair. "It's no bother at all." Her voluptuous lips retracted in a smile that revealed perfect white teeth. Tiny gold hearts decorated the front ones.

Patty stared for a second, having never seen orthodontia like that, then sat back and breathed a sigh of relief.

☼☼☼

Shalane mounted the stairs of the tour bus two at a time, thankful to discover Cecil was still out. She itched to answer the email she'd received from Mitch Wainwright. He had been out of the country since their brief, but tempestuous fling in Atlanta. Now he wanted to meet her in Asheville, North Carolina, the next stop on Shalane's tour.

Sinking into her desk chair, she flipped open the laptop, heart thumping as she clicked the link. Her crotch twitched in anticipation. Their last hookup had been mind-blowing, and not just the sex. Something had happened to Shalane that weekend, something unrelated to the physical attraction she felt for the mysterious man.

She reread the last paragraph. "I have news about Emily Hester's father. If revealed, it will serve to vindicate me, and likely bring an end to the Hester Empire. That will be a day of jubilation. I would like you to celebrate it with me."

She certainly would. Not because she knew or cared anything about the Hesters he spoke of. But because the attorney had captured Shalane's fancy, and possibly her heart.

She stopped short and replayed her last thought, horrified at the connotation. No way should she have feelings for that man. He was a misogynist who cared nothing for Shalane *or* her feelings. Or anyone else's for that matter.

Nevertheless, she tingled all over at the thought of seeing Mitch again. Which gave her further pause. For the first time since her coming of age, Shalane's insatiable sex drive had been nonexistent. And it had started after spending that night in Atlanta with Mitch Wainwright.

Fear ran roughshod over her anticipation. Shalane buried her face in her hands and pressed her thumb in her throbbing eye socket. Exhaustion descended, weighing her down. Even her head felt heavy when she lifted it to glance longingly at the bed.

Rising slowly, Shalane shucked off her clothes and peeled back covers the maid had straightened. She climbed in and stretched, luxuriating in the soft, expensive sheets. The image of a sexy blond-turned-redhead filled her thoughts. Mitch insisted the woman meant something to Shalane.

Sitting up, she stuffed the pillows behind her and called on Archangel Michael to show her the memories related to Ebby Panera and Emily Hester. She took three breaths, anchored, and entered a meditative state.

Shalane was in the Atlanta rental car. From the woods emerged a petite woman with curly red hair. Shalane followed her to a park, left the car, and hurried down the path to lean against a boulder.

Soon, Ebby Panera emerged from the woods. Shalane stepped into her path, excitement mounting. Only Ebby wasn't thrilled—she was angry. They argued and fought, then Shalane blacked out. But she'd seen enough.

Once out of the trance, Shalane's anger mounted. Ebby's real name was Emily Hester. She had found her power and had somehow managed to sock Shalane with a memory charm.

That's why Shalane had forgotten. That's why she had awakened in the park with no memory of Ebby *or* Emily. Grabbing her cell phone, she called Mitch Wainwright.

CLOSING IN

aw's thoughts churned. He hadn't notified Shibboleth about the fiasco in Agartha. Inanna was supposed to be dead at Maw's hand. Now, his mercs had let both her *and* Ishkur escape. On top of that, witnesses at the bar reported the presence of two other parties—a petite doctora, and a burly Draco wearing a black hooded-cape.

Not one of the bystanders admitted to getting a look at the Draco's face. And though he walked with a bent posture, and a pronounced limp, the reported-size matched. Inanna had survived. Now Maw was convinced that Nergal had too.

Furious, Maw half-walked, half-slid down the last hill. At the base, he signaled the others to wait. He strode to the place where the signal had originated. The clearing was empty. He circled, inspecting, but the ground was swept clean.

"Spread out," he barked. "Search high and low. The scum are here somewhere. Or at least a clue as to where they headed."

When that yielded nothing, the Dracos grumbled. Maw had marched them from the compound before breakfast. If he didn't let them eat, he'd have a mutiny on his hands.

"At ease. Eat. Drink. Fill your flasks from the spring."

Maw's hand-picked warriors settled haphazardly around the clearing. Presently, a recruit still wet behind the ears, a Draca who had proven her worth in the field, fished a handheld from the creek. Maw snatched it away and stared at the damaged screen.

Needles of impotent rage coalesced into one fiery inferno. He threw back his head and roared long and loud, then slung the broken phone in exasperation. So much for tracking Ishkur and Inanna the easy way.

Instead of slamming against the side of the mountain and bouncing off as Maw expected, the device disappeared. Curious, he charged in that direction and found a barely-visible path that appeared to lead into the mountain. He entered the bushes. His company followed as he navigated a series of switchbacks through the dense foliage. When he reached an opening, he signaled them to hang back.

Ducking into the cave, Maw detached a lightstick from his belt and shone it around the interior. The only clue of occupation was a faint aroma of smoke. Ordering his warriors to follow, Maw strode to the rear of the cave.

UNDER THE KAPOK TREE

Emily turned right onto the gravel lane that served as Zephyr Cay's thoroughfare. Once uninhabited, the island had become a self-sustaining, if tiny, community after the lower-lying islands succumbed to rising seas. Home to one of the world's smaller blue holes, Zephyr Cay hosted a plethora of plant and animal species, some of which were native to the Bahamas.

She strolled in the general direction of the blue hole, savoring the sweet aroma of jungle flowers.

"Got the pigs, the fixings, tents, lights, servers—"

Emily jerked around to see who was talking. Manny, the owner of the neighboring estate, appeared alone at the end of his driveway.

Had he been talking to himself? He shoved something in the mailbox and threw up a hand. Emily waved back, but kept her head down. When he didn't strike up a conversion, she breathed a sigh of relief. She needed every moment of her alone-time.

In no particular hurry, she walked slowly to the spectacular clump of pale pink trumpets she had seen the day before. As their intoxicating scent washed over her, Emily consulted the pocket guide Khenko had loaned her after poking fun at her endless questions. The healer was a wealth of knowledge, but when asked about this plant, he'd merely said, "Stay away."

Emily had seen similar blooms in California known as Angel's Trumpet. Pale white or yellow, they drooped toward the ground. These pointed upward. She rifled the pages of Wildlife of the Caribbean, and stopped at a picture of the pink flower. "Devil's Trumpet" the caption read. She sneezed and held her nose.

"Datura, or sacred datura, is a poisonous perennial plant that is also cultivated as an ornamental flower. Sometimes used as a hallucinogen,

Glad she had resisted the urge to pluck one, Emily stepped away from the dangerous beauty and slid the pocket guide in a fanny pack. She mopped her brow and resumed her walk, slicing through the hot, stagnant air.

The jungle teemed with birds unfazed by the tropical heat. They tweeted and chirped and chattered in the trees, calling to one another and zipping about. Peering eagerly from side to side, Emily tripped and almost did a face-plant in the rutted lane.

Regaining her balance, she consulted the guide, identifying flycatchers and phoebes and a West Indian Woodpecker that tapped out a dinner beat against a tall palm tree.

"Bob-WHITE, bob-bob-bob-WHITE." The shrill call from the copse near her feet startled Emily. Deeper in the jungle, the refrain repeated.

She wheeled as a quail family burst across the road, mama and babies running to escape an unseen threat. Relieved she wasn't under attack, Emily chuckled. The birds looked like the northern bobwhites that roamed the woods at Wren's Roost. She consulted her guide and darned if they weren't.

Turning back toward the blue hole, she almost collided with a black and white butterfly. It fluttered across her path and meandered aimlessly before lighting on a spray of red pentas. This one she knew. The Zebra Longwing was Florida's state butterfly. And poisonous, though not as deadly as Devil's Trumpet. Leave it to Emily to uncover the treacherous.

She took a long gulp from her water bottle. At least the pretty pentas were medicinal. She'd learned they were used as a natural remedy for snake bite, diarrhea, roundworm, and malaria. Gazing around at the beauty of the jungle, Emily sighed.

Some of the worry and anxiety that were her constant companions seemed to have melted away. She had sorely needed to be alone. Her wounds might be mending, but she was suffering from a nasty case of Not Enough Alone Time. Which usually meant too many people, for too many days in a row.

At the Atlantean Center, that included two bossy dragons. Talav and Ooschu were alike in many ways, but both had eccentricities. Talav was forward and acted without thinking about consequences. But she was also kind and gentle when she wasn't pushing Emily to connect with her inner Awen. Ooschu shared Emily's melancholic tendencies and her moods were as unpredictable as the wind. In the ocean, she was graceful and acrobatic but tripped over her own feet on land.

But both dragons exuded deep, compassionate wisdom that soothed Emily's demons. At times, the Keepers made her feel invincible. Especially when the Awen appeared.

Wishing she'd taken the hat Khenko had offered, Emily rounded a lazy curve and halted. The lane opened to a sandy beach she hadn't noticed on her previous walk. Had she taken a wrong turn?

She glanced back in the direction she'd come. There had been no turns.

Puzzled, she sighed when the wind kicked up to cool her sweaty brow and less-mentionable places. White hibiscus blossoms and tall grasses waved gaily in the newly-sprung coastal breeze. The creek that babbled beside the road detoured to rush downhill toward the sea.

Emily followed the path to a narrow strip that was strewn with Sargassum seaweed. Kicking off the borrowed sandals, she wiggled her toes in the hot sand, then tiptoed through the seashell-laced sargassum to the warm, gently lapping Atlantic.

She could get used to this life. Emily had always wanted to retire on the beach, or to a cabin on a mountaintop. Maybe she would combine the two. But that was somewhere in the far distant future. Assuming she lived that long.

She thought of Lugh MacBrayer, and her pulse quickened. Should she try to contact him again in the Otherworld? She'd been practicing. Her pre-bed ritual these days was a brief yoga session with Khenko in the activity room, lights out by 9pm-ish, then her forays into the Otherworld.

She'd gotten quite good at contacting the dragons and Khenko. But she'd also spoken to her Da a couple of times, and once thought she'd sensed her mother. Cu and Hope had yet to answer, or anyone else she'd tried.

A mewing seagull wheeled overhead, then soared out to sea. A family of iguanas she had disturbed upon arrival, crept cautiously back onto their rock, while a pair of squawking Cuban parrots played hide and seek around the trunk of a sprawling kapok tree.

Marveling at its enormous size, Emily left the water for the kapok. She crab-walked onto one of its larger roots, disturbing a willet and two tiny plovers. The willet took flight and the plovers dashed across a strand rippled by low tide.

Emily wasn't sure, but thought they might be Piping Plovers. She flipped through the guide and confirmed her suspicion. An endangered species that wintered in the Bahamas, the plovers should be in North America by now.

She watched them for a while, then leaned against the kapok to peer up at its high, umbrella-like canopy. Something she'd read niggled at Emily. A Mayan something or another. The smooth, warm bark cradled her body as she flipped to the middle of the pocket guide.

The Ceiba tree, pronounced SEE-ba, (Ceiba pentandra; also kapok or silk-cotton tree) is a tropical tree native to North and South America, as well as Africa. Its name is Yax Che ("Green Tree" or "First Tree") in the Mayan language.

"North America?" Emily wondered aloud. "Where in North America?" Then she remembered the ones she'd seen in Key West, Florida as a little girl. They'd looked so exotic, she'd imagined they'd come from a foreign land. Awed, she read more.

For ancient Mayans, the ceiba was considered the most sacred tree. It was the symbol of the universe according to Maya mythology, and represents a route of communication between the three levels of earth.

The three levels of Earth. Chills ran up Emily's spine and scalp, and down her arms. She shivered and kept reading.

The ceiba's roots were said to reach down into the underworld, its trunk represented the middle world where humans live, and its canopy of branches symbolize the upper world and the thirteen levels in which the Maya heaven was divided.

"So the Maya knew about the Underworld."
A large wave crashed against the sea bottom and rushed to shore, driving the willet and plovers before it. A sudden gust of wind sent the gulls screeching. It slammed against Emily and rattled the long leaves of the kapok tree.

A memory clicked inside her. Of what, she didn't know. The kapok trembled and a chill ran down Emily's spine as the willet, the plovers, the parrots, and even the iguanas all turned to face her.

"Hail, Awen, Queen of the Druids," they cried in unison. Then each of them bowed, including the iguanas, which was a sight to see.

Emily's jaw fell open, and tears sprang to her eyes. She stood and clung to the immense trunk as a surge of love filled her heart. Then Awen emerged and swept Emily forward to acknowledge the creatures. In that crystalline moment, Emily could feel Awen inside her, and they dwelt as one. It was odd, but not unpleasant like the times before.

Encouraged, Emily bowed again. "Hail Creatures of Zephyr Cay. I am pleased to make your acquaintance."

"And we yours, Awen," the willet cheeped. The other birds tittered and the iguanas did push-ups on the rock. The seagulls, not to be outdone, lifted from the sea in unison and formed a semicircle in the air around Emily.

"Hail Awen, Queen of the Druids."

Awen stirred and smiled upon them. "Hail humble gulls, seabirds of my heart."

Emily bowed her head and placed her hand over her heart. The gulls lingered in the air a few beats, then reversed direction and dove for the sea.

Touched, Emily twisted to wrap her arms around the kapok, though her reach was less than half its girth. "Thank you, dear Ceiba, for sheltering me. I am in your debt."

The tree shuddered. One of its leaves let go and drifted toward Emily. She plucked it from the air and turned it over. Eight separate, lance-shaped leaves were attached to one stem and formed a fan. Carefully folding them all together, Emily placed the gift in her fanny pack, then touched her lips to the kapok's smooth bark.

Awestruck by what had transpired, Emily stared out to sea until the peaceful soughing of water on sand was interrupted by the strident call of a Sandhill crane. Moments later, Khenko's metal bell clanged, calling her to dinner.

Wishing she could stay longer, she slid slowly from the kapok tree and started for the Atlantean Center. Her precious alone time had passed too quickly. But the Awen had appeared. And for the first time since this had all begun, the encounter left Emily with inner peace, rather than shaky in the knees.

WAYLAID

Aloud noise woke Brian. He sat up straight, disturbing Ethnui whose head rested on his shoulder. She looked around wild-eyed, then the chute lurched and came to a stop. The lights flared on and the alarm quieted. The doors slid open and without warning, they were ejected from the car.

Landing in a tangled heap on what felt like crushed stone, Brian wailed, "What the heck?" He extricated himself and leapt to his feet. He could see nothing, including Ethnui. "What happened?" He dug the lightstick from his pocket. Flicking it on, he extended a helping hand.

Ethnui took it and rose slowly, cap atilt, revealing one horn. When she saw him looking, she reached up and yanked it back in place.

"No idea. I was sound asleep." She drew her weapon and circled the car. Brian stayed close with the light. "I'm pretty sure this is not our destination," she said warily. "We're not even at a station. I don't like this one bit." She boarded the car, and Brian crowded in beside her. Together they studied the rudimentary map.

"Is it hot in here?" Ethnui tugged at her collar and fanned her face. She was beet-red. A wave of heat washed over Brian.

"Yes," he panted, shucking his jacket and tying it around his waist. His eyes widened, as terror crept into hers.

"Magma?" she squeaked.

"Magma," he gulped, nearly convulsing his body trembled so hard. "This is what it was like before the volcano spewed at the zoo. Eeeuww." He pinched his nose together as sulfuric fumes filled the car. "We gotta get outta here. But where is it coming from? It's not in the tunnel. We'd be toast."

The alarm clanged again, louder this time, and cycled through a repertoire of annoying sounds. They couldn't go back. The only way out was through.

Ethnui exited the car and strode in the direction of their destination, holding the other lightstick out in front.

"Wait!" Brian called. "Where are you going?"

"Come on, human. Hurry!" she yelled back.

Against his better judgment, Brian followed. With every step, the air became hotter and fouler. Soon they came upon the source. A gas vent beneath the rails. Steam billowed out, stinking of rotten eggs and camp latrines.

"Gross," he groaned and held his nose.

Ethnui hesitated. "We need to get past. There should be a station around the corner. I saw it on the map. I'm hoping there's another car. Or a switch that will help get ours moving."

Brian eyed the rank-smelling vent. It was too wide to skirt. Holding his nose and covering his mouth, he waited for a break in the steam. Sweat trickled down the back of his neck and he fanned his damp tee-shirt against his chest.

Sure enough, the steam soon thinned and he took a flying leap over the vent. He turned to gesture to Ethnui, but she was right behind him, one foot catching the edge of the rim. As she tipped backward, Brian reached in to yank her to safety.

"Are you okay?" he asked. "Did you get burned?"

"I'm good," she uttered against his cheek, then pushed away. "Thanks for saving me. That was close." She tentatively placed one foot in front of the other. "Be careful. There may be other vents. And pray the station is up ahead."

Luckily, it was. About a hundred yards from where their car had stopped, they found another terminal that was dark and looked abandoned. Ethnui took her weapon from its holster and reached into her boot to produce another.

This, she handed to Brian. "Just in case."

When he wavered, she frowned. "You know how to use a gun, don't you?"

Brian took the revolver with trepidation. He checked the chamber, the way his father had taught him, and made sure the safety was engaged. Clutching the loaded weapon, he nodded.

Ethnui's face relaxed and she smiled just a little. "Stay behind me. It's still a long way to your North Carolina, and I sense the

Reptilians may be close. With any luck, we'll be out of this mess shortly."

"If that vent doesn't blow and kill us first," Brian muttered.

Ethnui's face fell. "Yeah. There's that." Then she brightened and pointed. "Look, another car. Let's get out of here. Maybe the magma will trap the Dracos." Her expression turned thoughtful. "Heeeey. That thing's going to blow anyway. What if we helped it?"

Brian had wondered the same thing, then discarded it as too dangerous.

"I see where you're going, but no. First things first. That magma will kill anything in its path. Including us. I vote we get the hell out of here. And not mess with Mother Nature."

ASHEVILLE

Shalane stepped from the train in Asheville, North Carolina with a song in her heart. Rain pummeled the awning and the scent of spring filled the air. Shouldering her heavy hobo purse, she joined the debarking passengers and wheeled her carryon into the newly-updated depot.

She scanned the crowd, but didn't see the attorney anywhere. Disappointment dragged the corners of her mouth down. Shalane hurried to the restroom to freshen her makeup and reinforce the youthful-appearance spell.

Returning to the teeming lobby, she elbowed her way through the throng. Near the front door, she caught sight of Mitch Wainwright leaning against an empty counter. His arms were folded and his fingers tapped an agitated beat.

A frisson of anxiety made Shalane pause. The handsome face was lined in consternation; his vague blue eyes stared past her into the crowd. Mustering a smile, she strolled over nonchalantly.

"Hello handsome. Care to give a lady a ride?"

The steel eyes flicked over Shalane as if seeing her for the first time and not sure they liked what they saw. Then the eyes lit and a slow smile stretched across the attorney's face, igniting a fire in her belly.

"Well hello, Shalane." He leaned close as if to kiss her.

Instead, Mitch gripped the handle of her carryon and made for the door. Dismayed, Shalane had no option but to follow.

Outside the rain beat down even harder. She had learned that spring in the southeastern U.S. was incredibly beautiful—lush and green with prolific flowers—but it was only so because of its unpredictable rain. She dug in her purse for the compact umbrella and popped it open, then stepped from the curb. The attorney was nearly out of sight. He hadn't bothered to wait.

What the everlovin'? Why had he even asked her here?

She slogged through the lot, cursing Mitch in her head. If he was a gentleman, he would've pulled the car to the curb. The rain blew at a slant, soaking Shalane from the waist down. She caught up with him as he lobbed her carryon into the back of a BMW convertible.

Disgusted, Shalane climbed in on the passenger side and wedged her umbrella behind the seat. Regret and something akin to fear warred with excitement at seeing him again. When he continued to stare straight ahead, thrumming his fingers on the steering wheel, anger surged to the forefront.

"Is something wrong?"

For a moment Mitch remained silent, then he turned slowly and looked in her eyes for the first time. His own were drawn, but his lips curled in a half-smile.

"Not at all, it's good to see you." He pulled into traffic.

"Then tell your face. You look like someone pissed in your oatmeal." The face darkened and he scowled at her.

"They kinda did."

"Seriously?"

Mitch sighed and gripped the steering wheel, then glanced in the rearview mirror. "I found out my birth father screwed every Marie and Sheila he ever came across. Even paid for it. All in the name of siring a female child."

Shalane stared. Now that was a first. And not at all what she had expected. Usually, the aim was to continue the bloodline by fathering a male—not female—heir. On impulse, she reached over and touched Mitch's cheek. He flinched, but covered her hand with his and looked at her a tad woefully. Her heart softened. The man was obviously in turmoil.

But she was anxious to get out of her wet clothes. And into his pants. "Are we almost there?"

"The hotel's not far. Up by the Blue Ridge Parkway. I thought we'd stop and have a bite to eat first." He must've seen the dismay on her face, because he quickly added, "Unless you'd rather go change first."

She leaned back and tugged at her wet pant legs, ungluing them from her inner thighs. "Yes, let's."

The powerful vehicle shot forward, only to stop short when Mitch slammed on the brakes. Growling at the car that had stopped in front of them, he maniacally maneuvered through the late-morning traffic.

It took another twenty minutes of tailgating terror, but they finally arrived at the famous Grove Park Inn. Its winding drive wove through a forest and opened to a grand, rock-sided building that sprawled atop what was billed as Sunset Mountain.

Had Shalane not been itching to get out of her wet clothes, she would have been suitably impressed. As it was, not even the Taj Mahal could've taken her breath.

Mitch parked the BMW under the portico and left it running. The valet slid into the driver's seat, and the bellhop scooped up Shalane's bag. Leading her onto an empty elevator, Mitchell shoved her against the back wall and ravaged her lips as the door dinged closed.

For once, Shalane wasn't in the mood. She pushed him away and raked her fingers through her damp, flyaway hair. "Down, big boy. I'm wet and need a drink. A good stiff one."

Mitch leered and cupped his crotch with both hands. "I've got a stiff one here, and wet is exactly what it needs."

She rolled her eyes. "Not interested at the moment."

A dangerous glint sharpened his stare and her twat twitched despite her discomfort. She added with a smile, "But I can assure you that is temporary."

Finding the bathroom, Shalane shucked her wet clothes, toweled off, and pulled on a pair of loose-fitting palazzo pants with a crepe blouse that flowed past her tush. She fished for her pipe and added a measure of ground flower, then stepped onto the balcony.

The rain had stopped. Clouds enveloped the hotel, shrouding them in mist. Lighting up, Shalane inhaled deeply and held it until she couldn't any longer, then let go of a dense puff of white smoke.

Mitch stepped through the sliding door and reached for the pipe, taking it and the lighter from her hands. Inhaling deeply, he handed them back. They stood companionably on the balcony, smoking and gazing out at the cloud-blanketed landscape.

"Too bad it rained. When I arrived it was clear enough to see the Blue Ridge Mountains." He turned to face her. "Hungry?"

"Famished."

"Shall we get naked and order room service?" Mitch's tone sounded strained.

She peered at him from under her lashes. Something had changed since Atlanta. He was distant. Aloof. Uncaring. Not that he'd been a powder keg of emotions. But at least he'd wanted her. Now, she wasn't sure.

Rather than dwelling on it, she decided to give him the benefit of the doubt. Maybe he just needed food. Lord knows, she did. She hadn't eaten anything substantial since last night.

Instead of room service, they agreed on lunch at one of the hotel restaurants, where the host seated them by an imposing picture window. The view was likely grand here, and Shalane hoped to get a chance to see it exposed. She might have to conjure a spell to help it out.

The waiter appeared with an aged bottle of Seyval Blanc. He removed the cork and recited the pedigree. Not being a wine connoisseur, Shalane only half-listened, though she did catch the part about it being grown and bottled at a local vineyard. Mitchell, on the other hand, appeared intrigued.

As instructed, she swished her glass and inhaled, then took a sip. The wine was dry with citrus overtones, as their waiter had said. He poured more and took their orders. She opted for the Salmon Paillard salad, Mitchell for the Sunburst Trout. When the waiter scurried to turn in their order, Shalane studied her date.

"So what were you saying about your father?" she asked, batting her lashes.

Mitchell blanched and looked away. "Oh, nothing. I'm sorry I brought it up. Just some crap I've been dealing with."

"So tell me. I'm all ears."

He cleared his throat and started to speak, then shook his head. "No, I'd rather enjoy our lunch. I'll tell you later."

Shalane shrugged and let it go. For the moment, anyway.

Mitch's sides heaved. He lay atop Shalane, spent and winded. She groaned and rolled from beneath him. Mascara caked her lashes, but somehow it hadn't smudged. Curious, he looked closer. Her face was plumper and pastier than he remembered.

She opened her eyes and a look of pure terror flit through them. Then her features smoothed. The wear and tear disappeared behind wrinkle-free skin. Did she use magic to hide her flaws?

Rolling to his back, he gasped for air and fanned his face. Hauling himself up, he opened the slider and stepped to the balcony. Someone on the grounds looked up at him. Mitch covered his cock with both hands, returned to the bedroom, and yanked on his clothes.

It was a mistake to come here. Why he'd thought Shalane could help him was beyond his ken. He had more than enough information to out his birth father. But he couldn't shake the sick feeling in his gut. It had plagued him since hearing Hamilton Hester had done every druid female in the United States. And probably those in Europe, too.

That he had recompensed each was beside the point. The man was a letch if there ever was one. And he'd never even acknowledged Mitch was his son. Shuddering, he slammed the bathroom door, hit his knees, and lost his lunch.

☼☼☼

Shalane stared at Mitch over her mocha latte. They'd been having a companionable moment in a quaint coffee shop in Asheville. Up until his phone beeped.

"I have to go," he said again.

"But, we just got here." Pooching her lips, Shalane fluffed her hair to soften the impact of her shrill words, then bumped it down an octave. "I'm not ready to let you go."

Mitch raked an annoyed hand across his face. "Look, doll. I did tell you I'm in the middle of an investigation."

"So?" she pouted. Mitch buried his face in his hands. Shalane flashed to someone else doing the same thing—Ebby, when she was frustrated or down. Or thinking hard. Which was Mitch?

"That text conveyed a key piece of information. It won't wait. I have to go take care of it now."

From the steel in his eyes, Shalane knew he had made up his mind. "Can you at least tell me what's going on? Maybe I could help."

"Maybe. But not now. I can drop you at the rail station, or you can stay in Asheville until Thursday, as planned. The room's paid for."

255

Shalane snorted. "If you're not here, there's no reason for me to stick around. Tell me, Mr. Wainwright, is there any chance you are related to that Hester woman you keep talking about?"

Mitch's brows twitched and his glare sharpened, but he shrugged and paid the check. "I'll take you to the hotel. You can collect your things."

She bit back a retort, aching deep in the pit of her stomach, but angry, too. She knew not to let her heart get involved. Bad things happened when she did.

Silence filled the sporty car on the trip to the hotel. As Mitch maneuvered the long drive, Shalane fished again. "So, is she your sister?"

The response was silence from a profile etched in stone.

Shalane laughed so hard she snorted. "Sister it is. And now she's likely dead. But she didn't know about you, did she?" His bottom lip twitched. "No. And you hate her, loathe the ground she walks on."

He parked under the portico and leveled her with a demonic glower. Her smile morphed to a sneer.

"Daa-umm," she said. "You're a mean one, aren't you? You hate her that much?"

"Woman, you have no idea what you're talking about. Stop shrinking me." He strode from the car and held the elevator in silence.

Where was the man she'd fallen for in Atlanta? Packing her bag, Shalane noticed he only had a small duffel, including a shaving kit with a few toiletries. No change of clothes. Had he planned on ditching her all along? If so, why'd he bother to show?

She fumed in silence all the way to the station. When he didn't get out of the car to see her off, she leaned in his window for a kiss. Mitch glanced away.

"So long," she muttered, battling to keep the hurt at bay. He nodded and peeled away from the curb.

"Goodbye, asshole," she yelled after the car. "And good effing riddance." But the hurt sat heavy on Shalane.

Ignoring stares from passengers milling nearby, she wrangled her carryon into the station and exchanged her ticket for an earlier train. Lucky for her, there was one in forty-five minutes. She settled in an uncomfortable chair and opened her phone browser to read the news. The second headline caught her attention.

Ice spiked through Shalane's veins.

"What the hell?" she groaned. "That insolent twit went and blabbered to a reporter. My least favorite one. Dammit bitch!"

She clicked the link and recoiled at the picture of Patty with Shalane's hand on her tit. That damn photo had been bandied about by the religious right ever since the paparazzi had invaded what was supposed to be a private moment.

She scanned the brief, but damning, article.

Patrika Tolbert, the paramour of evangelist Shalane Carpenter, claims that during a session with Carpenter, a snake-like alien entered her body and took over her thoughts. Miss Tolbert states the alien eventually left her alone, but after recently parting ways with Carpenter, Tolbert began seeing into the alien's mind in her dreams.

According to Tolbert, the being is a leader of a race of reptilian aliens living inside Earth, in what they call UnderEarth. Tolbert says the aliens are plotting to kill humans and take over Earth.

When asked why she is coming forth now, the eighteen-year-old Tolbert insists something must be done to stop the aliens. Reverend Shalane Carpenter is away on a twenty-week evangelical tour of America, and not available for a quote at this time.

A blinding pain like a hot poker stabbed Shalane in the eye. Wincing, she dug a thumb into her socket and fumbled in her purse for the pain blockers.

Not available for a quote? The bitch hadn't even tried to contact Shalane. But out of all the shit Patrika had done, she'd gone too far this time.

Shalane's call to Patty went straight to voice mail. The reporter answered on the first ring.

WAY STATION

The meters crept by slowly and painfully for Nergal. If his band of exiles didn't reach the abandoned station soon, they would be forced to stop for him to rest again. And despite pretending otherwise, he needed the medicine to dull the pain. Plus, they all needed sustenance and water. They'd had neither since their hasty retreat from his hideout, and they had meandered for hours through an endless maze of tunnels.

Nergal kept his eyes on the provocative sway of the doctora's behind. It was the only way he could ignore the agony that increased with every step. That, and remembering her healing touch.

When she peered intently at him over one shoulder, Nergal got the fleeting sense that she'd read his mind. Only Dracos were not gifted with that kind of sight.

Brian and Ethnui gaped at the chute car. It was rustier and more ancient than the one that had left them stranded. She hopped inside it to fiddle with the controls, then looked up, frustrated. "This bucket is a no-go. I'm afraid we're stuck with the horse that brung us." Ethnui leapt from the car and hurried to a control panel on the far wall.

"How do you know that saying? Are there horses down here?" Brian asked, surprised.

The Fomorian chuckled. "Of course, Human. Pretty much everything up there has a counterpart down here. Aha!"

"Aha? Does that mean good news?"

Ethnui grinned in the meager light from the station. "Indeed, it does. My handheld synced with the chute's main controller."

Her fingers flew over the keys. A series of blue bulbs blinked on the wall console, then glowed steadily. The tracks hummed and clicked, then whirred and settled into silence again. They eyed one another.

"Wonder what that means? Is it fixed? Or—" A guttural bark sent Brian's heart to his throat. Yanking the pistol from his pocket, he crouched beside Ethnui, but no Dracos were in sight.

He pointed at the panel. "I think it came through that speaker."

Ethnui nodded. "I think you're right."

She activated the map on the wall panel and zoomed out to their surroundings. Four Dracos approached through a narrow corridor that led to the station. One appeared injured and required aid. They all looked harried, as if on the run, rather than the other way around.

Brian lowered his voice to a whisper. "Those are not the same Dracos we saw earlier. I don't remember any females."

Ethnui grabbed his hand and tugged. "Who cares, come on!"

But Brian had an idea. "Wait! A diversion!"

Closing his eyes, he consulted with Ham, then opened them to speak the spell. With a cracking boom, the ceiling collapsed, sealing the entrance.

Ethnui applauded. "Well done, Human. Well done. Now, let's get out of here before that vent blows us to smithereens."

The stench of metal and rancid oil tickled Nergal's senses. They must be nearing the chute station. Looking ahead, he could see a brightening in the gloom. His forked tongue flicked, tasting the air. There was something else too. Something…pungent. Odiferous.

He gagged, remembering the stench in Agartha. Though they were deep within the mountain, it was warm here. Too warm. Plus, they had reached a dead-end. The ground was strewn with boulders, evidence of a cave-in.

"Hold up," he barked.

✵✵✵

Ethnui and Brian ran for the chute car, leaping over the vent between blasts. Faint foreign voices drifted to them. The cave-in wouldn't hold them for long. Crossing her fingers for good luck, Ethnui silenced the clanging alarms.

☼☼☼

The doctora halted and pointed to the pile of stones. "This is the entrance. Or, it was when I was here two days ago."

"We've got bigger problems," Nergal grunted. "Smell that?"

"Magma," Ishkur said, looking pale and rather sickly.

Inanna sucked in a sharp breath. "Which is it, Nergal? Turn around, or hop a car? Whatever you choose, we've got to do it quickly."

Iskur prodded the boulders, searching for an opening. "The wall has caved in, but I think we can get through."

Nergal eyed the tiny gap, not sure if he could manage it in his present state. "That doesn't look stable." But he could see no better option. "How 'bout we move some of the larger boulders? If it doesn't give way, we can crawl through. Otherwise, we must retreat to higher ground."

Together, Inanna and Ishkur rolled several of the large stones out of the way, while the doctora moved smaller ones. When they were done, the opening was passable. Nergal pushed against the arch and it remained in place.

"You first," he grunted to Inanna.

On hands and knees, she wiggled through the opening.

One by one, he and the others followed and found themselves in the run-down lobby of the chute station. Nergal collapsed to the ground panting, and waited for the pain to subside. It was even hotter here. And the doctora was right. The place didn't look like it had been used in centuries.

A thought flickered through the back of his mind. Nergal strained to capture it. Something about the heat. Or Shibboleth's relentless goons, who'd been on their heels all day.

Taking charge, the diminutive doctora barked, "You two get the car running. I'll redress Nergal's wounds."

Inanna made a beeline for the chute. Ishkur lagged behind and reached in his belt. He produced a flask, unscrewed the top, and took a long swig. Nergal averted his eyes and crawled away from the opening. He had his own problems at the moment. As long as Ishkur held it together.

260

Gritting his teeth against the pain, Nergal leaned against the station wall while the doctora removed his bandages and repacked his wounds. She gave him a sparing mouthful of the pain decoction, then went to help Inanna and Ishkur.

Closing his weary eyes, Nergal slipped into a restless sleep. One in which a red-clawed Draco ripped his body from head to heel.

UNEXPECTED STORM

"You want me to do what?"

"Move that coconut from there to here," Talav repeated, "without touching it."

Emily stared at the dragon. The coconut lay beneath one of the palm trees, half-buried in the sand. They had been working on spells all morning, but none of them included moving objects.

"Okay, this is a first. Can you show me how?"

The earth dragon sighed and rolled her great, ochre eyes. The coconut jiggled and rose from the sand about a foot, then moved through the air to settle on the beach at Emily's bare feet.

Sweeping her arm in a flourish, Emily giggled and bowed. "See? Done!"

Talav groaned—that long-suffering sigh with which Emily was well acquainted. Every one of her druid teachers had made the same sound. Emily was a good student, but she could also be tiresome, something she hadn't previously known about herself.

"No, silly girl. Move it yourself. Getting me to do it for you doesn't count."

"But isn't that a sign of a great leader? Getting others to do things? Isn't that delegating?" Emily knew she was being literal, but still.

"Yes, but a great leader must be trained in that which she commands others to do. The time will come, Emily Bridget, when there will be no one to help. When you, and you alone, must stand and fight. You need to be prepared because that time is nigh. Now, move that coconut back to where it fell from the tree."

Emily threw up her hands. "I can't, oh great one. Tell me how, and I will do my best."

There was that huff of exasperation again. Draig Talav, whose face was sprouting horns similar to Ooschu's, shifted and stared at the roiling sea. Thunder rumbled and storm clouds gathered on the southern horizon. A seagull screeched and landed in the waves, inciting laughter-like cries from its brethren.

Lifting the hem of the lavender tank-top she'd gleaned from the center's stores, Emily wiped sweat from her face and tightened the jute belt holding up the too-large, cast-off shorts. Without the coastal breeze, the heat was even more oppressive than usual.

Talav swung her long neck back toward Emily. "Remember your meditation and trance-work? Go there. Use that state. Connect with the elements, synchronize your biorhythms, and direct your focus to the object you wish to move. Imagine seeing it in the spot you want it to be. It's that simple."

Emily snorted. "For you, maybe."

Talav stamped her front paws, and the ground quivered. "Deary, your snark has reached epic proportions. Maybe you aren't cut out for this."

Emily squirmed. "Or maybe I just need a break. We've been at it for hours." Her clothes clung to her frame uncomfortably, and the thick, wayward hair she had confined in a stubby ponytail escaped to tangle in sweaty strings around her neck. "I need a swim. I'm so hot my head feels like it might explode."

Of course, some of the pain was from the head injury. It had certainly slowed Emily down. She was only able to walk short distances, and couldn't yet jog. She had defied Khenko's orders and tried the other day, and ended up in bed wishing she hadn't.

Thunder rumbled, louder and closer. She glanced at the billowing clouds hugging the horizon. Talav's eyes followed Emily's gaze.

"If you must. But hurry. That storm will be here soon."

The breeze stirred, carrying the distinctive scent of rain—or petrichor as she had learned during her years as a disaster specialist. It was named after the oil the earth releases before it rains. That it was part of Earth's delicate dance with itself made the aroma all the more enjoyable.

Emily waded into waves that morphed from deep green to metallic blue as the sky darkened. She laid back to dunk her head between breakers, and let the surf cool and support her. Charged particles filled the air, followed by a deafening clap of thunder. Emily jerked upright as it rolled across the water.

The gulls lifted from the ocean, screeching. Their eerie cries blended with the crashing of the waves and reverberating thunder as she hurriedly sloshed to shore. The earth dragon was nowhere in sight.

Wringing water from her teeshirt and ponytail, Emily wondered if she would get used to the creatures appearing and disappearing without warning. At another clap of thunder, she squealed and dashed to the back porch with her beach towel.

She mounted the weathered steps as the first fat drops splatted on the wood. One landed on Emily's crown and trickled down her scalp as she ducked beneath the metal roof. Moments later, the bottom fell out and a curtain of rain descended upon the tropical paradise.

Grinning, Emily settled in a creaky cane chair, one of several rockers facing the sea. The storm's cooling effect was instantaneous. Wind-wafted rain drenched the porch apron, but its substantial width provided a haven for Emily. She draped the towel across her body and rocked with glee.

The door banged open and a soaked Khenko emerged from the center.

"What happened?" Emily laughed. "Get caught in the rain?"

The big man scowled, then shrieked like a banshee when a bolt of lightning struck the sand. Electricity sizzled and ozone mixed with the acrid scent of silica melting. Thunder cracked and shook the island sanctuary. Emily raced for the door, hair standing on end.

Khenko slipped inside and waited for her, then slammed the screen door and bolted the heavy, wooden one. Together they stood with their noses against the tiny window as the storm raged, tearing fronds and bark from the thrashing palms and hurling it in circles in the air.

An ancient, but sturdy, director's chair tumbled across the beach and slammed against a tree. The umbrella that had been firmly anchored in the sand ripped loose and caromed end-over-end into the cabana. Another stalk of lightning, this one shaped like an upside-down tree, flashed across the sky, followed by a deafening boom.

Something crashed in the back. Khenko tore from the kitchen with Emily close behind. In his office, the metal blinds twisted in the wind and slapped against the shattered pane. A mini-tornado upended furniture and swirled papers around the room. Khenko dove to rescue his open laptop, which lay upside down on the wet floor. Together they secured the storm shutters, though too late to save the contents of the room.

Another clatter sounded down the hall. Emily ran to Khenko's bedroom. The blinds fluttered and twisted here, too. Rain lashed through the open window, drenching the floor. Then Khenko was beside her, yanking the window shut and unclamping one of the storm shutters. She unclamped the other, and he latched them shut. Slumping against them, he surveyed the room with wild eyes. The storm raged overhead.

"Should we do the rest?" Emily shouted over the melee, shaking from head to toe. Khenko nodded. Together they secured the hurricane shutters in every room.

When finished, they sank into ladder-back chairs at the kitchen table and stared at each other while the storm consumed the island.

"Did you know this was coming?" She wiped her brow with the back of her hand.

Drops of water from his shoulder-length hair landed on her nose when Khenko shook his head. "Nothing in the forecast. A seventy-percent chance for our usual afternoon thundershowers. No mention of a squall of this magnitude."

Emily shivered in her wet clothes. Had Shalane recovered her memory and figured out where Emily was? Was this one of her Elementals? Or had Emily somehow summoned the tempest?

Suspicion played in Khenko's eyes. "Is there something I should know?"

"I was playing around with storm spells earlier. But I seriously doubt I did this."

Khenko glared. "You better not have. My computer is toast."

Emily traced the grain of the table with a finger and wondered how much she should tell the medicine man. Since he'd brought her back to life, she should probably come clean.

For the next twenty minutes, the storm raged outside the Atlantean Center and Emily told Khenko everything she knew about Shalane Carpenter and her Elementals. When she was done, he put his forehead to the table and banged it softly against the dark wood. When he finally lifted his head, Khenko wagged it slowly back and forth with a slightly-crazed light in his eyes.

The rain lessened, and the wind calmed from wild to unruly. Khenko stilled and stared blankly into space. When the thunder rolled finally off to the north, he roused to blink owlishly at Emily. "Anything else you haven't told me?"

She let go the breath she'd been holding. "Probably. But that's all I know about Shalane Carpenter and her Elementals."

The medicine man pushed away from the table, chair scraping on the wooden floor. Anger, despair, and a smidgeon of grief radiated from him.

"Where are you going?"

"To see if there's anything left of my laptop." He trudged out of the room.

Guilt seized Emily, though she was pretty sure she'd done nothing wrong. The tears she'd held at bay too long escaped to slide down her cheeks. Spying a salt shaker, she dashed away the tears, determined to do something right.

She squeezed her eyes shut and breathed deeply, synching with the four elements. When she was ready, she opened her eyes to stare at the salt shaker, imagining it on the table in front of her. Nothing happened.

Reflecting on her weeks with the druids, she focused on how it had felt to calm the volcano at Zoo Atlanta, end an untimely blizzard, and save Jocko's from the tornadoes. Allowing that energy to grow inside her, Emily stared at the salt shaker, then closed her eyes. When she opened them again, it sat accusingly on the stove.

Grinding her teeth, she growled in frustration. Then remembered the Awen. Sighing, she gave in and asked for help. "Okay, Awen. Show me your stuff."

Emily emptied her mind of everything, leaving nothing behind but quiet. Then she repeated the earlier exercise. This time she knew that when she opened her eyes, the salt shaker would be there. It was.

Wrapping her fingers around the cool metal canister, Emily clutched it to her chest and laughed hysterically.

THE HEAT IS ON

Inanna flipped the breaker. Nothing happened. The empty shell of a chute car remained silent and still. It might be operational, as the doctora insisted. But if so, it wasn't getting any juice. She followed the wires to a cable, then followed that.

Where it exited the bedrock, the wires had frayed and melted. Inanna repaired them quickly and wiped her brow. The air was fouler, and it was getting hotter by the minute. This far underground, it should be cool. Cold, even. Yet it was hot enough to make her want to curl up and take a nap. She shook her head to clear it.

"Anyone else having hot flashes?"

"Not hot flashes," the doctora corrected. "But it *is* hot. Where do you think that magma is pooling?"

Inanna shrugged. "No idea. But if we're to get out of here alive, we'd better hurry. Has anyone seen a maintenance closet?"

"Over there." Ishkur hurried to the opposite wall where the indicative symbol was etched on the stone. Prying open the heavy door, he held it for Inanna.

She felt in the dark for a screen, then entered a series of numbers remembered from her days as a maintenance tech, a code that would not be traced back to Inanna should anyone be looking.

There was a hiss, like a vacuum-seal breaking, and the screen popped away from the wall. Digging a light from her pack, Inanna inspected the inner workings of the power supply. She found what she needed, and switched the port connections. The station lights flared to life. The Dracos cheered, including Nergal, who had revived and taken a post as lookout.

Ethnui entered the instruction to engage the car's drive. She held her breath as it lurched once, then chugged up the tracks. It picked up speed quickly, and by the time they reached the vent, they were moving fast enough to avoid annihilation. The stench filled the car, and the station approached. Brian tugged her down beside him on the floor.

✵✵✵

Away down the tracks, a clanging commenced. The rails vibrated, softly at first, then increasing in magnitude.

"Get in the car," Inanna yelled and bounded to it.

They were about to climb aboard when a second car shot into the station. The helpless Dracos stared as it kept going, and sped away into the dark void, rear lights blinking haphazardly. The rumbling settled into a low vibration, then faded in the distance.

✵✵✵

Brian and Ethnui rose from their crouched positions in the back of the car.

"That was close," he shouted over the clatter.

They peered cautiously through the dirty back window at the four Dracos gaping in surprise. Not one of them had reached for a weapon. The car swayed as they rounded a curve and plunged into darkness.

"Wow, that could have been really bad." Brian plopped into a seat, grateful for the cabin lights even though they were dim. It was colder now they were away from the vent. He untied his jacket from around his waist and tugged it on.

Ethnui settled beside him, cap askew. Had her horns grown since the other day at the compound? It seemed an eternity, though it had been only a few days ago.

"Do you think we'll be safe now?"

Ethnui shrugged. "I hope so. That was a good plan, Brian."

His chest swelled with pride, then quickly deflated. "It could just as easily have gotten us killed. I didn't know they were so close." He averted his eyes. There was something in hers that terrified him. But what was she was saying?

"…it's a good thing the Dracos didn't know of our presence. We wouldn't have made it past them." Her big eyes blinked.

Brian's gaze went to the back window. The corridor was dark, the only light shed by the rusty car. "You're right, of course. What now?"

Ethnui sighed. "Now, we keep going. That magma could break through any minute. Hopefully, it won't short out the power to the tracks."

Brian peered into the oncoming darkness and shivered.

☼☼☼

"What in Hades?" Inanna growled. She was pissed they had missed out on a ride. She fingered the fresh scar across her right brow and herded the others onto the car. Maw and his warriors would be here soon. If the magma didn't get them first.

A sudden blast rocked the car and sent her flying. Dislodged boulders and debris crashed around them, striking the metal roof and bouncing off. Inanna ignored the pain tearing through her arms and chest, and struggled upright to see Maw and his warriors pour through the enlarged hole.

"Get down," she hissed. "It's Maw."

In desperation, she punched the button for the next station. The chute whirred, and the car came to life.

"Halt, deserters!" a gruff voice commanded, and shots rang out, exploding against the car.

"Go, go, GO!" Nergal barked.

The car crept forward.

"Stop!" Maw roared. With a mighty leap, he crossed the station and pried the door open to stand in the opening. The car moved at a snail's pace.

"By command of Warlord Shibboleth, you are all under arrest."

Ishkur leapt forward, weapon leveled on the Draco. Inanna pressed a button and the door slammed into Maw, sending him backward onto the landing.

"Go, go, go!" Nergal yelled again. Inanna stabbed the station button repeatedly.

The car shuddered as the rat-a-tat-tat of automatic weapons struck the side. A window shattered, raining shards of glass upon the cowering refugees. The firing continued peppering the car as it picked up speed.

Gingerly, Inanna crawled over glass to peer out the back window. Maw leapt from the landing and chased them down the rails, firing his weapon. But the car was faster, and Maw grew smaller until she could no longer see her litter-father's dastardly enforcer.

There was a roar behind her and a long, low keening howl. She wheeled to see Nergal gather the doctora in his lap and cradle her to him. His keen wrenched Inanna's normally-stony heart. She rushed to him and bent to check Magdalena's pulse.

"She's alive, Nergal," Inanna said softly, rocking with the chute car. "But she's losing blood. Ishkur," she barked, "see if there's a medi-kit in the forward cabinet. Nergal, can you lay Magda here on the floor?" She swept shards of glass out of the way, and he gently lowered the doctora to her back. Violet blood covered her chest.

Inanna swiftly found the bullet holes. "Looks like it went straight through. Luckily, it missed her heart, but blood is pouring from both the entry and exit wounds." She extracted a wad of gauze from the emergency kit and applied it to the hole in her back. Taking Ishkur's claw, she pressed it tight against the wound.

Looking into his rheumy eyes, she instructed, "Hold this and apply pressure. We've got to stop the bleeding or we'll lose her. And that's not an option. We need her connection to get us out of this mess." Inanna placed a wad of gauze over the hole in Magda's chest and pressed hard.

"Let me." Nergal moved to the doctora and pushed Ishkur aside. Wincing, he lifted the petite Draca onto his lap and hugged her close, holding the bandages in place.

Inanna swept glass from a bench and sagged into it to pick shards from her arms and chest. Ishkur dragged himself from the floor with a grunt and settled beside her to remove a flask from his belt. Nergal clung to Magdalena, as the chute car sped through the dark tunnels.

☼-☼-☼

While Brian and Ethnui slept, Hamilton searched the Otherworld, frantic for news of his daughter. He could feel her presence, but nothing more. He made brief contact with Hope at Wren's Roost and learned that Emily had contacted them via the

Otherworld. Lugh, Hope, and the resurrected Cu were preparing to fly to Beli at her behest.

That was enough for Hamilton. Excited, he returned to the rocking car. He studied the fierce Fomorian, fast asleep beside Brian. A warrior-type, she'd taken a shine to the boy and seemed committed to getting them back to AboveEarth, despite having an enslaved father in UnderEarth. Ham admired her courage. Brian could do a lot worse.

MELTDOWN

Maw roared at the rapidly-receding car. Rage coursed through him. They had been so close. He wasn't used to being thwarted, and this devil-spawn Nergal had slipped through his claws again. He pivoted and loped back to the station where his soldiers milled on the platform, waving to him frantically.

Bred more for brawn, than brains, these young recruits couldn't hold a thought between them. Maw leapt from the rails to the platform. The ten Dracos saluted, fist to chest. Ignoring the gesture, he yanked the closest up by his neck.

"What is it this time, you moron?" He itched to take his head off. Instead, he shoved him backward, bowling over two others. "Speak!"

The least of the warriors shouldered past the others. Saluting, she took a step closer. "Sir, it's the magma. It has punched through the tunnel. I don't believe we can get out the way we came."

Beneath their feet, a rumble began. Another chute car? Maw turned to peer up both ends of the tunnel. He detected no lights, but the rumble grew, vibrating the ground.

A thrill ran through Maw. Another car was coming. He strode to the keypad and the recruits parted to let him pass, each as incompetent as the last. Maw resisted the urge to slit every one of the idiot's throats.

The rumble increased to a roar, a car approaching from the lower chute to his right. The inept Dracos shouted something he couldn't discern. He leaned further from the platform trying to see the oncoming car. The temperature spiked. An acrid odor assaulted Maw's nostrils. The chute was on fire.

Turning, he plowed through the Dracos and dove for the opening to the outer tunnel. As the magma roared through the chute, it expanded to fill every crack and crevice, incinerating everything in its path.

AIR DRAGON

a-Ur exited the vortex upside-down in a cloud of déjà vu. As the dragon flies, he was near the Atlanta cemetery, where a-Ur had awakened three fortnights ago. For the life of him, he still couldn't remember how or why he had ended up encased in stone—or who had imprisoned him there.

His search for answers had sent him to Emrys, on the coast of Wales. Now he was back across the Atlantic. But the journey to Zephyr Cay had taken too long. Each moment wasted meant greater peril to Earth and humanity. The accursed wormhole had been unreliable, and twice flung him out in random places. So, a-Ur had flown much of the way.

Rain beat against his plate-sized scales. The front blew northwest, the direction he was headed. He rested inside the billowing thunderheads, glad to be carried by the winds for a while.

The question of his missing memory troubled a-Ur. It was worse than waking half his normal size and being trapped in marble combined. Dragons had immense brain capacity, especially air dragons. As a race, they carried all of Earth's collective memories. Now a chunk of a-Ur's was gone.

He flapped weary wings to right his bearings and jigged to dodge a lightning bolt. Back on course, he enjoyed the sensation of electrically-charged rain scouring his armor. a-Ur had enjoyed plenty of precipitation since the Awen had released him. The British Isles were awash in floodwaters; and in Beli, high in the mountains of Snowdonia, snow still blanketed their meeting place.

It was warmer there than a-Ur remembered, and that was concerning too. But more troublesome was the absence of dragons. He'd hoped to rally those wintering in the mountains, but none were to be found.

No dragons. No druids. No humans. And no sign of recent habitation.

Bewildered, a-Ur had flown south, passing high above the old villages. All he had encountered were structures similar to the modern, insensible ones crowding Atlanta.

The wind shifted, and an air pocket dropped a-Ur several meters. He recovered and discovered he had bypassed Zephyr Cay.

Digging in with his wings, a-Ur reversed direction and dove seaward. He broke through the clouds at a roar, juking when a lightning bolt sizzled past. It struck the waves with a massive clap, sending a waterspout upward toward a-Ur. The storm was more dangerous than he'd thought.

Weary to the bone, the dragon battled on, rain lashing him in sheets and obscuring his keen vision. When he sensed land, he dove and hit a narrow hardpack at breakneck speed. He tumbled head-over-tail, skidding to a stop against a stand of battered palms. The eye of the storm wobbled and careened off to the north.

Lifting his bedraggled head from wet sand, a-Ur spit out grit and let the deluge wash it from his mouth and eyes. Able to see again, he realized he had landed in front of a low, wooden building. He collapsed in a fit of exhausted laughter. He had landed in the perfect spot. The Awen was inside. And two Keepers weathered nearby.

☼☼☼

"Is that dragon laughter?" Emily rose from the chair. "It doesn't sound like Talav or Ooschu." She struggled with the latch and pried the shutters open to peer through the rain. A dragon with gossamer wings and a horned head stood on the beach.

"It is a-Ur!" The air dragon had grown substantially and was now the size of a large truck. Emily had first encountered him in Oakland Cemetery, the day after her weather-calming success at Jocko's.

a-Ur preened, bathing in the downpour like a bird. Of the dragons, he was definitely the most formidable. Not counting Tiene. Thoughts of the fire dragon still gave her the willies. Did

275

male dragons, like humans, tend to be the larger of the species? Notwithstanding the women who towered over most men. Aunt Morgan for one.

"What could they possibly be laughing at in this storm?" Khenko appeared from the hallway, damp and disheveled.

"It's not them."

"That's not a dragon? It sure sounds like one." Khenko's smoky eyes widened beneath the doo-rag he'd wrapped around his head.

"Oh, yeah, it's a dragon. Just not Talav or Ooschu." Emily scooched over to make room for the tall man. He wiped away the fog and bent low to press his nose against the pane.

"Well, I'll be." The reverence was unmistakable. "Another dragon." Khenko glanced down at Emily and his eyes were big. "That's one helluva big drake. He takes up most of the beach."

"It's a-Ur. He about scared the pee out of me in Atlanta. He was smaller then, and made of marble. Or rather, encased in marble."

"Huh?" Khenko's brows knit into one.

☼☼☼

a-Ur stopped laughing and scrambled to attention. A slip of a woman descended the stairs two at a time and strode toward him. This time, she recognized a-Ur and no hint of fear clouded the Awen's demeanor. His heart thrilled. One less obstacle to overcome.

With more reservation, a lanky man trailed behind her. The rain beat against their thin, plastic slickers as they came to a halt less than a meter away.

"Hail, Draig a-Ur, Keeper of the Air."

a-Ur trembled in excitement. He bowed deeply.

"Hail, Awen, Queen of the Druids." He straightened and blinked rain from his eyes. "I am relieved and honored, Dragon Master, that you remember me. Much you have grown since that day in the cemetery. I have come with news. And am at your service." He bowed again and settled on his haunches, front legs splayed out before him.

"This is Khenko, friend of Corr." The Awen gestured, and the tall man stepped in line beside her. "He rescued me from the Otherworld, and is nursing me to health while I train."

276

The man looked awestruck, as well he should. Not many lived to see a dragon and remember. The healer bowed with a radiant smile.

"Hail, Draig a-Ur, Keeper of the Air."

"Hail Khenko, Dragon Seer and friend of Corr. The world owes you for saving our Awen. But where are my other Keepers?" From the dense jungle surrounding the building, the earth dragon emerged.

"Here, Brother," the familiar voice rumbled.

The man's eyes widened and cut to the Awen. The rain lessened, calming to a patter.

Swishing a tail that had sprouted nubby horns since the last a-Ur had seen her, Talav scampered to his side and lowered her head. They bumped brows, his rigid horns brushing her new, supple ones.

"How different you are, Talav. You've grown fins. And horns."

"And I can swim." She rushed into the surf, splashing water everywhere.

When she didn't reemerge, a-Ur readied to save her. Earth dragons don't swim. Meters out, she rose from the surf, flipped an air somersault, and slid back beneath the heaving surface. a-Ur's jaw fell open. Never in his memory had he known Talav to swim. Always she had remained close to the earth. Just as all dragons adhered to their respective realms.

Talav crested the waves, abreast with a second dragon.

"Ooschu!" a-Ur trumpeted.

Sunbeams broke through the receding clouds, setting the Water Keeper's aqua scales ashimmer.

"Brother!" she called in a voice as liquid as her element. Ooschu sloshed to shore.

Talav hung back, undulating waist-deep in the rolling waves and throwing off sparks of colored light.

a-Ur's delight grew. He'd found the Awen *and* two of the Keepers. Now to get them back to Beli posthaste.

Ooschu plodded toward him across the rain-hardened sand. a-Ur stared. Since when did a water dragon feel comfortable on land?

"I know, right?" Ooschu laughed. "Talav taught herself to swim, so I had to learn to walk. Turns out, it's easy."

To prove her point, she scratched off and dashed around the building, appearing moments later on the other side, trailing palm fronds and mahogany leaves.

Unease settled in a-Ur's craw. Something peculiar was at play here.

☼☼☼

Emily smiled as the three dragons greeted one another. Not often had she seen such immense respect. There was much she could learn from them.

"Indeed, deary." Talav wheeled toward Emily. "That is why you are here, rather than with your druids. Any progress with transfiguration?"

"Oh, I don't know. Why don't you read my mind?" Emily hated it when they did that.

a-Ur roared and slammed his tail onto the beach, shaking the trees and making the backwash dance. Emily squeezed her legs together to hold back the pee.

"We have urgent matters to attend." a-Ur announced

"More important than the Awen's training?" Ooschu protested, unfazed by a-Ur's temper. "There's much she's yet to learn."

a-Ur's face horns quivered. "Let me share my news. Our victory depends on more than skill. The dragons must assemble or Earth is doomed. I flew straight from Wales, and the outlook is grim." A chill settled upon Emily.

"Beli has been forsaken. It lies in shambles; the dragons scattered far and wide. We must go now, raise the city before it's too late. There, Awen will regain her powers and call the dragons. Only then will we be able to stave off whatever Darkness threatens Earth."

"But, don't you think that's unrealistic?" Khenko scoffed. "How do you plan to restore a nonexistent city? And how will that return Emily's powers? Do you also think taking Emily to Wales will right all that's wrong in the world?"

"You make that sound like a bad thing," Emily snickered, then eyed the air dragon warily. The medicine man smirked and lightly punched her arm.

a-Ur groaned. "Please. This is serious."

Ooschu and Talav snapped to attention. Emily giggled. The dragons' "tricksy-effect" and their perpetually-sunny dispositions often managed to override her melancholic tendencies.

"Amen for that," Talav sniffed.

"Get out of my head. It's rude, Talav. I don't go poking around in yours."

a-Ur stuck his formidable nose in Emily's face. "Well, you could. And you *should*."

Emily couldn't help trembling. "I don't read minds." Which wasn't exactly true. She had heard others' thoughts lately. Not all the time. But now and again.

"It's excellent training." a-Ur whipped his head toward Talav and Ooschu. "Transfiguring is a good skill, but why do you not teach her to listen?"

"There's been little time," Talav huffed. "And this one balks at every turn."

"Aw, come on, Talav," Ooschu snorted. "The girl's not so bad. You make it sound like she's the worst Awen in history. Considering she's crammed several decades of knowledge and training into a few months, I think we should cut her some slack."

"Hear, hear." Emily threw back her hood and shook out her curls. Water still dripped from the palm trees, but the storm had passed.

She high-fived the water dragon's pinky claw—something she'd taught them yesterday. "Thank you, Ooschu. Thank you very much." She said it like Elvis, her Da's all-time favorite singer, and felt a pang in her heart.

Were Brian and her father still alive? She hadn't been able to contact them in a while.

a-Ur tutted. "Stop taking the blame for what's beyond your ken. Have faith, little wren. I suspect you will all come together in the end." But he sounded worried when he added in a mumble, "I don't remember how I know this, but I am reasonably sure we all will."

A sudden vision came unbidden to Emily—of Brian and a woman running for their lives. A sharp pain shot through her head, and the world spun. Her knees wobbled. Then her vision went cloudy, and she collapsed to the sand.

"We must leave at once for Beli," a-Ur commanded.

"No way," Khenko argued. "It's too big a risk."

"One we must take." a-Ur hunched forward, preparing to battle the medicine man if need be. He must get the Awen to Beli right away.

"She's not well enough to travel."

"Says who?"

"Says her doctor," the man fired back.

"To delay is dangerous. The Awen must call a Dragon Meet. It's the only way. And only from Beli can that be done."

They stared at the fallen druid. So fragile she looked, reposing in the sand as if asleep. But she had passed out and was still under.

"I concur with the medicine man," Talav weighed in. "She cannot be moved. Not yet, anyway. She needs time to heal. Plus, she has to master the essentials, a-Ur. She cannot travel between worlds confidently or without assistance. She's just learning transfiguration and knows nothing of shape-shifting. Nor has she mastered the concept of environmental magic, much less the science of creating storms. And as you said, she must learn how to listen."

a-Ur groaned and turned his eyes to the sky. The storm had moved on, leaving an azure canopy dotted with fluffy clouds. A moderate trade wind swayed the upper branches of the tallest palms, those not broken on his landing. The wind called the air dragon to action. But the girl wasn't ready. Or well.

He snuffed the breezes, lifting his snout to the moisture-laden scent of salty fish, and something else. a-Ur's dragon heart beat faster. Something was out there.

And whatever it was, wasn't waiting.

RUNNING ON EMPTY

Brian woke abruptly, pain echoing through his body. It took him a second to realize that the chute car had ejected them again.

"Stop doing that!" he growled, leaping to his feet and patting schmutz from his pants. He followed a grumbling Ethnui to a directory etched on the stone wall. At least they were in a lighted station.

"It's warm in here." He tugged off his jacket and tied it around his waist.

The Fomorian turned to meet his eyes. "Please tell me it's not the magma again."

"It doesn't smell like magma." He twisted to peer pensively down the tunnel behind them. "We must have traveled a long way by now." He had no idea how far, but prayed it was enough. The car hummed quietly beside him on the tracks.

"Hey! This spur leads to Blowing Rock," Ethnui called. "Look!"

He hurried to her and eyeballed the directory. According to the map, there was indeed a spur leading north and east out of the station.

Giving her a high-five, Brian flapped his elbows and crowed like a rooster. Ethnui giggled and danced, too, though hers was more sedate and sexier. He stopped to watch, grinning wide.

Hamilton interrupted them both. "Are you sure this place is deserted? And why is it so blasted hot?"

Ethnui drew her cloak close and peered around. "Good questions, sir."

They searched the station and the halls outside the sliding doors. The place was deserted, save them. Brian breathed a sigh of relief.

"The coast is clear. But if the magma is headed this way, we'd better hurry." He boarded the northeast-bound car. "This one should get us to Blowing Rock, right?" Ethnui crowded in beside him.

"It should." She reached for the destination button and a clanging commenced. They both jumped, then laughed nervously. Until another, more ominous, rumble sounded and the lights of a chute car pierced the shadows far down the tracks.

Brian nearly crapped his pants when a whoop of warning preceded the approaching car.

Ethnui grabbed their packs and leapt to the platform, dragging Brian with her.

"Hide!" She shoved him through the sliding door into the corridor beyond. "Which way?" she cried. Neither was the direction they needed.

She consulted her handheld as the chute car rumbled into the station and squealed to a stop.

"That way." She took off running. Brian followed.

They loped side by side as noiselessly as possible until they reached another junction and stopped to look back. Brian held his breath and listened intently, then let it go when there were no sounds of pursuit.

Ethnui checked their bearings and pointed to the right. "I think we should stay away from the chutes and walk from here. Just keep that gun handy and watch out for Dracos."

Brian stared at her. "Walk to Blowing Rock? That's a long way." His feet hurt. He needed to take a dump. And it felt like days since they had eaten a good meal.

"Yes, it is. But I think it wise. That station was well-used. If we're in Draco territory, we have to be careful." Ethnui didn't sound pleased, which made Brian feel a little better.

They left the well-lit corridor for a narrower, darker one that reeked of mold and decay. Finally, Brian could wait no longer. "Can we stop? I'm starving. And I need to use the john."

The Fomorian halted and stared. "John?"

"Toilet," he explained, massaging his forehead. He'd been nursing a headache ever since they'd leapt over the steam vent.

"Oh." She pointed back the way they'd come. "Go ahead, I'll wait."

He walked a way for privacy and found a shallow alcove, grateful for the paper Ethnui had packed. He did his business and hurried back to her dreaming of bacon and eggs with crisp toast and salty butter and crunchy hash browns, or even the grits he had learned to enjoy in Atlanta.

"I have *got* to eat," he announced when he reached Ethnui.

She handed him one of the hard biscuits and took one for herself. He could tell from the size of the bag there weren't many left. Brian thanked her and wolfed his down. With water, it barely put a dent in his appetite.

Ethnui resumed the lead, gobbling up the distance with her long stride. After a while, a buzzer sounded, and a door slid open behind them. They crouched silently in the shadows. A large being entered the corridor, speaking in an unfamiliar tongue. Several more followed. They moved in the opposite direction, toward the chute.

"That was close," Brian whispered. "Those didn't sound like lizard-men."

"They aren't. They're Ceruleans. Some of them are harmless. But most have thrown their lot in with the Dracos. They are not to be trusted."

Ethnui consulted the handheld. She tapped it, jiggled it in a figure-eight, and looked again. "Seems we're off the map. No GPS signal. But the compass indicates we're heading due east."

He rubbed his temples and pinched the bridge of his nose. Ethnui's thin eyebrows arched.

"Headache?"

He nodded, though he hated being a wuss.

"Come 'ere."

Brian sidled closer.

Standing behind him, Ethnui spread her fingertips around his skull. Lightly at first, then with increasing pressure, she massaged his temples and the top of his head. Her fingers circled slowly, covering every inch of Brian's skull, then hooked to perform a quick lift at the base of his cranium. Slowly, she bent his head forward as far as it would go, then did the same in the backward position.

As she worked, Brian felt the tension drain from his temples
and behind his eyes. In no time at all the pain was gone.

He swung around. "Wow. How'd you do that?"

"Easy. Just find the right points, apply pressure, and voila."

"Good to know." He eyed the Fomorian with growing respect.
"Thank you. I feel a lot better."

"Good." Her smile widened to a grin. "Let's walk a bit further
and find a place to rest. According to my handheld, we've been at
it for thirty hours."

Brian groaned. No wonder he was worn out. He hadn't stayed
up that long in, like…ever. Much less, walking.

He trailed her lean outline in the dim light, thinking about
being in AboveEarth and sleeping for days in his comfy bed.
Which made him wonder again how his Uncle Lugh had fared,
and whether Emily was still with the dragons.

Brian stopped short. How could he have forgotten? The
earthquake seemed so long ago. Would they never get out of this
nightmare?

PROJECT START-UP

Whatever had scorched them, Azi's assistant had taken the brunt. Azi escaped with a singed face and earholes. Randar remained in isolation in the medical ward, with deep burns over much of his body.

Still bandaged, Azi settled at the console to peruse the list of target candidates. He had gladly returned to the rarified atmosphere of the laboratory, assigning the search for access points to his best apprentice—a younger, more-dare-devilish version of himself.

Each crew he sent out had similar experiences, reporting back burned, the search abandoned. On the plus side, four of the worldwide human targets were now connected and ready to go live. Soon they would perform their first trial run.

If all went well, Azi would earn his family a seat on Shibboleth's council. His parents and siblings would be happy to accept the honor. Azi planned to remain in the lab.

Returning his attention to Nergal's brainstorm, he memorized the coordinates and names of each of the four locations, the corresponding target, and the connecting being. Shalane and the Fomorian lying on the slab in front of Azi made five.

He dictated a memo to Shibboleth, outlining his plan for the trial, and hoped the commandant would remain in Irkalla. The gruesome Draco gave Azi the creeps.

NOW WHAT?

Inanna checked Magdalena's pulse. It was racing and thready. They had staunched the bleeding, but hours had passed, and the doctora had not regained consciousness. Inanna would have to wake her soon.

The doctora claimed to have an ally in Araf—a loyal physician who would treat the Dracos and provide shelter and a place to hide. Magdalena had assured them he held no loyalty to Shibboleth. She had called him a miracle worker. They needed one.

Nergal's breath was shallow, and his face pale. He had passed out soon after they boarded, and slept next to the doctora on the floor. Inanna's own pain had been in abeyance for most of their flight from Agartha. The doctora's ministrations had worked wonders.

But Inanna was beginning to have other difficulties. Her breathing was labored from the ribs she'd reinjured in the haste to escape Maw, and blood oozed from a few of the puncture wounds inflicted by the glass shards. Worse, fatigue sapped her vigor. She and the others needed food and rest.

At least the electronics in the decrepit chute car had begun working. According to the overhead map, they were nearing the border between Agartha and Araf. Inanna moved to the panel and entered the code to stop the car at the next station.

At some point, they had left the abandoned tracks and crossed into a more populated area. The car had stopped at a couple of stations, and a few beings had tried to board. On seeing the damage and the four Dracos inside, each had opted to wait for another ride.

As the car approached the next station, Inanna spied two figures on the platform. They were fairly small and looked to be

Fomorian. Or maybe human, though that was a stretch. Humans rarely frequented UnderEarth. Most ended up as food for the more barbaric Dracos. The beings slipped through the station door and disappeared.

The car came to a screeching stop beside another that idled, doors open. It looked like the car that had roared past them earlier. They had encountered others, but all heading in the opposite direction. Inanna debarked to search for the beings and the facilities.

RENDEZVOUS

Exhausted, Emily sank into the narrow bed and dragged the covers over her head. As mattresses went, it wasn't half bad. She had slept on worse in remote areas of the world while a disaster specialist. But she sorely needed to talk to Lugh. a-Ur had arrived and was insisting the dragons take her to Beli at once.

She scooted upright and propped against the wall, then focused on entering the Otherworld. In the fog, her mind wandered to Lugh's celebratory kiss at Zoo Atlanta. It had rocked her world. Until the peak collapsed beneath them.

She pushed away the horror and concentrated on how the kiss had felt. Her insides went all warm and gooey, until she realized she was surrounded by strange, shadowy creatures. They advanced upon Emily, intent on luring her away from the path.

Out loud she repeated, "These are not real, these are not real," and focused her attention on finding Lugh. She charged through the apparitions and hurried along the passage, searching for the place where they last met.

Feeling a trifle silly, Emily called out loud, "Lugh! Lugh MacBrayer! Where are you?"

She wandered a while, searching and calling, but got no answer. When the umpteenth apparition climbed up her leg, a phone jangled, yanking Emily back to the real world.

☼☼☼

Lugh entered the house with Cu close on his heels. They were just getting home from another called meeting. Luckily for Lugh, Arthur Creeley had done the heavy lifting, standing in as Grand

Druid pending Emily's return. He'd taken most of the flak from the few dissenters, who were vicious and relentless.

Despite the evidence to the contrary, they contended Emily was dead and demanded the clan appoint a new Grand Druid. Thankfully, their de facto leader, Mitchell Wainwright, wasn't in attendance. He had crashed the first meeting, but as Emily had previously fired him as Order attorney, Arthur had kicked him out. Simon, the caretaker, had shown him the door.

The druids were all weary of the debate. Arthur finally conceded to schedule a motion for the following week. The two sides agreed to let the Order's vote stand, however it went down. Which worried Lugh, though Morgan Foster insisted the dissenters were a minority. Still, his trouble-radar was on high alert.

His healing brain throbbed despite the pain meds, and he was too wired to sleep. He wandered to Brian's room and half-heartedly folded a basket of clean clothes and put them away. A tear escaped, and he dashed it away, annoyed. He must get it together.

Overcome by a sudden need to lie down, Lugh shuffled to his room. He shucked his shoes and crawled under the covers. Shivering, he dragged the wool blanket at his feet up to his shoulders. Cu bounded into the room and leapt on the bed, taking up more than half.

☼☼☼

Emily came to in the small bed in the Atlantean Center. Down the hall, Khenko's phone rang loudly and insistently. He'd stuck his head in earlier to say he was going to Settler's Cove to service his boat. Had he forgotten to take his phone? Or had Emily been out of it when Khenko returned?

When the phone kept ringing, she slipped out of bed and padded down the hall. The ceiling fans whirled, stirring the thick air. She lifted her heavy hair from her neck as she entered Khenko's office. The phone buzzed and jangled on his desk, but Khenko wasn't there.

She hurried through the center, but couldn't find him. Nor did he answer when she called to him from the back door or the front. Butterflies did loop-de-loops in her belly. Khenko wasn't here, but his phone was. Dare she use it to call Lugh?

She thought of the dragons and their dire threats. If Armageddon was coming one way or the other, what could it hurt? She hurried to Khenko's office and punched the numbers Lugh had made her memorize. From the other end, a familiar, and sleep-drenched, southern drawl warmed her heart.

"Hullo?"

"Lugh, it's me. Emily."

"Emily, omigod! Where are you?"

"I'm still on Zephyr Cay, but I don't have long. Khenko will be back any minute, and I'm not supposed to use the phone."

"I've been so worried." Her heartstrings twanged.

"I know. I'm sorry I haven't called sooner. But, the dragons insisted all sorts of awful things would happen if I did. Still, I had an opportunity, so here I am. Have you heard from Brian and Da?"

"No, not yet. Have you?"

"Uh-uh. But I had a vision of Brian with a woman…" Her voice hitched and she swallowed hard. "Lugh, they were running for their lives."

There was a noise on the back porch and Emily's pulse raced.

"I have to hang up. But the Keepers are taking me to Beli. If not tomorrow, then soon. a-Ur says the dragons have scattered far and wide, and only I can bring them together." Her heart thudded at the audacious undertaking. "They say the gathering place is the source of their power. But it's fallen into decay and must be restored." The weight of the world sat heavy on Emily's shoulders. Her voice took on a high-pitched edge.

"Can you bring Awen's handbook and meet me there? I don't think I can do this without help, Lugh. I need you. And Hope and Cu. Can y'all meet me in Beli?" Knowing how the druid priest felt about Wales, she added sweetly, "Pretty please?"

Lugh didn't hesitate. "Of course, Emily. Anything for you. The Elders and I will meet you in Wales and I'll bring the handbook. Where is it?"

She hastily explained, then a chill came over her, and she was standing on the face of a snow-covered mountain. Shivering, she blinked and was back in Khenko's office with his phone in her hand. "Lugh, are you there?"

"Uh-huh." The back door slammed.

"Gotta go," she whispered. "I love you."

Laying the phone where she'd found it, she slipped through the door and back into her room. The ever-present uneasy feeling in her gut reared its ugly head.

☼☼☼

Lugh vaulted out of bed and danced in place. "She loves me!" Cu yapped and danced with him.

But Emily had sounded frightened. Lugh stopped dancing and rubbed Cu's head. Oh goddess, he'd promised to meet her in Beli. With the Elders. His brother Jake had never come home from there.

Lugh conveyed Emily's news to the wolfhound and slid a pain pill from the vial on the nightstand. His head throbbed, and he needed help if he was going to Wales in search of dragons. He was about to pop it in his mouth when Cu spoke aloud.

"Put it away," the Elder ordered. "That is not the help you need."

Lugh stared slack-jawed. He'd never heard Cu talk except as Hamilton Hester. Speechless, he stared at the enormous dog.

Cu licked his lips and sat back on his haunches. "Young raven, you must pull it together. This quest depends on you. The *world* depends on you. Get rid of those pills. Throw them away, remove the temptation. It's time you accept your destiny."

Lugh stared into the solemn brown eyes. He knew Cu was right. The pills didn't help that much anyway—plus, they clouded his thinking and made him sleep. Like Emily and the two animal Elders, Lugh was bound to the Awen Order and its affairs.

His life, like hers, was no longer his own. Not that it ever had been. Once a druid, always a druid. Which meant relinquishing the importance of one's life in deference to that of the Order. Since its primary purpose was to protect and defend Earth, Lugh couldn't well do that medicated.

Cu was right. Lugh had to pull it together.

He stared at the pill and returned it to the vial, which he threw in the wire waste can. But the amber bottle lay accusingly at the bottom of the receptacle. He stared at it, then dug it out and buried the bottle in his sock drawer.

Electricity washed through the room and the hairs stood at attention on Lugh's arms. He twisted to scan for his deceased parents. "Mom? Dad? Are you here?"

Cu reared to put his paws on Lugh's shoulders, and he almost collapsed beneath the dog's weight. Regaining his balance, he hugged the dog tight.

"Thank you, big guy. I needed that. I'll try not to let you down." Cu licked Lugh's face and retreated.

Lugh wiped away dog slobber. "Emily sounded frightened. But I'm not sure I'm up to meeting her in Beli."

The wolfhound yipped three times and ended on a long howl.

"And what exactly does that mean?"

The dog shook until its jowls flapped, then gazed steadily at Lugh. "Whether you are prepared or not, we must go to our Grand Druid."

The scent of lilacs wafted to Lugh then, and the chills ran up his spine. His mother floated through the closed door, and his father appeared out of nowhere at Lugh's side.

"Son," he said with a woeful expression, patting Lugh's shoulder. "Your mother has news." Lugh's throat tightened. Whatever it was, it was not good.

"Ma?"

She floated to Lugh, and her normally-twinkling eyes were solemn pools. She brushed his cheek with an otherworldly hand.

"You may want to sit down for this, son."

He plopped on the bed, and Cu sat at his feet whining.

His mother addressed the animal Elder first. "Hello, Cu. I am glad you're here. My news is startling."

Lugh cleared his throat. He eyed his parents' ghosts, not sure he was ready to hear what they had come to tell him.

"Your brother is alive. We've located him."

Lugh's jaw fell open. Except for that. "Jake? Where?" He leapt from the bed.

His parents exchanged a look. "You're not going to like it. He's still in Wales."

Lugh gulped. "Not Beli, by any chance? That's where the dragons are taking Emily. She wants us to meet her there."

"His exact location is unclear. But, the Alien Intelligence Agency sent Jake to search for dragons. Beli is a good place to begin your search."

"Alien *what*? I thought he was working for a corporation."

"The Alien Intelligence Agency. It's a branch of the U.S. Space Force dedicated to finding and communicating with extraterrestrials. Or in Jake's case, dragons."

Lugh expelled a long breath, not sure whether to be relieved or angry. He had suspected as much. Jake had always been obsessed with dragons. He'd insisted they still lived and were hiding in plain sight.

"Did you know this all along?"

She lovingly brushed his cheek again. "No, son. Not until recently."

"Why would Jake let me think he was dead?" Lugh buried his face in his hands.

Never one to coddle, his father tutted. "Maybe something happened and he couldn't. Secrecy was a crucial condition of his employment. You know now. And there is work to be done."

His mother nodded vigorously. "Emily needs help. Your help." She nodded to Cu. "And that of the animal Elders. But, there is more. You know Rona Wainwright?"

"Your friend? Mitch's mother?"

She scratched her ethereal head and cut her eyes to his father, then back to Lugh. "Rona is also Emily's mother."

Lugh's stomach lurched. "Rona is…*what?*" He stood to pace. "So, Mitch *is* Emily's brother? For real?" Lugh had suspected as much and had shared his theory with Emily at Zoo Atlanta. The two shared more than one mannerism, and Mitch had Hamilton Hester's eyes.

His mother nodded. "Not only her brother, but her twin brother."

Lugh sank back to the bed. "I don't understand. How can that be?"

"Oh, sweetie, there is much you don't know about the Awen Order, and the sacrifices we make to preserve its integrity. In generations where there is no daughter, the duty falls upon the father and sons. They must each sow their seed until a worthy heir is born. And technically, Hamilton Hester was an only child."

"But, Morgan is his sister."

"Morgan was adopted. She doesn't count. Nor was she Awen material. The burden fell entirely on Hamilton to produce a female heir."

This was getting weirder and weirder. "So you're telling me that Rona and Hamilton…" He couldn't finish the sentence. "Ma, that is messed up."

Her laughter ricocheted around the bedroom.

Cu twisted his head to gaze at Lugh with compassion. "Like it or not, young raven, that is the druid way. It is not about any individual druid, but about the Order as a whole. To fulfill its duty—to protect Earth at all costs—the line of succession must be preserved, and its ways kept intact. We lose our selves to preserve the whole."

"But, why Rona?" Lugh held his head and wished he could take a pain pill. "She was like a second mother to me."

"I know, son. And a good friend to me. But Rona wasn't the only one who agreed to be a conduit. Many druid women volunteered to allow the Awen to come through them. It's a great honor. And it was Ham's duty to keep trying until a viable one was birthed. I myself—" Her voice broke. His father wrapped his arms around her and drew her close.

"There, there," he comforted, patting her back.

"Anyway," she said over his shoulder with a sniff, "the Order must be preserved. Put your feelings aside and go to Rona. Tell her everything you know about Emily *and* her mission. Emily will need all the help she can get, including from her mother."

GETTING SERIOUS

The breakfast crowd was beginning to thin when the restaurant manager hailed Patty between tables. Patty wiped her brow on her sleeve and balanced her tray on the other hand.

"Can I drop this first?" She nodded toward the waiting table.

"I'll take it," her manager said brusquely. "I don't think they're willing to wait." She gestured over her shoulder to two men in suits, one balding and thick around the middle, the other dark with glasses. They both eyed Patty intently.

"Can I help you?" she asked, as her manager retreated with the loaded tray.

"Patrika Tolbert?" The bald man stepped forward flashing a badge. "I'm Special Agent Warner, and this is Special Agent Jeter. We're with the Federal Bureau of Investigations. Could we have a minute?"

Patty resisted the urge to bolt. It would only delay the inevitable. Besides, she'd been expecting this. Since talking to that reporter, she'd been getting odd calls and visits. This was the first official one, and it was a good thing. Someone had to stop the aliens.

She tossed her head, enjoying the way her new hairdo cascaded and framed her face. "I guess so."

"Come with us." The second agent's voice was smooth like peanut butter, and he was kinda cute. She didn't mind much when he took her by the elbow and guided her out the front door. When he directed her into the back of a waiting sedan, Patty protested.

"I assure you it's all aboveboard, miss." The brown eyes gleamed. "We're just taking you somewhere private to chat."

At least they hadn't handcuffed her. Not that they should. She hadn't done anything. They wound along Sunset Boulevard through Pacific Palisades, past Will Rogers State Park, and kept going through Brentwood.

When they crossed over the 405 Freeway, Patty became alarmed. "Where are you taking me?"

Agent Jeter glanced over his shoulder reassuringly. "We're almost there."

Within minutes, they were parking at the Federal Building. Ten minutes later, they had passed through security. In the lobby, Agent Warren held out his hand.

"Cell phone, please."

Patty's heart raced. She slid the phone from her purse and held it, uncertain. "Maybe I should call someone and let them know I'm here."

"Sure, go ahead," the agent said, and they turned their backs

Not knowing who to call, she tried Shalane. As she'd suspected, it went to voicemail. Patty left a short message and hung up. Should she call Latoya? Probably not. The actress hadn't been thrilled about Patty's interview. The crazies were targeting her, too.

"Why can't I keep my phone?" She handed it to Agent Warren reluctantly.

"It's not allowed in interrogation."

"Interrogation? Like in TV crime shows? Why there? What have I done?"

"As I said before, we need to ask you a few questions."

"You could have done that at the restaurant." Patty backed away, terrified now. "Why did you bring me here? I am not a criminal." Her insides churned, and she suddenly needed the bathroom. Clenching her butt cheeks, she looked around frantically for a ladies room sign. "I need a toilet. Now."

A look passed between the agents. The cute one said, "Follow me," and walked her a short distance back the way they'd come.

Face blazing, Patty ducked inside, did her business, and splashed water on her neck. Blotting it with a paper towel, she gazed at her frightened reflection in the mirror. The tears she'd been holding onto so desperately, trickled out.

"You haven't done anything wrong," she told herself. She dabbed away the tears, took a deep breath, then marched into the hall, chin high and defiant.

The Interrogation Room was brightly lit, like in the shows, and devoid of furniture except for a small table and three chairs. They seated her facing the window and took the opposite side. Opening a file, Agent Warren cleared his throat and looked up.

"According to this," he pulled a copy of what Patty assumed to be the L.A. Times article from the file, "you've been visited by an alien that claims to live inside the earth, and is part of a race seeking to destroy humans and take over Earth." The gray eyes fixed on hers, brows raised with a slight smile. "Is that correct?"

"Yes, it is," Patty nodded.

Agent Warren scratched his nose and glanced at his partner, then back at her. "Will you elaborate?"

"There's not much else to tell. A few months ago, Shalane was teaching me to meditate and I started having weird thoughts. It made Shalane mad. She didn't believe me." Patty sniffed, thinking back.

"She was having awful headaches during that time and always in a bad mood. We fought all the time, but mostly about the crazy stuff that came out of my mouth—stuff I had no idea about. Then one day, it stopped. The weird thoughts *and* Shalane's headaches."

Agent Warren wrote something in the file and motioned Patty to continue. Agent Jeter stroked his handsome chin.

"A few weeks later, I left Atlanta and flew back to California for my brother's wedding. While I was here, I had a dream about an alien named Nergal." The agent scribbled furiously. "Only it didn't seem like a dream. It seemed real. And I *was* Nergal. I was hurt and looking for a doctor. Then everything started rumbling and shaking like an earthquake, and I woke up. But it happened again later when I was taking a nap."

"So you're having recurring dreams."

"No, not really. They keep changing. The second time, I was running away from a strange city like none I've ever seen in real life. It was awful. Everything was on fire, and the smell was so disgusting I nearly threw up. Oh God," she almost sobbed, then tried to continue, "I-I couldn't..." she hesitated and took a deep breath like Shalane had shown her when she was upset.

"I could never have imagined anything so horrible. People were burning in the buildings." She wrung her hands. "I could smell them burning and..." Patty shuddered, remembering. "And this time there was another lizard-creature helping me. Or helping Nergal. It was a lady lizard, much shorter and smaller. A doctor—doctora, he called her. I—he—was in so much pain, but they made it to a cave and hid. Someone, or something, was after them."

She stopped talking. Agent Warren's eyebrows had remained pasted in an arched position the whole time. The asshole didn't believe a word she'd said.

In contrast, Agent Jeter gave her an empathetic nod. "And is that all?"

She turned to face him and ignored his boss. "Almost. The last time it happened, there were two more lizard-men and the doctora. They call themselves Dracos." Agent Jeter blinked and his left eye twitched. "You know about them, don't you?" Her heart skipped a beat.

Jeter glanced down and shook his head. "Please continue."

Disappointed, she told him the rest. "Nergal is hurt and might be dying. They are running from a warlord named Shibboleth. And they are all plotting to kill us humans and take over Earth. Please," she leaned forward imploringly, "you have to do something. If you don't stop them, we're all going to die."

Agent Warren nearly choked on his laughter. "Sounds like the plot of a Hollywood movie. You should pitch this to the studios, young lady. You'd likely have a blockbuster on your hands." Patty slumped in her chair, defeated.

But, Agent Jeter held her gaze. "Can you tell us about the appearance of these lizard-men, as you call them?"

She straightened, nodding. "Nergal is tall, maybe seven or eight feet."

Warren coughed behind his hand, and she could swear it sounded like "bullshit". Jeter rolled his eyes and motioned her to continue.

"Nergal has scales all over his body like a snake. They're small and whitish, olivey-greeny colored. And really soft and silky. Except for his chest and ab scales," she gestured to those parts of her body. "Those were much larger, like plates, and a creamy shade of yellow. His ears and nose are slits," she gestured to hers, "and his eyes are large and red with black pupils, like a cat's."

"Is that all?" Warren prompted snidely.

Patty bit her lower lip and wrinkled her nose. She was going to tell him about the others, but screw that. He was being too pissy.

"You sure?" Jeter asked.

Patty smiled at him sweetly and batted her eyes. "They have claws. On their hands *and* their feet. Oh, and pointy teeth." She shuddered. How could she forget?

Special Agent Warren leaned back in his chair and clapped slowly. "Kudos, young lady. I believe you have just delivered an Oscar-winning performance."

Agent Jeter blinked behind his stylish glasses and leaned near to say softly, "Thank you, Patrika. Is there anything else? Anything at all?"

Ignoring Warren, she ransacked her memory. "No, I think that's it. But you believe me, don't you?"

The dark man studied her with eyes that were kind and wise. Then he blinked, and the strict agent-persona returned. Special Agent Jeter pushed back his chair. "Come, Patrika. Let's retrieve your cell phone and get you back to work."

☼☼☼

The girl was telling the truth. Derek Jeter had known about the aliens since childhood when his FBI-agent mother was stationed at the complex beneath Denver International Airport. He'd had a fever and couldn't go to school, so Derek went to work with her instead. He spent the day in sick-bay and saw things he wasn't supposed to see, enough to give him nightmares for years.

Only later had Derek learned he was a half-breed, part human, part reptilian. The blood of the creatures he'd thought of as monsters throughout his youth ran through his veins. His mother had shared her secret on her death bed—a secret Derek would carry to his own grave.

He had no idea how he had managed to avoid being tapped for the Watcher program. But he kept ending up on their cases, nonetheless. Derek felt sorry for the girl. After his last case, he felt inclined to push her agenda with the higher-ups. As long as it didn't land him in hot water again.

Special Agent Warren was clueless. Or was it an act? Derek suspected he knew more than he was telling. How else could he be an FBI Watcher? It was their job to squelch rumors and information regarding the aliens. And if that was the case, Derek must tread lightly. Otherwise, Warren would have his head.

Knowing what he knew about the Draconians, Derek shuddered. He finished recording his observations on his private tablet, secured it in its hiding place, and went back to work.

☼☼☼

FBI Special Agent Becket Warren slowly spun his coffee cup and stared into its murky depths. He'd give anything not to make this call, but as head of the Watcher Division, it was up to him to report directly to Washington.

"Anders," he instructed his assistant, "have SCIF round up the Director for me. Tell them I'll be right down."

Warren boarded the elevator to the basement, and traversed the long corridor to the Sensitive Compartmented Information Facility. Holding his hand in front of the pad, he waited for the ding, then looked into the iris scanner. The door buzzed and Warren entered SCIF. He nodded to the three specialists on duty.

"The Director is on," Joaquin advised. Warren crossed his arms and nodded.

FBI Director Katarina Hobbs appeared on screen, hair pulled back, expression severe. "What is it Warren?"

"Director, we have a problem." He summarized his conversation with the girl and finished with his assessment. "We need to nip this in the bud, Director. From the intel we've gathered, Patrika Tolbert has two powerful allies in Reverend Carpenter, an up and coming evangelist, and Latoya Cloud, a singer-turned-actress. I recommend we discredit the girl quickly before people start to take this seriously."

"Are you sure that won't make things worse?" the Director drawled. "Because from where I stand, if we start hootin' and hollerin' about one silly little girl, the world is gonna think we protest too much. If you get my drift, Special Agent Warren."

Inwardly, he winced. He had been dead set against the appointment of a woman to the post of Director. Especially this woman. She had the personality of a viper, in a sugary-sweet skin.

300

Which made her perfect for keeping the reptilians in check. But she made life hell for everyone else.

"I do, ma'am. But I stand by my assessment. One statement is all we need. Patrika Tolbert will go back under the rock she crawled out of and this will all go away." Director Hobbs looked skeptical.

"Are you willing to bet your career on that, Special Agent Warren?"

"If I have to, ma'am."

"Then so be it. The statement will come from the Los Angeles Field Office. Do not mention the Director's Office. If this goes sideways, it's on you." She made the throat-slitting motion, and the no-signal pattern replaced her on the screen.

A TRIP TO TOWN

The dragons drilled Emily relentlessly, despite her need for frequent breaks. Her headaches were still of the raging variety but happened less often. And while her energy ran out quickly, she'd not passed out since the day a-Ur arrived.

Still, she had reached her breaking point and had finally convinced the air dragon to give her a day off so Khenko could drive her into town.

They made a morning of it, including a visit to the salon for Emily's first haircut in a year. She'd forgotten how good it felt to be pampered. The stylists ooo'd and ahh'd over her gold-tipped scarlet curls, and when Sylvi finished and handed her the mirror, they all clapped. Then Khenko joined her for a mani-pedi, jack-knifing his brown legs into a spa chair.

Afterward, Emily followed the medicine man down Main Street to a small boutique, owned by his friend, Randall. It didn't take a detective to recognize the sparks flying between them. And to think she'd suspected Khenko fancied her.

While Emily tried on the clothes they handed her through the curtain, the two men bantered over dinner plans. The unanimous choice was a pig roast hosted by Khenko's neighbor, which must've been what he was planning the day she'd seen him on her walk. Randall winked and assured them in his smooth, French-Guiana accent, he would see them there.

When they were done, Khenko flashed his FlexCard. It panged Emily's conscience, but before they'd left the Center, she had agreed to let him pay—despite her mother's voice in her head telling her to depend on no one, and take care of herself.

But she needed clothes. And other necessities. And though Khenko wouldn't hear of it, she'd resolved to repay him if ever her life returned to normal. She only hoped that day would come soon.

They stopped by the tiny post office, where Khenko retrieved a package from the states, and by the local Pescadero for fresh-caught halibut and stonefish. At a produce stand, Emily ran inquisitive fingers over the ripe melons and stocky bananas while Khenko loaded a basket with coconuts and fruit.

Thanks to his excellent care, and the flavorful, nutrition-packed smoothies he prepared daily, Emily was beginning to feel herself again. Remarkable, considering she'd been on his tiny island only two weeks. And seventeen days ago, she'd been sucked into the earth and damn-near killed.

Their final stop was at a shop that doubled as the local liquor store and mercado. It smelled of exotic spices and mysterious brews and was stuffed to its thatched ceiling with oddities and island trinkets.

Khenko spoke in hushed tones to the wiry proprietress, a hunched woman who looked a hundred if a day. Lined features molded from darkened leather arranged themselves around her toothless grin. A headful of grayed dreadlocks bobbed vigorously, and her beady eyes twinkled. But not a word did the wizened owner murmur.

Until Emily reached for an amulet.

It hung from a stand with a variety of others, on a table full of bracelets, earrings, and assorted bangles, all cloaked in a thick layer of dust. The crone cackled from behind her, and Emily jumped.

"Dat's yurz den, izzit?"

In a flash, the woman had snatched the necklace from its wire hook and motioned Emily to lower her head. Emily obliged, shivering when the chain caressed her neck. She straightened and fingered the deep-red stone that rested below the hollow of her throat. A wave of energy surged through her body, much like when she wore Aóme.

Emily patted the pocket of her new jeans, seeking and finding the outline of the emerald ring that had belonged to the first Awen one thousand years ago. Her father, Hamilton Hester, had bequeathed the powerful heirloom to Emily when he'd installed her as the new Grand Druid.

Her throat tightened. An image of the once-rugged druid appeared in her mind, waving and sporting his patent smile.

Beside him stood the young Brian MacBrayer, whose rare, toothy grin was reassuring. The two were still alive.

The crone passed a weathered hand before Emily's face. "Yo'kay, Mamselle?"

Khenko tugged at her arm. "Emily?"

With a shudder, her thoughts returned to the mercado. Pooh-poohing their concerns, she took the smoky hand-mirror the crone proffered and admired the amulet resting on her chest. She lifted the stone in one hand and was surprised at its heft. On her neck, the pendant felt weightless.

Catching the proprietress's scrutiny in the mirror, Emily asked, "How much?"

The crone wagged her dreads and backed toward the ancient register, crossed her hands in front of her face. From her lips poured a string of unintelligible words. She bowed, as in obeisance, then turned and spoke to Khenko in the same, incomprehensible tongue.

The medicine man paled and nodded, smile tight. Not sure what had transpired, Emily protested when he pulled her to the door.

Down the street a way, she paused to look back. The crone peered from a boarded-up window, gnarled hands clutching a string of prayer beads. She made the sign of the cross and backed out of sight.

A chill ran up Emily's spine and spread across the top of her head. She had an urge to remove the crone's necklace, and put her hand to the clasp, then changed her mind.

Why not wear it? Even if fake, the ruby lent color to her cheeks. And Khenko seemed okay with the whole thing, though he'd been evasive about the meaning of the crone's words, and her refusal to accept payment.

Whistling an off-key tune, he loaded the jeep, making use of every nook and cranny, while Emily buckled in and laid her head against the seat. The oppressive heat and the day's doings had worn her thin.

She quietly hummed a tune of Taliesin's adventures and stared out the window, though she didn't see the colorful market stands, or the villagers, or the beaches as they passed. Amergin's ballad had been the first of many lessons her Da had taught. And it'd been stuck in her head all day.

Was it his way of reminding her to have faith? Of letting her know she was on the right track? All his lessons had focused on Emily's druid heritage, on their responsibility to the Earth, and its salvation. All things she'd been taught by her mother to shun. Now Emily would be traveling to Europe soon; Amergin's stomping grounds, the land from whence their druid line had sprung.

The island receded further, and for a moment she was Awen, the last Druid Priestess, searching for William, future Conqueror and King.

Intrigued by the convergence of past with present, Emily grasped at Awen's thoughts. She stared out the window at the thick jungle spiked with coconut palms, mahogany trees, and other exotic plants, as the jeep bounced over the mucky ruts left behind by the rains. A macaw flapped majestic blue wings and screeched from its perch in a lone teak. But the vision was gone.

They spun sideways and Emily grabbed the chicken strap with both hands, glad she'd buckled her seat belt. Her thoughts churned as Khenko righted the jeep. Was Awen trying to tell her something about the trip to Beli?

Emily's stomach flip-flopped. Whether from excitement or anxiety was anyone's guess. She was as conflicted about leaving the safety of Zephyr Cay as she was about the Awen. On the one hand, the priestess was great in a crisis. On the other, Emily loathed having her mind hijacked.

She thought of seeing Lugh and her tummy flipped again, this time in a more delightful way. The druid priest had a manner that calmed her inner demons. She remembered her parting words on the phone and wondered if he was spinning over her declaration of love. But if something happened and she never saw him again, she wanted him to know.

The jeep bounded over a deep rut. Emily gripped the strap and squealed when Khenko slammed on the brakes and swerved to the shoulder so that a rickety red bus stuffed bumper-to-grill with grinning locals could squeeze past. Haphazardly-parked cars, jeeps, bicycles, and mopeds left little maneuvering room on the narrow approach to the Atlantean Center.

So the rumors were true. The whole island was turning out for Manny's pig roast.

A savory aroma tickled Emily's nostrils as they bounced into the driveway. But there was something more, something she couldn't name, that made her shudder from head to toe.

Khenko parked and ran up the stairs with his arms full of groceries. She exited more slowly with her clothes purchases and stood by the jeep to peer through the jungle. Based on the cars and the noise level, the party was already well underway, but the jungle was too thick to get more than a glimpse.

Goosebumps danced along the nape of Emily's neck. They ran across her shoulders and down her arms, eliciting a shudder. Something, or someone, was out there.

SECRETS AND LIES

Lugh hadn't been to the Wainwright residence in years. He rang the bell and fiddled with his button-down collar. When he, Mitch, and Jake were friends, he'd practically lived at Canongate. The door opened and Rona, Mitch's mother, bustled out.

"Lugh!" She enveloped him in a bear hug and held on tight, rocking him back and forth. Then squeezing hard, she pulled him into the house. "I'm thrilled to see you. Can I get you some sweet tea?"

"No ma'am, I'm good." Lugh fidgeted with his jacket zipper, running it up and down absentmindedly.

"Can I take your coat?"

"Oh, no ma'am. I'm okay." He let go of the zipper and tried to smile, though he was filled with trepidation. He wasn't sure how Rona would react to what he had to tell her.

"Well, come on into the living room and tell me what's on your mind." She motioned to a chair and settled on the couch. He sat facing her.

"Still no word about Jake?" she asked.

Lugh cleared his throat, not sure where to start. "Well ma'am, that's what I wanted to speak with you about. I talked to my ma and pa yesterday—" Rona's eyebrows shot up. "I mean, well, I know they're dead, but they come to visit me now and again." He smiled wryly. "Mostly to warn me about things."

The eyebrows remained raised, but at least she was smiling.

"I know you probably think I'm crazy, but I promise it's true."

"You're right-handed, yes?"

He nodded, and Rona took his left hand. She turned it over and inspected his palm. "You see this line here?" She traced an arc from his pinky to his wrist.

"Yes, ma'am."

"This is your intuition line. It's well-defined, prominent even." She held his fingers together and traced the outer edge of his hand. "And your hand is pointed. This, my dear Lugh, is known as a psychic hand; small and slender, with smooth, long fingers and narrow fingertips."

"Huh. I had no idea." He smiled genuinely for the first time in what felt like forever. "But what does that mean?"

"That, with this combination, it would be natural for you to talk to your deceased mom and dad."

"So, you believe me?"

"Of course, dear. You never were one to make things up, unlike my son who tends toward flights of fancy. Speaking of, I just got off the phone with Mitch. He has something he needs to discuss, too. He's on his way." Lugh's gut churned.

"Then, I will hurry so y'all can visit."

"Oh, take your time. He was at the office, so I'm sure it'll take a bit. What did your parents say?"

Lugh hesitated, then plunged right in. "For the sake of simplicity, I'm just going to say it." He sucked in air. "Ma told me that Emily is Mitch's twin sister. And that you are her real mother." Rona's face went pale and her lip trembled. She took a deep breath and blew it out slowly.

"Yes, I am. Only Mitch doesn't know, and I'm not sure I want him to know."

"I understand," Lugh assured. "Ma explained the whole duty to the Order thing, which I never truly comprehended until now. So, I'm not here to judge or criticize. Just to tell you that Emily is alive, and she's in trouble." Rona's eyes crinkled, and he hoped she wouldn't cry.

"Since the earthquake, she's been hiding in the Bahamas, training with the Dragon Keepers. Now they are taking her to Wales, to the Isle of Beli." He shook his head, knowing he sounded crazy. But Rona's eyes never wavered from his. "I'm not even sure such a place exists." A tear escaped to roll down her cheek.

"My poor baby," Rona whimpered. "Oh Lugh, if you knew how hard these years have been. Not knowing where she was. Not able to acknowledge her. Or tell anyone. When she came back to Wren's Roost, I wanted to rush over there every day. And when I thought the quake had taken her, my heart broke a million times. Now you tell me she survived, and maybe even thrives. Is she the Awen, Lugh? Did the Awen really come through my baby girl?"

"Oh, yes ma'am, she did. It's true." Rona smiled through her tears, and Lugh couldn't help grinning.

"She is amazing, Rona. When the whole block was demolished by those tornadoes, Emily saved Jocko's. And that was before she knew how to use magic. She stopped that blizzard in March, and when we were at the zoo, she kept the earthquake and volcano from destroying Atlanta and wiping out our Order. Yes, ma'am, the Awen has come through your daughter loud and clear."

"You have a *daughter*, Mother?" a brusque voice growled. "One you hid from me?"

Rona hurriedly wiped away her tears and turned to Mitch. He stood in the doorway, anger twisting his normally-handsome face. He advanced into the room, and Lugh stood to leave. Mitch pushed him back down and rounded on Rona.

"Is it Emily Hester? Because I know Dad is not my real father. And I know Hamilton Hester is. Would you care to explain? Tell me, Mother. Tell me about Hamilton Hester. Tell me why he worshiped Emily and made her Grand Druid, even though she had no magical powers and had never been trained. Tell me why he couldn't bother to acknowledge me as his son, even after hiring me as the clan's lawyer."

His hands and voice shook, but he wasn't done venting. "Yes, Mother. Tell your *son* why you hid this all these years." Tears of anger started down Mitch's face. He swiped at them and turned on Lugh. "And what in holy hell are you doing here?"

"Mitchell Albom Wainwright the Third," Rona scolded, rising to face him. "Mind your manners. *And* your words. You will not talk like that in this house." Mitch crumpled to the chair Rona had vacated and buried his face in his hands.

Lugh squirmed on the sofa, wishing he could leave, then decided there was no reason he couldn't. He stood and cleared his throat. "Rona, I need to tell you one more thing. Could you walk me to the door?" He nodded to Mitch, whose head was still cradled in his hands. Rona followed him to the foyer.

"My apologies, ma'am," Lugh murmured, genuinely sorry he had caused her more grief.

"It's not your fault, Lugh." She touched his cheek. "Mitch is right. This is all fubar. But it is the way of the druids, and though I no longer practice, I am still, and will always be, a druid. Now, what did you want to tell me, dear?"

"The Dragon Keepers insist Emily must call the dragons together. After that, I don't know what they plan. I also don't know what Ma thinks you can do, but she insisted I deliver the message that Emily needs you. If you want to talk more after Mitch leaves, you have my number." He gave her a quick hug. "I'll be flying to Wales in the next day or so. And I'm taking Cu and Hope with me."

"Thank you, hon. And please thank your Ma and Pa for me. I miss them something awful." She hugged him close. "You are a wise man, Lughnasadh MacBrayer. Tell Emily I love her. Stay strong and be safe. My prayers are with you both. Now, I must go comfort my son."

☼☼☼

"I am shocked, Mother. Shocked and outraged. I understand you were doing your duty to the Order. But it is still messed up. Royally." Hi mother had just finished pouring her heart out. The Order needed a female heir, and Mitch's father, the one who raised him, had desperately wanted a male heir. And was shooting blanks.

"If Father was willing to go to such lengths to have a son, why didn't he love me? He was never around. And nothing I did was ever good enough for him, even when I excelled. Which you know was often. I even joined the service because of him. But, never once did I feel love from him, only disapproval. Why is that?"

His mother dabbed at her still-flowing tears. "I've asked myself, and him, that same question many times over the years. Truth is, I think he's done the best he could. He's not a lovey-dovey man, even with me. And as a surgeon, he basically lives at Emory. But that doesn't mean he doesn't love you, Mitchell. He does. And he's proud of the man you've become, even though it

310

broke his heart when you chose to become a lawyer rather than a surgeon. He hates it, but respects that you stood up to him."

Her words didn't make him feel any better.

She cradled his face between her hands and lightly kissed him on the forehead, nose, and chin. Then she kissed his eyelids, his cheeks, and his lips.

Energy surged through Mitch, and his hurt bubbled up and out in a wail. "Mother, why didn't you raise me as a druid? You knew I wanted that more than anything in the world. Lugh and Jake had to teach me what little I do know. From what you just told me, both you and Hamilton were powerful druids. Wouldn't it have made sense to let me train?"

"Yes, and I regret that to this day. But once I fulfilled my duty to the Awen Order, your father made me promise to stop practicing. *And* to not raise our son as a druid. He wanted you to be 'normal'—like him." She wiped his tears with her knuckle. "Not that there was anything normal about you, Mitch. You were always extraordinary and still are. I just wish you hadn't 'inherited' your dad's arrogance."

Stung, despite the good things she'd said, Mitch decided to hit her with Hamilton's dirty secret—which was why he'd come over in the first place. "Did you also know that you're only one of the many women Hamilton had relations with? All in the name of a female heir?" She had the grace to blush and look away.

"Yes, Mitch, I do know. It was Hamilton's duty to produce a viable heir for the Awen Order. As the lineage is over a thousand years old, it was a heavy burden for one man to bear. If it makes you feel any better, it ruined his marriage. And from what I understand, Alexis was the only woman Ham ever loved. But most of his progeny turned out to be boys. Or girls that weren't Awen material. Until Emily." A light sprang to his mother's eyes, along with more tears.

"Though we had signed a contract, it nearly killed me to give your sister to the Hesters. But you must understand, it was an *honor* to be chosen. For every one of us women. *And* our spouses. Because without the Awen, our Order loses its power to protect Earth. And protecting Earth is the reason the Order exists."

Mitch shuffled his feet, anger spent. He felt hollow inside. Calm, even.

"I hope you can forgive me," his mother lamented. "Can you see that this is bigger than any one person?"

Mitch nodded. He did understand. But that didn't mean he had to like it. Or approve.

"Plus, sweetie, every one of those families was financially compensated. Quite handsomely, too. Especially us, because your sister turned out to be the Awen." There was a flash of pride in her eyes before she stood and held out a hand. "Come with me. I want to show you my secret room."

☼☼☼

Mitch squealed out of Canongate's driveway and floored the BMW down the avenue, before slamming his brakes at a stop sign. The anger that had been eating him alive was gone. Instead, he felt empty. And he still reeled—Emily Hester was not only Mitch's sister but his twin. Mitch felt nauseated.

He lowered the window and sucked in a breath. The day he took Lugh home from the hospital, Mitch had placed an illegal tap on his cell phone. Sure enough, Emily had called Lugh a couple of days ago. She was hiding in the Bahamas, and Mitch planned on seeing her soon.

He would fly to Nassau and meet Shalane. Then, together they would haul Emily back to Georgia. Not for the reward money, though money was always good. But because Mitch was determined to show the druids that he was better than the one they had chosen as Grand Druid.

MANNY'S PARTY

After too many winter weeks indoors, Shalane turned her face to the sun. The speedboat skipped over the tops of the waves, spewing salty spray. She stiffened her arms on the seat behind her to keep from bouncing into the rowdy sea.

When Mitch had called with news of Emily's whereabouts, Shalane had booked the first flight to Nassau. There, she paid a small fortune to an islander to motor her to Zephyr Cay, where Emily was reportedly holed up.

One of Shalane's loyal devotees had grown up in the Bahamas. As chance would have it, he still maintained a beach home—of all places—on Zephyr Cay. When she'd contacted him about her trip, he'd told her he was throwing a shindig. And according to Manny, the entire island turned out for his famous pig roasts.

Which meant Ebby, aka Emily Hester, should be there.

Her heart beat faster. Nobody ran out on Shalane Carpenter. Not without giving up something dear. Plus, she now knew that Ebby had a brother. And if the hatred was mutual, Shalane would relish being the one to deliver her to him.

☼☼☼

Shalane prowled the perimeter of the party. Dark had fallen, and still no Ebby. Maybe she wasn't coming. Maybe Mitchell's intel had been incorrect. Either way, Shalane had pulled a lot of strings to be here. Enough, that both Cecil and her manager were livid.

Her devotee Manny didn't know she was here. Shalane had called from the airport with the news she couldn't make it. Now she was Lolita Lozano, a singer-songwriter. The clueless Manny

313

had flirted relentlessly with Lolita since Shalane had walked through the door.

The night was hot and sultry. True to his word, a couple-hundred people roamed Manny's estate in various stages of drunken undress. Miniature lights threaded around the dance floor and through the palm grove, lighting the path to the beach where the crowd spilled over, dancing, laughing, drinking, and necking.

Her Bahamian driver and several of the locals had formed a drumming circle on the beach near the drink hut. The beat resonated in Shalane's chest, and her twat responded to the gyrations of the scantily-clad men and women. After weeks of not much feeling down there, she welcomed the lust growing in her loins. Still, she refrained from taking a partner.

Most were intoxicated on Goombay Smash, a potent punch laced with several different types of rum. Shalane had abstained from that, but she had taken a few tokes from the bongs as they passed. The Sativa did little to calm the edge vibrating her nerves.

Annoyed that she couldn't join the revelry, Shalane tapped her foot and swayed with the beat. She would like nothing more than to lose herself in the throng of islanders engaged in the singular pursuit of fun. But she couldn't forget her primary purpose was finding Ebby.

But what if she was never coming? What if Emily really *was* dead?

Grabbing a drink from the bar, Shalane downed half. If Ebby wasn't coming, she might as well let her hair down. Maybe she'd partner with one of the sexy locals. Or more than one. Then tomorrow, she would scour Zephyr Cay. She wouldn't leave until she found her quarry, or determined Mitch's lead had been false.

At the edge of the lanai, Shalane kicked her slides atop a pile of sandals. She glided to the improvised dance floor and wiggled her way to the center. The song changed and the cadence slowed. Sweaty bodies bobbed to the bongos and strings.

Someone caressed her shoulder, and Shalane turned to find it was her glistening host. She let him take her hand and twirl her around, then dance her across the crowded floor to a corner partially hidden from the partygoers. There, he pulled her against his muscular form and a delicious sensation flooded her tummy.

When he rubbed his hard cock against her clit, Shalane gasped. And when he lifted her off the ground onto his exposed bulb, she came then and there. Groaning, she tightened her arms around him and sawed up and down. He moaned and collapsed into her, pumping jism inside her spasming cunt. Shalane bounced and came again and again.

Devouring her lips, Manny held her against his still-hard cock and thrust harder. She surrendered to his plundering tongue, and came one more time, hard and heavy, as the music crescendoed and the dancers howled.

Breathless, Shalane regained her feet and clung to Manny to get her bearings. He guided her onto the dance floor and sashayed her to the liquor tent. With a knuckle tap to his ebony chin, Shalane disengaged, pulled her skirt down, and bellied to the bar as her host disappeared with a wink. Smiling, she used a napkin to wipe his cum from her bare crotch, then tossed it in a flaming metal drum.

The tempo of the music intensified. The entire clearing was a sea of people—the dance floor nearly indistinguishable from the surrounding area. Scantily-clad partiers grated to the frantic beat. Those standing on the sidelines swayed or bounced in time to the rhythm, absorbed in conversations impossible to hear.

Accepting a drink from the cheeky bartender, Shalane fished out a chunk of ice and rubbed it on her chest. It melted quickly, joining the pool of sweat between her breasts. Grateful for some relief from the sweltering heat, Shalane tilted the plastic cup and let the sweet rum punch cool her insides.

Her unsuspecting devotee had resumed his station greeting new arrivals beneath a cascade of white lights. A flash of scarlet caught Shalane's eye, and an electric shock jolted her system. Manny's arm was around none other than Emily Hester.

Ebby was alive. And here.

The redhead glanced in Shalane's direction, scanned the crowd, then back again. Reacting quickly, Shalane lowered her face and let Lolita's long hair fall across it. When Emily's scrutiny passed her over and returned to their host, Shalane exhaled and stared.

Red hair looked good on Ebby. The mass of riotous curls was swept back and pinned. But something else was different. When they had first met, Ebby had no inkling of the power Shalane sensed within her. That had changed.

She seemed tired and anxious and worn around the edges, but Ebby Panera exuded an air of command. She had somehow managed to embrace and develop her latent powers—and without Shalane. That stuck in Shalane's craw.

Towering over Ebby, was a lanky man of obvious American Indian heritage. The hooked nose and sandy hair didn't quite match, but the man stood with an unconscious dignity and grace; the demeanor of one born into power and privilege. Shalane might like knowing him under different circumstances. But tonight, he was her competition.

She watched them together for another minute, envious of the way Ebby stuck to his side. Then a dark, petite man sidled up to the couple and put an arm around Ebby's date, drawing him close for a quick embrace and warm kiss.

Satisfaction curled Shalane's lips as Ebby greeted the newcomer, then stood alone, resignedly eyeing the revelers on the dance floor. Ebby panned the crowd again, and Shalane ducked, then the redhead followed her companion and the native through the writhing mob. Shalane shifted to keep the dancers between them and twisted her ankle, nearly falling on her ass.

Why, oh why, had she given up and gotten toasted? Her head was woozy from the Goombay Smash and too many bong hits. Now she'd probably sprained her ankle, and if she didn't pee soon, her bladder might burst.

Speaking a spell to keep Ebby on the premises, Shalane fished her shoes from the pile, dangled them in one hand, and hobbled through the crowd keeping her head down. She took a last look and entered the house via a side patio, then wove her way through the rambling bungalow.

"Great. There's a queue for the bathroom," she mumbled, crossing her legs. "And no air conditioning." Sweat beaded on her upper lip and dribbled down her décolleté. Her ears buzzed and her face flamed. It was hotter in the Bahamas than Hades.

But Ebby Panera was here. Alive and in person.

Fanning her skirt, Shalane schvitzed and waited. Christ, it was hot. Schnockered or not, it was time to put her plan into action. Then, Shalane would meet Mitch and fly Emily back to the mainland. And blessed air conditioning.

☼☼☼

Emily waded through the cannabis haze that extended next door to the Atlantean Center. The neighbor's backyard was crammed with half-naked people—drinking, smoking, and gyrating—all in manic party mode. Uneasy in crowds, Emily crossed her arms.

Her stomach growled. She hadn't eaten since lunch in town. Emily trailed Khenko and his friend Randall down a short path to the beach, where the rich aroma of spiced pork overtook the pot smell and made her mouth water.

At the roasting pit, a young Bahamian with laughing eyes and a smile that showcased perfect, white teeth, spooned pulled pork onto a paper plate. Beside it, another cutie added the traditional peas n' rice, creamy potato salad, coleslaw, and a hunk of Johnny Cake. Emily carried it to a seat at the nearest table.

Like his namesake the stork, Khenko folded his long frame onto the wooden bench. Randall slid a heaping plate next to him and went off to get their drinks from the nearby tiki hut.

The meat was succulent, simmered for hours in the roasting pit with smoky spices. The potato salad and sweet coleslaw she pushed to the side, but ate every morsel of the peas n' rice, and nibbled half-heartedly at the Johnny Cake. Randall returned with three plastic cups and claimed a newly-abandoned seat.

When the rum and grenadine concoction struck her palette, Emily gagged. She managed to swallow the strong, sweet liquid, shuddering when the burn trailed down her throat all the way to her belly. Shaking like a poodle, she pushed the rest aside.

The sense of impending doom she'd had all afternoon was quiet for the moment. Emily was almost enjoying herself, despite the late hour and unyielding heat. The long nap had helped with the fatigue that had dogged her since the earthquake. She breathed a heavy sigh, grateful the air was fresher out here.

Blotting sweat from her face with a napkin, she unfolded it and spread it over her food. The meat was tasty, but it was the first she had eaten since her arrival on the island, and her stomach felt queasy. She was wondering if another helping of peas n' rice would calm it down when Randall passed her a bong.

Having never smoked Bahamian weed, Emily was curious. She took a small tug from the tall, cylindrical pipe, coughing when it overfilled her lungs. When it circled again, Emily took another, more tentative hit. Still, she coughed, hacking until the pork rose to the back of her throat. She waved it away next time, and giggled at Khenko cutting up with the others.

Until chills danced on the back of her neck and arms. Her spidey-senses flared to life, and the unnerving feeling returned full-force. Emily scanned the wide beach, searching for anything out of the ordinary.

Instead, she spied a row of recycle-potties. Excusing herself, she headed for them, weaving a bit in the shifting sand. The weed-rum combo had been mighty potent. She normally abstained, so it didn't take much.

Wedging herself into a portable potty that stank of vomit and fresh excrement, she unrolled a fistful of toilet paper and held it to her nose to quell the stench. Gagging, she finished and escaped into the warm night air. On the fringe of the party, beyond the reach of the lights, she could hear the waves slapping against the shore.

Emily kicked her flip-flops at the edge of the jungle and strolled to the sea, stopping when a wave washed over her toes. As the water receded, tiny crabs scrambled from hastily-dug holes.

A late-rising thumbnail moon hung low on the horizon. Its meager reflection played on the surf and gently lit the underbellies of the breakers. Sinking to her heels in the warm sand, Emily squatted and rested her elbows on her knees, looking out across the ocean.

Where were Ooschu and the others? She hadn't seen them since early that morning when Khenko convinced the bossy air dragon to give her a much-needed break. a-Ur's plan to escort Emily to Beli scared the crap out of her. Even after all the training, Emily had no idea how to be a champion, much less a savior.

Thinking of the impossible task before her, Emily's heart kerthumped, and a band tightened around her chest. Her hands began tingling, and soon the sensation traveled up the inside of one arm.

Was she having a heart attack? In the middle of nowhere? Please God, no. She was on a tiny island, one of the few remaining vestiges of the Bahamian chain, and it likely had no real doctor. Terrified of dying alone on the beach, Emily tried to stand, but the world tilted sideways and she stumbled forward. Saliva filled the back of her throat.

Falling to her knees, she barfed up the pork and peas n' rice. When the waves brought it back to swirl around her, Emily groaned and tried to move out of the way. Round and round the world spun. She retched on hands and knees in her own vomit until nothing was left, then heaved some more.

When the vomiting finally subsided, Emily dragged herself a few feet to one side and splashed water on her face and mouth. She waited another minute just in case, then crawled ever so slowly on hands and knees toward the coppice. She kept her head down and breathed in and out, trying to convince herself it was an anxiety attack.

"My heart is fine. I am safe and secure. I am protected by a medicine man and three dragons. There is nothing to worry about at the present moment. Nothing at all. I am safe. I am secure. God's holding me in his arms. God's got me."

By the time she made it to the edge of the jungle, Emily's breath was ragged. She collapsed in the sand, sweat pouring from her brow and down the front of her thin dress. She tried to sit, but her head started spinning, so she flopped to her back.

Soon the world settled and stood mostly still. At least until Emily opened her eyes long enough to see a couple strolling in the surf holding hands. On the speakers, Bob Marley and the Wailers belted out "Jamming". The local band must be taking a break.

When the tingling and tightness were mostly gone, Emily decided it was time to get back to the party. Khenko would be worried. But when she tried to stand, the symptoms came racing back.

Reciting Taliesin's poem to calm her nerves, Emily stared at a star twinkling blue in the heavens above the palm fronds. Her eyelids grew heavy, and she gave in to the insidious fatigue.

A HELPING HAND

What if they couldn't get out? Or what if they did, and everything changed between him and Ethnui?

Something sighed in the shadows behind Brian. It was barely audible, but his hearing had sharpened in UnderEarth. And he could almost feel whatever it was breathing down their necks.

He wheeled to confront it, but nothing was there.

"What is it?" Ethnui stopped walking and stuck her head next to his.

"I heard something." He pulled the pistol from his pocket. "Stay here, I'm going back a short way to see what it is." She grabbed his arm.

"Be careful, Brian."

Steeling his nerves, he moved slowly and stealthily, one step at a time, listening with all his senses. The darkness closed in around him. He was thinking about Emily when he heard her whisper.

"Brian?"

He stopped walking. He shined his light all around, seeing nothing but tunnel walls. "Emily? Are you there?"

Hamilton roused. "Emily, we're here. Are you okay? Where are you?"

"I'm at a party on the beach. But we're leaving the Bahamas for Beli soon. How did you find me, Brian?"

"Huh?" Brian said, confused. "You found us. Didn't you just call my name?"

"No. But I'm glad you're here. Where are you?"

"In a tunnel heading for Blowing Rock, North Carolina. There's supposed to be a portal. We're hoping to get back home from there."`

Hearing a snap, he released the safety and held the gun in both hands. "Emily? You there?"

She didn't answer, but something crept toward him. The hairs on his arms stood at attention. A light flashed on. It was Ethnui.

"What the hell? You almost got shot!"

"Did you find anything?" She flicked her beam in the direction he'd been heading.

"No."

"Then let's go." She turned on her heels and strode down the tunnel.

With a glance back over his shoulder, Brian hurried after her, wishing for the well-lit, polished halls surrounding the Dracos' prison below Atlanta.

"Emily?" he said inside his head.

"She's gone," Hamilton said. A flash of light made him stop short as Ethnui's beam reflected off something shiny.

"Hey, hold up! There's something over there. On the wall to the right."

Ethnui ran her lightstick along the surface, and sure enough, there was a directional sign. They studied the map.

"It looks like there's a settlement here." She pointed to a spot labeled "Mu" not far from the tunnel. "Should we check it out?"

"Yes, let's. We need food and water." He shook his almost-empty bottle. "And a bed would be nice." There was a snuffle behind them. He whirled, but saw nothing.

Still uneasy, he followed her down the side tunnel until it opened to a clearing. Daylight was just breaking.

"Hal-le-effing-lujah!" he crowed, eyes adjusting to the brightness. They were finally, *finally* out of the infernal caves.

"Stay close," Ethnui warned. "We don't know who or what might be waiting in this town."

Brian's elation dampened. He shadowed her through a sweeping grassland dotted with horses, cows, goats, and chickens.

"Hey, we have these same animals in AboveEarth."

"Of course, silly. What did you think?"

"Oh, I don't know. I keep hoping to see something new and exotic." Ethnui chuckled, then stopped, finger to her lips.

A woman who looked a lot like Ethnui approached from the village. She wore a burgundy robe and had flowers in her hair and said something in a lilting language. Ethnui answered eagerly. All Brian understood was "Ethnui" and "Brian".

"What did she say?"

"Good morning, basically. But Brian, you won't believe it! Her name is Petra, and she's a Fomorian, like me. She says there are many of them living in this village." She spoke to the woman, who said something else and turned toward town, motioning them to follow.

Delighted, Ethnui translated. "She's going to feed us and let us rest in her home."

Brian hesitated. "Are you sure it's safe?" After what they'd been through, the last thing they needed was an ambush. Especially this close to escaping UnderEarth.

"Pretty sure. Like the rest of my people, she's not a friend of the Dracos. She says the nearest reptilian base is mostly deserted, and a good fifty kilometers away. How about we have a bite, take turns sleeping, then get back on the road?"

☼☼☼

They spent the morning in Petra's home in the village eating and drinking copious amounts of water. When they were finished, she gave them a sweet dish of cashew flowers and crème. While Brian slept, Ethnui refilled their water bottles and conversed with Petra.

The town of Mu was a peaceful Fomorian village. Its older population had been lost to the slave trade. But since then, they'd been mostly insulated from the horrors Ethnui's kin had experienced. The remaining residents consisted of a few old crones, and the rest were younger than Ethnui.

"Do you have computers?" Her handheld's kinetic battery had worked well, even in the tunnels, but it needed to be synced to the main-brain periodically.

Petra nodded cautiously.

"Can I take a look?"

The woman hesitated, then shook her head. "It is better you don't. The Dracos monitor our activity. If you plug in to their system, they will know you are here and attack our peaceful village."

"So you are under scrutiny, but they leave you alone? How do you manage that?"

"One of the more-civilized Dracos mated a girl from the village. He took pity on her and spared us, but the reprieve is tenuous. We dare not rouse their attention or make them suspicious. They marched in and killed the last ones who did. And several others. Plus, you travel with a human. That automatically makes you a target. They hate humans, except as food and a source of the negative energy that keeps them going."

"Negative energy? What do you mean?"

Petra eyed her warily. "You did not know this? The Dracos thrive on negative energy. They beam high-frequency waves that create despair and anxiety. The beams penetrate Earth's crust and keep humans on edge and fighting one another. It's what creates the anger and greed and feelings of futility that drive their wars, which further fuel the Dracos."

As she spoke, Petra became more agitated. She stood abruptly and moved to the window to peer through the thick curtains. "It is best you go. The villagers are beginning to gather outside. Wake your human companion. I will show you the back way to the tunnels."

Petra clutched her breast and wheeled. "Hurry, Ethnui! Jhondu approaches. He will be angry that I took you in. You must go now, or who knows what punishment he will mete."

Ethnui hurried to the window. The Fomorian Petra spoke of strode toward the house, and looked angry indeed. The crowd parted to let him through. Ethnui slid her handheld in her thigh belt, grabbed their replenished packs, and went to wake Brian.

"Come, we must go."

Brian protested and rolled toward the wall. She shook him harder.

"Hurry, human. Trouble approaches."

That got his attention. Wide-eyed and wary, Brian leapt from the bed, slipped on his shoes, and raked fingers through his thick, black hair. As they slipped out the back door behind Petra, angry fists pounded on the front one.

PUZZLING DEVELOPMENT

Shalane had searched Manny's estate and Ebby was nowhere to be found. She'd asked the two men with whom Ebby had arrived, but they had no idea. Not wanting her to know someone was looking, Shalane put a temporary spell on both of them, just in case.

After that, Shalane danced with a young stud from Zephyr Cay, necked with a sweet hotty from Surry doing a stint at the Oceanic Observatory, and conversed with an aging Rasta who claimed to be descended from Bob Marley. All the while, she kept a lookout for Ebby Panera.

She hadn't imbibed since Ebby's arrival, and her head was clear. Leaving the dance floor, Shalane searched again, weaving in and out of the thinning crowd. She peeked in every room of the bungalow, startling more than one couple. But no Ebby Panera.

Trudging to the beach, Shalane found a few stragglers, most of whom were necking or passed out on the sand. The tiki hut and drink tent were closed. She circled the roasting pit and peeked behind the serving platform. No Ebby. Not that she had expected to see her there.

Frustrated, Shalane stopped to regroup. She took three deep breaths and called on Archangel Michael to help locate the woman, then leaned against the tiki hut and waited for direction. When none came, she slogged through the fine, crystalline sand, first in one direction, and then the other.

How could Ebby have disappeared? Shalane's spell should have confined her to the property, or at least signaled Shalane if Ebby tried to leave.

The beach was deserted. The lights had been doused, and the outdoor speakers switched off. Shalane wandered down to the hard-pack just above the waterline, where it was easier to walk.

She stopped to scan the dark beach in both directions, fighting anger. This was getting old. The woman was here. She had to be.

Mitch had been adamant. His plan hinged on Shalane locating Emily, so they could take her back to Atlanta tomorrow.

Shalane plodded through the infernal sand back to the jungle as a cooling wind sprang up, blowing the synthetic black tresses. Grateful for relief from the oppressive heat, she lifted the hair from her neck and went sprawling face-first into the sand.

What the hell? Had she tripped?

Someone moaned. Pivoting on hands and knees, Shalane felt along the dark sand and encountered skin—first a leg, then a thigh. A woman's.

Could this be Ebby?

Crawling closer, Shalane found an arm and followed it to a boob and on up. When her fingers tangled in a mass of curls, she knew it had to be Mitch's sister. Sliding one hand beneath the heavy head, Shalane leaned close and peered at the oval face. Ebby was out cold. Had Shalane done that?

She dragged the woman into her lap, brushing sand from her hair and dress. The body seemed frail beneath the thin material. Shalane remembered her having more curves. Was Ebby sick?

She jumped when the surf slapped against the shore. It crashed and fell, then receded to the sea. Thunder rolled, far away. The breeze stiffened. Shalane looked to the sky. The stars that had shone so brightly earlier, had disappeared. Lightning flashed, backlighting the clouds.

Shalane hugged Ebby to her, rocking slowly to the rhythm of the tide. Ebby's face against her breast should make Shalane hornier than a teenaged boy at an orgy. But she felt no heat. Not even a spark.

Instead, she felt a heavy sense of duty. She'd promised to bring Mitch's sister to him. But Shalane hadn't expected this. *This* was Mitch's sister, Emily Hester, not the Ebby Panera that Shalane had loved.

Settling Emily's head on the ground, Shalane rose to trudge back through the sand to tell the driver to ready the boat. Thunder rolled, louder and closer. Shalane eyed the distance to the house and groaned. Oh, how she detested the beach. A soft rain began to fall.

"Oh, great. Sand in my crotch *and* I'll soon be drenched."

Emily woke to water dripping on her face. It took a moment to realize she was still on the beach and in the rain. And another to remember why. The dread and doom came rushing back, threatening to keep her down.

But she sat up anyway, groaning when pain shot through her head above her right ear. She cupped her temples and pressed, momentarily keeping her head from bursting and spewing gray matter everywhere. Or so it felt.

The pain hadn't been this bad in a while—at least a couple of weeks. Rising to a squat sent the knife deeper. Emily waited for a second, then hauled herself up bit by bit, and braced her hands on her knees. With every breath it hurt like the dickens. She scanned her foggy memory for a pain-relieving spell and mumbled the words.

Nothing happened.

She stood up straight, shoulders back. The pain ratcheted up another notch. Focusing as best she could, Emily connected with the beach, the rain-filled sky, the vast, churning ocean, and the fire burning in the belly of the earth. Feeling a burst of energy, she whispered the spell as rain dripped from her chin.

This time, the pain eased a little. Her labored breathing calmed. From the corner of one eye, Emily caught a movement. She glanced toward the pit and spied a silhouette lumbering through the rain in her direction. Danger meter maxing, Emily edged closer to the jungle and crouched low. The black figure neared, huffing and growling in a familiar voice.

Emily's heart pounded. It couldn't be.

Shalane stopped and looked behind her. She should've come across Emily by now. Had she walked too far? Frantic, she peered into the night. The rain had ceased for the moment, but clouds still shrouded the thin moon, and the lights from the house had been extinguished. She could see no further than a few feet. Shalane doubled back, weaving from jungle to hardpack, searching for Emily Hester.

The witch passed her, muttering profanities. Emily shifted in the thick underbrush, timing her movements to the crash of the tide. Briars slashed her bare arms and legs. Biting her lip to keep from crying out, Emily debated whether to make a break for the house. She was about to do that very thing when the mumbling ceased and Shalane halted midstride. Emily held her breath.

Shalane turned and walked in her direction, then veered toward the beach. It was now or never. Gathering her courage, Emily parted the brush, gouging her arms. She sneaked out of the coppice and edged along the border, darting back in when Shalane turned and walked her way.

☼☼☼

Losing patience, Shalane peered through the darkness shrouding the beach. She inched toward the jungle, shrieking when the bushes parted noisily, and Emily Hester materialized.

"Leave me alone, you psycho witch!"

"Psycho?" Shalane chuckled.

"Stay away from me, Shalane. Or, you'll wish you had!" Emily knocked her flat and ran toward the house.

Still on her backside, Shalane spoke an incantation to hog-tie Emily's legs. Her quarry cried out as she hit the sodden beach. Shalane smiled. Another spell bound Emily's wrists and taped her big mouth shut.

Satisfied Emily couldn't escape or call for help, Shalane hauled herself up and huffed across the beach to leer down at her captive. She nudged her with one toe. The whites of Emily's eyes gleamed, and she strained against her restraints.

Now to get her to the speedboat.

Levitating Emily a few feet off the ground, Shalane marched behind her to the dock, cursing the wet, shifting sand every step of the way.

SEARCH AND RESCUE

Khenko raked his winnings to him. He might be sloshed, but he could still beat a bunch of amateurs. Randall sat next to him rubbing his back. He had gone all-in earlier and lost.

"Ready to head home?" Randall might not be much of a poker player, but he was good at plenty of other things.

Nodding, Khenko rose, and for the first time in hours, wondered what had become of Emily. Frantic now, he and Randall searched the bungalow. She wasn't there, or in the yard, or on any of the patios. They hurried down the path to the beach, but Emily wasn't there, either.

"Maybe she got tired and went back to the Center," Randall suggested. "She wasn't all that keen on coming in the first place."

"True," Khenko replied. "Only I don't think she would leave without telling me first." A chill went through him. Something was wrong.

They interrupted the poker game, but no one at the table had seen Emily. Thanking Manny for a kick-ass party, Khenko and Randall stumbled down the verandah stairs to the gravel drive. Drunkenly weaving their way toward the center, Randall stopped to take a piss in the jungle, and Khenko joined him.

Arm-in-arm, they stumbled up his driveway, snickering and helping each other walk. When a wild sow squealed nearby, scaring them both, they squealed in answer and raced up the stairs.

The door was unlocked, the way Khenko had left it. But Emily Hester was not inside. Holy Mother of God, he'd gotten drunk and lost the Awen.

☼☼☼

The boat sped over the choppy sea. In the bow where Shalane had dumped her none-too-gently, Emily worked to unbind her hands. She was getting nowhere, and thanks to the unmerciful pounding she was taking, the headache had come back in full force.

"I've got our girl." In the stern, Shalane talked on the ship-to-shore, her silhouette visible in the scant light.

Our girl? Who could Shalane be talking to?

Emily craned her neck, hoping to enlist the driver's aid. He'd seemed surprised and uneasy when Shalane brought her on board, but he was out of sight in the forward compartment. Emily tried again to do a spell, but her mouth was taped shut, and her arms and legs bound.

Remembering Losgann the frog Elder's instructions, Emily squeezed her eyes tight and silently called the dragons, focusing on her predicament and whereabouts. The boat skipped over a large wave and slammed into the trough so hard, Emily yelped and nearly fainted. She shifted an inch to cushion her head on the life jacket Shalane had thrown at her after tossing her in the bow.

Her mind raced, working on an escape plan in case the dragons didn't hear or respond. But the boat was speeding through rough waters, and every thud racked her head until the pain became an ungodly roar.

The sickle moon disappeared, and the drizzle started again. It soon settled into a downpour, every drop a stinging torture against Emily's exposed skin. Her body temperature plummeted, and an uncontrollable shiver set in.

☼☼☼

Dragon roar startled Khenko awake from the alcoholic stupor into which he must've fallen. Hauling his bones off the sofa, he rubbed his eyes and hurried to the back porch. There in the drizzling rain, with her front paws planted on the top step, Talav howled loud enough to wake the island.

"Alright, alright, I'm up. What is it?" Khenko yawned. Then his eyes opened wide. He vaguely remembered calling the dragon. Emily was missing, and he was to blame. "Oh crap! It's Emily. She left the party, and we can't find her."

The dragon roared, long and loud, then lowered her jeweled head to stare at him "You had one task. One tiny task. Now you've lost the Awen. Do you have any idea how long it took to find her in the first place?" Her angry roar shook the back porch.

Khenko hung his head. The drizzle turned to rain that pelted the tin roof. "Yes, and I'm sorry," he said over the noise. "I know you're worried, Talav. I'm worried, too."

The dragon's new face horns stood erect. "As well you should be, young stork." Khenko had never seen them do that before. "The Awen could teach you a thing or two. She contacted us before you did. Ooschu and a-Ur are on their way to rescue her."

"To where? Where is she?"

"On a boat heading toward the big island." Talav shook her mighty head, drenching Khenko. "The witch named Shalane and a local man have her bound and gagged. The witch has a grudge, and is up to no good."

Mentally chastising himself, Khenko turned toward the kitchen to grab his slicker and the keys to his boat.

"No, healer. You will stay here with me. The Awen may require your care when they return."

"But I don't understand. How did Shalane get to Emily? She was with us."

Something crept into Khenko's memory. The sultry singer with long, black hair had interrupted the card game to ask about Emily. After that, he had forgotten all about Emily until the game was over.

How long ago had that been? They could already be in Nassau by now.

☼☼☼

Surfacing, Ooschu spied the boat and swam faster. Far above him, a-Ur soared. As they approached the watercraft, a-Ur dropped lower. Together they closed on the kidnappers.

Pulling flush with the speeding craft, Ooschu signaled readiness. Seconds later, the air dragon dove in a whistling trajectory to snatch the Awen from the prow, then flapped its wings to disappear behind a cloud.

Taking his cue, Ooschu lunged beneath the boat and came up quickly, catapulting the vessel out of the water. The powerful motor growled as the boat somersaulted end-over-end. The Awen's kidnappers flew clear, their screams abruptly ending when they hit the waves. Then, the boat crashed upside down, sending a plume of seawater sky-high.

Ooschu ducked beneath the waves and swam for Zephyr Cay.

Shalane rolled to her back and treaded water, sputtering when a wave broke over her head. Clutching her skirt to keep it from tangling around her legs, she said a spell to right the speedboat and bring it to her. At least the rain had stopped for the moment.

Clamoring up the ladder, Shalane squeezed the brine from the hem of her skirt and spoke another spell to stall the motor and restore the vessel to its previous condition. When a simple locator spell failed to reveal Emily's position, a sick feeling plundered Shalane's gut.

The islander swam toward the boat, bobbing in the rough surf. He climbed the ladder and shook his dreads, sending water everywhere. Shalane readied to try another spell

"Wha' hoppen mon?"

"I have no idea. Don't you know? Didn't you see what hit us?" The dreads shook vigorously.

"No'ting, mum." The whites of his eyes grew larger as he peered suspiciously at the vast ocean, then restarted the engine. Shalane held up a hand.

"Wait! Give me a minute."

The motor idled, but she could tell the islander was not happy with the command.

Ignoring him, Shalane found her center, called on Archangel Michael, and reached out energetically in a circle for miles. There was no trace of Emily Hester. She searched deep down into the sea, yielding the same results. No Emily.

Shaking with rage, Shalane threw back her head and screamed into the night, while the driver cowered beside the purring motor. She reached up to the sky, stirred the clouds into a frenzy, and sent them shrieking in the direction of Zephyr Cay.

Feeling only slightly better, Shalane collected her wits and motioned the driver to get them to dry land.

READY OR NOT

Flying back to the Atlantean Center was exhilarating, though a-Ur's claws sliced into Emily, and her head screamed bloody murder. Despite all that, she was grateful to be free from Shalane, who was crazier than ever.

The sickle moon broke through a cloud, sending sparkles across the sea. Emily lifted her gaze. The Center was just ahead. Thunder rumbled behind them as a-Ur propelled them to the beach. He gently released Emily and landed beside her.

"Are you okay, Awen?" The air dragon blinked his silver eyes and the tape over Emily's mouth disappeared.

"Yes. No. I guess so. But, my head is screaming and my body aches. Thank you for coming, and for rescuing me." She tried to stand, then gave up and held out her hands. "Plus, I'm a little tied up at the moment."

"Silly Awen," a-Ur eyed her with disdain. "Why didn't you conjure a protective spell?"

"I couldn't use my hands."

a-Ur stared in disbelief. "You what?"

"I couldn't use my hands *or* speak." Emily squirmed when a-Ur laughed.

"You don't need your hands for a spell, deary. Do you talk with your hands? No. You talk with your mouth. And if you can't speak out loud, what do you do? You say the spell in your head."

Emily blinked as a-Ur's revelation sunk in. "You're saying all I have to do is speak the spell? I don't need to do all that other stuff?"

"You are the Awen, deary. No one on Earth is more powerful than you when you *are* you. Remember that. And use it to push your limits. You are capable of doing things most druids cannot. Go ahead. Get rid of your bonds."

Emily quieted her mind, then silently spoke the spell to free her limbs. The bindings disappeared. Astounded, she peered up at the air dragon.

"Why has no one ever told me that? And why hasn't it worked before? I usually have to try spells two or three times. And even then, they only work if I connect with the elements. Otherwise, nothing happens."

"Maybe you're getting better. Or maybe you just needed to know how powerful you are. Practice makes perfect. Isn't that the saying?"

Emily nodded and hummed Taliesin's ballad. Thunder rumbled as the storm moved closer.

"What's that you're singing?"

"Just a tune that's been in my head all—"

A roar sounded, loud and near. Talav ran toward her with Khenko on her tail.

"You found her. The Awen is safe." Talav bowed her head in salutation, then scrutinized a-Ur. "Well done, brother, well done."

Khenko helped Emily to her feet and slung a supporting arm around her. A fine rain began to fall. Khenko gasped.

"What the heck? You're bleeding, Emily."

Emily arched her back and moaned. The cuts were deep. Blood dripped down her arms and legs. But first things first.

"I'm sorry, Khenko. Shalane must have been at the party. When I left the table and went to the bathroom, I got sick from the punch and the rich food. Then I had an anxiety attack. The vertigo was so bad, I laid down on the beach and must have passed out. Shalane was searching for me and stumbled over my head. Literally." She fingered the nasty scrape on her temple.

"Does Shalane have long black hair?"

Emily nodded. "Not usually, but she did tonight. You saw her?" Khenko let go of a string of expletives before he answered.

"Yes, but I had no idea it was Shalane. Come to the house and let me tend to those cuts." He turned her in that direction.

Ooschu emerged from the surf and waded to shore growling. "The witch escaped and sent a storm this way. We must get Awen out of here. If she knows her whereabouts, others will too."

Terror ripped through Emily. Her temperature was dangerously low, her head was splitting in two, and she was one big, gigantic ache. Hunkering close to Khenko, she pressed her hands into her temples and rounded on the dragons.

"I am not going anywhere until one of you gets rid of this blasted headache. And for the love of God, would you magick away these lacerations? a-Ur, I am grateful to you and Ooschu for rescuing me, but your claws are deadly."

She glared at the air dragon, not giving a rat's ass that he towered over her menacingly. When none of them obliged, Emily clenched her fists and stomped her feet—which made the pain worse and brought tears to her eyes.

Khenko moved to scoop her into his arms, but a-Ur forbade it.

"If Emily wants to be the Awen, she must stop being pitiful and learn these things." The air dragon lowered his horned snout in front of her face. "Heal your wounds, Awen."

A brilliant stalk of lightning split the heavens over their heads. Thunder exploded and rolled away across the waves. Emily fell to her knees and hid her face in the sand. The engorged clouds let go and pummeled her with rain. The reek of ozone filled her senses, and nausea threatened.

Focusing on the earth supporting her frame, the rain against her skin, the air heaving in and out of her chest, and the fiery pain consuming her being, Emily drew a rasping breath and summoned the spell. It came to her from the depths of memory, or maybe from that of her ancestor.

Saying the words inside her head, Emily imagined a cloud of white light enveloping her body. It grew stronger and brighter until she went limp in the sand. Khenko was beside her in a heartbeat, lifting her head.

"Emily, you did it. Look! Your arms and legs are healed. The blood is even gone. It worked. You did it!"

She rolled onto her back and marveled at the skin covering her arms. No welts. No bruises. No lacerations. And no longer did her brain pound mercilessly against her skull. She checked her back and legs. They, too, were whole. Khenko was right.

"Well, I'll be blessed." Emily leapt from the sand, raised her arms to the heavens, and twirled in the rain squealing.

With a triumphant roar, Draig Ooschu proclaimed, "The Awen is ready."

"Aye, the Awen is ready," Talav and a-Ur chorused.

FATE STEPS IN

Nergal paced the living quarters, though his gait was little more than a hobble. The petite doctora with violet eyes was on the table in the next room fighting for her life. According to her doctor friend, the bullet had missed her vital organs. But she'd lost a lot of blood during the long flight to Araf.

The doctor's familiar had provided the use of this room before disappearing to assist her partner. They had both eyed Nergal and his companions fearfully and would have turned them away. But Magdalena was like family, they said, and they had made an exception.

Nergal wobbled and limped the other way. Pain and fatigue slowed his steps, but he would not rest until the doctora was safe.

The headlines scrolling across the ancient screen confirmed what they had learned on the streets of Araf. Shibboleth had issued a warrant for Nergal's arrest for the murder of Maw the Punisher. Ishkur, Inanna, and Magdalena were similarly charged, with a fifty-thousand-credit reward on the head of each. According to the feed, the Draconian army was searching for them in and around Agartha and Xibalba IX.

"Great," Inanna snorted. "Two more places I won't be able to frequent. At least they didn't mention Araf."

Ishkur snored lightly in a nearby chair. Nergal sank into the one beside him, then hauled himself back up to pace.

☼☼☼

"Magda is stable, but her condition is serious," the doctor announced. "A projectile had lodged near her spine, but I was able to get it out. I'd like to keep her here under observation for the new few days." His familiar bustled in.

"Come. Eat. I've laid a simple meal in the back hall." She peered intently at Nergal and Inanna's injuries. "Those wounds need tending." She glanced at her partner, who nodded and touched Nergal's arm.

"Come with me."

In a room that seemed out of place in a residence, the doctor gestured to a stone ledge. Nergal climbed onto the uncomfortable table and laid on his back as instructed. The doctor positioned a bright lamp to inspect his wounds, then moved to his face.

"General Nergal, you are lucky to be alive." He probed the gash that had closed and reopened several times over the last weeks. Nergal roared in pain and lashed out at the doctor.

Nimble for one so old, the doctor leapt back, then peered at Nergal through magnifying goggles. "Must I secure your limbs to the table, Sir? Or will you lay still and refrain from maiming me while I treat your injuries?"

"Proceed," Nergal grunted. "I am a Draco warrior. I can handle pain."

"Well, I cannot. Shall I engage the restraints?"

"Nay. I will cooperate."

"In that case," the doctor chose an instrument from a nearby shelf, "I will numb the wounds before I proceed. That will make this easier for us both." He paused and peered at Nergal intently. "Not that I care about your comfort. Your warriors laid waste to this village centuries ago. You killed my life partner and much of my family."

Nergal growled. It wasn't in him to feel remorse. "Then do it for Magdalena, and I'll let you live."

The doctor's laugh taunted Nergal. "You dare threaten me? Your life is in my hands, Sir. Be careful, or you'll find yourself dead, rather than healed. Now, may I proceed?"

Disgusted by his own pathetic weakness, Nergal nodded and turned his head away. He felt the sting of the needle, then the pain eased. Inside of a minute, he was out cold.

☼☼☼

Nergal couldn't believe his pain was nearly gone. His wounds were healing at a remarkable pace, aided by the treatment the doctor had administered. He could even stand tall, though he listed slightly to the right. The slash across his face added a terrifying feature that would prove useful in battle, but it wouldn't win him any points with the ladies.

Aware of the doctora next to him, Nergal felt an unfamiliar warmth creep into his cheeks. Without Magdalena's help, he would've died in Agartha. The violet-eyed medic had not left his side since they'd fled the city—until Maw shot her. Now it was Nergal's turn to watch over the doctora.

Part of him hated what he'd become. It was not in his nature to need, or give, help. But long had he hovered at death's door, and without Nergal's permission, something had changed, even softened, inside him. His will to exact revenge on Shibboleth remained, outweighing his contempt. If help was what he needed, then help he would accept.

He glanced at Magdalena. She was pale and feeble but recovering, thanks to her doctor friend. The door opened, and the white-coated Reptilian bustled in. Nergal eyed the aging Draco with distrust. His ministrations had given Nergal new life and saved Magdalena, but he'd also threatened to kill Nergal.

After examining them, the doctor declared their progress satisfactory. He gave each another healing injection and declared the last would be administered the next day. After that, they would be on their own.

There was a commotion in the back, and the doctor hurried from the exam room. Nergal shepherded Magda to the hideout in the basement, then hurried upstairs to find the uproar had been caused by the return of Inanna and Ishkur. They sat wide-eyed and breathing hard.

"Nergal, we must flee," Ishkur gasped. "We were scouting the area, and Shibboleth's goons saw us."

"You're bleeding!" Inanna cried. "They got you." She applied compression to Ishkur's wound. Her own were barely visible after receiving the doctor's miraculous treatment, but Ishkur's yellow blood spotted the shiny floor.

"I'll be fine, we must go. Now!" Ishkur barked.

"That's a deep tear. At least let me wrap it so you don't bleed out. Come," the doctor ordered, pulling Ishkur toward the exam room.

The Draco grabbed Nergal's arm. "Get our packs and take the females. Head east and north. Shibboleth's men lie in the opposite direction. Hurry, they will soon be here."

When Nergal hesitated, Ishkur pushed him toward the door. "Go. I'll catch up with you."

Nergal drew the hood closer and shrank into the midday shadows. Shibboleth's spies were everywhere, and Ishkur had yet to find them. Seeing a wanted poster hawking the foursome's guilt, he ripped it down, tore it to shreds, and scattered the pieces underfoot. It felt good to be himself again.

"We should wait for Ishkur," Inanna pled, not for the first time.

"No. We keep going. He will find us."

Magdalena took his claw in hers. "Please, Nergal. I need to rest."

He noted her pale cheeks and looked around for a hiding place.

"Over there," Inanna pointed to a collapsed structure.

They scurried from the shadows and wiggled through an opening at the base. Finding a large pocket in which to hide and see the street, they settled down to rest and wait for Ishkur.

Presently, there was a racket nearby. Nergal rose to attention but remained in the shadows. Draco warriors were knocking on doors and inspecting the area.

Hissing quietly, he roused Inanna and Magda, both of whom had fallen asleep, something they all sorely needed. But they couldn't leave the ruins without attracting attention.

Huddling close, they stayed low and waited for Ishkur. Or worse, to be captured.

SPEAK THE WORD

Brian and Ethnui walked for hours in silence. Her handheld had resynced at the edge of Mu, before ducking into the tunnels. Neither spoke of their experience in Mu, or of their harried flight to escape the villagers.

Brian switched his heavy pack to the other shoulder. "How much further?"

Ethnui consulted her wrist unit. "Another few minutes, I think."

A half hour later, Ethnui halted. "We should be there by now." She pointed to a notch dug into the granite. "I recognize this mark. We passed it earlier. I think we must've missed a side-tunnel." She blew out an exasperated breath.

"Great. We're lost." Brian nibbled at a nail.

"Shhh!" Hamilton shushed, startling them both.

In the quiet, they heard it. A soft slithering in the tunnel behind them.

"Alexis?" Ham called.

The slithering continued, growing louder. Taking Ethnui's hand, Brian pulled her with him to investigate. The sound stopped, and they stood quietly for a long minute before it started again.

"Sssssss…"

Brian's neck tingled. "It's behind us."

He turned in the direction they'd been traveling and shined his light. Where the wall met the floor was an opening, but nothing else. Brian inched closer. The hole was just large enough to shimmy through.

He waved his light over it. "Should we see what's in there?"

Ethnui's nose scrunched in distaste. She looked at both ends of the long, dark tunnel and wagged her head. "I guess we should. If it's a dead end, we can retrace our steps."

"You first."

"Manners, Brian!" Hamilton scolded out loud.

Ethnui squatted and shined her light into the hole. "It looks like it goes through to the other side." She scooted closer and slung her legs over the edge, rolled her eyes at Brian, and slid inside. There was a scraping whoosh, a thud, and a grunt. Then nothing.

Brian dropped to his belly and yelled into the hole, "Ethnui?"

"Uh-huh?"

"You okay down there?"

"Yes. Come on down. There's another passage, and it leads in the right direction."

Brian twisted to sit on the edge, legs dangling. Slipping his lightstick into the side pocket of his pack, he yelled, "Geronimo!" and pushed off, falling a short distance onto a pile of rocks.

"OUCH!" he groaned and scrambled to his feet.

"Shhh!" Ethnui warned. "I hear something."

"Like what?" Brian dusted his hind end and picked a chunk of gravel out of his elbow.

"Shhh!" she repeated.

Realizing he was panting, Brian held his breath. A slithering came from the tunnel to their right.

"Isn't that east?" he said quietly.

"Yes." Ethnui flicked her flashlight down the tunnel, then over Brian.

"Oww," he whined, clamping a hand over his eyes. "Why'd you do that?"

"Making sure you're in one piece." Her tone was light. Which calmed his skittering nerves just a little. "Ready?"

He drew his light from his pack and trained its beam on hers. "After you."

The path climbed steadily and was steep in places. Before long, Brian broke into a sweat. He stopped to tie his jacket around his waist and shove his sleeves up, then hurried to catch Ethnui. She stood in front of an enormous mound of rocks that blocked the path.

"What the hay?" Brian came up beside her. "Looks like a cave-in or something."

"It's another dead-end is what it is." Her tone was heavy with disappointment. "We'll have to go back."

"Wait! Listen!" Ham interjected, making Brian jump.

A scrabbling sound echoed through the chamber. On the other side of the mound, something scratched at the rocks. Brian and Ethnui looked at one another, eyebrows raised.

"A rat most likely." She waved a dismissive hand. "Or some other furry creature. I doubt it would hurt us."

Tackling the pile, Brian hefted rocks and chunked them to the side. "Help me, Ethnui."

"No. Stand back. Both of you," Hamilton ordered. "Remember that spell you memorized? The one we used to get the stones off your legs?"

"Yes!" Brian thumped his forehead with his palm. "I keep forgetting I know magic!"

Ethnui flicked the light over his face, and he clamped his eyes shut.

"Do it, Human. Get us out of this hell."

With a confidence born of having done it before, Brian spoke the spell. The rocks rolled from the opening as easily as they had lifted from his legs the other day.

"Way to go!" Ethnui cheered. Brian took a sweeping bow.

Together, they stepped through the opening into a large chamber. On the far wall, their lights illuminated a series of crude steps that were carved into the bedrock. Approaching the earthen staircase, they directed their beams up toward the ceiling. Eyes the size of saucers blinked amber in the light.

Shrieking, Brian dropped his lightstick and backed away quickly. Ethnui stumbled into him and grabbed his hand to keep from falling. An electrical shock shot through Brian, giving him the strength to face anything.

Until a deep, gravelly roar shook the chamber, and dirt and pebbles rained on their heads. Brian's knees knocked together, and he was grateful for the reassurance of Ethnui's hand. He squeezed and held tight.

"Approach, young raven," the voice boomed.

Trembling all over, Brian consulted Hamilton. "Sir? We could really use your help about now."

"Whoever it is, must know you. They called you 'young raven'. I say we approach."

"You are wise to do so, Master Druid." This time, the gruff voice came from the other side of the chamber.

They wheeled, and Ethnui shined her light in that direction.

The cave sprang to life as rays of colored light shot from thousands of mirrors and danced upon the walls. Huddled amid the flamboyant prisms, the amber eyes gleamed. And below the eyes was the largest collection of teeth Brian had ever seen.

"It's a dragon!" he gasped and backed through the opening with Ethnui. His legs trembled, and his heart pounded. This was worse than lizard-men—and a heckuva lot bigger. Its enormous gemmed body filled the chamber.

"Leaving already?" The dragon sounded amused. "You just got here." It bowed politely. "Hello, lovely lady. My name is Talav. Might I have yours?"

"E-Ethnui," the Fomorian sputtered.

"Such a pretty name. Pleased to meet you, deary." The dragon's long neck swung back toward Brian. Its eyes gleamed. "Where is the master druid?"

"You are a dragon," Ethnui gasped in disbelief. "I've heard about dragons, heard they still existed. But I didn't believe it. Not until now." She moved a half-step closer to the scaled creature. Rudimentary horns stood at attention atop a crocodilian face that swerved toward the Fomorian.

"No, Ethnui. Come back." Brian grabbed a handful of her robe and tugged hard. "That thing will eat you."

"Bwahahahaha, heeheehee, hahahahah!" Its booming laughter reverberated through the chamber, dislodging more stones.

Brian ducked and clapped his hands over his head. When the laughter died away, he stepped to the middle of the available space and faced the dragon. Since the beast hadn't fried them, and it had enjoyed a good laugh at their expense, it probably wasn't planning to eat them. At least, not yet.

"Who are you, Sir?" Brian demanded. The dragon roared, but Brian stood his ground when its hot breath seared the hair on his head.

"I am Talav, Queen of the Earth Dragons, Keeper of Earth's portals. It is my job to keep UnderEarth creatures inside where they belong and AboveEarth beings out of harm's way."

Brian's excitement grew. "I know you! Hope, the cat Elder told us the story of Awen and the Dragon Keepers. You're one of them. You're Talav!"

The dragon's eyes glittered. "Aye. That was no story, but pure truth." It burped and flames licked the ceiling. Brian and Ethnui ducked. The dragon chuckled.

"I thought Emily was with you. Can you help us? Can you get us back to AboveEarth?" Brian held his breath and prayed she would help them. If not, they'd have to make a run for the tunnels and hope for the best.

Talav stretched her long, jeweled neck toward the carved staircase. "You stand before a portal between the worlds. As I said before, it is my sworn duty to keep all from passing." Colored lights danced about the cave when she settled on her haunches.

Brian's nerve wavered, but he stood tall. Ethnui stepped up beside him and slipped her arm through his. Strength coursed through him. Nudging him with her elbow, she nodded toward the tunnel. He winked understanding and turned slightly in that direction.

"Halt!" the dragon bellowed. "I shall not harm you. In fact, I intend to help. Assuming you are indeed a friend of the Awen." The yellow eyes twinkled.

Brian held tight to Ethnui's hand. Awen was Emily's ancestor, the source of her power. "You mean Emily?"

The dragon cocked its head to one side. "Yes, that is her earthly name. Or so she keeps insisting."

Brian's hope rekindled. "Where is she? We were separated in the earthquake."

"She is safe beyond your ken, young raven. Do you want my help? Or would you retrace your treacherous steps to nowhere to escape my good intentions?"

Ethnui stepped forward, keeping a firm grasp on Brian's hand. "Losgann the Frog Elder sent us here. Can you get us through the barrier between the worlds?"

The dragon towered over them now, wing-nubs lifted, horns extended, and scales flinging kaleidoscopic-colors everywhere.

"Speak the word, friend of Awen, and I shall let you pass."

The word? Brian's heart beat so hard it might burst from his chest.

"And what word would that be, Queen Talav? I am tired, hungry, and in no mood for games. What word could I give you that would grant us passage from this miserable place? Uncle? Abracadabra? Beam me up, Scotty? What word is it that you seek, oh wise one?"

The dragon laughed, a long, throaty, rumbling roar that echoed through the chamber and dislodged more rocks. Brian and Ethnui crouched and covered their heads. When its mirth was spent, it settled on mighty haunches.

"You have a sense of humor, young raven. Speak the word of passage and I shall clear the way for you and the Fomorian."

Frustrated, Brian growled and stomped his feet. He let go of Ethnui's hand and a word formed, tickling his senses.

"Please?" he mumbled.

THE FERRY

Emily showered quickly and donned the casual linen pants and kiwi-colored blouse, then stuffed underwear, tank tops, and assorted toiletries into a hemp shoulder bag. Though the storm seethed overhead, a-Ur had demanded they leave for the vortex at once.

Zipping the bag closed, she removed Aóme from its hiding place and slipped the emerald on her index finger, feeling stronger right away. The ruby amulet she placed around her neck, and the otter and frog stone she tucked in each of her pants pockets.

Eyeing her reflection in the full-length mirror, she hummed Taliesin's song and pulled her wayward hair back in a bun. She fastened it with the ivory pin Khenko had presented her with loving tenderness. He'd said it was one of his prized possessions and would be an asset to Emily should the need arise.

On the beach beneath the shelter of the cabana, the dragons gave Emily final instructions. One by one, they schooled her on setting protective spells, wormhole logistics, and what to do when they reached Beli. Then they waited impatiently in the driving rain while Emily said goodbye to Khenko.

Promising to keep in touch, she hugged and thanked the new friend she owed so much. She eyed the Center and its surrounding grounds, gaze lingering on the back porch and narrow beach where they had spent so much time. With a resigned lump clogging her throat, Emily tied the plastic hood close to her head, waved to the dragons, and turned to follow the medicine man.

They wound along the shore a short way, then cut through the jungle to a cove Emily had not visited before. The wind howled in from the ocean, whipping the palms into a frenzy and driving the rain sideways against her plastic slicker.

The craft Khenko used to ferry seekers to the vortex rocked in its mooring. He climbed over the side and into the enclosed cabin. Admiring the vessel's workmanship and size, Emily climbed in, grateful for the dry, air-conditioned interior. She removed her rain gear as the motor roared to life. Its throaty purr competed with the drumming torrent on the fiberglass roof.

"Here goes nothing," Khenko yelled above the din.

The boat inched backward through the churning water until it cleared the floating dock. Forwarding the throttle, Khenko maneuvered the vessel out to sea, where Emily could barely see Ooschu and Talav cavorting in the swells. The dragons would escort them to the vortex.

Overhead, the storm raged, drowning the thrum of the powerful engine. Emily gripped the seat as waves crashed against the sturdy boat, swamping the gunwales. Tropical rain strafed the cabin, and the wind wailed through the flapping ensign flag.

The ship pitched from side to side. Emily's queasiness returned. When they hit a deep trough, her stomach lurched and she held on tight. The smoothie she had downed threatened to come back up. She fought the nausea and tried to keep her eyes on a horizon that wasn't visible.

"Hey!" Khenko yelled, leaning close. "You healed your wounds back there at the center, and you've been working on weather spells. Think you could calm this storm?" His bushy eyebrows conveyed fear and hope.

Emily blinked like a paralyzed owl.

He backed off the throttle. "I'll set the engine to idle if you want to try."

Terror clutched at Emily's heart. She stared at Khenko, remembering the tornados that had spared Jocko's Restaurant while ripping Druid Hills apart, and the blizzard Awen had quelled at Wren's Roost. What he asked was possible. But could she do it?

Emily wavered, too frightened to move.

"I'm here," Awen whispered. "You can do it."

Courage shot through Emily like the lightning that ripped across the sky. She stood, determined, as thunder cracked and rolled. "Why the hell not?" she yelled over the noise. "The worst that can happen is nothing, right?"

Donning the wet slicker, Emily tied the hood under her chin, and exited the cabin. Wind and rain slammed against her. Clinging to the handle, she reached for a stanchion and held on tight, squealing when the door slammed behind her. She peered over the side into the raging sea and almost barfed.

Gathering her wits, she swallowed hard and nodded to Khenko through the cabin window. Blinding rain lashed her face and streamed down her chin. Emily recited the Lord's Prayer and squeezed between the cabin and bulwark. A stalk of lightning lit the heavens and thunder boomed. The sweet scent of ozone filled the air.

Wedged in place, she planted her legs to absorb the pitching. Dawn infused the gloom with light, but all she could see was driving rain. Emily stroked the emerald ring on her forefinger and inhaled deeply, then exhaled before sucking in another long breath.

Holding Aóme against the amulet on her chest, she thought of the ancestor from whence she had sprung. A warmth spread through Emily's limbs. Her heart soared. Feeling Awen's power gather within her, Emily flung her head back to beseech the sky.

She reveled in the wind and rain upon her face, and the vast ocean cradled by the earth. Tapping into the fire that burned within her, Emily spoke the spell, adding her own twist, "I increase the witch's storm and send it back to her."

The rain ceased.

The wind stilled momentarily, then changed directions.

The storm barreled off to the east.

The ocean stopped churning and settled into a gentle swell.

Emily squealed. Her invocation had worked. And without being controlled or possessed by the Awen.

Thanking her Maker *and* her ancestor, Emily ratcheted out of the tight space and ducked into the cabin.

"I did it!" she shrieked to the grinning medicine man.

Khenko delivered a sopping bear hug, then high-fived her proudly. "You certainly did. Way to go, kid."

a-Ur swooped down and tipped a wing in homage. Ooschu and Talav breached the ocean and saluted Emily from the air. Grinning, she breathed a sigh of relief.

"I sent the storm back to Shalane in Nassau," she muttered sheepishly to Khenko. "I hope we don't have to go that way."

STAYING BEHIND

After showering and changing clothes at the resort, Shalane buzzed the front desk for a bellhop and waited impatiently. Her trip to the Bahamas had been a bust. Well, not totally. At least she knew that Emily was alive.

Only where was she now? And how had she escaped? The woman's powers must be strong indeed, to magick herself from a tied-up position in the bottom of Shalane's boat and vanish into midair. Her disappointment was bitter. Shalane had wanted to deliver Emily to her brother. Now she would be forced to tell him she had failed. Not the greeting she had anticipated.

Shalane took a motor cab to the tiny airport, which consisted of two runways and one small building. There was a surprising amount of activity, considering the early hour. It was still dark.

Making a beeline for a tiny cafe that had just opened, she ordered a cup of coffee and a muffin. But, before it was delivered, she was confronted by Mitch Wainwright. Her heart quickened, in spite of his obvious temper.

"What took you so long?" He grabbed her by the front of her shirt. Pulling her to him, he planted a kiss on Shalane lips, then held her away. "Where have you been? I've been waiting forever."

"Miss me?" she sassed.

"Only a little." The ice-blue eyes searched the terminal behind Shalane. "Where's Emily?" His tone was menacing.

Her own anger spiked. "Gone. I had her. I had Emily, Mitch." Color sprang to the attorney's handsome face. "Then, she disappeared. From the front of the boat. She was tied up, too. And she vanished, right from under my nose."

His brow crinkled into a surly scowl. "Then we're going back."

"No use. I searched. She's gone. It's time to go home, Mitch."

"But—"

"She's gone, Mitchell. Do you feel her energy?" He was silent a moment.

"No. Not particularly. But I'm not all that good at feeling energy." He looked out at the brightly-lit tarmac, at the bronzed Bahamian shuttling luggage into the hold, and the Learjet taxiing between two commercial liners waiting to take off.

Shalane studied his profile and wondered what he was thinking. She could read most men. This one, not so much. He slid his cell phone from his pocket and held up one finger, then spoke into the phone.

"Rochelle, this is Mitch. Clear my schedule for the next two days. This is going to take longer than I expected. If anything needs handling, give it to Scotty. And if you need me, call my cell. See ya soon."

He turned to Shalane. "I'm going to Zephyr Cay to talk to that healer. See if I can get a read on where Emily went. Want to stay another day? Maybe two?"

Shalane was sorely tempted. But she had to get back. They had already rescheduled several shows and her fans weren't happy. Not that she cared all that much about that. But Cecil and her manager were another story. She tucked a curl behind Mitch's ear and ran a nail over his cheek and chin.

"I wish I could. But I can't. I've got to get back to the tour."

Disappointment flashed in the blue eyes, then relief. He'd acted like he wanted her to stay. But did he? It was frustrating trying to read the man. He was as closed a book as any Shalane had seen.

"Suit yourself," he said brusquely and nodded toward the tarmac. Your plane is boarding. I plan to charter a boat to Zephyr Cay. Were there any decent hotels on the island?"

"I don't know. I would imagine." Shalane slung her purse over her shoulder and repositioned her carry-on. "I didn't stick around long enough to find out." The attendant gave the last boarding call. "I gotta go, Mitch. Be safe. And good luck finding Emily."

The flight attendant began closing the gate.

"Wait!" Shalane called. To Mitch she said, "I ordered coffee and a muffin if you're hungry. My order's up." She kissed his cheek and scurried to board. Scanning her pass, Shalane turned to wave goodbye, but the attorney was gone.

UP IN THE AIR

Lugh MacBrayer woke with a start. Dread curled in his gut. In his dream, Emily was trapped in a cave beneath a castle. And something was wrong. Unbuckling his seatbelt, Lugh climbed from the pod to stand in the aisle. The cabin lights were low and snores rose from sleeping passengers.

Through the opposite window, stars winked against a brightening sky. Lugh checked the time. 6:02 a.m. He hadn't slept long. The plane shuddered in a pocket of turbulence. Lugh grabbed the seatback just in time to keep from pitching into a muscular man who spilled over the side of his pod.

The PetJet leveled, and Lugh made his way to the midsection to check on Cu and Hope. It had cost a fortune, but Morgan's assistant had secured them first-class passage on a specialty-liner designed for traveling with larger pets. The wolfhound slept curled in his cramped, but sufficient quarters. He had made the journey without complaint, good nature intact. The dog's usual snores were dampened to a gentle snuffle.

Lugh reached inside the cage and ruffled the long face. Cu twitched and stretched his long, lanky limbs, then flopped to the other side and went back to sleep. In the adjacent cage, Hope's luminous eyes stared unwavering.

"Can't sleep?" Lugh caressed her black cheek stripes through the wire. Her answer sounded in his head.

"Barely a wink. I'd forgotten how much I hate flying." Lugh tickled the sweet spot behind her ear and was rewarded with a purr.

"I've got a bad feeling." Lugh's gaze flicked over the other cages.

Hope shifted positions, coming up into a crouch. "Me, too. Another reason I can't sleep."

"I had a bad dream. Emily's in trouble."

"Yes, I feel it, too. But there is nothing we can do. For the moment, at least. We're thirty-five thousand feet in the air and on a plane." She rolled her eyes. "My least favorite thing to do."

"But this was your idea." Lugh ran his hand across his sandpaper face. His five-o-clock shadow had turned into the beginnings of a beard.

"We do what we have to do for the Order," she purred. "And the Awen."

LIVE LONG AND PROSPER

Thirty, smooth-sailing minutes after Emily magicked the storm east, they reached the edge of the vortex. a-Ur arrived first. Ooschu and Talav brought up the rear. Lightning split the morning sky, followed quickly by a cracking boom. Emily jumped. The storm must've reached Nassau by now.

Khenko killed the motor and dropped anchor.

"What now?" he asked a-Ur, who hovered above the bow.

"Now *we* enter the wormhole. You, Khenko, must stay behind."

"But—"

"Dear crane, you cannot go," Talav said from the starboard side of the vessel. "Your path lies in a different, less dangerous, direction than the one that we must tread. Your service to the cause will not be forgotten. Be well, gentle sir. Live long and populate the earth with your kind."

Emily watched the tall man, knowing how much he hated goodbyes. He hung his head to hide his tears, then looked up at Talav.

"Will I see you again? Will I remember, if I do?" His words were strangled.

Reaching into the boat, Talav caressed his cheek as if it were one of her jewels. "You may, Khenko Blitherstone. It is my fond hope that it be so." She chuffed and sank slowly into the warm Atlantic, but not before Emily saw a tear slip from one ochre eye.

Ooschu rose out of the water and used her powerful tail to balance on the port side facing Khenko. "Our time together has been edifying, my wise friend. Live long and spread your peace throughout the lands." Then she, too, slid into the drink.

The fierce a-Ur settled on the stern, tipping the vessel precariously. "You have delivered the Awen, mighty stork." He bowed to Khenko. "Now your service is complete. We'll take it from here. Live long and prosper through these dark times." a-Ur nodded to Emily. "Little wren, say goodbye to your friend. It is time to take your place as the Awen."

Tears blurred Emily's vision. Turning to Khenko, she threw her arms around his waist and buried her face against his chest. Long arms circled and held her close to rock her gently back and forth. Her heart nearly burst, so full was it with love for the man who'd brought her back from the dead.

"What can I say, Medicine Man?" Her smile wavered and tears trickled down her cheeks. The golden eyes gleamed. Chucking her under the chin, Khenko leaned close.

"Here's looking at you, kid."

She burst out laughing and returned the gesture, grateful to him for lightening the mood. Turning to a-Ur, she swallowed hard.

"I cannot believe I'm saying this, but I think I'm ready. Or as ready as I am going to be. What now?"

"Now, you cast a spell of protection so you don't get hurt. I will carry you into the vortex. Once inside, I will let go," a-Ur told Emily. "You must navigate this journey on your own. Remember to keep your mind on Beli, our destination. That is the key. The wormhole will do the rest."

Chest tight and heart racing, Emily set the protection charm, then reached impulsively for Khenko's hand. He smiled, nodded, and nudged her toward the dragon. Belief and something akin to reverence glowed in his eyes.

"Take care of Awen," he yelled to a-Ur, who snatched Emily up, quick as a wink.

DIVER DOWN?

Khenko stared at the newly-risen sun and wondered what he was doing at the vortex. Had he lost someone? That would explain the tears clouding his vision. Only there was no sign of an expedition.

Where were Sajak and Ke'nani? He would never take seekers out on his own. And what about the diving buoy? If someone had gone down, a buoy would be set. And the divers' flag. Plus, the boat was swamped, evidence of a nasty storm. So why in the world would he be out at sea? Alone? In a storm?

Engaging the bilge pump, Khenko stared at the ocean in every direction. No craft was in sight, not even the fishing boats that put out daily from Zephyr Cay at the crack of dawn. In the distance, he could hear a flight taking off from Nassau.

Khenko watched it climb, a C20-20 loaded with vacationers heading back to the states. He ducked inside the cabin to consult his captain's log. There it was, in Khenko's concise handwriting:

Departure—5:30am
Destination—the Vortex
Passengers—1
Name—Awen
Weather Conditions—squall

Khenko stepped outside to scan the sea again. He would never, ever go out in a squall—or in the dark, for that matter. It was just past sunrise. Where in the Devil's Triangle was this passenger named Awen? And why couldn't he remember anything?

The Arcana rocked on its anchorage, waves slapping against the hull. A capricious wind alternately fluttered the ensign flag and whistled through it. The scent of gardenias on a summer morn lingered just outside Khenko's awareness. Unable to pinpoint it, he went back inside.

It was quieter here, the gardenia more evident. He inspected the cabin for other signs of a passenger and came up empty. Pausing to ponder his next move, Khenko wondered why he didn't feel anxious. Why was he only slightly worried, when a woman was likely missing, and he may well have ferried her to her death? Assuming, of course, that Awen was a she.

The wind shifted, and a knowing came to Khenko, the sense that whatever he had come to do was complete. He fought the urge to start the engine and motor home, reaching instead for the radio. He must notify the coast guard.

"No!" Khenko heard inside his head.

He looked around. The voice was familiar, but no one was there. Silence reigned briefly, a pregnant silence full of answers. Or commands. They came at Khenko in rapid-fire succession.

"Go home. Pack your clothes."

"Go to Princeton. Your family awaits."

"It's time to become the leader you are meant to be."

"Time is short. The Darkness is nigh."

Khenko shook his head to clear the oddly-familiar voices, and used the binoculars to scour the ocean in every direction. The words cycled back.

"Go home. Pack your clothes. Go to Princeton."

"Be well. Live long. Populate the earth with your kind."

Feeling an urgency now that he couldn't explain, Khenko started the motor and raised the anchor. The words kept coming.

"Live long. Spread peace. Be strong. The world needs you."

Nudging the throttle forward, Khenko circled the perimeter and even ventured a short way into the Vortex.

"Your service is complete." That struck a chord.

"Go home. Pack your clothes. Live long. Prosper."

Turning toward Zephyr Cay, Khenko gunned the inboard motor. The ferry leapt eagerly for home.

ANOTHER WORLD

Brian stood atop a boulder overlooking a wide canyon. A hot wind whistled up from the valley floor, taking his breath. Sweat popped out on his brow. Beside him, Ethnui squealed—a peal of happiness that thrilled Brian's heart.

They slid from the boulder and landed on concrete beside an interpretive sign. Its bold letters read THE LEGEND OF BLOWING ROCK. Underneath, it elaborated.

"Look!" he crowed. "We're in Blowing Rock. We're out, we're out, we are finally out!" He grabbed Ethnui and spun her in a circle, then hugged her close, letting go when her scent tickled his nose. "But how did we get here?"

Ethnui slapped him on the back. "The last I remember, you used magic to clear the rocks from that entrance. Great job, by the way!"

A bead of sweat trickled down Brian's cheek. The sun shimmered through a haze of humidity, and though it appeared to be early morning, it felt like it must be a hundred degrees. But at least they were back in AboveEarth.

Which was weird, because Brian had no recollection of climbing any stairs, scaling any shafts, or anything else. His last memory was the same as Ethnui's—him performing the spell. For a fraction of a second, large yellow eyes flashed in his mind, then were gone.

Ethnui's gaze darted about. She clung to Brian's arm, wide eyes taking in everything. He glanced around to see what she was seeing—heatwaves radiating from the concrete, cloudless blue sky hemmed in by towering trees, the granite monument, the canyon below, the cars whooshing by on the highway passing the entrance to the park.

"What happens now?" Fear lurked in her big blue eyes.

Brian took the Fomorian's hand. It was as sweaty as his. With the back of his other arm, he swiped his bangs from his eyes.

"Christ, how long was I down there?" he moaned. "It was still cold when I left, and barely spring." The fear pinched Ethnui's features and she clung to him tighter. He was scaring her.

Brian had better pull it together. They were in his world now.

"Okay. First, let's get out of this heat." He fanned the front of his shirt. "And find a phone. We need money. And transportation to Atlanta." Brian stuck his nose to his underarm and sniffed. "And it would be great if we could take a shower and change into clean clothes."

Ethnui laughed and the pinched look disappeared.

But, Brian had no idea how they would pay for all that. Then, the hundred-dollar bill his mom had tucked into his wallet for emergencies, came to mind. He was pretty sure this qualified. And, miraculously, Brian still had the wallet.

A hundred dollars should be enough to buy a cheap phone. And he was betting his Uncle Lugh would take care of the rest.

They didn't have to go far. A hundred yards from Blowing Rock Park was an old, rambling hotel named Green Park Inn. Brian and Ethnui entered through a side door and ducked into the restrooms.

At the gift shop, Brian purchased a prepaid cell. He called Lugh, whose voice mail message said to call Morgan Foster. Morgan made arrangements for rooms at the hotel for him and Ethnui, clothes, and a ride to Atlanta.

Lugh, Morgan said, was on a plane headed to Wales. Brian told her about the Dracos plan to overtake Earth, then waited at the front desk while she paid for the rooms over the phone. Thirty minutes later, he was in the shower, washing off the grime of UnderEarth.

Morgan stared at the notes she'd written based on Brian's description of the Dracos. She had seen the article and resulting hullabaloo, but hadn't paid much attention until the FBI made a statement denouncing it on television. Which meant it was likely true. This could be the Darkness of which the Elders warned.

She hurried to her office and used the secure line to call the Director's personal number.

"Hobbs," the familiar voice announced.

"Kate, it's Morgan Foster. How in the world are you?"

"Ahh, you know, Morgan. Just up here sticking it to the bad guys. How're things back Atlanta? I see you're having a heat wave. You'd never know it was spring in D.C., there's an ice storm forecast for the weekend.

"But I know you didn't call to discuss the weather. What's up, my friend?"

"I'm afraid I have bad news."

"Dahlin', you always have bad news."

"Well this tops the chart. Remember the young druid caught in the earthquake at Zoo Atlanta? Brian MacBrayer?"

"Uh-huh."

"Well, he was captured by what he describes as lizard-men— scaled, green, clawed, pointy-toothed, nasty, evil lizard-men—who are plotting to escape and take over Earth."

The FBI Director groaned. "Not you too, Morgan."

"I'm afraid so. Only this is not a hoax. This is real, Kate. It's time to initiate the protocol."

"Aw, hell." There was silence, then a heavy sigh. "You're sure, Morgan? I damn-near fired my L.A. Field Director for telling me the same thing."

"Yes, I'm sure."

"Damn, damn, *damn*. I'd hoped we'd make it through life without having to deal with anything like this."

"Yeah, me too. Yet, here we are. Who woulda thought when we were in druid training that the next big war would fall on us?"

"I did," Kate snorted. "I know you were always the optimist. But, even as a child I had a feeling something big would go down in our lifetime. And as the years have gone by, seeing what I see, I have become even more certain.

"Now, let me get to work on this. And Morgan? I'm glad Brian made it home safe. We'll need to debrief him. Keep him close. We'll be in touch."

GOING LIVE

The flight from the Bahamas was brutal. Shalane missed her connection in Atlanta and had to hop a flight to Dallas-Fort Worth. But, heavy lightning and monsoon rains closed DFW Airport after they landed, and it took hours for the weather to break.

To make matters worse, Shalane was running on no sleep and had indulged too much at the pig roast. She'd taken pain pills chased by Alka Seltzer, and managed to snatch a few restless hours of sleep on the plane and a couple more in the Dallas Aero Lounge. But the bags under her eyes were epic, and her mood was that of a baited bear.

Then, somewhere between DFW and McCarren International, the drilling pain behind Shalane's eye returned with a vengeance. After a several-week reprieve, she had hoped it was gone. But her eye ached horribly, even after the two Tapentadols she had swallowed with breakfast.

Eggs and bacon had seemed a good idea at the time. Now, Shalane was not so sure. She belched and groaned, checking the clock. Only a few minutes until curtain call, but at least she had made it here in time. The orchestra struck a chord and played the opening strains of "Hallelujah".

Shalane took a last look at her costume in the mirror. Not liking what she saw, she refreshed the appearance spell. Then, with a deep, centering whiff of Dragon's Blood oil, she exited her dressing room and stood behind the red velvet curtain.

When the band reached the first chorus, Shalane stepped out on the stage. The audience went wild. Catcalls, applause, and rhythmically-stomping feet greeted Reverend Shalane Carpenter as the crowd exploded in adulation. Shalane held her arms wide, encompassing them all. They clapped harder.

When the next verse started, Shalane lifted the microphone from its stand and a hush fell over the arena.

She glided to the front of the stage and opened her mouth. As usual, the crowd reacted, whistling and calling Sha-lane, Sha-lane. She belted out the verses of her signature song, nuzzling the microphone like a lover.

Buoyed by the energy of her adoring fans, Shalane finished the last verse and gave her opening remarks. When she was satisfied she had them eating from her hands, she climbed onto her throne chair and crossed her legs in lotus pose. Her assistants quieted the crowd while she got settled.

Today was the first trial run. Azi stood to do the honors. His fingers flew over the keyboard, initiating the first phase of Project Takeover. The Los Angeles, Paris, Istanbul, Jakarta, and Osaka feeds went live simultaneously. He studied the overhead screens broadcasting the action.

On four of the five screens, the Connector-beings lurched and arched. Something was wrong. The UnderEarth Connectors writhed and moaned. Azi twirled the knobs and buttons on the console. When nothing changed, he hit the kill switch.

But it was too late.

One by one, the Connectors went still. Flat lines showed on every monitor, save that of the Fomorian. The Connector attached to their first target, Shalane Carpenter, was still alive. But its vital signs were failing.

"Call a medic!" Azi yelled to the nearest assistant. "The Fomorian is alive, but needs care."

Switching the feed to that of the Targets, he saw that they were all dead too—except for the one attached to the Fomorian. With shaky claw, Azi hurriedly placed a call to Paris.

Within minutes, he had contacted all four centers and had confirmed the worst. The new Connectors and Targets had all perished. His Fomorian and Shalane Carpenter were the only survivors.

Baffled, Azi stared at the being on the onyx slab, then up at the screens. What had gone wrong?

Shalane gazed out over the sea of people and forgot what it was she was supposed to say. Alarmed, she waved like a beauty queen instead. Amid another round of frenzied applause, she renewed her connection with Archangel Michael. Then her eye twitched, and the pain sharpened, an ice pick scrambling her brain.

Forgetting everything but the twisting agony, Shalane pressed her hands against both sides of her head. A wave of nausea struck her, and she pitched forward. Then her body went rigid, and Shalane collapsed in a heap in the middle of the stage.

☼☼☼

Yanked out of sleep, Patty fought back. The Draconian warrior dragged her by the scruff of her neck into the light. Only she wasn't Patty. She was Nergal. As pain shot through her, she roared and flew into a rage. Backhanding the assailant, Nergal watched the Draco fly through the air and bowl over two others diving to attack. Inanna downed two more with a machete in one hand and a sword in the other. Where had she gotten those?

Nergal wheeled and caught a Draco by the throat and yanked hard, gratified by the crunch of the worm's windpipe ripping away in his claws. On the street, several soldiers marched Magdalena away at gunpoint. Nergal lunged after them.

Inanna screamed, a blood-curdling cry of terror and pain. Nergal swung around in time to see a lance skewer Ishkur. Only one Draco carried a weapon like that. Mot. Maw's arrogant brother.

Inanna screamed again. "Nergal, duck!"

He dove for the pavement and came up on the defensive, raining blow after blow upon three of Mot's henchman. He had to get to Magdalena. Over the thuds of his fists and the grunts of his targets, excited chatter filled the streets. Dracos and Ceruleans, Fomorians and Jacquadis emerged from the nearby buildings.

"Kill, kill, kill," they chanted.

Patty shivered awake. As the horror of what she'd witnessed washed over her, she sat up in bed, heart pounding. Wrapping her arms around her sweat-drenched shoulders, she rocked back and forth trying to push the sights and smells out of her mind.

She gulped air and looked around, trembling. Patty was in one of the many guestrooms in Latoya Cloud's mansion on Sunset

361

Boulevard. But the sight of the lizard man with a spear stuck in him was all she could see. Sobbing, Patty rocked and cried.

THE VORTEX

Emily rested comfortably in a-Ur's talons, grateful not to be in pain. She had watched until Khenko's boat disappeared. Now, with each flap of a-Ur's mighty wings, dread grew in Emily's gut. A fuzziness enveloped her entire body, and her head felt thick. They must've entered the vortex.

One moment, her body felt it would burst its very bounds, the next, it was being sucked into her center, squeezing the meat, and the life, from Emily. The atmospheric pressure assaulted her eardrums, and her teeth ached as if she had a mouthful of aluminum. The air dragon pressed on.

Straining to look down, Emily thought she caught a glimpse of Ooschu. Or was it Talav? It was hard to tell them apart from this distance.

Then the pressure changed. The wind swirled, forming a gale. It gathered upon itself and doubled around, swirling and flip-flopping back and forth. Emily held her breath, anxious to reach their destination. a-Ur had warned her to stay focused on that, so she didn't end up somewhere else. She repeated the name to herself. Beli Castle in Wales. Beli Castle in Wales.

They flew into a thick cloudbank, and the world disappeared. The air was close and filled with unshed water that gathered on Emily's eyelashes and curls. Then her stomach was in her throat as they plummeted into an air pocket. a-Ur gained control, but they encountered another, and another, dropping lower and lower.

Frantic, Emily peered down at the ocean, sure they would crash. All she could see was rain-laden fluff. Steeling herself, she braced for impact, but they were yanked skyward by a powerful updraft, and she chomped down hard on her bottom lip. Extending his wings, a-Ur soared higher.

From this vantage point, Emily could see their surroundings. And almost lost her breakfast. They were in the clutches of a powerful maelstrom, so large the revolutions weren't evident as such.

"Take heart, little wren," a-Ur's voice rang in her head. "We're nearing the heart of the vortex. Soon we shall be on our way to Beli, and I will let go."

"No! Don't you dare!" Emily cried, terrified of being at the mercy of quantum physics.

"Aye, child. You'll be fine. I must."

The pressure increased, and Emily's ears popped. Around and around in wide circles a-Ur rode the whirlwind, clutching Emily in his talons. Below them, it swirled deep into the ocean. She saw Ooschu and Talav, then pods of dolphin and whales.

"Long live Awen, she who hails from Druantia," the mammals chorused, before swirling out of sight with the dragons.

Lightning flashed, and for a moment, Emily got a three-sixty view from bottom to top. The funnel was so enormous, the dragons and sea creatures appeared small. Then the maelstrom collapsed upon itself with a loud, sucking explosion.

Expecting to be crushed, Emily held her breath. Lightning flashed, and the resounding boom split the cyclone apart at the seams. Ozone saturated Emily's senses as a brilliant pink hue suffused the passageway that opened before them.

Only Emily was no longer anchored in a-Ur's clutches.

She panicked for a moment, then realized she was supported by something else, something Emily couldn't see or touch. But she felt its presence. A lively, breathing, playful essence that pulsed all around her, carrying her through one looping passage after another.

No longer afraid, Emily marveled as the pink morphed to iridescent blue, then canary yellow. Wondrous awe filled her with an indescribable ecstasy. She twirled like a feather in all directions, alone, riding a pipeline of fluffy gauze.

She didn't recoil when her mother's face appeared on a snake's body, so large it extended back into the tunnel. "Dear child, please forgive me for everything," her mother said. "I am sorry and wish to make it up to you. Your companions are safe, and will meet you at the mouth of the giant." Then, Alexis Mayhall vanished.

In her place, Da's smiling face appeared. "I am with young Brian, little wren. We will join you soon. Stay the course." And he, too, faded away.

A raven appeared, Bran the Elder—both Lugh and Brian's totem. Flapping mighty wings, Bran lit on Emily's shoulder. "Be brave, little wren. You have come a long way since that night in the park. The prophecy is nigh. Keep the faith, young Awen. The Elders are with you, cheering you on." Then Bran flew off into the clouds.

The pressure against Emily's ears let up, and the air changed. No longer did it reek of ozone, but salt and sea. A grassy marsh. A gritty bog. The edges of the tunnel thinned and wavered. But she saw no sign of her dragon Keepers.

A loud screech split the sky, and an unfamiliar drake roared into view. It bore down upon Emily, blazing-red scales telegraphing death and doom. Terror bloomed in the pit of her stomach, and her limbs went weak. It was Draig Tienu.

The dragon roared again, and fire poured from its jaws. The pathways shimmered with dragon fire—effervescent oranges and fervent, unrelenting, crimson flames that consumed the very air.

With an abruptness that made Emily gasp, the wormhole burped and spit her out into the blackness of space. Terrified, she hung, motionless, and weightless.

Where was Beli? Her Keepers? The earth?

MYSTIFIED

The sight of the Atlantean Center greeted Khenko as he rounded the bend from Settler's Cove. His head throbbed from last night's rum. His heart thudded for fear of having left someone at the Vortex, then calmed with the conviction that all was well. His work in the Bahamas was done, and it was time to go home.

What once was the worst thing that could happen to Khenko, now filled him with anticipation. The morning was bright, with spring in the air, and his step. He bounced up the stairs to the kitchen and whipped up a smoothie, adding cacao and coconut butter for a pick-me-up.

Wandering to his bedroom, Khenko was surprised to find Randall sleeping soundly, one leg outside the covers, and an arm flung over his face. A memory stirred in the cobwebs of his mind, then slipped away.

Why couldn't Khenko remember?

At the sight of his party clothes crumpled on the floor, and his leather thongs upside down with Randall's, he had a flash of being at Manny's pig roast, raking in the pot, staggering back to the Center, and skittering up the stairs with Randall after a wild sow frightened them both.

He remembered looking for someone in one of the bedrooms. His passenger from that morning? Hurrying to the room, Khenko poked around. The bedclothes were rumpled and the sheets slept in. Someone had been here. Heart thumping, he opened the drawers, checked the closet, and desk. Nothing. Not one damn thing to tell him who had slept in the bed.

He raced to his office and rifled through the mess on his desk. There was a receipt from Randall's boutique for a pair of women's linen pants, two shorts, two women's blouses, some undies, and tank tops. He also found a receipt from Madame Bouvee's and another from the hair salon. All were in a manila folder with nothing written on the label. There were also several sticky notes and sheets of folded notebook paper, but these were all blank.

This was getting weirder and weirder.

Plopping down in his desk chair, Khenko opened the laptop and powered it up. He combed through his desktop and document files, including his daily journal. There were entries for every day for the last months, but no mention of anyone staying at the Atlantean Center. He opened his calendar and likewise found no notation. Nothing about a guest named Awen.

Khenko queried the name. There were lots of hits, including a definition: inspiration, inspired thought, flowing spirit. Another said it was the originating substance of the universe, as in "the word". There were also mentions of the rays arcing up or down from the sun, and a symbol drawn by druids. But no mention of a person named Awen.

Hearing a toilet flush, Khenko hurried to the women's bathroom. No one was there. Frustrated, he wandered down the hall, poking his head into each of the bedrooms, scanning for signs of habitation. He jumped when Randall exited the men's bathroom.

"Morning, handsome," Randall said, grabbing Khenko's butt. "I had a blast last night. That was one helluva party, and you raked in some dough. Did you count it, yet?"

Khenko wagged his head. "Was anyone here with us last night?"

"No baby, it was just you and me." The swarthy man grinned and rubbed his forehead. "At least I think so. To tell the truth, I'm a little fuzzy on the details. We were pretty sloshed. But I don't remember anyone else."

"Me neither." Shaking his head, Khenko went to the kitchen and looked around. Nothing seemed different. But he couldn't shake the feeling he'd had since coming-to at the Vortex. Someone was missing. Someone important.

"Go home, Khenko. Your time here is done."

His head snapped up. "What did you say?"

Randall's black eyebrows cocked. "Me? Nothing."

"You didn't just tell me to go home?"

Randall laughed nervously. He took Khenko's hand. "You *are* home, baby. Are you okay?"

Unease filled Khenko, and he laughed it off. But whose voice had he heard?

"I have to go to Princeton, Randall. Right away." Surprised at his own pronouncement, Khenko blinked foolishly. The words were not his, but he knew them to be true.

Pain flashed in Randall's eyes, squeezing Khenko's heart. But the resolution had taken hold. "I'm sorry sweetie, but something has come up. My family needs me."

"Right now?" his partner cajoled. "I was hoping you would make a batch of your famous coconut pancakes."

Khenko's mouth watered. He opened the cabinet for pancake fixings. "That, I can do. Then, I need to run into town to take care of a few things before I leave."

He would ponder the matter of the disappearing guest on his way to make arrangements for the Center. At the least, it would require maintenance during Khenko's absence. If they could rent or sell it all the better.

A pang of sadness washed over him. The Atlantean Center was his island baby. Of course, the market sucked, so neither of those scenarios were likely.

Ladling batter onto the hot skillet, he thought of the folder of receipts and blank messages. He turned to Randall and felt another pang. His friend-with-benefits slumped in the chair, morosely staring out the window.

"Do you remember me coming to the boutique yesterday?"

"When we made plans for the pig roast?" Randall perked up. "Sure. Why wouldn't I?"

"I have a receipt for lady's trousers and tops. And underwear."

Randall's eyes widened. "Now that, I don't remember. In fact," his face scrunched, then his head wagged slowly, "nope. I don't remember you buying anything." His voice lowered suggestively. "You bought women's undies?"

"No." Khenko chuckled. He flipped the pancakes and popped the syrup in the microwave, then spooned coconut butter into a serving dish and put it on the table between the plates and utensils Randall had set. Scooping the pancakes, he slid them on a warming plate and poured three more. "Will you watch these for me?"

Randall nodded and stood to prop against the counter.

"Be right back." Khenko hurried to his office and retrieved the mysterious folder. Carrying it to the kitchen, he picked the receipt for the boutique from the others. Handing it to Randall, he flipped the pancakes and watched his friend's reaction.

The olive features creased in puzzlement. "The register code is mine. But I don't remember making this sale. Or ringing it up. And I certainly don't remember you shopping for women's things." His eyes met Khenko's. "This is very weird. What's going on, dear?" Fear flickered in the earnest black eyes and found a reflection in Khenko's.

Puzzling the mystery, Khenko flipped the pancakes on the warming plate and carried them to the table. "What indeed?"

His trip to town yielded mixed results. The real estate office wasn't open yet, so he made the rounds to the other stores whose receipts he held. The answer was the same at each place. Shifting eyes, raised brows, and, "No. No lady. Just you, Khenko."

Until he entered Madame Bouvee's. The wizened owner ducked behind a shelf and edged toward the back of the store.

"Wait," Khenko begged. "I need your help. Please. My friend is missing."

The woman hesitated, visibly wavering, as if uncertain of what to do. Finally, Madame Bouvee moved from the shadows like a reluctant wraith and glided to Khenko. Her dark, beady eyes peered from the wrinkles, seeking an answer, rather than questions.

Khenko held out the receipt for the booze and herb. "I came here with a woman yesterday." The proprietress ignored the slip and kept her eyes on his. "Madame Bouvee, the woman has vanished. A woman named Awen. Just Awen. No last name."

He hadn't meant to tell her so much. But she was Khenko's last hope of solving the mystery. When her shriveled hand clutched his forearm, Khenko jumped. Then the crone sagged against him and the light went out in her rheumy eyes.

Alarmed, Khenko held the frail woman up. The eyes rolled back in the aged head and the crone gurgled. Then, just as quickly, her sight returned and the bright eyes stared into Khenko's. Her nails dug into his forearm.

"She is beyond my sight, young stork."

Khenko's jaw fell open. How had she known to call him that?

"I sense your Awen has moved on to another land." She sniffed and looked away. "I am told you should, too." Madame Bouvee let go her death-grip and turned to the register. "Is there anything in the store I can help you with?"

"That's all? She's gone? Forget it?" Khenko's volume rose with every word.

The owner stared at him for a moment, then dropped her gaze. Head down, she shuffled to the back of the emporium. Hand to the curtain, she turned and said, "Khenko, you must speak of this to no one. The Awen's life, as well as yours, depends on your discretion." With that, the wizened woman disappeared behind the heavy drapes.

A weight lifted from Khenko's shoulders. There *was* a woman. And her name was Awen. He wasn't going crazy. For a moment, he felt better. Then another thought squeezed the wits from him. He had left her at the Vortex. He had to go back.

Hurrying to Randall's boutique, Khenko rushed through the front door and nearly knocked over a departing customer. Apologizing profusely, he made a beeline for Randall, who was dressing a mannequin.

Dragging his lover to the back of the store, Khenko gushed, "There *was* a woman. I have confirmation. But I can't talk about it."

Randall opened his mouth, but Khenko leaned close to place a finger on his lips.

"No questions. I can't talk. See you later?"

The exotic eyes widened. "Sure. I'll swing by after close. Don't do anything crazy. Or stupid. I'll be there as soon as I can."

Nodding, Khenko left and climbed in the jeep. Seeing that the real estate office had opened, he slammed on the brakes and slid sideways in the mud. The road was even sloppier after last night's rain. Waving apology to a couple of locals carrying baskets of wares, Khenko pulled to the side and parked. He would take care of business, then run back to the Vortex. Just in case.

But as it turned out, he didn't get a chance. After making arrangements with the realtor, Khenko went back to the Center and fell asleep on the hammock in the shade of the palms.

While he slept, he was visited by three dragons—one silver, one sea-green, and the other a multicolored rainbow. Each strongly insisted Khenko Blitherstone drop everything and go home to his family.

Apparently, he was sorely needed.

☼☼☼

The flight to Princeton, New Jersey, via Atlanta, Georgia, was crammed full. Khenko tucked his long legs beneath the seat in front of him and opened the window shade. He watched the light play on the Caribbean as the plane taxied and took off, then circled low over Zephyr Cay.

Spotting his beloved Atlantean Center, Khenko's heart swelled and flooded over into his eyes. Dashing away the tears, Khenko craned his head until the Center was gone. But in his mind's eye, he was on the beach with a red-headed woman and her dragon friends.

Khenko gasped and sat up straight. Emily. Her name was Emily.

So who was Awen?

DRAGONS OF BELI

The dragons exited the wormhole near Dinas Affaraon. Ooschu landed in the frigid waters of the Northern Atlantic, which was angry this day, heaving and churning, with a powerful undertow. She rode the waves gleefully, happy to be back.

From the shore, Talav bellowed, offering a benediction to their old homeland. a-Ur soared above them, and dipped on one wing, coming to rest near Talav. Ooschu dove beneath the rowdy surface and swam ashore, noting with surprise the sparsity of sea life. She picked her way over the rocky beach to where the others gathered.

a-Ur roared, "Where is the Awen?"

The three dragons eyed one another, then turned toward the jagged peaks of Yr Wyddfa.

"The castle maybe?" Talav said.

Ooschu eyed a-Ur. "You could fly up and check," she suggested. "Talav and I will have a look down here."

a-Ur circled the sharp ridges of Crib Goch and Y Lliwedd, and climbed the lofty peaks of Yr Wyddfa. He came to rest beside what was once a moat. Castle ruins littered the landscape, a pile of crumbling stones with few remaining walls. Lifting off, he hugged the skeleton of a parapet, sweeping the castle remains with his keen gaze. The Awen was not here.

Anxiety growing, he took flight again, soaring low above the mountains. Not only was the Awen not in sight, but he detected no trace of her energy signature. Returning to the rocky beach, he found Talav and Ooschu as agitated as he. None could fathom what had happened to the Awen.

"Maybe she forgot our instructions, and thought of some other place while in the wormhole." Talav suggested. "That girl is as wayward as they have come. And while I often enjoy her tantrums, this is no time to run astray. I say we check the Otherworld, in case she got confused in the maze."

a-Ur shook his horny head. Something had occurred to him, and he didn't like it. "It's Tienu," he muttered. "That conniving drake has intercepted the Awen."

Ooschu squealed, a sound most unbecoming to a dragon. "You're right, a-Ur. That's exactly what happened." She pounded the rocky strand. "I suppose it was bound to happen sooner or later."

Talav looked sheepish. "Did I mention to either of you that I saw Tienu?"

a-Ur's angry roar echoed from the cliffs.

"Okay, I didn't exactly see Tienu. But, I did talk to him. It was he who told me what to do to get the Awen's attention. Where to shake the earth." Guilt gave way to horror as awareness dawned in Talav's ochre eyes.

"That devil played me, didn't he? He wanted me to create that earthquake and eruption so he could escape. Do you think he's stolen the Awen?"

"More than likely. So, what now?" Ooschu wondered.

a-Ur heaved a heavy sigh. "We find the Awen. I will backtrack through the wormhole. It may have kicked her out somewhere, and she would have no idea how to proceed. It's not your fault, Talav. It's mine. I should have foreseen this. That damn wormhole is unreliable. It kicked me out twice on the way to the Bahamas."

He prepared to take off. "You two stay here. Maybe Ooschu can scan the Otherworld and Underworld. Talav, could you check the rest of the island? Look for Tienu, too. Find him and we'll find our Awen."

a-Ur's eyes roved the rocky beach. Guillemots, cormorants, and kittiwakes combed the rocks, looking for a meal. He hated to leave Beli so soon. But without the Awen, their cause was lost.

"Wait!" Talav called as a-Ur lifted off. "I sense the old witch's presence. Maybe she has news of the Awen."

The Cailleach tottered to the window. She parted the heavy curtains to peer up into a cornflower-blue sky. The screech had summoned her. That, and a roar that brought a thrill to her old heart.

The dragons of Beli had returned.

She watched the air dragon soar over the crumbled remains of the castle that had once belonged to her consort, Beli-Mawr.

Donning her wrap, she pulled the hood over thinning gray hair, then hobbled outside to tap her alder cane on the rocky ground. Ice fanned out before her. She waved her cane over her head, and a frigid wind swooped down from Yr Wyddfa.

The Cailleach clutched her robe tighter and watched the dragon pick through the castle's icy remains. For what did the drake search?

Putting two fingers to her lips, the Cailleach whistled. The wind shrieked, a keening cry of hope delayed. The temperature plunged and fine snowflakes whipped along the airways.

The dragon's head snapped toward the Cailleach. No surprise registered on its horned visage. Cautious, as dragons are wont to be, the drake approached.

"Hail, Cailleach, keeper of winter."

"Hail Draig-athar," she welcomed the shimmery creature, who was both a bestower of dreams and the bringer of destruction. "You have returned."

"Aye," the dragon roared.

Eyes born of the stars themselves scrutinized the Cailleach, then the dragon bowed before her. "And you have remained, Cailleach. Your presence brings pause to an old dragon's heart. The time is nigh."

a-Ur flapped his translucent wings, and a ray of sun penetrated the clouds to sparkle and play with the swirling snowflakes. Thunder boomed and rolled across the land.

"Show off." The Cailleach cackled, and relaxed her wary stance.

The air drake bowed, and the snow gathered about him. It whirled into a long, narrow spiral that stretched up into the clouds. Then the funnel closed upon itself, and the winds abated. The snow ceased.

Nodding in approval, the Cailleach planted her cane firmly. At its tip, ice formed and emanated out in concentric circles to cover the ruins. It ran up the tors, spreading quickly and freezing any vegetation the early spring had coaxed from the earth.

A bolt of lightning struck the ground in front of the Cailleach. Startled, she blinked and the ice receded.

Draig-athar's laughter, gruff and melodious, echoed off the jagged peaks. The Cailleach leaned heavily on her cane, glad for the support for her old bones.

"Truce, dragon. We've both made our points. What is it you seek, a-Ur?"

For the third time, the dragon bowed before the Cailleach. "I seek the Awen, old one. The time is nigh. The darkness lurks beneath our feet. Without the Awen, all is lost."

Fury twisted in the Cailleach at the mention of Awen. For a twinkling, she dwelt in memory, in a time when her cohorts had ruled the land. When humans were few, and mostly meek. Save the druids.

"Who is this Awen, and why should I care?" the Cailleach lied. "Short are the days before Brigit claims my rightful place and ushers in the warm summer season. Already she threatens, poking her head from the earth in crocus spikes. But I am resolved to stay until Beltaine, as is my right. Begone with you, and this interloping Awen."

She struck the earth with her cane, and ice crystals flew into the air dragon's face.

a-Ur roared and prepared for battle.

FALAISE

The wind whistled through the dragon's wings as it sped up behind Emily. She wheeled to face it, and fire streamed from its great maw. Cringing, Emily tucked and gathered around her center, but the flames bypassed her to sear a new passageway. This one was gray, tinged an ominous blood-red. Unable to change directions or stay her course, Emily flew into it.

The dragon soared ahead of her, burning a new channel through the densely-forming clouds. Lightning flashed, and the world tilted sideways, spilling Emily into a dark place filled with dust and decay. All motion ceased.

She was no longer in the wormhole.

Feeling around with her hands in the dark, Emily hoped she wasn't in another freaking cave. At least she wasn't frightened, for the moment. The space reminded her of Talav's underground lair. Had she been hijacked by Tienu? The fallen Keeper? Emily shivered.

The wall was clay, damp and slimy beneath her fingers. Had something happened to her in the vortex? Was she knocking on death's door, again? Or was she actually dead this time?

A gravelly chuckle echoed through the chamber, bouncing off the ceiling and reverberating all around Emily. Low, light, amused laughter. Dragon laughter.

"Tienu, is that you? Are we in Beli?"

The laughter grew louder, deeper, more mirthful.

As Emily's eyes adjusted, she could just make out an enormous form, larger than any of the other dragons. Even a-Ur.

"Hello?" No answer.

Feeling around the perimeter, she remembered she had matches and a lighter in her backpack. Shrugging the straps from her shoulders, Emily opened the side pocket and fumbled for the disposable lighter.

She held it high but couldn't make out the dragon's details. At least the chamber was larger than the one beneath Zoo Atlanta. A layer of fine dust covered the floor, and when Emily stood, it tickled her nostrils. She sneezed, and the flame went out.

Digging in the compartment for a stubby emergency candle, she lit that, and held it aloft, cupping her hand around the flame when it flickered and almost died. She inched cautiously toward the silent dragon, wondering why she felt no fear. She was underground, in the dark, and worse, a hostile dragon was here.

Bran the Raven was right. Emily *had* come a long way.

Of course, she wore the ring and the amulet. Maybe that was why. She touched Aóme to the ruby resting lightly against her chest. In the shadows, a motion caught Emily's attention. Then the dragon shambled into the light, its blood-red eyes fixed on her.

Emily shuddered. Its face was horned, and a line of sharp spikes ran from the center of its crimson forehead, down the length of its spine, to the tip of its deadly-looking tail. She crouched and waited for the dragon to strike.

"Fear not, young Awen." The booming voice rolled around the chamber and echoed deep into the earth, as if through a cavern system. "Sleep. You are weary and will need your strength for what is to come."

The dragon lifted its great head. Its nostrils flared, testing the air, and its thick, mahogany tongue flicked across leathery lips, revealing sharp fangs.

Emily shivered and wrapped her arms around her shoulders. Then the dragon bowed.

"I fear we have not been properly introduced. I, Master Awen, am Draig Tienu, ever at your service. We are in your cave beneath Chateau Falaise."

SEEING STARS

Wrestling with the shame of his failure, Azi trudged through the tunnel. Shibboleth had not executed him this time, but if he failed again, Azi wouldn't be so lucky.

As a punishment to himself, he had come alone to search for the access point. No Chupacabra sightings had marred his passage, and he was nearing the shaft of the defunct volcano. He'd brought a stun gun and attached a video camera to his vest. Should there be any hocus pocus, he would have the playback.

Evidence of the chimney's incendiary origins appeared in the beam of Azi's headlamp. He approached with caution, claws clicking over magma flows that had hardened in uneven ripples and waves. Reaching the endpoint of his previous expedition, Azi paused before taking another wary step.

The base of the vent gaped before him, surrounded by boulders and debris. Dropping his pack at his feet, Azi clattered over the flow to duck inside the opening. As he'd anticipated, the chimney was blocked. He retrieved a concussive device and placed it center mass, then retreated into the tunnel to detonate. He covered his ears and head.

Rocks ricocheted off the walls of the passage and dust filled his nose and the tunnel. He sneezed several times in quick succession. When it had cleared sufficiently to breathe again, Azi looped the pack over his neck and shoulder and entered the narrow passage to begin the climb.

For the next thirty minutes, he scaled the stack easily until he reached another blockage. Azi planted a concussive and climbed down the vent a short way to hide beneath a small outcrop.

Flattening his body as best he could beneath the ledge, he shielded his face and exploded the charge.

An avalanche of rock and debris cascaded down the chamber. Azi clung to the wall, grateful when the outcrop held and deflected the largest boulders. When the barrage was over, he lifted his head to peer above him, and barely avoided a large stone that tumbled lazily behind the rest. He waited another minute until the dust cleared, and cautiously peered upward.

And almost plunged to his death at the sight.

There, above him, was a purple sky filled with dancing stars. Losing his grip, Azi slid a half meter before gaining a handhold, then a foothold. Heart galloping, he gazed skyward. The celestial lights blinked, steady and real.

With a rush of excitement, Azi hauled himself up, hand over hand, the last several meters. He clamored over the edge and kneeled, ignoring the shards that tore at his scales. Inky sky surrounded him, and it was filled with glorious, sparkling stars.

A coyote howled, answered by another, then the rest of the pack added their voices until the ululation sent chills down Azi's spine.

He had breached the worlds.

The howls coalesced into hungry yips, then quieted. Azi listened closely, and could just make out the sound of the beasts fighting over their kill. The scent of blood mixed with the spice of fir.

Azi shivered. The chill air was crisp against his face, and cooled his core rapidly. Standing slowly, he turned in all directions, searching for signs of danger.

When he was sure there was no immediate threat, he retrieved his communicator. The signal was weak but active. Calling up the message he had prepared earlier, Azi sent it to the base commander and copied his assistant.

An hour later, four Draco warriors poured from the old volcano in the middle of California's Panamint Mountains.

On the other side of the world in Varanasi, India, Ramananda sat very still. So still, the grasshoppers and dragonflies perched upon him like he was a statue or part of the landscape. He was very old and wished only to spend his last days in this special place, the Well of Sheshna, where he could gaze for hours into the waters. On a good day, the water spoke to him. Right now, what it said astounded Ramananda.

His eyes flew open. A ripple disturbed the usually-placid surface. Amid a flurry of gossamer wings, the dragonflies took flight. The water churned and parted. The steps to the legendary Patala appeared.

Ramananda knew without seeing, that there were forty steps. They descended into a stone grotto that terminated at a door covered in bas-relief cobras. In the past, the pool was drained for special celebrations. But the door hadn't been opened in a century, or more.

A green head with crafty red eyes appeared on the steps, and Ramananda suppressed a surprised breath. The head was followed by a plated chest, lean muscular arms, and a long torso and legs. Snake-like scales covered the man-sized creature that wore nothing but a wide belt from which weapons dangled. Its feet and hands ended in sharp claws that could tear Ramananda to shreds.

What was this creature? A lizard or a man? It looked like a combination of both.

He shivered as another emerged, then another, and another, until four of the beings crouched beside the statue. Water dripped from the sleek, scaled bodies to the dry stones, where it sizzled and released its vapor into the air.

Were these the Naga? The snake men of yore? With fearful awe, Ramananda said a silent prayer from his ancestors designed to make himself undetectable.

They filed past Ramananda silently, walking upright. The shortest was easily seven feet tall, with a mouthful of sharp, pointed teeth.

When they had passed from Ramananda's failing sight, he released a pent-up breath and rose from lotus position to creep toward home.

CONTINUED IN AWEN TIDE

NOTE FROM O. J. BARRÉ:

I know, I know! Another cliffhanger! You expected that, right?

But you'll be happy to know that the action continues and builds to a rousing finale in *Awen Tide: Book Three of the Awen Trilogy*.

In *Awen Tide*, Emily, Lugh, and Brian, along with their friends and allies, new and old, will face frightful conditions and challenges in their quest to save Humanity from the Reptilians—and more.

Are you ready for the climax? Read *Awen Tide*. (And be prepared for another sleepless night.)

HAPPY READING! O. J. Barré

SNEAK PEEK

AWEN TIDE, Book Three of the Awen Trilogy:

Chapter One - TURBULENT TIMES

Lugh MacBrayer surveyed the animals in the compartment tucked behind first class. The last-minute fares for the PetJet, designed for travelers with large pets, had cost the Order a pretty penny.

"I've got a bad feeling."

Hope, his Druid Elder, shifted in her cage. "Me, too. Between it and this infernal airplane, I have not slept a wink."

"I slept, but not well." He glanced at Cu, the Irish wolfhound, snoring upside down in the next cage. "A bad dream woke me. Emily is in trouble again."

After being sucked into an earthquake and disappearing for weeks, Emily Hester, the love of Lugh's life and the head of his Order, had finally resurfaced on an obscure island in the Bahamas. Now Lugh was optimistic his nephew Brian would turn up next.

Letting go of a heavy sigh, Lugh scratched the underside of Hope's neck.

"You may be right." The Scottish wildcat licked her lips, a nervous oddity for Hope. "But we're seven miles high, and there's nothing any of us can do. Did I tell you flying is my least favorite thing?"

"You did. Several times. But this was your idea, Hope. Go to Wales, you said. Find the dragons, you said." Lugh ran his hand across his sandpaper chin. Last night's shadow had become the beginning of a thick beard.

Hope tossed her head. "We do what we must for the Order, Lugh. And for the Awen."

How well the druid priest knew. He wouldn't be here if not bound by duty. But Emily needed him. And in the process of searching for her in Europe, he hoped to stumble across a clue about Jake.

"At least you didn't have to ride in the cargo—"

The plane dropped unexpectedly, throwing Lugh into Hope's cage.

The wildcat yowled her displeasure, and the bell dinged overhead as the jet bucked and pitched. Lugh clung to the cage. The cabin lights flicked on, and the captain's voice crackled across the intercom, cautioning passengers to return to their seats.

Jarred awake, Cu howled, and the other animals joined in.

Wild-eyed flight attendants emerged from their pods. One staggered to the mic and instructed passengers jarred from sleep to lock seatbelts and stow electronics and tray tables. A first-class attendant appeared at Lugh's elbow.

"Sir, you have to return to your seat." He pressed a button that unfurled padded ticking insides the cages, and the animal Elders disappeared from view.

Lugh gripped the steel mesh tightly and slowly, precariously, moved toward his seat.

The loudspeaker hummed. The pilot was taking them higher to get above the system. The plane shuddered, and the bucking grew worse.

Bracing his thighs against the armrests, Lugh clung to the seatbacks and pulled himself forward row by row until he reached his pod. He buckled in, then gasped, recoiling, when an overhead bin sprang open.

The attendant reached up to close it, but the plane lurched, throwing him sideways into the aisle. Carry-ons, briefcases, and a diaper bag rained down on him and an adjacent passenger who cried out in shock. The baby that belonged to the diaper bag squalled.

The juddering plane climbed, bucking turbulence.

When it leveled off, Lugh peeled clenched fingers from the armrest and breathed a sigh of relief. The seat-back monitor showed they now cruised at an altitude of forty thousand feet.

The attendant hoisted himself up, checked on the abused passenger, then wrangled the cases back into the bin. But despite the welcome calm, the seatbelt sign remained lit.

Lugh eyed it and debated whether to obey the command or chance a visit to the bathroom. He'd been bound there earlier before stopping to talk to Hope.

His aching bladder won. Unbuckling the belt, he hurried to the head, took care of business, then splashed cold water on his face.

He blotted it with the thin paper towel and studied his drawn features in the mirror.

Purple splotches pooled in the hollows beneath his eyes. Lugh raked his fingers through thick ebony hair in perpetual need of a trim. As usual, he had a whopping headache, courtesy of the head injury he'd sustained the day Brian and Emily disappeared in the quake at Zoo Atlanta.

A pocket of nothingness opened beneath the plane. Lugh's stomach lurched as they fell toward Earth. Grateful to be wedged between the sink and wall, he held his breath for several scary seconds until the trough bottomed.

The captain's voice blared from the speaker above his head.

"Ladies and gentlemen, please remain in your seats. We have received word that this storm extends across the entire Atlantic seaboard. We are currently over the Azore Islands and have received clearance to land in Caen, France, the nearest airport with favorable ground conditions. Please hang tight and keep your seatbelts fastened. The ride promises to be—" he went silent for a long moment while the plane tossed from side to side. "—bumpy," he finished.

Which was an understatement, to say the least.

Lugh opened the door cautiously and clung to it as the plane lurched and shuddered. Then he pulled himself along the seatbacks avoiding the contents of another spilled overhead bin.

Distressed passengers peered up at him with terror in their eyes—terror that matched Lugh's own. He hated flying, hated it with a passion. Now his loathing had ramped up exponentially.

Reaching his seat, he collapsed into his pod, but the plane seesawed, and he overshot, landing on the woman in the next seat. She screamed bloody murder and shoved at him.

Apologizing profusely, Lugh dragged himself into his seat and buckled the belt, then craned his neck. Hope and Cu were hidden by the padding. He prayed it and their restraints would keep them safe.

Then the plane tilted and descended at a steep angle.

KEEP READING IN:
AWEN TIDE

WHAT'S NEXT?

Awen Tide, Book Three of the Awen Trilogy (available soon)

Also, be on the lookout for:

Awen Rising, Book One of the Awen Trilogy
The Druids of Marduk, Part I: An Awen Prequel
The Druids of Marduk, Part II: UnderEarth
The Druids of Marduk, Part III: AboveEarth (available soon)

PLEASE LEAVE A REVIEW

Honest reviews help grab readers' attention when deciding whether to read a book. If you enjoyed *Awen Rising*, please take a few minutes to leave a review. It can be as short or as long as you like—even a star rating without comment would be helpful.

Thank you for reading *Awen Rising* and for your review!

Olivia/O. J. Barré

ABOUT THE AUTHOR

O. J. Barré hails from the lushly forested, red-clay hills near Atlanta, Georgia where much of this story takes place. From birth, O. J. was a force of nature. Barefoot and freckled, headstrong and gifted; she was, and is, sensitive to a fault.

Books became her refuge as a young child, allowing O. J. to escape the confines of her turbulent alcoholic home for adventures to untold places and times.

Her daddy's mother was a Willoughby, making O. J. a direct descendant of William the Conqueror. Her Awen series is a love letter to that distant past.

O. J. currently resides in Cheyenne, Wyoming, with her twenty-four-pound mixed Maine Coon cat, Rambo.

www.ingramcontent.com/pod-product-compliance
Lightning Source LLC
Chambersburg PA
CBHW030827110726
47900CB00006B/1783